CHLOE CATES
IS MISSING

MANDY McHUGH

SCARLET
NEW YORK

CHLOE CATES IS MISSING

Scarlet
An Imprint of Penzler Publishers
58 Warren Street
New York, N.Y. 10007

Copyright © 2022 by Mandy McHugh

First Scarlet edition

Interior design by Maria Fernandez

Library of Congress Control Number: 2021920529

cloth ISBN: 978-1-61316-268-2
eBook ISBN: 978-1-61316-270-5

10 9 8 7 6 5 4 3 2 1

Printed in the United States of America
Distributed by W. W. Norton & Company

To Sean, Mackenzie, and Jack, Always

JENNIFER

Fourteen clicks.

I stare at the numbers. Surely, there's been some mistake. I hit refresh and watch the graphs slowly rematerialize on the screen.

Nope. No change. The numbers stay the same.

We missed our thousand-dollar bonus by fourteen lousy clicks.

"Shi-oot," I say, catching the cuss on my tongue. I used to swear like a sailor—words that'd make a pirate blush, Jackson used to tease—but that was before we had kids.

Mothers aren't awarded the luxury of profanities. I know from personal experience.

After I had JJ, I tried to make mom friends. I did. The few women I'd stayed friendly with after college were too busy chasing shots or building their careers to even think about kids. They didn't want to spend their free time cooped up with a screaming newborn. I didn't either, until it was my child. With our tenuous ties and shifting priorities, it was easy to drift apart.

No friends. Jackson was working overtime to account for our newfound single salary income. I would've rather chewed my arm off than ask my mother for help.

I was alone.

More than alone. I was becoming a maternal hermit. I'd go days without showering. Ate peanut M&Ms by the handful at 2 a.m. Binge watched *Criminal Minds* to distract myself from the agony of mastitis while JJ was cluster feeding.

One particularly stressful morning, JJ wouldn't stop crying. I was so tired I shaved the same leg twice. I decided I needed to get out. I hadn't seen anyone besides Jackson and the cashier at Target in weeks. People would help, I thought. Connection. Getting out would fix the crater-sized hole in my soul. I dressed JJ in this adorable two-piece set from Gymboree—blue and white nautical stripes with a smiling cartoon whale wearing a sailor hat, one of my favorites—and we headed to the only place I knew there would be a chance for me to meet a mom friend.

The playground.

Ever tried having an adult conversation at a playground? Small talk is a feat of endurance.

I found myself standing near three women, JJ at my feet playing with a leaf because he couldn't walk, let alone use the playground equipment, when one of the moms turned to me. Brunette waves fell effortlessly around her shoulders. She wore a cashmere V-neck over stylish jeggings and sensible black Sperrys. Not movie star pretty, by any means, but compared to me in my clearance Old Navy leggings and too-tight tunic, she was a knockout. She gave me a warm smile. We exchanged pleasantries about our cute kids, the weather, coffee, and traffic.

Then, she asked the same question every mom inevitably gets when she's new to the group. Well, besides the *are-you-married* question.

What do you do?

I don't know why this always made me uncomfortable. There's nothing wrong with customer service or freelance work, both of which I was doing before I had JJ. But now, I didn't even have that. Admitting my new role as a stay-at-home mom was still surreal. *Temporarily*, I would add, because that was a double-edged sword I hadn't quite learned how to wield: how to be in between.

Before I could voice my hesitant reply, though, her son toppled off the ladder. He landed on his belly with a soft thud and smacked his face into the chopped-tire mulch. It really does happen in the blink of an eye.

Fuck, I said, *is he okay?*

The attention swerved from the shrieking toddler with a bloody lip onto me. Like I had sucked that air out of the atmosphere.

Ah, we don't speak like that here, said one of the women, lips pinched in disapproval and shouting a bit to be heard over the scream-cries.

We try to make this a safe space, said the third, all bouncy blonde curls and eyelashes. *Kids are exposed to so much already, you know?*

No, the fork, I didn't, but I kept my mouth shut anyway, not wanting to broadcast my new-mom ignorance. I apologized and gathered JJ up in my arms while he fussed to get back down. Always fighting me, JJ. He's as stubborn as I am. I counted one more painfully awkward minute so it wasn't entirely obvious that I was fleeing and bolted to my car.

That was fifteen years ago, but if there's one thing I've learned since then, it's that no one is more judgmental of mothers than other mothers.

Which is why it's so important that I stay on top of my game and why losing that bonus makes me want to chuck my laptop out the window.

Instead, I close it gently and push it aside. Better.

No. Closed or not, I can't erase the knowledge. The failure. My hands tremble despite the fact I haven't had my morning caffeine fix. I stretch and curl my fingers trying to knead the nerves away, but knowing we won't get that extra grand this month . . . fork, I was counting on that money.

How am I going to fix this?

Jackson stirs in his sleep, one arm thrown above his head, the other curled beneath his chest. He grunts then exhales deeply. He's a restless dreamer, sleeping or awake. Constantly searching for an outlet that's going to bring him satisfaction. I used to give him that. Satisfaction.

The shades are drawn haphazardly, and a thin line of sunshine streams through, casting a white mark across his back. It's an eerie resemblance to a rope drawn taut around his neck.

A chill shivers through me. Will we ever be like we used to be?

If the stars align? If we renew our vows? Maybe take a trip?

With what money?

Crust, even my own mind is working against me today. My alarm buzzes. I swipe it off and roll my head from shoulder to shoulder before padding across the room. I don't have time for hypotheticals. I leave Jackson to his dreams and close the door behind me.

The hallway smells like vanilla and soap. I'm glad we had the carpets cleaned last week, soft and factory-new in the cozy morning light. I haven't always noticed details like that, but it's important to take in the little things. The difference between getting a hundred thousand likes and getting over a million comes down to the small stuff. The wrong color, the wrong angle—one wrong choice and we can kiss our incentives goodbye.

Fourteen god—*gosh*—darn clicks.

There's no way around it. Abby's going to have to do a second shoot today. On top of everything else, she won't be happy with the news.

Why does it seem like raising girls is so much more difficult than raising boys? Everybody talks about being a Boy Mom like it's some badge of honor, but there should be a Nobel Prize and national holiday for moms of girls. Do you know how difficult it is to teach your daughter the ins and outs of womanhood?

With JJ, I had no idea how lonely being a new mother would be. I thought we'd have this huge support group, a village who wanted to help raise our bundle of joy. Instead, most of my days were spent covered in spit-up and poop and comforting a colicky baby boy. Parenting websites were no help, full of suggestions like, *Go for a walk! Have a barbeque! Jog through the park! Beach day!* That's all well and good if you live in Florida, but winter outings aren't doable on the East Coast. We live in upstate New York. Can't build a sandcastle when you're knee-deep in January snow.

By the time I had Abby, though, I'd adjusted to the loneliness. JJ had his tiny friends and was a genuinely happy kid. Jackson had his work and his ever-changing hobbies. And I had Abby. I didn't need anyone else as long as I had my baby girl.

I stop in front of JJ's room and press my ear to the door. Some acoustic song I don't recognize is playing. Must've forgotten to turn it off before he went to bed. He works so hard to maintain his average during baseball season.

Knocking gently, I turn the knob and enter. The room smells of cologne and boy sweat and I immediately know he forgot to put his uniform in the wash. His back is to me, blankets tucked all the way to his ears. Pillow on the floor. I pick it up and lay it at the foot of his bed, listening to his snores in a singular moment of peace.

The emo song ends and is replaced by "Chicken Fried." Geez, his playlist is weird. I close his laptop, organize the notebooks scattered on his desk into a neat pile, and drop the pens into the holder. JJ loves to write. I'd be lying if I said I wasn't proud of that. He wants to tell stories just like I do with my blog. His are full of vampire legions and flesh-eating zombies, but still, following in my footsteps.

Ah-ha. His clothes basket overflows in the corner. I stuff an errant shirt sleeve deeper into the mix and lug the hamper down the hall. One more load. At least JJ appreciates me. Can't say the same for everyone else in this family.

Setting the basket down, I raise my hand to knock on Abby's door. I hesitate, suspended in dread, then let it fall back to my side, thinking of the hard talk that's waiting for us.

I pick the hamper back up.

I'll let her sleep just a little longer.

Abby's Journal

Mom says keeping journals is dangerous. I think she's just worried about what I might say when she's not watching. Add it to the list of stuff she won't let me do. No video games. No unapproved labels. No junk food. No free time.

That's like a million nos, *in case you're keeping track, and I didn't even get to the big stuff.*

I never ask for anything. But the one time I tell her I don't want her to post pictures of me on the blog—the ONE time—you'd think I stole a car or something. Big mad. Raging. Spit flew out of her mouth and landed on my forehead, it was so gross.

"You have no idea the repercussions *of what you're saying!" Throwing around dictionary words like I'll be more scared because they're bigger. "Think of what you'd be doing to us—to* me!*"*

Always about her.

Sorry, I'm getting ahead of myself. We should have a "proper" intro. My name is Chloe Cates, also known as CC Spectacular. Chloe because of my grandmother, Dad's mom. I never met her, but I've seen pictures. Pretty in that sepia-filter way. She lives somewhere in Florida with my grandfather George. Dad says they like the heat and the politics, and idk what most of that means, but they didn't even try to see us that one time we went to Disney.

But that's a whole other story.

So, Chloe from my grandmother. Cates because, well, this part is sad. Mom's obsessed with this old movie Gremlins. *From like the '80s. Anyway, the woman who starred in that movie was named Phoebe Cates. Mom says I have the same wavy brown hair as her, so we ran with it.*

Of course, Chloe Cates isn't my real name. My real name is Abby Scarborough. It feels good to write it down. Good, but super weird. Everybody knows CC Spectacular, but Abby Scarborough doesn't exist, not on Facebook, Twitter, Instagram, Snapchat—nowhere that counts. Why would she? Who cares about me when Chloe is the star?

I don't go anywhere without my trusty Chloe Cates cape. I'm positively spar-kling! *That's my catchphrase. One of them anyway.*

"SIGH." I miss friends. I thought Willa Forest from around the corner was going to be my BFF but she stopped calling for no reason. So really, I haven't made a real friend since I was like 4. Sucks. Eating popcorn in pajamas under a pillow fort at a sleepover. Four-year-old me didn't know how good she had it.

Then all of this started.

I was 4 when Mom started her blog. "CC and Me," it's called. Quick, cute, and best of all, catchy. When someone asks her what it's about, she tells them *clears throat and uses best Meryl impression* a mother's personal reflection on parenting and what it means to be a good mom. *What she should say is A MOTHER TRYING TO CONTROL HER DAUGHTER'S LIFE!!*

Four years old. Almost 10 years I've been on camera.

I liked it, at first. The attention and happiness. So many smiles. It was like a game. Mom bought crazy photo props. She set up shoots for whatever she was writing about that week. I remember the first one best. "A Mother's Galaxy," was the title. She made her own backdrop. Took her 2 days to finish. She painted it black and added like 4 layers of sparkle. Dad was so mad she got glitter everywhere. He calls glitter a virus because it spreads and sticks to everything. He's not wrong, but Chloe is basically made of glitter so ¯_(ツ)_/¯

Then she glued on papier-mâché planets and comets and finished with a glossy topcoat. I got to help with that part. I remember being so happy she let me use the big girl paintbrush.

And the cherry on the sundae was me. I was the sun. The biggest star of all.

Dressed in a tutu made of gold tulle and bedazzled with cosmic gems. The leotard was gold, too, custom made by an Etsy shop. I loved that outfit. I wanted to spin and twirl and never take it off. But I couldn't get it dirty. Couldn't rip it. Everything had to be perfect for our debut.

Mom did my hair, straightening it in sections until it fell to my hips. Curling the ends like birthday ribbons and dousing me with gallons of hairspray. SO bad for the environment, tbh, but it was cute.

She did my makeup too. Not the kid stuff. Real makeup. Eyeshadow, mascara, lipstick. A little pink blush on my cheeks. "You're ready," she said with one last dab of color. I didn't know what I was ready for, though, only that I had to smile pretty and give attitude.

"People like attitude when it comes from toddlers," she said. "It's sassy and cute and guaranteed to get traffic."

I remember being confused b/c I thought traffic was bad. Funny how many different meanings there are for words. Dad's always pointing out bad drivers when we're stuck in traffic. I know for a fact anyone driving a Subaru is going to be a bad driver. When I get my license in a few years, we won't be shopping for one of those. I pay attention.

JJ might, though. He's def gonna be a bad driver. He'd rather ride around on his dumb scooter or whatever he does with his friends when he's not here. And he's *never* here.

Anyway.

Mom showed me every time someone liked her posts or subscribed. "It's so good!" she said. "We want that number to keep getting higher. Sponsors will come in droves, Abby-girl!"

Abby-girl. Who I used to be before the blog went viral.

"It sounds better, right?" Mom said. "Someone might call you Abby Scabby or Abby Dabby Doo. We don't want that. Chloe Cates is magical. Like a princess name. Think of it as part of your costumes. When we do our skits, you'll pretend you're Chloe Cates and all your heebie-jeebie jitters will float away." She swooshed her hand like rainbow. "To the sky, Abby-girl. When you're CC, send those nervous bubbles to their castles in the clouds."

I never got nervous. I never had a choice. What if I don't want to have a brand? What if I don't care that other kids could make fun of me? Some days, I'd rather be Abby Scabby than the fake me she wants me to be.

My life isn't mine. It's not real. I just act out a bunch of stories to make our subscribers happy.

I'm tired of being make-believe.

JENNIFER

I shuffle awkwardly down the stairs and plop JJ's laundry next to the other overflowing basket. It sits there casting judgment, like it's my fault I ran out of time to wash everyone's dirty clothes. With a sigh, I start shoveling bunches around the basin, recoiling at the ripe stench. Jesus, does it always stink like this? Okay, family, you win. I cannot miss a week again; this is outrageous. I throw in a pod—two pods, definitely two pods—and a heaping cup of softener.

I close the lid. Press start.

Task complete. My real day begins.

No one sets out to be a blogger. I certainly didn't. But at the time I decided to give it a go, I was treading water. Sending up flares and praying someone was watching.

We can't make her do this if she doesn't want to, Jen.

I blow the hair out of my eyes, blonde and crimpy from sleeping weird, and pretend Jackson's words fly away with the strands.

We can't make her do this if she doesn't want to. It's not right.

How could Jackson say that to me? After everything we've done. All the hours and late nights and sacrifices I've made? Blood, sweat, tears, pounds—you name it, I've given it to this blog. Everybody loves CC Spectacular, and that's not because of dumb luck.

If this next promo series goes viral, a lot of doors will open. *A lot.* TV. Movies. Merchandise. A recording contract. Chloe could be the next JoJo Siwa if we play our cards right.

Opportunities—isn't that what every parent wants for their child? To give them a chance for a better life? Options we didn't even dare to dream about?

It's killing us.

The clock on the stove reads 7:07. My eyes skim the kitchen for any signs of disorder, and, finding none, land on the wall calendar. I review my schedule.

It is Saturday, April 25th, and the day is long indeed.

Bow-tastic! photos are due at one. Flipping fantastic.

Blog post is scheduled to go live at three. No trouble there unless the pictures are late, in which case I could technically push it back an hour or two, but I don't like doing that, especially when it pushes us out of our optimal posting time slot. Fourteen clicks.

Moving on.

Blog tour interview at five followed immediately by #OOTD picture and stories for Insta and Twitter.

Phone interview with JV Fashion at seven.

JJ also has practice at 11:30, which complicates our shooting timetable. Jackson will have to drop him off while I finish the edits. I select a marker from the metallic container next to the fridge and make a note to text Denise Fletcher across the street about carpooling. Her son, Ryan, plays varsity with JJ, and the boys have been friends for years.

At 7:10, I take two mugs down from the top shelf, pour water into the coffeemaker, and add a second scoop of grounds. I need the extra caffeine.

Usually, I'd run to Starbucks and get a grande Americano for me and a flat white for Jackson. Not happening today.

Today, we're short on time.

And clicks.

Fork.

The numbers slag is eating at me. We were killing it this time last year. Incentives are great until traffic wanes and money goes into someone else's pocket. I'm left working twice as hard with nothing to show for it except a moody teenage daughter who uses it as cannon fodder to be difficult.

A sizzling hiss from behind me. I spin and realize I forgot to put the coffee pot underneath the flow. Shoot, shoot, shoot.

Another mess to clean. Another mess is not what I need. Seems like all I do lately is clean up other people's messes.

I sop up the hot brown liquid with the nearest dish towel and hope my careless mistake hasn't left a permanent stain. Pottery Barn linens don't grow on trees. Even on garage sale sites, PB raises asking prices to unaffordable heights.

"Get your shirt together," I say to myself. I have to calm down before Abby sees me.

I bury the thoughts of the sponsor bonus we won't get, add BUDGET to my list, and focus on the most pressing obstacle.

Bow-tastic!

One exclamation point is still too many, but they're paying, so exclamation point it is. What's left to do on my list so that we can get paid? I haven't finished prepping the drop. The ring light has been flickering and the smaller one just won't cut it for a shoot this important—of course, perfect timing—and if we're going to get the outdoor shots done, Chloe needs to be up ten minutes ago.

Makeup, hair, wardrobe, accessories. Those are supplied in the perk package today. The dresses and leggings they sent are hanging in Abby's closet, boat-necked and a playful mixture of sporty and flirty. She shouldn't fight me on that, but everything is a fight with her lately, so I'll probably have to run interference too.

A cumbersome magenta-striped box sits on the counter opposite me. *Bow-tastic!* the top reads in obnoxiously perky italic lettering. Outlined in glitter, and it's already shedding everywhere.

"I'm too old for bows, Mom," Abby whined when I presented the offer to her.

"Nobody's too old for bows," I said, accepting the contract.

"JJ is!"

"JJ's a boy."

"She's just worried they'll look better on me, Abs." He nudged her in the side and they both laughed. He's a good big brother. I'm glad she has him.

Abby's going through a rebellious phase, at least that's what I keep telling myself. Talking back. Arguing with every single direction I give. Foot-stomping and doors slamming and *no way*s when we both know that when it comes to "CC and Me," the answer is going to be *yes*. Totally normal at her age. I was the same way. She's a little young for the drama perhaps, but kids are growing up faster nowadays.

And I sound like I'm one prune shake away from a hip replacement.

One of the other things nobody told me about motherhood was how stressed I'd be all the time. You stress about your children fitting in. About teaching them the difference between right and wrong. Making sure their needs are met, toeing the line between selfish and self-sufficient. Am I helicoptering? Too distant? Am I giving them too much screen time? Do I need a minivan? Do I need to get a mom cut? Am I allowed to wear shorts or does my wardrobe consist solely of athleisure wear once I hit thirty?

If only—*if only*—the trouble stopped there.

Bullying. Sexual pressure. Failure. Healthy diets and exercise. I mean, I lived on Ellio's pizza and Hot Pockets. Busted my shins on pogo sticks and Skip-Its. Was made fun of for numerous reasons, really, but the point is, none of it was anywhere close to the expectations we have for our children today.

I open the Bow-tastic! lid and wipe glitter on my thighs.

A row of hot pink eyeshadow, aptly named Orchid, Fairy Power, and Madness. Imagine being the marketing director of a major cosmetics brand, perched at a sprawling conference table discussing which names would most appeal to teenagers, and the *best* idea your A-Team can muster up is Fairy Power. Stunning.

Next to those, two bottles of lip gloss (Berry Berry and Yeah Right), a nude shimmer stick (Bow-tastic! Shine), a trial size bottle of foundation with a squishy applicator and a contour kit—you know, for all those super important galas thirteen-year-olds need to contour for—two pairs of heart-shaped rhinestone earrings, and twelve bows.

Fuck. Fork.

"Abby!" I slam the lid shut and jog up the stairs, my knee clicking with every step, another delightful reminder that my body's not what it used to be. "Abby! Rise and shine, pretty girl!"

Crust. How did it get so late? We're going to have to dive right into this shoot and save the heart-to-heart for later if we want to catch the light. Less than ideal, but I don't see what other choice we have.

These pictures can't be just great. They need to be perfect.

Abby's room is to the left of the landing next to the bathroom she shares with JJ. The door is decorated with large ombre block letters spelling out CHLOE. A black and white sketch of the old oak tree in our yard, rope swing swaying lazily in the wind, hangs beneath them. Not bad. Abby's always loved art.

It used to be stick figure families and construction paper hearts. Her scratchy just-learning-to-write letters naming her creations. MOMMY. DADDY. JJ. ABBY. Holding hands under a sunny sky. I have a box of them stored somewhere. Not all of them—she made hundreds and I couldn't save them all—but a few favorites I couldn't bear to throw away.

Stick figures gave way to the Disney princess phase, one I never had to endure with JJ. Every picture was ball gowns, princes, and castles. We had a playlist of all the major princess hits on repeat, lyrics burned into my brain to this day.

But we were happy then.

She was happy. My Abby-girl, dancing through the house, begging Jackson to be her prince, skirts trailing glitter clouds behind her.

Abby has always sparkled.

And I've loved being here for everything. While I admittedly had a rough initiation into mom world, I've come to cherish this identity I've crafted for myself. Mommy and blogger. Mother and entrepreneur. Having the chance to record it all, share her sparkle with the rest of the world, it's special.

She's special.

"Abby." I knock. "Abby, time to get up."

No response.

My heartbeat kicks up a notch. "Abby?"

Crickets.

"Abby, we're not doing this again." I open the door and prepare for her protests as I've invaded her privacy without permission. I fight the moment of déjà vu, expecting to see her burritoed in her comforter, wrapping it around herself to block me out. The puff of her brown ponytail visible through the top like a spring roll.

But everything I see is wrong.

Her bedding is tangled and tossed to the floor. I touch the spot on the pillow where her head should be. Cold. As is the rest of the bed. Like it hasn't been slept in.

Her window is wide open. Beads of condensation gather along the edge, growing fat and dripping down to the sill.

I try to rationalize the empty bed. She's in the bathroom. In the shower. Went for an early morning run. There's a perfectly logical explanation to explain her absence.

But my gut is screaming. *Something is wrong. Something is very wrong.*

"Abby?" I call, my volume rising. "Abby!"

Jackson appears in the doorway. His boxers are twisted and his dark hair is disheveled, but his eyes are alert. "What's going on?"

"Have you seen Abby?"

"Uh, no, I just woke up."

"Why are you being so loud? It's Saturday." JJ stands behind Jackson now, sleepily tugging his practice jersey over his head. He studies my expression with naked curiosity.

I'm rushed by a wave of claustrophobia. Abby isn't in her bed. She isn't here. I can't get out of this room with them blocking the doorway. I have to find her. "Abby!"

I push through them to the bathroom, my breathing harsh and ragged. I haven't had a panic attack since college graduation. Sitting in the middle of hundreds of other polyester-clad graduates waiting for our names to be called. Surrounded by people. No way to leave without drawing attention to myself. The overwhelming certainty I was going to faint as my vision clouded and sweat popped on the back of my neck.

That same thick urge to collapse hits me as the bathroom door smacks against the wall. "Abby?" Not at the sink brushing her teeth or beating me to her primer. The curtain rings catch on the bar and I yank them free. Tub, dry and empty.

She's not here. "Abby!"

Jackson and JJ follow me, gentle curiosity replaced by growing concern.

Jackson tries to grab me. His hand clutches at my shoulder before I jerk out of his reach. "Jen, what's the—"

"I can't find Abby," I say.

"She's—she has to be here somewhere. Abby-girl? Where are you?" He leaves my side, hands falling off his hips, heading toward our room.

Why would she be there? Does he think she's hiding in our closet like she did when she was five? He marches out seconds later, hands open in a beats-me gesture.

"I'll check downstairs," JJ says. "Abs! Come on, mom's freaking out, this isn't funny!"

I follow behind him. He goes from kitchen to living room to the half bath and the study. Nothing.

I open the basement door and stare into the darkness. "Abby?" I call.

I wish for her voice, but I hear a loaded nothing.

Fork. This isn't happening. I close the door a little too hard and jump as I turn directly into Jackson. I glare at him and tread back upstairs to her room.

When was the last time I saw her?

Why can't I remember?

I'm freaking out, that's why. "Get a grip," I tell my reflection in Abby's mirror. I close my eyes. Inhale, exhale. "Get it together, Jen." Three, two, one. "Get. It. Together."

I don't feel better. I climb over her bed and peer out the window as JJ comes into view in the backyard. He shakes his head and shouts, "She's not out here!"

Fork.

Jackson runs in, breathing hard and phone in hand. "I'm going to call her."

Of course. Why didn't I think of that?

He rakes his fingers through his hair and paces while we wait for the connection to blare through the speaker. "Come on, come on."

We both jump when her phone rings. Charging on the corner of her side table where she plugs it in every night. A picture of her and Jackson flashes on the screen. A close-up of the two of them last summer riding Splash Mountain just as the boat hit the biggest drop.

He looks at me, slack-jawed and desperate.

I think I'm going to be sick. The walls shrink. The floor sways. I reach out to steady the melting reality but find nothing to grip for purchase. I collapse to my knees, taking fistfuls of her purple comforter and pooling it back onto the mattress. This isn't right. I have to make the bed. That will fix everything. If I can just put things back the way they're supposed to be—yes. Abby will appear, smiling and wonderfully present, and we'll all laugh at my moment of panic.

"Jen," Jackson says.

I can't get the blankets to stay on the bed; they cascade around me until I accept the futility and moan.

"Let's not overreact," Jackson insists. "We don't know for sure anything is wrong, and getting this worked up doesn't help. Stay calm."

Calm. He has no idea what he's asking of me. "Did she say anything to you last night?" I ask. "Before she went to bed?"

"No," he says. "Just goodnight."

I stare at the window. Why is it open? Abby hates the cold. "We should call the police."

Jackson's face drops. "Jen, hold on, that's a little premature."

"She doesn't have her phone. She'd never leave her phone."

"Maybe she went to the park. Weren't you guys talking about taking pictures outside today? Let's just give it a little while before we make any rash decisions."

"If something happened to her . . ." I shake away the thought.

"Don't get ahead of yourself," Jackson protests. "I think we should—"

My ears feel clogged. The ringing blocks out Jackson's voice. "This isn't right," I mutter. "This isn't right, this isn't right, where is she?"

"—check around the neighborhood," Jackson says.

"Call the police."

"I'll call the Fletchers and ask if they've seen her, and—"

"No," I cut him off. "Not the Fletchers. Not the neighbors. Call the police. Call them now, Jackson."

When he doesn't move, I rip the phone out of his hands and dial the number myself.

It is 7:21 A.M., and Abby is missing.

EMILINA

I smell the coffee before my eyes open, dark roasted and heavenly. Drew, my coffee angel, clinks around in the kitchen, and I take a second to breathe it all in.

Dragging the pillow over my head, I groan, not ready to abandon the brief happiness in order to tackle the day's events. Debriefing. Reports. Paperwork. There should be a law against busy Saturdays, but then again, I've never had a normal work schedule. I throw the blankets to my feet and send a mental farewell to my bed. Papers aren't going to file themselves.

Reaching the landing, I rub the sleep from my eyes and yawn. "Morning."

Drew stands at the stove, poaching a couple of eggs to go over the toast he's already stacked on two plates. Wrapping my arms around him from behind, I nuzzle into the sweet spot between his shoulder blades. He smells like cinnamon and butter. I could breathe him in all day. "What's the occasion? Did I forget our anniversary?"

"Yes," he deadpans.

"Seriously?"

He turns and smiles. It's one of his best features. Full of dimples and unabashed glee. When Drew smiles, it lights up his whole face, every crease transformed into a mark of positivity. The world needs more of that. "It's April. We got married in October."

"We're married?"

"I like to think so," he says, and pulls me in for a real kiss.

I slap him away. "I have morning breath."

"Just how I like you."

"Gross and smelly?"

"My woman." He gives me a playful squeeze on the hip and delicately stirs the egg. I've seen him do this enough times to know that if he moves the spider too quickly, the yolk will break open.

I take a big bite of toast and pour myself a cup of steaming goodness, wrapping my fingers around the warmth of the mug.

"To what do I owe this surprise, then?" I ask, settling into the corner where the counters come together.

"Can't a guy do something special without having a reason?"

"He can, yes, but I find that highly suspect."

"Taking me in for questioning?"

"Maybe after you serve up those eggs," I say.

Drew slices a tomato and half an avocado, scoops the eggs out of the boiling water, and serves his creation with a dash of salt and pepper. Avocados have been the butt of millennial humor lately, but I don't care. They're delicious.

We have a few bites in comfortable silence.

Drew sets his plate on the counter and sips from his own mug. "We have to talk about this eventually," he says.

"I know." I move to the table. I love this spot in the morning. The view of the mountains is crisp, and I swim in the shades of blue. Cornflower sky. Cerulean ridges. The vast line of trees, so close together they blend to murky navy-black.

At the base of the mountain are the railroad tracks, rusted yet functioning.

Trains pass at all hours of the night, shaking the windows and blowing whistles. I wonder what's on them. Oil, I think some days. Others, viruses. That one, I admit, is a guilty pleasure from the *X-Files* movie I watched as a teenager (embarrassingly in love with Mulder and secretly wanting to be Scully). Absurd to admit, I know, but I love making up crazy doomsday scenarios, pondering how I'd handle each apocalyptic event. Mutant viruses. Zombie outbreaks. Creating hypothetical disasters is easier than dealing with the hardships I encounter on a daily basis.

"Emilina," he says.

"Drew."

"Did you take your vitamin?"

"I haven't even brushed my teeth yet," I remind him. It's just after seven. I might have time to shower and plait a halfway decent braid before the meeting.

"Em." His eyes are translucent in the light. Amber and beautiful. They scuttle over my body, hoping today is the day we finally talk about the elephant in the room.

"We will," I acquiesce between mouthfuls. "Tonight. I have to finalize this case and then I'll be able to focus."

He sets his fork down and holds out his pinky. "Promise?"

I lock mine in his. "Promise."

That's been our dealmaker for as long as we've been together. Pinky promises may be old-school, but for us, they are sacred.

"Good," he says, sending another smile my way before chomping half his toast in a single bite. "I'm excited. Thank you."

"You're welcome," I say. He's so good to me. I'm not sure I can say the same.

Patrick would've loved him. Dad too.

When I was growing up, we used to play Clue every Wednesday night. It was just the three of us: my dad, me, and Patrick, my older brother. I was Miss Scarlet, even though green was my favorite color. Everybody knows Mr. Green is the worst character. Patrick was Colonel Mustard. My father, Professor Plum. We'd mix up the cards and use broken pencil stubs to tally our sheets, carefully deducing who the murderer was. The conservatory was my favorite room, the candlestick my favorite weapon. Is it weird to have a favorite weapon? It just seemed so . . . . dependable. In a murdery way.

Maybe that's why I ultimately chose to become a detective. I never really grew out of story weaving and strand pulling.

Or sussing out the bad guys. That comes with the territory, too, although the ones I chase aren't as easy to spot as a bloody murderer in a board game.

"Quarter for your thoughts," Drew says.

"Dollar for my time," I respond. We're on a roll this morning.

"I'd gladly pay double."

I snort laugh. Sometimes he sounds like a sonnet. Number 310, Ode to a Goofy Husband. "I'm just going over what I need to do when I get to the bullpen."

"Busy day?"

"No busier than yours." Drew manages an almost–Fortune 500 software company. They're supposed to be revolutionizing the online world. I don't understand half of what he tells me, but I listen nonetheless. It's a welcome distraction from the work I carry home. Missing kids don't make for a good night's sleep.

"Let's hope it stays that way," he says.

"Fingers crossed." I move to take another bite and my phone rings from the catchall nest on the counter. "See what you did," I say, wiping crumbs from my shirt.

He holds his hands up in defense. "Wasn't me, ma'am."

"Emilina Stone," I say, flipping him a loving bird.

"Stone, you on your way yet?"

Cap Suter, commander of the Children and Family Services Unit, the local division that handles missing persons cases. His actual title is Detective Lieutenant, but Ossian Suter has gone by Cap for as long as I've known him, a nickname he allegedly earned in youth when he started handing out tickets to his family. Hogging the remote, clothes on the floor, eating the last snack—all ticketable offenses.

Cap's a lifer, and our department loves him for it.

"Getting ready," I say. "I'll be there in twenty."

"Need you on site. We got a call."

Drew stares at me. I nod and mouth, "Sorry." He finishes chewing and clears the table. Our brief foray into normal-couple-who-eats-weekend-breakfast coming to an abrupt close. Another dance we've mastered.

"Where am I going?" I ask Cap.

"Upper Madison. This one's sensitive, Stone. High profile. Some sort of Internet celebrity."

"Text me the details," I say, disconnecting.

Drew scrubs the stuck-on bits of food down the drain and piles the dishes into a neat stack on the side of the counter. I appreciate his thoroughness.

"Sounds like your day just got busier," he says.

My phone dings and I open the message. An address in Upper Madison, the historic part of the city. Our house is in between Upper and Lower; the tracks serve as an unofficial border. Disappearances aren't relegated to arbitrary boundaries, though. Rich or poor, old or young, anyone can go missing.

And today, I'm going to the suburbs for a missing kid.

"I'll try to be home at a decent hour."

"Waiting up is my specialty, Em. I'm a pro." His hands disappear into the soapy water. I can't tell if he's joking or hurt. It's a fine line, being the supportive husband, the one who hungers for the missing children's safety as much as I do, and the loving husband, who understands the importance of my job, but at the end of the day, wants nothing more than for me to be able to leave all that heaviness at the office.

Sometimes, though, heavy can't be shaken. It sticks to your bones and spreads.

Like I said, Drew's good to me. He finds a balance, and he tolerates my dives. How detached from us I become at the start of a new case. Swimming the depths of depravity no one should ever have to see. Time crunched and greedy and—more often than not—angry. Angry at the people who think it's okay to mistreat children. Sickened by the things people do to one another. Frustrated that my normal depends on the abnormal impulses of predators.

I can't change when the calls come in. There's no way to conveniently schedule absconding or abductions. Doesn't make the routine any easier.

"I pinky promised. We'll talk about it tonight."

"You better get a move on," Drew says. He kisses the top of my head, a giant in his own right. I'm tall for a woman, six feet on the rare occasion I wear heels, and he still looks down to meet my gaze.

"I'll text when I get a chance," I say.

The separation has started already. My body is here, but my mind is racing. My thoughts have turned to the little information I've been given. The seconds tick by on an invisible clock.

Click, click, click.

Numbers tumble over one another, fast and ever moving. A constant reminder that every minute counts. Every minute it takes me to brush my teeth and get clothes. Every minute I sit in morning traffic listening to the radio announcer. Every minute a child is involuntarily absent from their family.

I pick dark jeans and a light blue button down that reminds me of the mountains, figuring it must be a good omen, and fasten my weapon, no longer a candlestick, but a dependable semiautomatic that I've never had to use. Toppling my hair into a messy bun, I glance at the mirror hanging by the door. By no means perfect, but presentable. I don't have time or patience for purses, so I shove my wallet into my coat pocket along with a pack of breath mints and a small notepad.

I freeze at the top of the stairs, Drew's hope wheedling through the veil of the concentration. I jog to the bathroom, dry swallow a vitamin, and run out the door, shouting, "I love you!" as it closes.

Cool breeze whacks me in the face. Clouds roll at a steady clip, but the sun is breaking through. Finally. It's been a long winter.

I press the phone button on the steering wheel and command, "Call Cap."

Siri complies, and Cap's deep voice reverberates off the dashboard. "Stone, what's up?"

"On my way. Should be at the address in fifteen minutes, but break it down for me. What am I looking at?"

"Call came in from the mother. Allegedly went in to wake the daughter a little after seven. Chloe, thirteen years old. She was apparently gone at that time."

"Witnesses?"

"None as far as I know. Mother said the room looked like it hadn't been slept in and the window was open."

Wouldn't be the first kid to sneak down a gutter pipe. "You said this was high profile."

"Mom's a *blogger*," he says, and I can hear the disdain. "Runs some sort of horse-and-pony show with her kids. CC something."

"CC Spectacular?" I ask.

"That's the one."

"No shit."

"You know it?"

Yes. More than I should. "Kind of. Pops in my Facebook timeline every so often."

"Well, good, maybe you'll have some added insight. Keep me apprised, Stone, and tread carefully. We have to stay on top of this or shit could go south real quick."

"Understood, sir."

One of the most popular mommy blogs in the country. Run by a woman calling herself Jennifer Cates. A woman who, decades ago, I knew only as Jen Groff, my middle school best friend.

Until the night everything changed—and then we weren't friends. Or enemies.

We were something worse.

JACKSON

I should've gotten out of bed when I first heard Jen moving around. Hunching over the laptop trying to block the glare from the screen. She thinks I haven't noticed the downward trend, and I've let her believe that. No point arguing about it now. Her—*our*—numbers are struggling. They've dipped before and we've been fine. What concerns me is how she was trying to hide it. Pretending everything is okay when it's so clearly not.

Nothing is okay. Today is all the proof I need.

This is a nightmare.

Jen hasn't stopped crying. I hear her sobbing downstairs. Sitting at the kitchen table. Waiting for the cops to get here.

The thought rocks me. Cops. In our home. I suppress a gag and turn away from the mirror. I can't stand what I see.

Jen cries louder. "I don't know where she is, Mom. If I did I wouldn't be on the phone with you!"

Carol. Great. Just what we need.

Why did she even bother to call her mother? It's not like Abby would go there on her own. They've interacted maybe a handful of times in her entire life.

Jen's relationship with her mother is tumultuous. Parasitic. They feed off each other's drama. Jen blames Carol, and Carol, in turn, tells stories about how difficult Jen was as a child. The sacrifices she made to ensure Jen didn't turn out like the "other kids" from their neighborhood.

Always in air quotes. Like they were fictional but still dangerous.

It's not *just* Carol who's the problem, though. Jen would never admit it out loud, but she can be just as bad.

Jen thrives in conflict.

She reined it in a bit when JJ was born, but I don't think it's possible to completely eliminate the part of her that loves misery and all its company. A person's character can wax and wane, but it's as indestructible as the moon. Once a mean girl, always a mean girl.

That sounds terrible, a really shitty thing to say about your wife, but it's the truth. People sugarcoat who their spouses are far too often. They plaster their perfect relationships on social media and act completely shocked when everything falls apart around them.

But who's surprised? Divorce parties are marketed on Hulu, on cart handles at the market, on the back of receipts. Hell, there's a billboard five minutes from my office advertising a law firm that specializes in speedy divorces. Next to their pricing and contact info—YOU can be FREE and SINGLE within a DAY (for the cool price of four hundred and fifty dollars)—is a graphic of a three-tiered wedding cake. Each layer has a separate saying. **I DO. I DID. I'M DONE.**

Where's the accountability? The obligation to work through problems? I knew Jen had that mean streak when I married her. I loved her in spite of it, maybe even because of it, if I'm being honest. Nobody wants to be brutally honest today. But Jen does. Maybe she doesn't have a heart of gold, but I'll settle for brass.

And she's a good mother, other than her obsession with the blog.

I don't want to think about the blog.

Too late. Abby would be taking photos for the new sponsor right now. If she were here. Instead, we're scrambling around like headless chickens.

I slog down the hall to JJ's room. He's sprawled on his bed scrolling through his phone when I enter. "I'm going through her Instagram," he says without looking up.

"That's a nice thought, but I doubt she'd post on 'CC and Me' without your mother knowing."

JJ stops scrolling. "No, Dad. Not the official account."

The hairs on the back of my neck prickle. Call it a father's sixth sense, an alarm that goes off whenever your kids are about to tell you something that reaffirms they are people. Not just your babies, but growing beings with their own thoughts, feelings, and motivations that might be totally different than your own.

"JJ," I say, with a hint of fatherly admonition. "What account are you looking at?"

He frowns. I can see the man he's becoming and part of me swells with pride. His whole future rests in that look, focused and cautious. A burgeoning moral compass guiding him to this point: do I tell him, or do I keep a secret?

Because there is a secret; I see that in his face too.

JJ is quiet for almost a full minute before he decides. "Abby has her own account."

Shit.

All the assurances Jen gave me about how careful she was, how she handled the issue, JJ is able to destroy that illusion in a single sentence. "Are you sure it's hers? Mom was pretty clear that Abby wasn't allowed to have her own socials. She knows the rules."

"It's hers," he says flatly. "I helped her make it." He adopts an accusatory tone I've never heard in my son before this moment. "I know Mom got pissed when she signed up before, but I don't care. It's not right. She can't go to regular school, doesn't go out of the house unless it's for the blog. Can't go online unless Mom says yes. It's like a prison. You guys are killing her."

Killing her.

"We're protecting her, JJ. You guys think you're invincible, that nothing bad can touch you. But there are a lot of bad people out there who'd take advantage of that in a split second. Boundaries are important. Someday when you have your own kids, you'll understand."

"That's a cop-out, and you know it."

I close my mouth. He's right.

"She's not doing anything crazy. She just wants to be able to post her own stuff," he says. "Without Mom telling her how to do it."

"I get that, but you should've told us you helped her."

He's angry. The sudden shift in his mood reminds me, again, that he's not the same little boy who used to hold my hand walking through the market. Leaning into my knees for safety as the floor cleaner passed, afraid of its loud noise and size.

I can't imagine JJ being afraid of anything anymore. But then I realize that's not true.

He's terrified that something has happened to Abby. And for perhaps the first time in our lives, I can't assuage his fears.

"Why?" He throws himself off the bed, stumbling over one of his cleats. With a grunt, he chucks it across the room. It thumps into the wall, leaving a black scuff and a sizable chip in the paint.

"Jesus, JJ," I snap.

He turns to me, tears glazing his eyes through the adrenaline. "Why would I tell you shit? You would've taken her phone again or her Internet privileges or whatever Mom wanted you to do because you always do what she wants. You guys treat her like a baby, it's messed up."

My own anger is rising. Frustration, worry, fear—a big ball of emotions careening down a mountain, gaining traction as it plows forward, and JJ is directly in its path. "Hey, don't speak to me like that. I'm your father. Show me some respect."

He scoffs and gives me this smug look, full of scorn and hatred that only a teenager can manage. "What the hell does that matter? You want to talk about boundaries? Bad people?" He throws air quotes around the word, and spit flies from his mouth. I watch the spray in the sunlight, wishing I was somewhere, anywhere else. "Abby's gone. What did you do to stop it?"

Fuck, this is the last thing I wanted.

Heart hammering in my chest, I stare at the cleat mark, too ashamed to meet JJ's gaze. I open my mouth to apologize or at the very least find some common ground, so he'll stop looking at me like I'm the enemy.

The doorbell rings, saving me from the rest of this conversation.

"Jackson! The police are here!" Jen shouts.

I glance at my son. He's breathing hard, nostrils flaring and jaw working. When did he become this young man? This whole person not afraid to stick up for his sister and talk back to his father.

"We'll talk about this later," I say. "Right now, we need to find Abby."

"I guess." He shuffles past me, runs a hand through his hair and clears his throat. He doesn't want to be emotional in front of strangers, in front of Jen. Trying to be strong.

"We'll find her," I say.

He stops, eyes fixed on her door. "What if we don't?" he asks.

"We will." I say it like I mean it. Like it's the only option.

"I'm not so sure," he says, turning to the stairs.

A hot wave of guilt washes over me, and even though I know it's stupid, I can't believe we've reached this point. He doesn't trust me.

The thought that follows doesn't make me feel better either.

Maybe he's right not to.

JENNIFER

I was arrested once.

Jackson doesn't know. I've never had the guts to tell him, but it's true. Only three people were there when it happened, and one of them is dead.

The other is dead to me, which is basically the same thing.

I was in eighth grade, and as is so often the case at that age, I wanted to impress the older girls. Mary and Nicole. They were in tenth grade. The epitome of cool: Spaghetti straps. Clinique Happy. Body glitter and blue eyeshadow.

Mary lived next to my aunt, and Nicole lived two doors down from my grandmother—all on the same block. Most of Albany was like that, generational neighborhoods where children grew up but never left, buying houses and raising their own families on the same street they spent their childhoods. So, while we'd known one another our whole lives, they never invited me to hang out. Never asked me to join them when they rode bikes or celebrated birthdays in their backyards.

They had massive parties, too, bashes that made me ache with jealousy as a kid. Piñatas and ponies. Balloon-tying clowns. One year, they had an actual circus tent.

I watched from my stoop, pretending to be busy. Pretending I had friends.

I wanted so badly to be part of their group. I chalked their attitudes toward me up to the age difference. Three years makes all the difference when you're a kid trying to prove how grown you are. I thought maybe if I could show them I wasn't a little kid anymore—if I could prove I was one of them—they would accept me. I was thirteen by then, practically an adult, and having older friends—*high school* friends—was guaranteed to make me popular too.

Thinking back on it now, I have no idea why I was so determined to befriend them. They tormented me for years before that horrible night, and it started before I even understood the rules of the game.

When I was seven, maybe eight, I was on my porch building a puzzle while my mother unpotted marigolds for the planter. I was piecing together the fluffy pink ballgown when they appeared. They smiled sweetly and politely asked if I could come out and play.

A dream come true.

That would never happen today, by the way. Now it's all playdates and dance classes and scheduled practices. I'm one to talk, I know. The Calendar Queen. But back then, we were left to our own devices, completely responsible for finding our own friends.

I still wore sticker earrings. They came on a cardboard sheet, like forty shapes for three bucks. Hearts, ice cream cones, diamonds, everything a girl could want to be fashionable in the early nineties.

That day I had chosen sparkly rainbows. I remember being super excited to put them on because I'd learned about ROYGBIV in school. But Mary and Nicole, they had pierced ears, something we couldn't afford and I was afraid to get. So when Nicole asked me where I had gotten mine pierced, I lied. Instinct. Or self-preservation.

"Oh, um, I don't remember the name of the place."

"Was it in the mall?" Nicole asked.

"Uh huh."

"Old Navy?"

"Um, yeah. That sounds right. Definitely Old Navy. I remember the sign now." I didn't even know what Old Navy was. We shopped exclusively at Walmart. My mother's idea of splurging was two pairs of Jordache wide leg jeans.

They exchanged a look. I was too concerned with getting my story right to notice that I'd made a big mistake. Always keep your lies simple.

"I got mine at Claire's," Nicole said. "They gave me the choice of studs, and I picked pink for my birthstone. What did you get? You know. At Old Navy."

I ignored the ridicule in her voice. "I got pink, too, but I lost them," I explained.

I had never been to Claire's. I knew some of the girls in my class went there for best friend necklaces and scrunchies, but my only scrunchie was a hand-me-down, an outstretched faded blue one that mother never wore. And the only jewelry I owned was made of string.

They laughed, but I was laughing, too, so I naively assumed that I'd gotten away with it.

They liked me.

Later that week, I sat on my front porch, legs dangling over the concrete foundation, staring up at the clouds, and they appeared again. Asked if I wanted to walk up the hill behind our houses to the field. The field was just that: a wide-open meadow straight out of a poetry book, with summery greens, long stalky grass, and fuzzy white dandelion buds dotting the brush.

It anchored a square mile of dense forest.

I eagerly agreed and followed Nicole and Mary up the hill, across the meadow, and through the woods to a clearing. It sounds like a nursery rhyme when I say it that way, but this place was far from idyllic.

The ground was littered with wrappers, broken bottles, and cigarette butts. Magazine pictures of celebrities I didn't recognize were stapled to the tree trunks. This was where the older kids hung out, and Mary and Nicole wanted to bring me with them.

Even at seven or eight, I knew how important something like that was. When you're a kid who doesn't have friends, every chance to fit in becomes important.

They claimed the two stumps that served as chairs. In tandem, they crossed their legs, folded their arms, and locked eyes on me. Standing before them, I awkwardly tried to figure out what to do with my hands. On my hips? In my pockets? Behind my back? What did a cool girl do with her hands?

"Should we?" Mary asked, her high-pitched tone betraying her excitement.

"Oh yeah," Nicole said. She reached behind the stump and pulled something out of a plastic bag. "You like *Playboy*?"

I didn't know what *Playboy* was, but I figured it was another test. Like the earrings.

"Sure," I said, hoping I didn't sound too eager.

Nicole handed the magazine to Mary. The corners were burned almost to the spine, like someone had lit it on fire but changed their mind at the last minute. "Have you ever seen someone naked before?" she asked, eyebrows arched.

I mean, yeah, I had. My mother used to change in front of me all the time. But I knew that wasn't what she meant. She was trying to trick me into the wrong answer.

"Have you?" I asked.

Both of them smiled. Foxes in the henhouse.

"Here," Mary said, holding the magazine out. "Have a look."

"No thanks," I said, taking a step back. "I think I should get home. My mom'll kill me if I'm late for dinner."

"Are you scared?" Nicole asked. She flicked her hair over her shoulder, and her earrings sparkled in the sunlight.

Those damn earrings. A shining reminder of my baby status. "No, I'm not scared."

"Then take it."

"I shouldn't."

"Do it," Mary said, and shoved the burnt papers into my chest.

The magazine crackled in my hand. That's how it felt at the time. Wrong. Forbidden. I could see outlines of women, breasts pointing in the air, legs splayed open on beds of silk sheets. I held my arm out wishing one of them would take it back.

They snickered and ran around me.

"I can't believe you, Jennifer," Mary chided.

"What?"

Nicole, still smiling, every tooth on display. "Ugh, that is *so* gross."

"What? What did I do?" I couldn't hide the panic. I had done something wrong.

"Why would you show us that?" Mary asked, shouting now.

"I didn't do it!" I shrieked.

But they were already running through the trees, a singsong rhyme echoing in their wake. "Pervert! Pervert! Jennifer's a pervert!"

"I'm going to tell my mom!" Nicole said. "You're trying to show us naked pictures!"

I dropped the magazine and ran after them. "You gave it to me! It's yours!"

Not knowing how I messed up, I watched them run toward their houses and retreated to mine, proverbial tail between my legs. My mother was watching one of her shows in the living room, as usual. I rushed past, ignoring her questions and throwing myself onto my bed. If Disney movies are good for nothing else, they've mastered the art of teaching girls how to collapse and cry on cue.

It wasn't ten minutes later that Nicole's mother came pounding on our front door—which we never used. Front doors were reserved for salesmen and guests. We left the back door unlocked and used it accordingly. There wasn't as great a concern for break-ins in the nineties. Lots of inflatable furniture.

Nicole's mom was livid. Screaming at my mother that she didn't know what kind of parent let their children run around doling out pornography, but she certainly wasn't going to tolerate such abhorrent behavior. I was a terrible influence on her *beautiful angel*. She didn't want me hanging around anymore, corrupting her innocent child with my smut.

There was no point defending myself. Even if she had believed me, the inconvenience of having to answer the door and deal with another parent was enough to have my freedom revoked. My mother is many things, but flexible has never been one of them. The rules were clear: be home when the streetlights came on, and don't get into trouble.

I was grounded for two weeks. Nicole and Mary schemed the entire time about what their next "trick" would be, and it continued that way until I was thirteen. Until I stopped them. Innocent angels.

Girl-world is such a crazy place. I thought I was sparing Abby from it all, shielding her from that toxic mentality. I don't let her read the comments section. Ever. That was one of *my* first rules when I started writing "CC and Me." No reading the comments. She has some input over which pictures are posted, and she's allowed to see the metrics—although lately, I've been keeping them from her when she asks. Putting it off until she forgets. Making excuses.

But never the comments. Never the horrible things people write when they can't be held accountable for their actions. What better way to voice an opinion than lurking behind some generic username with a gray-box avatar?

There's no short supply of trolls. They crawl out of the woodwork from all directions. Mom shamers. Religion shamers. Body shamers. Some perverts, but those are mutually hated by everyone in general. When our platform started exploding, I was genuinely floored by the sheer number of people who felt entitled to airing their two cents.

Stage mom. Fat kid. Gold digger. Slut. Momager. Ugly kid. Boring.

It's one thing to scroll through Yahoo Celebrity and laugh at the Who Wore It Best comparisons and plastic surgery rumors. It's quite another when you're the subject of public scrutiny and the shit is directed at your children.

Imagine what they'd say if they knew I'd been arrested. The very foundation beneath our feet would quake and shatter.

Anyone can make a video. Hashtag their way into a split second of Insta-fame. But the ugly truth is that most vanish into the matrix, a blip on the algorithm radar. It takes thick skin and perseverance to maintain a presence in the online world.

I've protected Abby from what I could.

I couldn't shield her from real life, though.

That's the world we live in, and that's what I hoped to keep out. Having a flexible homeschool schedule instead of trudging off to the local public junior high was one more way to buffer her from cruelty. Have you *met* teenage girls? That was a gift.

The Bow-tastic! box taunts me. *See how happy it is in here! Rainbows and butterflies and cupcakes and YES!*

So forking cheerful. Like everything I've worked for isn't on the verge of catastrophe. Like Abby's going to walk in any minute and pin a giant bow to her ponytail.

She's not here, though. And as I drum my fingers on the kitchen table, I find the what-ifs invading my thoughts. What if I had listened more? What if I had given her way a chance? *What if I were different?*

If I had made different choices—left instead of right, forgiveness instead of revenge—would I be the person I am today?

Am I the reason this is happening?

Like I said, I'm no stranger to consequences.

Should I tell the officers about my past? Isn't that how these things drag out in the movies? The main character hides some indecorous detail from the rest of the cast, when what she really should be doing, as the audience knows, is confessing it all. The seemingly useless detail is the key to solving the whole case.

My mother rants in my ear. Shrill, dog-decibels of grievances. I can't take it anymore. Cutting her off, I promise to let *her* know when *I* know anything and hang up. She's still ranting about the *dangers of city living* when I hit END. We're in the suburbs, I want to tell her, but there's no convincing Carol when she's got her coat of righteousness on.

The doorbell rings. Pleasant chimes announce my worst nightmare as I pad to the foyer.

"Good morning, ma'am. Albany Police. We received a call about a missing child. Are you Mrs. Cates?" Two officers stand at attention, thumbs hooked into their belts like a hoedown is about to rev up. This, I know, is an unkind assumption, but their lackadaisical stance is irritating. How are they so nonchalant when my girl is missing?

"Jennifer, yes that's me. Please, come in. I'll show you to her room."

Jackson and JJ appear on the landing, and I can tell they've been arguing. Jackson's shoulders are tense, and his jaw is clenched so hard I think he'll bite right through bone. JJ is red-eyed but trying to hide it.

"That won't be necessary yet, Mrs. Cates," the man says. "We've got a detective from the Children and Family Services Unit on the way. We're here to take your statements and gather some information. We need to assess whether there's just cause to issue an Amber Alert."

"Amber Alert." I can't believe this is happening. I've gotten those buzzes on my phone a number of times. Never once did I think I'd be issuing my own.

"Yes, Mrs. Cates. The sooner we can work through your account of what happened, the better."

"Jennifer. Yes, better."

"What's your daughter's name?"

"Abigail," Jackson says.

"Chloe." I give him a death stare. "Chloe Cates."

The officer on the right hitches a breath. She thinks I don't notice, but I'm hyper alert. Her roots are overgrown, for one. The dull shade of brown is mousy in comparison to the richer chocolate pulled into a low knot. She's also wearing too much perfume. Sweet Pea from Bath and Body Works, I think. Spit up stain on her shoulder and heavy bags under her eyes, pitifully disguised by the wrong shade of concealer. New baby at home, if I had to guess. And she recognizes my daughter's name.

A follower.

"Jen, we should use her real name."

"It *is* her real name, Jackson. To everyone outside this house, she is Chloe Cates."

"Mrs. Cates," the spit-up officer says. "I'm a big fan."

Nailed it.

"Call me Jennifer, please. Or at the very least, Mrs. Scarborough. Cates is a stage name, not our real name, as my husband so aptly put it. We usually try to keep a low profile."

The second officer, a red-faced man with a sturdy no-nonsense demeanor dominated by burly black eyebrows, shakes his head and takes out a small black tablet. "Let's start at the beginning. Chloe with a C or a K? And can one of you get me a recent photo?"

"C," the other officer answers for me.

Why haven't they told me their names? Rude.

I push the attitude away. They need a picture. They're here to find Abby. I grab the 8 x 10 headshot from the gallery wall.

"This is the most recent, Detective, um?"

"I'm Officer Katherine Welsh," she says. "And this is Officer Brian Downy."

Downy and Welsh. What is this, a British period drama?

Officer Downy enters a description, snaps a photograph of the picture, and drags the image to a blank white box in the corner of the screen. She gazes out at the world. Brown hair styled in thick ringlets and pinned with a butterfly clip. Glitter around her blue eyes, glossy pink lips.

This used to be done on a milk carton.

Looking at the picture now, I can't believe how vulnerable she looks. The timidity crawling behind her confidence. Her smile isn't genuine. It stretches more than slides. How could I have missed it?

"Oh god." I clap a hand over my mouth as if that could stop the emotions from pouring out. This is really happening.

JJ puts an arm around my waist and leans against me. "It's going to be okay, Mom," he says reassuringly. "We're going to find her."

I smile at his bravado, but I feel nothing, like I'm watching this unravel through frosted glass instead of living the moment firsthand. Part of my brain is categorizing these little details for the post. How to best describe this moment to our subscribers. The smells, the twitches, and quirks.

Because when they find Abby, we're going to go viral again.

I don't know if thinking all this makes me a genius or a monster.

"Mrs. Scarborough," Officer Downy asks, "when was the last time anyone saw Chloe? To the best of your knowledge."

Viral.

"Um," I say.

"Mrs. Scarborough?"

"I said goodnight to her around ten," Jackson says, turning his attention from me to the officers.

"Nothing unusual? Did she seem off?" Officer Downy asks.

Our eyes meet briefly, then Jackson looks away, furrowing his brow and scratching his chin. "No. No, I didn't think so. She was just listening to music."

"What was she wearing?"

"Is that important?"

"We need an accurate description for the report."

Viral.

"I . . . I don't remember," Jackson says, shaking his head.

"A pink sweatshirt and matching sweats," I say. The voices around me unmuffle, the conversation suddenly up front, fast forwarding to the correct spot. "It's one of her favorite sets. Light pink. SELFIE in block letters on the sleeve with a little red heart. She wore it every night before a big shoot. Kind of like a lucky charm."

He taps on the tablet some more then looks to me again. "Nobody saw her after ten?"

What I don't tell him is why I didn't check on her. Why I avoided her.

"No," I say instead. "I don't know. Maybe JJ?" I turn to him with a questioning lilt.

"I, uh." He looks from me to the officers. "No. By the time I got home, her light was off."

I pause. "What do you mean, by the time you got home? When did you go out? I thought you were home all night."

Officer Downy exchanges a look with Welsh, so brief I almost miss it. The same one those miserable women used to give me at the play groups. *Bad mother.* Bad mothers don't know where their kids are.

"I was across the street at Ryan's working on a global project."

"You didn't tell me you have a project," I say. Immediately, I regret it. I'm making this worse.

"Would you have cared if I did?" he retorts. "When was the last time I had to ask permission to go anywhere?"

"JJ, go easy on your mom." Jackson pats his shoulder, but I hear the strain in his voice.

"What time did you get home, son?" Officer Welsh asks.

"After midnight."

"Mm-hm," he nods. "And did you see or hear anything strange?"

He shakes his head, shaking off Jackson's paternal hold in the process. "It was dark and I wasn't really looking. I had my pods in and didn't take them off until I got upstairs."

"Mm-hm, and you, Mrs. Scarborough?" Officer Downy turns to me, vacant yet assessing. "When was the last time you saw your daughter?"

The memory flashes, a split second of pure rage, and I force it away before it takes hold. "Dinner? I'm not sure. I took a melatonin and went to bed early. Before Jackson. I had to be up first thing this morning and wanted to be well rested. We have—*had*—a super busy day planned."

Shoot, what am I going to tell the Bow-tastic! team? I'm sure they'd be understanding given the circumstances, but not so understanding that they won't turn around and hire an alternate by this afternoon.

"Can you think of anyone off the top of your head who might have a reason to hurt Chloe?"

Would flat lays work? Probably not, but I have nothing else to offer to keep them interested. I don't even have test photos to work with. *Shoot.*

"Mrs. Scarborough?"

I feel Jackson glaring at me. Like this is my fault. "I'm sorry?"

Officer Downy clears his throat. "Do you have any reason to suspect someone might want to hurt Chloe?"

"No," I say stiffly. "I mean, we've had some eccentric fans throughout the years but nobody that stands out. You think someone hurt her?"

A few more waves of letters enlarge and fade on his screen, and Downy taps a single word: CONFIRM.

"We've got to consider all options at this point, ma'am. A formality." Tap, tap, tap. I could scream, why is he using one finger to enter this information? A toddler could do this faster. "Okay, ma'am," he says, finally shoving the tablet into a carrying case on his belt. "We're going to review this and look around a bit. If the CFSU detective determines there's sufficient grounds to issue the Amber Alert, we'll get that out and rolling. There won't be a cell phone, radio station, or TV outlet from Vermont to Massachusetts that doesn't sounds the alarm."

TV outlets. Right. I need to put makeup on.

"We should also take your prints, if that's okay," Officer Welsh says.

My previous arrest heavy in my mind, I cast her a shrewd look. "Why?"

"We'll cross-check them against any latents the guys might find. Helps us eliminate from the pool. Super easy. We use a mobile scanner now."

Jackson gives me a "why not" gesture and nods.

"Okay then," I say.

"Why don't the three of you take a seat on the couch and I'll get what I need," Downy suggests. "CFSU should be here any minute and they'll want to talk to you in more detail."

Jackson looks like he's about to speak but remains quiet. He ushers JJ to the beige sectional, and they sink into the cushions together. It would have been a darling photo op under other circumstances. Soft natural light filtering through the windows. Jackson with his arm around JJ. The practice jersey prominent against the neutral background. There's such love in their one-armed embrace.

"Mrs. Scarborough, can you show us Chloe's room?"

"Her name is Abby," Jackson repeats.

"Knock it off, Jackson," I snap. I pivot to Downy and Welsh, who are missing monocles, pipes, and tweed, and gesture to the stairs. "Right up the stairs. Can't miss it. The one with her name on it."

"Thank you, Jennifer."

"Sure, Officer Welsh."

"Please, call me Katherine." She dips closer. "I know this is hard. Everything is going to be just fine. Most of these cases resolve on their own very quickly. I'm sure Chloe will turn up soon." We stand a foot apart, but I feel her desire to reach out. That eager energy seeps through.

The doorbell rings and *Katherine* excuses herself. Are you supposed to be on a first-name basis with the officers charged with finding your child? Seems wildly unprofessional.

Another squad car has arrived. More uniforms crowd into the room. The noise increases tenfold—beeps, clicks, heavy footfalls—sensory overload. I plop down next to JJ and watch the madness begin. Even without an Amber Alert, they're taking it seriously. They'll find her.

A flurry of radios. Badges. Pitying stares.

"Mom, I need to tell you something," JJ whispers in my ear.

I squeeze his hand.

We just had the carpets cleaned, I think, staring at the shoes trampling wet leaves and dirt through the foyer.

You're terrible, that voice in my head mutters. I don't disagree.

Abby's Journal

Sorry I haven't written in so long. I've been cr-aaazy busy. With what, you might ask? Movies? Friends? Boys?

Nope. Sorry. Wrong answer. Thank U, next.

We've been doing *a lot* of skits. The last one she posted was me talking about, quote-unquote, the rise of Valentine's Day. Because I'm an expert on that, right?

Who says you need an S.O. to celebrate? I asked the camera, flipping my pony-tail over my shoulder (as Mom whispered at me to give more face). This should be a time to celebrate friendship. Embrace the girls in your life that give you joy. The ones who see you at your best and your worst. Support you when you're being dumb, crying over that jerk who won't call you back.

I've never had a boy call me, but none of them know that. I wonder if Dad has ever bought Mom roses or diamonds or chocolate-covered anything.

She let me watch the replay when she worked on edits. So much pink, I told her. Can't we tone it down a bit? The hearts flying around, the glitter—it looks like I'm throwing up cupids left and right.

That's the point, *she told me.* You're CC Spectacular. There has to be an abundance of sparkle.

Vomit.

Apparently "CC and Me" is booming. More subscribers every day. She's loading my schedule. Appearances and interviews. She thinks it's time I get an agent. Someone who has "an in" with the big studios. And that means an uber glam sesh. Teeth whitening. Subtle highlights. Gel mani (no tips, though, too tacky for my brand *eye roll*). Spray tanning because, duh, we live in New York.

It's not me doing these things, though. It's Chloe.

Some days I hate myself. I hate her.

And Mom doesn't get it. Doesn't want to see it. Even when I flat out tell her she just ignores me. Says I'm cranky or bratty and goes right on putting my face on the internet for all the world to see.

She's crazy focused on getting me in a movie. Any movie, as long as it's made in HOLLYWOOD. It's your dream! Your name on the big screen!

But that's the thing: it won't be my name. Nobody's ever gonna put ABBY SCARBOROUGH in lights. Why can't she see that?

Take away the spectacular and all you've got is me.

EMILINA

The circus is in full swing when I pull up to the house. Something I'm not expecting. How'd the press find out already? I haven't even talked to the family. White vans line the curb, their sides stamped with blocky station logos that seem out of place compared to the sleek black sedans and SUVs parked in most of the driveways. Despite the brassy sunshine, reporters shiver behind sawhorses on the lawn.

More crews than a usual missing kid attracts. Somebody must've tipped them off. That's good for us in some ways. More exposure means a greater chance of return. But kidnapping, if that is indeed what we're dealing with, is unpredictable. Someone who takes a child can't, under any circumstances, be seen as stable. Rational. Holding to normal measures of society and common sense.

Which also means the added coverage could be inherently dangerous.

Onlookers have formed small huddles around the reporters trying to glean an inside scoop into the chaos. Ambling toward the privacy fence, necks craned and shoulders shrugging when peeking through the cracks proves to be futile.

I've seen the house on the blog, but it looks different in real life. Stately colonial, white with black shutters. Two stories. Front door painted red—an eyesore to me, but trendy if the renovation shows on HGTV that Drew makes me watch are to be believed—with a wreath made of eucalyptus leaves punctuating the vibrant welcome.

From all outward appearances, the family who lives here is comfortable but not ostentatious.

As I cross the street, the throngs descend. Dodging under microphones, I politely, but deftly, ignore their questions, again wondering how the news broke so fast. I flash my badge at an officer flanking the steps. He offers a hushed greeting and lets me through.

My palms are clammy, and I can't remember if I put on deodorant. Missing kids are the worst, for all the obvious reasons and then some, but I'm not sure if I'm more worried about Chloe Cates or my own secret.

Our secret.

Get your shit together, Emilina, this isn't about you. Or Jennifer. Or any childhood grudges the two of you might harbor. This is about a girl in danger.

Right. Jennifer being her mother doesn't change the fact that a child needs help, and the odds stack against her every minute I spend stressing about our sordid history.

Examining the door frame, I see no signs of forced entry. The locking mechanism is intact, no scrapes or digs at the wood.

The majority of the action is focused on a room at the top of the stairs. Cap sent guys early, probably anticipating the publicity this could bring to the squad, and it looks like they've got a decent start. Cameras flash like lightning on the ceiling as officers jot notes in the hallway. Someone calls out numbers, clamoring to be heard.

I stare at the collection of Jack Vettriano reprints on the foyer wall, an elegant couple waltzing on the shore at sunset. Not the sort of thing she would've picked out when we were friends. The girl I knew wore cotton shorts under her dresses and ate Spaghettios out of a mixing bowl.

My gaze flicks to the gallery wall opposite the dreamlike beach paintings.

Strange to see them in person. Smiling faces, vacationlands, sport candids. The Scarboroughs. I read about their engagement in the paper, that's how I know her real name. Scanning the *Announcements* while shoveling Oreos in my mouth two at a time to distract myself from the case I was working, I stumbled upon Jennifer and Jackson, a classically handsome man proud of the woman on his arm. I hadn't seen her since high school graduation and had stopped talking to her long before then, but I recognized her immediately.

You never forget the face of your first best friend.

They looked happy, relaxed, but I wondered how much of herself she had shown. Which version she'd chosen to share with him.

All these things give me an uneasy *Matrix* vibe. I've been here before, but really, I've never set foot in this house. I've seen this wall before, dozens of times, it seems. On "CC and Me." On Jennifer's Instagram page. Tagged in family gatherings on her Facebook.

This observation sticks like a pinpoint. This family is overexposed. There are no privacy settings on her social media accounts. She's posted every inch of this house in videos and photos. How many other people has she given access to by documenting their lives? How vulnerable has Jennifer's blog really made her family?

I make a mental note to ask Luke, our tech savant, to comb through their follower and subscriber lists.

I pause at the last photo of Chloe. She has beautiful brown hair pulled into a mini bun and blue-gray eyes. She's missing a tooth, but her smile is radiant. Arms curled into parentheses above her head, she stands on tiptoes in a golden tutu.

An officer squeezes by me with a Faraday Bag. Cell phone, I register. That's a good start. Kids trust their phones more than their friends.

So why didn't she bring her phone with her?

Good freaking question. I move to the stairs when a commotion from across the room stops me cold.

"Oh my god, oh my *god*!" a woman screeches.

Even with the surrounding volume cranked to ten, even with years and miles and long-dead secrets between us, her voice remains the same.

Everything seems to shriek to a halt. Heads snap up at the sudden outburst of emotion. A hush covers the room like a weighted blanket. I gaze through the parting crowd and lock eyes with Jennifer.

Father and son sit shoulder-to-shoulder on the couch as Jennifer jerks out of her seat. No longer the doting, shiny blogosphere mother, her fists are clenched and disbelief oozes from her staggered movements. Wrinkles deepen around her eyes as she lets them roam up and down my body.

"You," she mutters.

"Hello, Mrs. Cates," I say slowly. I debate holding out my hand but think better of it. "I know this must be an incredible shock."

"Who let you in? Why are you in my home?" She lowers her voice, perhaps understanding how closely she's being observed. Police everywhere. The press right outside. People talk. "You can't be here."

"Jennifer!" Jackson, trophy husband, steps to her side and gruffly takes her elbow. "What's gotten into you?"

Jen wrenches out of his grasp and swoops back to me. "I want you out of my house. You don't belong here."

"What's your problem?" Jackson asks. "I'm sorry," he apologizes. "She's just—we're under an enormous amount of stress. Are you the investigator they told us about? I'm Jackson Scarborough. Abby's father."

Abby? Huh, should've known she'd lie about her daughter's name too.

I'd hoped to do this *introduction* under more contained circumstances. I should've known better than to think she'd react with anything other than rage. I hold up my badge. "My name's Emilina Stone—*Detective* Emilina

Stone—and I'm with CFSU. Can we speak in private for a moment, Mrs. Cates? Scarborough?"

"No, I'm not going anywhere with *you*." She points a tastefully polished finger at me, releasing a wave of memory so strong it almost knocks me down. I see her at thirteen making the same gesture in the darkness, surrounded by trees and crowned by the full moon.

You can't tell anyone, she says, a broken record, *you can't tell anyone. Promise me, Emilina. You can't tell a soul.*

"Okay," I say, staring her down but keeping my composure. "We can do this here. In front of everyone." I nod toward the reporters outside.

That does it. "Fine. *Fine*," she says, swallowing the worst of her anger. "This way." Like the flip of a switch, Jennifer rolls her shoulders back and smooths the frizz from her hair. Prim and proper Jennifer Cates is in control once again. "Follow me, please. Detective Stone."

She pats her husband's chest and whispers, "I overreacted, I'm sorry. I thought she was a follower. My mistake. I'll be back in a moment."

"Okay," he says, more of a question than a statement.

I meet his eyes, dazed and terrified, a gut-punch I've seen too many times. Not on "CC and Me," though. His are the eyes of a parent hanging on by a thread.

Jennifer leads me through the dining room and out a sliding door, nodding solemnly to an officer taking pictures. We step onto a large deck. The weathered wood is the rusty color of a rooster. A covered grill, empty flowerpots, and patio furniture are stacked beneath a window.

This door, too, seems unscathed, but sliding doors are notoriously easy to crack. "Do you have a security system?" I ask.

"No, we looked into it when the kids were younger, but the options were so expensive, they didn't seem worth it. Besides, we've always felt safe here. Neighbors run a watch and communicate on the Nextdoor app. And two of our closest neighbors have dogs that bark at their own shadows. Most nights, we don't even have to lock up."

"Did you lock them last night?" I ask.

She shrugs. "Honestly, I can't remember. I went to bed early."

Three stairs dip down into the wide expanse of yard. It is entirely fenced save for a roughly six-foot section that opens into the woods.

"Something happen to your fence?" I ask.

She glances over her shoulder dismissively. "Oh, no. We left that open for easier access to the woods for photos. Some of the equipment and props are pretty bulky. Plus, I keep a garden right on the other side. Nothing extravagant, herbs mostly, but I do have a bit of a green thumb. Chloe likes to explore while I pick weeds and water. Our property line extends back a ways, but it's too marshy to build on."

"Is she always supervised out there?" I ask.

Upper Madison's forested areas aren't as ominous as our old stomping grounds, but they are similarly secluded. I'm struck by the absentminded security. The degree to which they've underestimated, or dismissed, their vulnerability. I guess that's the bottom line, though. No one thinks something like this will happen to them until it does.

"Mostly," she says. "It's just the woods. What's there to be afraid of?"

A knot forms in the pit of my stomach. "There's plenty of reason to be wary of the woods." I'm looking at one of them.

I wonder if she sees that thought on my face, if my fears are as real as they used to be. Jen regards me severely. "You haven't changed," she says.

"I could say the same for you."

"How long has it been, Emilina?"

"Not long enough."

"I heard about the accident. Thought about sending my condolences, but it didn't seem right," she says, her face somber.

The accident.

It happened about a month before I met Drew. My dad had just had knee surgery and was learning how to get around with this massive black brace. Called himself the Terminator. I found it so annoying, but I would give anything to hear his shitty Arnold impression one more time.

I was working crazy hours trying to make detective, and an emergency came across my desk. Six-year-old boy abducted by his uncle. One of my first Amber Alerts. Mandatory OT. All hands on deck. I couldn't say no, but it was my turn to pick up my dad from physical therapy.

Patrick volunteered. *No problem*, he'd said. *Go save the kid.*

I had no idea those would be the last words my brother ever spoke to me.

My memories might've softened with time. I may look at our history through rose-colored glasses, but I have no doubt that Patrick was as good in real life as my mind makes him out to be. He was the guy you'd call to help you move your entire apartment on a Sunday afternoon—who would spot you his last twenty and not hold it against you if you didn't pay him back. He put his carts back at the grocery store and organized community cleanups, and he always reminded me to drink more water and wear sunscreen.

He wanted me to save lives, but I couldn't save his.

Five minutes from home, right around the time I was responding to a witness sighting of the uncle at a downtown Denny's parking lot, a distracted driver crossed the double yellow going seventy miles an hour and hit Patrick's car head-on.

There were no survivors.

I was told they died instantly, felt nothing, but that doesn't make it any easier to accept. If anything, it felt like karma catching up to me for what we'd done. Me and Jen, that night in the woods.

"I appreciate the sentiment," I say, pushing thoughts of the automobile carcass from my mind.

Jennifer props herself against the railing, arms crossed over her thin white shirt for warmth. "I think we clearly have a conflict of interest here, Emilina. You can't be the only investigator in Albany."

"Conflict of interest?" I ask, stepping toward her. "Your goal isn't to find your daughter?"

"That's not what I said. Don't put words in my mouth."

"Then let me do my job. You've trusted me this long. Why stop now?"

She considers me for a moment before offering an exasperated shrug. "What do you need to know?"

I exhale, finding confidence as I slide into detective mode. "Let's start with the basics. Has Abby ever gone missing before?"

She looks like she might not answer, pinching her lips together and tasting her options before replying. "Chloe. And no. She knows better than to run off without telling us."

"Have you checked with her friends? She might've stayed the night with one of them and forgot to tell you?"

Jennifer tugs at a delicate silver chain around her neck. Two circular charms with the initials J and C are engraved into the surface. She drags them back and forth then stuffs it under her collar. "No."

"Okay, I'm going to need the name and address of whoever she's closest to, Jennifer. I'd like to start there and eliminate the possibility this is just a miscommunication. We don't want to send officers on a goose chase if she's just at a sleepover and forgot to grab her phone."

"You're not listening, Emilina. She doesn't have anyone she'd go to. She doesn't have local friends. There was Willa Forest around the corner, but they lost touch a year or two ago and she really hasn't met anyone else."

This surprises me. Chloe's friends are frequently featured on "CC and Me." Perfect, curated selfies. Screenshots of their texts. Where are those girls? "What about someone from 'CC and Me'?"

She issues a breathy laugh and puts her hands on her hips. "You've read my blog?"

I give a noncommittal gesture, somewhere between a shrug and a wince. "Once or twice."

Jennifer smiles. "Of course you have. Why am I not surprised? No. She wouldn't go to those girls. I mean she can't." She sighs. "They're not real."

"What do you mean?"

She scans the area before speaking. "We use stock photos. Sometimes a model, but I haven't been able to—" She shakes her head as if to scold herself for almost revealing too much. "They're not real. Chloe takes the picture or records a short video and I use various photoshop programs to alter them after."

I recall the images I've seen on the blog, their warm hugs and beautiful faces, covered in sparkles and duck-lip posing. I've heard of deep fakes, but I didn't know you could fabricate pictures and videos to that extent. Who would photoshop friends into her daughter's pictures?

"They're all fake?"

"I mean, if we attend a brand event, no, she'll tag herself with other influencers. But Chloe can't be in school and maintain her presence on the blog at the same time. It's a full-time commitment for both of us. Her work would suffer. Her schedule's demanding—especially with the new branding opportunities we've received lately. We have to be available, and to do that, we have to be flexible. So, we homeschool, which means yes, the girls you see on our accounts are not real. I trust that information stays between us. The repercussions could be devastating if the truth got out."

"Jennifer, she's thirteen. She needs to socialize."

She rushes toward me, another flip of a switch. "Don't tell me what my daughter needs, Emilina. Chloe gets plenty of socialization. We go to influencer luncheons and networking events several times a year. Plus, the mall tours and—you know what, I don't have to explain myself. I know what's best for Chloe."

Officer Downy sticks his head out the door. I've worked with him on quite a few cases. He's good. Honest and reliable. I'm glad he's here for this one.

"Everything okay out here, Stone?" he asks.

I cock my head at Jennifer, watch the anger melt to worry then morph into a subtle pleading. There's more at stake than her reputation and we both know it. "Peachy," I say without breaking eye contact.

"Holler if you need me."

"Hey, Downy," I call after him. "Have one or two of the guys head back to the station for tip line duty." I have a feeling we're going to need all the manpower we can get.

"On it," he says. The door slides shut.

Patchy sections of blue sky peek through the stubborn clouds. I pace the deck, measuring my next words. "Look, I'm not here to cause trouble, Jen. My job is to find Abby."

"*Chloe*. You don't know her. You don't get to use her real name."

I can't offer the full branch, so I go for an olive twig. "Fine. Chloe, then. She needs someone in her corner."

"I'm her mother. I am in her corner no matter what."

"Yes, and because of that, you can't look at this objectively."

"And you can?"

She's not wrong, even though I hate to admit it. I should hand this off to someone else. Someone with a less complicated past with the mother of the missing girl.

But I can't. For Chloe's safety, and for my own.

"I know what I'm doing, Jennifer," I say. "I wouldn't risk your daughter's life because of what happened twenty years ago. So you can keep fighting me, or you can trust that I'm here to help. And if blind altruism is too much of a mystery, then trust that I wouldn't put my entire career on the line for you."

Reluctantly, she nods.

"Good. Can you show me where her bedroom window is? I'd like to see it from this vantage point."

Recoiling her muscles like a darting snake, Jen motions over her shoulder. "This way, Emme."

My old nickname. *Em-me.*

It's funny how memory works. You forget what friendship used to be like before the days of cell phones and social media. Inside jokes are forgotten, the ties that bind you fade into oblivion, taking the faces of those you used to know with them. No one's called me Emme since I was a kid, but that one word resuscitates the past I'd very much like to forget.

Maybe it's not the name, but the person it comes from. Like a scent memory. A Pavlovian response.

Or maybe it's that some secrets refuse to stay buried.

Abby's Journal

Today sucks.

I didn't plan on it sucking, like I actually woke up in a good mood, but rn everybody else is trying so hard to make it suck for me. First, Mom wants me to write a *wait for it* LOVE POEM. She printed out a bunch of these famous sonnets for me to read and said it would be ~so cute~ if I wrote one too.

So. Cute.

I'm like, oh, good idea, but we have a HUGE problem. How am I gonna make a "swoon-worthy sonnet guaranteed to bring your beau to tears" if JJ is the only boy I know.

Just pretend, *she said.* Think of it as an audition. There's so many shows to pull inspiration from. *To All the Boys* meets CC Spectacular. Think of the hits, Chloe. It's going to go viral. We might even get a call from Netflix.

I can't even with her.

Anyway, speaking of JJ. UGH. Are all brothers stupid or just mine? He's rly going hard on this whole Older Brother thing. I get that he wants to protect me, but I'm 13. I make my own choices and the fact that he thinks it's ok to step into my business is full stop annoying.

I set up my own IG and made the dumb mistake of telling him. He came in when I was doing a boomerang and I was like shit. *He promised he wouldn't tell and I believed him. I thought he'd be cool about it since he's always saying I should get to do more stuff without Mom. But what does he do?*

Tells MOM. Literally turns around and rats me out. She just barged into my room and snatched my phone out of my hand. Deactivated my account and refused to give my phone back.

WTF JJ. I don't say anything when he sneaks out of the house to go hang out with Ryan and the girls from Courtland Circle or wherever the hell he goes. I know how to keep a secret.

And instead of just owning up to it, he lied. Right to my FACE. He said he didn't say anything to her.

THEN HOW DID SHE FIND OUT?!!?

He goes, whatever it's not a BFD. She'll give it back in a day or 2.

And I'm like it IS a big deal. I just want something that's mine. Why is that so freaking hard to get? Half the time he doesn't even tell Mom and Dad when he's going out. Just like where's JJ? Oh, probably at Ryan's, la dee da. *He can do whatever he wants but I can't even post an unfiltered selfie without losing my phone.*

So now we're not talking at all.

Ugh, and now SHE'S calling me. Time for Chloe to do the VDay confessional. Chloe needs more sparkle in her cut crease. Chloe needs more energy. Come on, Chlo, don't let me down.

Sometimes I think she'd be much happier if Abby just disappeared.

EMILINA

The day I met Jennifer, she was sitting on her front porch staring up at the sky. She did that a lot. I lived around the corner, but the street was short, so our houses were adjacent. I could look out my bedroom window and see the back of her house—which was exactly where her bedroom window was. One time we tried to connect tin cans on a string to make an old-school telephone, some build-it-yourself prompt we found in a Nickelodeon magazine. It didn't work; the string was way too short, but we each kept our can as a kind of memento to our experiment.

I was coming home from basketball practice. She was one of the only kids who didn't participate in some sort of after-school activity. The other girls said she was too fat or weird—all the explanation needed for outcast status in the nineties—but my dad told me to go easy on her. Her mother worked nights, he said, and they probably couldn't afford it.

That stuck with me. Compassion can be a completely foreign idea at that age, but I remember feeling this tug, this connection to Jen. In a world where nuclear families reigned supreme, finding someone who knew the unique kind of sadness that comes with being the kid without a parent at a class recital is rare. None of my other friends understood what it was like to budget or buy generic.

Anyone who could handle Toaster-Tarts was okay in my book.

So, instead of walking past her, I hitched my ball under my arm and stopped. "Whatcha lookin' at?" I remember asking her.

"Water tower," she said after a minute. The big blue water tower stood at the top of the hill. Shaped like an oval—or an eye, as I imagined—it was a neighborhood landmark. Unmoving and reliant. No matter which direction you entered Albany from, its powder blue orb marked the way home.

It's still there today, more brown than blue, but just as present.

"Oh. Cool," I said.

Sometimes, I miss the days when all it took to make a friend was a single word. No asterisks or terms or conditions, years away from festering secrets that disintegrate pieces of your soul in the middle of the night. That's what no one ever tells you about friendships. They can be great, sure, but they can also create the scariest monsters of all.

"Want to hang out?" she asked.

"Sure, but I can't be out past dark."

"Me neither." Jen smiled then and brushed her dirty blonde hair out of her eyes. She's platinum now, which suits her, but it's hard to picture her as anything but dirty. "I'm actually playing a game."

"What kind of game?" I asked. We were in second or third grade. Games meant hopscotch and TV Tag and, my personal favorite, Ghost in the Graveyard. Drew tells me that no one else knows what that game is. Most kids played SPUD or Red Rover and hide-and-seek. We, however, chased each other pretending that if we were caught by "The Ghost," we joined the dead and were doomed to haunt the earth until someone who was "alive" tagged us back in, saving us from immortal damnation. Last one alive won.

Simple.

Our games always took on a note of the macabre, it seemed. And here we are, twenty years later, playing the same game. But instead of bragging rights, I'm trying to save a child from a fate worse than haunting.

"Do you remember the vampire hunt?" I ask.

Jen chuckles. "Blast from the past, Emme, wow. Haven't thought about that woman in ages. She was pissed."

"Well, you did accuse her of being a vampire."

"She had purple eyes and only came out of her house after the sun went down. What other explanation could there have been?"

"She was old," I say. "Maybe she had cataracts."

"You were the one who hung garlic on her stoop."

"You told me to. It was better than sharpening those twigs into stakes," I say in defense.

"A necessity when fighting bloodthirsty vampires. What did you want me to use? Popsicle sticks?"

We come to a storm entrance, and our childhood slips quietly back into its box. I study it, the rusted latches and splintering boards. "Could she have come out through there?" I ask.

"Technically, sure, but it's been locked since we moved in. I don't even know where the key is for it, and we've got so much stuff in the basement, I doubt the kids could even get to the door in the first place." Jen points to an open second-story window. "That one," she says. "Her room was freezing. Chloe hates being cold."

I estimate the distance from the ground to the bottom of Abby's window to be between twenty and twenty-five feet.

"Hm," I say, parsing through options. There's no eave. No gutter close enough to shimmy down. She could've jumped and survived, but the breaks would've been nasty—and there's no way she did any of that in complete silence. But maybe she didn't have to. JJ got in without being heard which makes it just as likely that Abby could sneak out without anyone realizing. But why leave her phone? Why the open window?

On the other hand, an unlocked door would provide easy access for an abductor. How easy would it be for someone to stake out the Cates house? Figure out their routine and pick apart their weak spots? What could be easier than slinking through an unlocked door in the middle of the night?

Above us, the curtains flutter with movement as someone photographs the window seams, the flat sill, carefully pulling down the screen in search of fingerprints. I'm curious about their findings, but my skepticism is growing. I just don't see how someone could've abducted her through the window without disturbing the area.

Slowly, I pace alongside the house toward the deck, eyes fixed to the ground, searching for footprints or signs of struggle.

Nothing.

I reach the deck stairs, Jennifer trailing behind me, and head down the hill toward the fence. When I was a kid, Patrick and I used to search for four-leaf clovers. It seemed like every time we walked to the field, he'd find one, but no matter how much I strained, I always came up short.

You're trying too hard, he said on one such occasion. *Let your eyes relax. See the bigger picture. If you try not to focus on any individual leaf, your brain will pick up the shamrock that's not like the others.*

One in ten thousand chance, but it worked. After a few minutes, I saw a deviation, an extra leaf. I heed his advice now, letting my mind clear and ignoring the urge to study each individual blade of grass. The bigger picture. What am I really seeing? Footprints? More than one set? It's possible, and I don't want to take chances. We'll need forensics to perform their magic.

"Hey, Downy, you still there?" I call.

The door slides and he steps out. "What's up?"

I meet him halfway up the hill. "Get a headcount of who's available. I want two guys canvassing the neighborhood and a search team prepped. Loop DL Suter in, too, so he's not blindsided by the news, all right? And get someone from forensics here to tape off the yard."

A hand on my bicep, and I jump.

Jennifer retracts, but the feeling of her grip, strong and unexpected, burns through my jacket.

"Sorry, I—what's going on?" she asks.

"You should go inside," I say. "Wait with your family, and I'll be in to speak with you momentarily."

"I'm not going anywhere."

Downy gives me an inquisitive look. "Stay with Mrs. Scarborough," I say.

Jennifer calls my name like a broken record.

Concentrate, I tell myself.

What am I really seeing? Jen said they use the area beyond the fence for gardening. Photo shoots. It's not out of the question then that there'd be a discernible trail that withstood the winter thaw.

Something catches my attention as I'm turning for the deck, and I freeze, tilting my head to make sure it's not just a trick of the light.

A blotch. A smear of brownish red the size of a quarter.

Blood?

"Shit," I mutter. Now that I've seen it, there's no mistaking it. Like the viral dress that was *definitely* black and blue until someone pointed out the white and gold; then you couldn't unsee it.

There's more. Dots varying in shape and size splattered around the opening in the fence.

"What?" Jen asks. "What is it?"

Two officers make their way to me.

"Watch your step," I say. "Here, here, and here." I point out the tracks and the blood. "Get this immediate area secured. Might want to set up some tents. Thanks. Let me know if you find anything else."

"Search party should be ready for instructions in five," Downy says, sweating despite the light wind and April chill. I realize I am too. He huffs and coughs into his fist.

"Thank you," I say, lowering my voice. "Pretty sure we've got blood. Take her inside with you, please. I'll be up for a briefing in five."

Jen's eager glare breaks through my concentration. "I'm right here, Detective Stone, don't talk about me like I can't hear you! What's going on? Answer me!" Her pleas become hoarse. Frantic. Downy ushers her toward the house, but she fights him. I hear him tell her to *calm down* before I'm lost in my world again.

The largest spot I see stains the bottom of the fence post, a stark contrast to the sterile picket white. I squat for a closer look. There's something stuck to the corner, mixed with the blood. Could be grass clippings or micro roots. I pull the pen from my pocket and loop it through the thin, chocolate brown strands.

Hair.

I see her, then. Abby, conjured from the depths of my imagination. Lifeless. Her beautiful brown hair is knotted and clumped with dead leaves. Mud and blood slimes her ears, cheeks, and neck.

"Not real," I tell myself.

Claws dig into her calves, monstrous and inhuman. Patches of the creature's coarse bark-hair bristle against Abby's exposed skin. Pustules form and burst from the pressure. Its chest balloons out and sinks in, revealing chunky outlines of organs, cartilage, and bones.

There are no horns, no forked tongues, but I recognize the evil for what it is.

I blink repeatedly until the air clears and the dark side of my imagination finally goes back to sleep, but the omen lingers in my peripheral vision. Not quite visible, but always there.

Promise me.

I signal one of the guys to collect the hair sample, but there's no denying the strands are the same color as Abigail Scarborough's.

With a shudder, and before I lose my resolve, I step beyond the fence.

JACKSON

This must be what hell is.

Officers pass papers back and forth, collecting evidence and taking notes about my daughter. Our home. Our life. No one bothers speaking to me, but everybody looks. Sad. Sorry. Suspicious. Like we're some bleak, mystifying painting. *Study in Stress* would be the title. *Father and Son Contemplate the Missing*.

Up and down the stairs, they come and go. Modern J. Alfred Prufrocks. No one speaks of Michelangelo though. There's only one person at the heart of this matter.

Abby.

I need to *do* something. What use am I twiddling my thumbs on the couch like an asshole? My chest swells, all this nervous energy and nowhere to direct it. I'm ready for action, for a brawl, anything that gets me off this damn couch.

As quickly as it starts, the rage is walloped by crippling fear. An insistent whisper that I'm not good enough, strong enough—*capable* enough to handle this. It wouldn't be the first time I balked at a pivotal moment.

Officer Downy has been watching Jen and the CFSU detective from the deck door for the last few minutes. Poised. Alert. I'd also like to know what's happening out there.

JJ looks at me expectantly. I'm his father. I should be able to give him answers. That's what parents are for, right? Instead, I'm gripped by that familiar need for escape. To run away. Blind myself to the present and put as many miles between me and Upper Madison as I can before they realize I'm gone.

I pat JJ's shoulder, wanting to give reassurances that aren't mine to give. "I'm going to check in with the officer." I nod in Downy's direction. "I'll be right back."

Isn't that what they tell you not to say in scary movies? *I'll be right back.* People who utter those cursed words never return. Offed by a chainsaw-wielding murderer.

Abby didn't say anything like that.

"Dad," JJ interrupts my thoughts. "I'm coming with you."

I read once that goodbyes are difficult, no matter how small, because deep down we're convinced that we'll never see that person again—that every time will be the last.

Yesterday, I would've said that was bullshit.

I'm not the same person I was yesterday.

"Dad."

Daddy.

I pinch the bridge of my nose, a swaying sense of reality flooding my mind. I nod. "Okay."

We stride toward Downy. I refuse to let my children have a coward for a father. "Officer," I say, clearing my throat to get his attention.

Downy swivels to me. He gives JJ a curt smile and brings his gaze back to me. "What can I do for you, Mr. Scarborough?"

"I was, uh . . ."

Daddy.

What was I doing?

"Mr. Scarborough?"

"Dad?"

I shake out of my stupor to their staring eyes. "Sorry. I uh, I was thinking. Wouldn't it be smart to have someone going around the neighborhood?"

"I think that's a solid idea," Downy agrees, "but let's wait to see what Detective Stone says."

"I don't mind getting a head start." I hitch a thumb toward the garage. "I can just hop in the car and do a few laps around the block. See if anyone's seen anything. Should've done that before calling you, really, when you think about it," I say. Rambling. I can't seem to stop. "I mean, how silly would this look if Chloe's been at the park or something? Yeah, I think I'll do that. JJ can stay here and call me if you hear anything, right?"

"Dad, no," he says, frowning.

Downy scratches the corner of his chin. "Look, your heart's in the right place, but at this point, Mr. Scarborough, let's wait for Detective Stone."

"Downy!"

A nearby shout, and Officer Downy is out the door.

I peer out the glass. The detective is motioning in a wide circle around the yard. She leaps down the stairs and Jen calls after her. She sounds borderline hysterical, although I wouldn't say that to her face.

Everything goes silent, the uneasy stillness that comes a second before the disaster, and I think I'm going to vomit.

This is it. The end of life as I know it.

Downy reappears, flushed to his ears. He excuses himself between me and JJ. "Luke."

A man with a full beard and a buzz cut steps forward. Luke, I presume, with wiry muscles straining against his uniform shirt. "Downy, my man, what's going on?"

"I need you to get someone from forensics and let the rest of the team know."

"Got it." Luke and his muscles swagger down the hall to a small group of officers.

Forensics?

"Welsh?" Downy calls.

"Here." She strides from the kitchen.

"Grab two of the newbs and get them on foot patrol. See if anyone saw or heard anything that might give us a clearer picture of our timeframe. And put the word out that a search party needs to be ready to roll out in five."

A search party? I check the clock above the sink, my lesser muscles cringing at how much time has already passed.

Welsh is off, following her orders, and my head spins at the sudden momentum.

"Dad, what's going on?" JJ asks.

"I don't know, Jay," I say. "Let's find out."

We follow Downy out the back. He's corralling Jen, and—not surprisingly—Jen is putting up a hell of a stink.

Detective Stone squats to inspect something at the bottom of the yard, then disappears into the woods.

Why? What did she find?

Jen is starting to lose it. I thought she was breaking down when she realized Abby was gone, but this is a different beast rearing.

I probably shouldn't think of my wife as a beast, either.

We have to stay united.

"Jen. What is it? What happened?" I ask.

"I don't know." She cries in hitched breaths. "I don't know, I don't know."

I wrap my arms around her. She smells like sweat and strawberries.

Jen allows me to hold her for a moment then leans away anxiously, smoothing her hands through her hair and sniffling. "She, the detective wanted to see Chloe's window, and then she—I don't know—she completely shut me out. I think she found something, Jackson, but they won't let me down there." Jen looks at Officer Downy, daggers in her eyes. "You can't keep me from going down there."

"Mrs. Scarborough, you need to calm down."

"Don't tell me to be calm. That detective found something, and you won't tell me what it is. Why is she in the woods? Why did she go down there?"

JJ presses the home button on his phone then clicks it to sleep. The screen lights up rhythmically. On. Off. On. Off. A picture of him at the plate, perfect stance, waiting for the pitch. He hit a homer that game. "Um, Mom? Can we talk for a minute?"

Shit. Not now.

Jen glares at me like I'm the one who interrupted her, but when she realizes it's JJ, her mood softens. She kisses his forehead like she did when he was a toddler with a scraped knee. "Not really a good time, Jay, okay?"

His voice wavers, the picture flashing faster. "Mom, I'm sorry. This is all my fault."

Jen's smile falters. "What are you talking about?"

Welsh joins Downy and whispers that everything is on standby. The officers clamber around us. So many people. JJ wipes tears from his eyes and hardens his face. So unlike me at that age. Jen thinks I'm exaggerating when I tell her I was a shy kid. Not a loner; I went to parties and did all the things you're supposed to do as a fifteen-year-old boy, but none of it came naturally to me. I had to work to fit in. Fake it. I never would've been able to do what he's about to do.

"I'm the reason she's gone," he says.

I marvel at his courage, however misguided, but the thought is marred by a voice in my head. Whispering, leering.

He's like this because she chose Abby.

JJ's part of the blog, but he's never been the star of the show. He has friends. Plays sports. Goes to school. Other than being the brother of CC Spectacular, JJ has a relatively average life. He has space to make the mistakes that Abby does not.

Jen's smile slides away, mottled by confusion. "Honey, I know this is difficult and scary, but none of it is your fault."

"I signed Abby up for her own socials."

Her eyes flicker from him to me and back again. "You what?"

"After you took her phone. I felt bad. So. I." His gaze roves over the audience, but he doesn't lose his nerve. "She asked for my help, so I signed her up for Instagram and TikTok."

Shit. I realize, not for the first time, that I have no idea what Jen is going to do.

Jen tilts her head. Narrows her eyes. Opens her mouth. Closes it again. She rubs her temples. "JJ, what were you thinking?"

"I wasn't thinking. She was miserable—"

"Your sister is not miserable," she interrupts. "Why would you say something like that?"

"Because it's the truth!" he shouts. "It's true and you're too caught up in your blog to see it. She cries all the time but pretends to be happy because she's afraid of what you'll do if she's not."

This isn't good. The weight of our audience presses down on my chest.

"JJ, that is enough," she says through gritted teeth.

"Always taking pictures. Always on your phone. Even today. You've posted three pictures in the last hour." He scrambles in his pocket and shoves his phone at her, loaded to the CC Spectacular Instagram account.

The top picture, already amassing thousands of likes, shows the unidentified officers gathering in our house.

Jesus. "Jennifer, what the hell is this? Are you insane?"

JJ shakes with adrenaline. "See, you can't even deny it. Why would you post them? You care more about 'CC and Me' than Abby and—"

I hear the crack before I see it. The loaded suspension of Jen's palm. Her handprint dominates JJ's face, a stinging red blob.

Welsh and Downy grab Jen and pull her away. She kicks and screams at them to let her go. Jesus, she's going to get herself arrested if she doesn't calm down.

The phone lies forgotten at JJ's feet. I hug him and it's like sand running through my arms. I think that if I can hold him tight enough, I can erase the damage. I'm shoveling spoonfuls of dust as mountains fall around me.

JJ doesn't move, doesn't reciprocate.

They say—whoever *they* are—a person's true colors show in moments of unimaginable hardship. I thought I knew who we were. I thought I knew what our family was.

For all the Spectacular we've cultivated in the past eight years, we aren't having a very good showing.

Detective Stone appears in the commotion and jogs to us. I didn't see her come out of the woods. "What the hell happened?"

Downy replies for me. "She slapped the kid. What do you want me to do with her?"

Stone's gaze goes from the handcuffs on Downy's hip to the shadow covering half of JJ's face. I'm not sure what she finds there.

"Keep them separated," she says, waving at JJ and me.

The rage seeps from Jen's face. "JJ, I'm sorry, baby, please, I didn't mean it."

He flinches from her outreached arms.

Jen drops to her knees. "Please, JJ, I'm so sorry."

"JJ, are you all right?" Stone asks.

JJ's eyes glisten. His mouth is clenched tighter than his fists. The muscles in his arms tense and relax, tense and relax.

Jen reaches for him again. "JJ, I screwed up, I'm—"

"Don't touch me!" he shouts, and for a second, I'm convinced he's going to hit her back. Instead, he whirls and slams both his hands through his hair. He grunts, chest heaving. Face red. Each word a punch. "Don't touch me."

Stone approaches, hands in front of her like she's taming a bull. "JJ, hey, focus on me, okay? Everything's going to be all right."

"I wish everyone would stop saying that," he says. "Nothing's all right, and the more you say it, the less I believe it. This is my fault. I signed Abby up for Instagram and TikTok. That's on me. I wanted to help," he says.

"Okay," she says. Placating. "Okay, that's good to know. Let's chat for a second." She pulls him aside, angling him away from Jen but still within my earshot. "I understand wanting to help your sister, that's a noble thing to do, looking out for a younger sibling. I get it."

"Yeah," he says, looking at the roof, the trees, anywhere but at her.

"Did Abby tell you she was leaving?" Stone asks.

JJ jolts. "No, she didn't say anything like that."

"Did she talk about anyone she'd met on socials recently?"

My ears prick, and I feel the clammy slick of sweat under my arms. "What's this about?" I ask, coming to JJ's side. He nonchalantly brushes me off, not wanting to be too close.

"JJ, please, talk to me. I'm so, so sorry," Jen sobs into her hands. The initial charms dangle against her skin. A Mother's Day present that's become a signature "CC and Me" accessory.

Stone regards her with an incredulous expression before shifting her attention to the group. "Officer Welsh, get the others for a briefing, please. We have a lot to discuss and very little time." She pivots back to my son. "JJ, I have a few more questions I want to ask you later, but for now, I need you to sit down with one of my friends." She motions for another uniform to join us. An endless supply of police. "We need to see Abby's profiles—anything you helped her set up."

"Luke's here, Stone," Downy adds. "Cap sent him."

"Oh, great, that makes this a lot easier. Detective Luke is a good friend and a wiz with phones. He likes the Sox, but don't hold it against him.

Maybe you could teach him a thing or two about good baseball. One Yankee fan to another."

JJ scoffs but I see how he tries to suppress his smile. "All right." He scoops his phone up with the enthusiasm of a root canal and gives it to the officer. "They took her phone. Her stuff's saved on mine, though."

Detective Stone confers with the officer and Detective Luke appears in the mix. She gives him the rundown, and he exits through the house with my son. I watch JJ go, overcome by the urge to yank him back, keep him in my sight. Instead, I rub my face for the thousandth time and saunter to the group.

Stone swipes a loose hair out of her face and addresses those officers awaiting instructions. "Before I make an official statement to the press, I'd like to go over a few things."

She doesn't seem too happy about the press. I don't blame her. Around here, we're the Scarboroughs. Few people know us as the Cateses, and the ones who do don't make a big deal about it. I can't help but wonder how the reporters knew Abby was missing and found out where we live—although I have a pretty strong guess.

"The press?" Jennifer straightens. Her hunger for the limelight is unparalleled. "Emilina," she says, "you have to let me talk to them."

Detective Stone holds up a hand.

"Please. I can help. I'm good at this, being on camera. I can speak to the kidnapper directly, show him that Chloe is a real person with a family who loves her. Doesn't that make sense?"

"Kidnapper?" I ask.

"Absolutely not," Stone says. Nice to see someone not bending to Jen's wishes for once.

"I'm giving a brief statement to cut off whatever misinformation may be making the rounds, and that's the end of it. We will not turn this into a spectacle."

Spectacle. The irony of her statement isn't lost on me.

"Emilina, *please*, let me help," Jen says, finding her feet.

"I don't have time for this."

"What does she mean, kidnapper? What did you find?" I ask, hoping my redirection takes the edge off Jen's plea to put herself in front of a dozen news outlets.

Two men carrying black cases emerge from the house. FIU written in bright yellow letters beneath the badges on their vests. I recognize the acronym from the news. Forensics Investigation Unit. Why would we need forensics? Stone gives them directions and they take off toward the officers taping off the yard near the fence.

Stone holds Jen steady in her gaze. I wonder what she sees. Whatever it is, she doesn't deviate from her plan. "There's quite a bit of ground to cover," Stone says. "We're going to break up into teams."

"You think someone took Chloe in the woods?" I scan the trees, their twisting branches swallowing up all the light. That's no place for my daughter.

"We may have reason to believe so." She doesn't elaborate further.

We're broken up into smaller groups, with each group given a walkie-talkie. I'm with Welsh. JJ returns after a few minutes and joins us. Welsh looks like she wants to give him a big hug and repeatedly tells him how fine everything is going to be. Fine. What a terrible word. Nobody who says *fine* is ever telling the truth. Fine is always bad.

While we work out search assignments, Detective Stone continues. "Luke will be sending Chloe Cates's details to all of you momentarily, but if there are any questions about parameters or specifics, go to Officer Downy until I'm done with the news. Now, I've mapped out the area surrounding the Cateses' property. Primarily, we'll be focusing on the grounds closest to the house and the surrounding woods. That's approximately two miles of rough terrain between here and Western Park, which borders the property." Several phones around us ding with updates. "We assume she was taken between the hours of ten P.M. and seven A.M., and we don't want our window getting any smaller."

"We are operating under the belief the girl's been taken, though?" a young officer with a buzz cut asks.

Detective Stone sets her gaze on me. "At this point, we'll be pursuing Chloe Cates's disappearance as a possible kidnapping. Pending forensics, I think it's safe to assume she didn't leave of her own free will. You all have your assignments. Be alert. Work smart. Stay vigilant. Let's remember why we're out here."

With that, she excuses herself and ducks into the house.

"Let's put a glitter shake on that," Welsh says, and the phrase surprises a gargled chuckle from my throat. Another Chloe colloquialism. Chlo-lloquialism. Abby loves my puns. I can almost hear her laugh.

Daddy.

No one else makes a sound, separating somberly in their respective directions.

Welsh secures the walkie-talkie and together we move to the woods. The search for Abby has officially begun.

Abby's Journal

Happy Valentine's Day! Thank god that's over and done with. VDay skits are v v annoying.

BUT I have the most awesome news. JJ made me an Instaaaaa. I know, I know, I totally put him on blast in my last entry, but it's whatever. He hooked me up with IG and tiktok and lets me use his phone if he's home since Mom's still searching through mine every day.

And suuuure. Yes. I do this stuff ALL the time. I should be sick of selfies and posting, but this is different. This is mine. I use my own name. I post my own pictures. My own stories. Mine. I've even done some of the viral dances. I'm getting better at recording them, I think. IDK. But it's literally the most fun I've had in forever.

I don't want anyone to know that I'm Chloe, which is super weird. Me keeping her a secret instead of the other way around. I'm like Hannah freaking Montana. And since I'm in a good mood, I'll share something else.

I met someone. !!!! Not like, met *met, but in my DMs. His first message was sweet.* **You have nice eyes.** *Nobody's ever complimented me like that. Me.*

Ugh, Mom's calling. Time to read skits. More later.

I can't believe this is my life. Being Chloe is so much easier when I get to be Abby too.

EMILINA

In fifth grade, I finished second in the annual spelling bee. Albany elementary schools don't have names; they have numbers. I went to School 19, and we prided ourselves on our traditions. The Bee was revered most of all, two classes competing for the title. The whole school jammed into the auditorium/gym/cafeteria combo in metal folding chairs made in the 1940s. They gave us special color-coded hats so we all had a side to root for.

Winning the Bee is the first goal I remember setting for myself.

I know it might sound like Jen was the only outcast, but I wasn't popular either. Boys criticized my weight. The other girls made fun of my clothes, always the wrong style or ill-fitting. My curly, often frizzy hair. When I was most desperate, I straightened it with an iron. Laid my head on the floor and prayed I wouldn't burn myself in a misguided attempt at vanity.

It wore me down. Kids can be cruel, intentionally or not. Jennifer isn't the only one who had to fight for her place at the starting line.

I was in Mrs. Lowery's class. We practiced our spelling words every day in the months leading up to the competition. Definitions, parts of speech, sentences, and mock bees. When the day finally arrived, I was ready. My last five tests had all been perfect scores. I was the front-runner.

Until the last round, it was everything I'd dreamed it would be. Other kids dropped like flies. *I've got this*, I thought as each student left the stage. Totally got this. That trophy was as good as mine.

My rival speller was Matt Bellamy, and our word was dealt.

I blanked.

"Dealt," I said, feigning confidence. "D-E-L-T."

The moderator shook her head. "I'm sorry, dear, that's incorrect. Mr. Bellamy, if you spell this word right, your class wins the Golden Buzzer."

Gasps from the audience. The kids who'd already been disqualified stomped their feet until the principal shushed them.

I wished with all my heart that he would spell it wrong. I'd get another shot. Any other word. I was prepared. Why did it have to be the one word I didn't know?

Matt Bellamy strutted to the microphone, absurdly confident with his mushroom haircut and Umbro shorts, and shot me one last snooty smirk. "Dealt. D-E-*A*-L-T. Dealt."

Who knew there was a silent *A* in dealt? That one letter crushed my hopes. I lost and cried right there on stage. One of my most cringeworthy memories. The thing that floats into my subconscious just as I'm about to fall asleep.

Standing in front of the press makes me feel like I'm losing the spelling bee all over again. I know if I get too cocky, that silent *A* is going to bite me in the ass.

There's always a silent *A*.

And the stakes are much higher than a plastic trophy.

"Good morning," I say, making eye contact with the array of cameras. "My name is Detective Emilina Stone, speaking on behalf of APD, in conjunction with the New York State Police, who have generously agreed to provide additional tactical support."

Another unexpected order from Cap. CFSU doesn't work with the state police often, but on a national stage thanks to Jen's premature posts, we have to put up our best front.

"At approximately seven-thirty this morning, Albany police received a report of a missing thirteen-year-old girl. Officers were dispatched to the home and conducted a preliminary investigation until CFSU arrived. After thorough examination of the facts, we have reason to believe Chloe Cates was abducted from her home sometime after ten P.M. yesterday. Chloe was last seen wearing a light pink sweatshirt and matching sweatpants. If you or anyone you know has information leading to her whereabouts, please contact local law enforcement or call the number on the bottom of your screen. I'll be taking questions at this time."

There's an explosion of activity from the reporters.

"Detective Stone, do you have any suspects?" the guy from News 9 asks. He's a redhead with an accent. Says suspects like *soos-pects*.

"We're in the process of interviewing witnesses and looking into several possibilities."

Truth-adjacent. I don't have much physical evidence to go on that Chloe was actually abducted besides the blood spatter and the hair at this point. And a strong hunch. But I've learned not to ignore a hunch. A good gut suspicion is almost as reliable and I trust it a hell of a lot more than Jennifer Scarborough's word.

"Have any ransom demands been made?" asks the rep from News On-the-Go. She's a pleasant woman, part of the grassroots movement on Facebook trying to even the playing field of misinformation with impartial reporting. What's her name? Rachel or Racina.

"No, no ransom demands but we're not discounting the idea that this could be connected to the family's Internet fame," I say, pointing to the next reporter.

"Last week we covered the alleged disappearance of Missy Crawford. Given the proximity, could there be a link? Should the public be concerned?"

This I haven't considered. Thirteen-year-old Missy Crawford, a well-liked cheerleader and active member of Our Lady of Sorrows Church according to her family and friends, was reported missing after she failed to return home from a late-night study session. Her parents claimed she'd been spending more time with this study group, but when her friends were interviewed, they claimed to have no knowledge of the group or what Missy was doing. They assumed she had a boyfriend and didn't press her for details.

That investigation is being handled by South District, not Central where I work, but the jurisdictional borders are close. No more than ten minutes apart.

"Detective?"

"I won't comment on an ongoing investigation, but at this time there's no reason to assume these instances are connected. The public has no cause for alarm, but again, we're asking anyone with information to come forward or contact the numbers on your screen." Saying any more than that could cause a panic, but I'm only delaying the inevitable. It won't be long until the couch detectives make the jump for me.

A renewed eruption of flashes and shouts catches me off guard.

From the corner of my eye, I see Jennifer emerge from the house. She's flushed and puffy, but combined with her fresh tears and the softness in her features, the effect is heartbreaking. A mother desperate to find her child.

Son of a bitch.

She glides to my side, giving solemn half waves to the reporters.

I hold her arm like I'm showing her where to stand and lean into her. "What the hell do you think you're doing?" I whisper.

With a sympathetic smile, she lifts my hand off her arm. Her grip is hard and cold. "What any good mother would do."

"Jen, don't—"

"Thank you, Detective Stone," she announces and turns to address the crowd. "And thank you all for being here. Some of you may know us from our blog, 'CC and Me.' But for those of you who don't, my name is Jennifer Cates. Chloe is my daughter. She's a beautiful, sweet soul. Selfless, compassionate, and generous." She trembles but remains composed. "We are devastated. And more than anything, we want our girl back. So," she inhales, holding the anticipation in the palm of her hand. "I'm speaking directly to the person or persons who took her from us. I won't say you're a monster. Chloe would tell me it's wrong to call people names, no matter how mean or troubled they are. That's how spectacular she is. I beg you, please . . . don't hurt her. Let her go. Chloe is every sparkle in our day. She brings light to so many people." Sob. "And to steal that light is to crush the dreams of young girls everywhere. Her father and I are offering a reward to anyone who comes forward with information that leads to her return. Ten thousand dollars and a guaranteed spotlight feature on our blog. Please. If you see something, if you know something: tag us on Instagram, Facebook, or Twitter, or post to the blog directly. Help us find our CC."

Holy shit.

Shouting her name, shouting questions over one another, vying for the best sound bite, the reporters eat it up.

Before she can say another word, I guide her toward the door. "That's it for now, folks," I say to the crowd. "Thank you for your time."

I don't push her into the house but I want to. Closing—not slamming—the door is a show of restraint I'm grateful I still have.

"The hell were you thinking?" I ask. "This isn't a game, Jennifer, you can't just pull a Maury and walk out on stage with a big reveal. A reward? Tagging your socials?"

She peeks through the blinds. "I told you I could help, Emilina. Look at them. They're invested now."

"The only thing you've accomplished is a media frenzy. I can't do my job when you're inciting random people to join in the investigation like it's some goddamn treasure hunt. I'm here to find your daughter. Let me do my job."

"Okay," she says flatly. "No more junkets."

I'll believe that when I see it. "Stay with Officer Downy. Do not say another word to the press."

"Okay," she repeats, with a twitch of a smile and heads down the hall. I watch for Downy and give him a wave.

One big circus.

I stand in the foyer collecting my thoughts until I'm fairly confident my anger's in check. Replaying the conference, the part before Jen railroaded me, at least, I consider the facts.

What do I know?

No ransom.

No witnesses.

What about the other missing girl? Missy Crawford. I don't dismiss it, but I'm hesitant to link the two together. Serial offenders develop patterns, preferences they stick to with superstitious force. I usually don't miss the markers. Like seeing an actor in a movie and remembering he had a guest role in one episode of *Law and Order: SVU* eight years ago. And neither of these disappearances strikes that chord.

I push the idea to the back of my mind to chew on later. I need to join the search party, but I have one thing to do first.

It's about time I saw Abby's room for myself.

The CHLOE letters are too cheerful in contrast to what I've learned today about this girl's life. It's like I'm looking for two different people. Everything I think I know about Abby is what I've seen on "CC and Me," and that's worrisome. I'm putting a lot of trust in a social construct. Chloe Cates isn't real. She doesn't have a family or friends or life outside the four-sided screen. Her personality is brainstormed and plotted by Jennifer to correspond with the needs of whichever demographic best suits their financial situation.

Has anyone checked their bank statements?

I text Cap to get a subpoena for the money trail. And phone records.

I skim through the report Downy uploaded to the case file. Jen fell asleep early. Jackson was the last one to see her but can't remember any specific details. JJ was unaccounted for.

Well, that doesn't help my suspicions.

Something about their account of the disappearance doesn't sit quite right, but I can't put my finger on what it is. Studies show that the majority of abductions are committed by someone the victim knows. A member of the inner circle. I'd feel better if I could definitively eliminate the Scarboroughs from my list of suspects.

Tick tock.

Shoving my phone into my back pocket, I push the door open.

Abby's room is nothing like her perfectly styled blog posts. The expensive bedding is stripped to the mattress. Unfiltered light shines through, but the space feels gray. Dreary and cold, an Amityville level of malevolent. I wouldn't be surprised if millions of flies started leaking from the crevices.

A Hydro Flask with various stickers sits on the desk. Her laptop's gone, as well as her phone. I hope Luke and the digital forensics guys are able to get something we can use. Until then, where else would a kid keep her secrets? Dresser? The drawers are a mess. Limp shirt sleeves and pant legs hang sadly over the edges, as if they're wilting without the girl to bring them sparkle.

Nothing strange. I move to the closet, organized by color and occasion. I'm sure this is Jennifer's doing. Velvety hues flow into pastel pinks, lavenders, mints, muted tangerines.

Five baskets line the shelf above the rack. I tip the first toward me and peer inside. An assortment of scrunchies, elastics, and clips. The second is full of nail polish. The third holds various enamel pins. Rainbows and cartoon characters. Butterflies. Birds. Cheeky slang. BAE and SHOOK and STAN and TLDR.

Basket four, however, is empty. I tip it farther until I hear a thunk. Something is hidden underneath the linen lining.

I place the basket on the desk and untie the bows which secure the cloth to the handles. I used to hide things from my brother and father when I was Chloe's age. Snacks I didn't want to share. Allowance money. My diary.

My stomach flutters and cramps. I fight the onslaught of nausea, swallowing the rising lump, and lift the cloth to examine the contents. A butterfly necklace glitters in the corner. Costume jewelry, but not with the other cheap necklaces and bracelets she's got stacked on top of her dresser. Why is this one special?

There's also a plain red notebook. Single subject and spiral bound.

Flipping through the pages, I regard the loopy handwriting, young and slanting. Hearts sketched into the borders. Song lyrics stretch in wavy arches, bypassing paragraphs in their artistic defiance. Not constrained to the blue lines.

I lift the notebook and freeze when I see the small square that lies beneath. A Polaroid.

I lift the picture gently from the basket.

Even though the image is fuzzy and her face is distorted, it's definitely her. Abby. She's wearing a bright pink tank top and wrapped in what looks like a sheet. The butterfly necklace hangs from her neck. Her hair is loose and frizzy like she'd taken braids out recently—nothing like the polished facade she sports on her Instagram feed.

The background is dark and offset by an indistinguishable blur.

I thumb the glossy print, but the smudge doesn't wipe off. What is that? A person? I turn the picture over. It would be incredibly lucky if someone had written a name, a date—a gimme clue, is what I call them.

No gimme clues here. That would be too easy.

I dial Cap's number and stare at the image until the line connects.

"What's up, Stone?" he asks. "Saw the press conference. Wasn't expecting to have to address the public this early in the investigation."

"They were here when I got here, Cap. There've been posts on social media, too, which I'm sure is fanning the flames."

"Less than ideal. And allowing the mother airtime to pitch a reward and call for the public to be involved? Jennifer Cates is—"

Unpredictable. "It's handled. Won't happen again."

"Every move Central makes is going to be scrutinized from this point forward," he says.

I shake my head. "I know. I don't like this, Cap. Something doesn't feel right." I glance at the picture. "I think I found her diary. And a Polaroid."

"Polaroid?" I know where his mind went. Mine went there, too.

"Nothing X-rated." Thank god. "But . . . suggestive. Looks like she was cozy with someone, but it's too blurred to make out who it is."

I stare out at the woods, the tops of the trees swaying gently, back and forth. No troubles, no worries.

You never get used to it, the horrible things people are capable of doing to one another, and it doesn't get easier. You learn how to compartmentalize better. You find an outlet—someone to talk to, a sport, a vice—whatever it is to help you sleep without nightmares gnawing into your brain every night. You grow a certain level of immunity—just enough to protect you from a breakdown. Like a fish in an anemone building up resistance against the stings.

"We've got three guys working the tip line," Cap says. "Want to know how many psychics have claimed to know her location?"

"Alive or dead?" I respond. I don't know what it is about tip lines that bring out the crazies, but give them a number to call and a semi-interesting case, and they flock. Ninety percent of the tips we receive are pure bullshit.

Crackles from the walkie-talkie interrupt my thoughts. "Detective, Welsh here. I think we've got something. West of the fence. Quarter mile. Over."

"Cap, I gotta go." I tuck the photo into the notebook and stuff the whole thing into the lining of my coat. With one last look around Abby's room, I pull the door shut and make my way outside.

Downy and Jen look out from the deck, fixated on the woods. She's been crying again, skin blotchy and bags sag under her eyes. Wet hair sticks to her cheeks, the platinum strands drenched to their natural state.

"Emilina, what's going on? What did they say on the radio? Did they find her?"

I pause on the steps. "I don't know," I say.

Her chin trembles. "Oh, my god, is it her?"

"Downy, take Mrs. Scarborough inside, please."

"Emilina," Jen starts, but I keep moving down the slope. I take a deep breath and step into the trees, steeling myself against the cold likelihood of a young girl's death.

Abby's Journal

JJ did a TikTok with me today. It's dumb, but it's great. I can do stupid dances. Or show off my contouring skills while lip synching to Billie Eilish. You can do a lot less on TikTok and still get millions of followers.

I tried explaining this to Mom. We've been doing the blog for-ev-er. IG too. Nobody uses Facebook anymore. It's like, for old people. Grandma Carol has it and that should tell her everything she needs to know. Even the gram isn't as popular as it used to be. They're gonna start hiding likes soon. Dumb. I don't get it. People only care about impressions.

I told my mom we can't keep doing the same thing over and over. It gets played out. People get bored. I get bored. Skits were cute when I was 5, but no one wants to watch me diss Starbucks or insult the food at Applebee's anymore. It's not cute, it's rude. Spoiled. Entitled. Idk how she doesn't see that.

We need TikTok. It would be FRESH. New catchphrases, new material, new followers.

She bugged, of course. She was all, You don't know what you're talking about *and* JJ shouldn't be showing you this stuff, it's not appropriate.

That rly pisses me off. Like, suddenly you're worried about me seeing something I shouldn't? I'm "mature" enough for you to make me—sorry, CHLOE—wear a bikini for a boutique ad on IG, but I can't duet with Addison Rae?

I told her she can't keep posting my pictures without my permission. That's, like, illegal. It's my body. It's my life. If I want to start a TikTok and link it to the blog, I should be able to. Because that's my choice. But she can't post my pictures without me saying OK.

Her response? I'm your mother. I can post what I want because I'm your mother. And, in case you forgot, this is my blog. It's about *me.* My goals. My writing. When you're old enough, you can make your own accounts and post whatever you want. Until then? *SHRUGS*

REALLY? All about her? Is her name in the blog title?! She would think that. Me, me, me, she's so selfish. How is it hers *when all she talks about is ME?*

I said cool, if it's ALL ABOUT YOU, don't write about ME. Don't put me in your stories. Don't take my pics. Don't ask me to model for sponsors. None of it.

She told me I was being a brat. Name calling. Cool, Mom. It's not like she has a real job. How hard is it to edit and click? Mom is seriously taking me for granted.

Can't have "CC and Me" without Chloe Cates.

Don't my feelings matter? Why doesn't she ever listen to what I say? I literally never ask her for anything. It's not fair.

UGH. Anyway.

I talked to *him* tonight.

Unlike Mom, he's a great listener. I don't want to jinx it, but I think he rly cares about me. He asks questions b/c he wants to get to know me and doesn't make me repeat myself a million times. I look forward to his messages more than, like, every other part of my day.

He said it might be cool to meet up soon.

JACKSON

We trek through the thicket, overgrowth scratching at our clothes as we scour for signs of Abby. We call her name sporadically, but aside from the haunting mimicry carried on the wind by the other groups, there's no response.

Welsh shines her flashlight into a cluster of thorny bushes. Meanwhile, I'm stuck on the phone with my boss, Marco. I've been the Associate Director of Marketing at Ignita for six years. For the most part, I like it. Some traveling, good benefits, and the flexibility to work from home—a plus when Jen has Abby wrapped up with the blog and JJ has practice or away games.

Marco's wife saw Jen's posts, and now I have to deal with Marco's sympathy.

I fight through a fresh surge of frustration as he delivers platitude after platitude like he's interviewing to work at Hallmark. Marco *understands*. Marco *relates*. He babbles about a time when his dog snuck under the fence and ran away. Marco doesn't have children and refers to his two ugly boxers as "fur babies."

A missing daughter isn't quite the same as an escaped mutt, but I don't tell him that.

I kick at a pile of leaves as JJ flags me down. "Dad, over here."

I hold up a finger and mime a chattering mouth.

He lunges toward me and grabs the phone out of my hand before I can react. His strength and speed surprise me. "He'll call you back, Mr. Garbinetti."

"JJ, you can't just take my—"

"I found something," he says. Only then do I register the fear spinning in his eyes.

"What is it, JJ?" Welsh asks. She bats broken twigs away from her arms. Bits of crushed leaves are stuck in her hair, and there's a small scratch on her already-ruddy cheek.

He points to the grove and kicks away some of the debris as we walk, me second in line, with Welsh following close behind, head swiveling in both directions, hand drifting around her hip.

There's a small clearing beyond the bramble. Secluded. Several smaller trees have been shorn and stacked into pyramids, an effect, I admit, that makes this place feel extra creepy. Nobody's out here roasting marshmallows.

In the center of the clearing is a large oak tree with rough, aging bark and a sturdy trunk. The blackish-brown branches are thick and knotted like octopus tendrils.

Situated in its nooks and crevices is a tree house.

The walls are solid and extend upward, blocking any view of the inside save for the black rectangle of darkness where a door should be. The planks are weathered. Splinters peel off and chunks are missing in spots where animals have clawed and climbed.

It's old, but the stepladder beneath it is not; twenty-two feet and aluminum, it's the kind of ladder you'd find in every garage in Upper Madison.

"Whose is it?" JJ asks.

"No idea," I say, staring at the planks. I can just make out a sliver of color. At first, I think I'm imagining it. An odd reflection. Trick of the light. Is that . . . pink?

We approach it like soldiers disarming an explosive device. Sweat pops on my brow. Gulping down my heartbeat, I call her name. "Abby?"

"I'm going up there," JJ says.

I throw an arm in front of him like I used to when he was smaller and we'd hit a sharp turn in the car. "No, you're not."

Welsh shines her flashlight at the door. The angles aren't right, though. She grabs the ladder, tests it against her weight, and ascends. Flashlight still in hand, it clacks against the metal like a metronome counting beats in a meter. Tick, tick, tick, tick. Each one that passes nicks a lump out of my patience.

Four rungs short of the top, Welsh steadies her balance and reaches up to the platform. Slowly, the flashlight rises. I see it in slow motion, dragging like molasses.

Shadows dance along the walls and ceiling. I jog to the outer edge of the clearing, craning my neck to peer inside. Welsh takes another step and jerks to a halt. Her head rotates, pained and gagging. I hear her curse under her breath, but my mind struggles to catch up. She does another quick swoop with the light before reaching for her radio.

She scans the trees. "All officers be aware, we've got a possible 187. I repeat, possible 187. We're going to need a bus and the ME, copy."

Static garbles the reply before Welsh alerts Detective Stone and signs off. She lingers, not looking inside the tree house but suspended in thought.

"What's a 187?" JJ asks.

Welsh climbs down. "Why don't you take JJ home, Mr. Scarborough?" She can't hold my scrutiny. Her eyes search the tops of the trees as if the answers are perched along their peaks.

Dread puckers my nerves. "I'm not going anywhere, Welsh."

"Mr. Scarborough."

"Officer Katherine."

"Mr. Scarborough, please get JJ out of here."

"What's in that tree house?"

JJ sidles past me. "The hell with this." He's up the ladder before we can reach him.

"Damn it," Welsh exhales. "Damn. JJ, don't touch anything else. Climb down carefully, please, before you compromise the scene."

The scene?

"Oh my god," JJ peers into the tree house and gags. Once. Twice. He covers his mouth and rests his head against the ladder, and I realize that he's crying.

I climb up and gently touch his calf. "Jay, come on down."

For a minute that drags on for a lifetime, he doesn't move. His hands press against the ladder, inching against the surface like caterpillars.

JJ descends. If he weren't my son, I would have thought him to be a ghost. In the dank woods, ashen and forlorn, it's suddenly vital to know that he is real. That he exists and he is here and is still my son. I take his hands in mine, rubbing the chill out of them in smooth circles. "JJ," I say. "I'm here."

"Dad," he says, just once, and collapses into my arms, staining my shirt with his tears.

Above us, the tree house groans.

JENNIFER

Half a dozen news crews loiter out front. They're waiting for something to happen—good, bad, they don't care as long as they're here when it unfolds.

Most people in my situation would probably consider them to be a nuisance, but not me. Their presence gives me a strange comfort.

Precisely the reason I sent in the anonymous tips.

I know what my critics would be thinking: Why? What kind of mother would do that?

A mother who knows what it takes to get ahead, that's who. Jackson would never have agreed if I told him what I was planning, but he doesn't understand the value of an audience.

They care about her story. Hundreds of comments are pouring in on the news sites. Well-wishers. Thoughts and prayers. People have become so quick to dismiss the power of those messages. I understand thoughts and prayers aren't tangible. They won't find Chloe. They don't pay bills or heal wounds.

But they do provide solace. Connection. The knowledge that we aren't in this alone.

Chloe Cates's abduction is breaking news on every local station and has spread to several national outlets, thanks to my quick thinking and early posts. #CatchChloeCates and #SearchforCC are trending on every major platform.

Viral hashtags are always so alliterative.

I check the blog analytics. Much like the reporters, the graphs calm my nerves. Traffic has spiked thirty-six percent since my impromptu appearance. The sponsored posts bounce rates have risen thirteen percent. We've gained three thousand new subscribers since this morning. A thousand new followers on Twitter and Instagram.

Holy shirt.

You care more about the blog.

JJ's words weigh me down. The accusation in his eyes. The animosity. How could he think I'd put the blog before our family? I'm doing this for us.

He'll forgive me, though, when this is all over. He will.

We have a platform. We should use it. It's that simple.

Getting the word out is our best shot, and we can't do that if I'm keeping everyone in the dark. We have a responsibility to our subscribers to keep them apprised.

I certainly don't put my faith in Detective Stone.

Oh, Emilina. My nails dig crescents into my palm. Emme, strolling in here with her condescension and pseudo-authority. Pretending to take her job *so* seriously. I guess that will never change. Leaving me high and dry in order to save her own bony behind is kind of a pattern for her. The only good that comes with Emilina Stone is the badge she carries.

I doubt she's been completely honest to get where she is. They wouldn't give her a rank if they knew what she did.

I power up my laptop and open a new browser in private mode. I go to the blog Admin page, tap on the DRAFTS folder, and reread what I've written so far.

Hello, Spectacles! I have some terrible news to share. I've talked a lot over the years about the difficulties that come with being a mother, but I've never experienced anything like this. We woke up this morning to every parent's worst nightmare.

Chloe is missing.

The police are on their way.

But, Spectacles, I am scared. Other than slumber parties, Chloe's never spent more than a night away from home on her own—and those were prearranged with parents/guardians ahead of time. I always know where she is.

My mom-heart is screaming that this is more than an unannounced sleepover. Anyone who's felt that intuition will understand.

I'm not in love with that last line, but I leave it for now. Might be laying it on too thick. Plus, they'll probably expect me to have talked to the parents of Chloe's imaginary friends. It'll need to be tweaked.

I'll be honest with you, Spectacles. You deserve as much for sticking with us through our highs and lows. Chloe's been a little off, as some of you have noticed (yes, I've read the comments), since the mall appearance. I've apologized repeatedly, but as with any mother/daughter relationship, we're going through a phase. There's nothing nefarious or unseemly about it. How many of you have had fights with your daughter? In public? They're awful. The guilt's been chomping at me like alligators.

Decent imagery, but I let the cursor hover before moving on. Editing while I write is a bad habit.

She's thirteen and growing into an independent young woman, which I'm so happy about.

Kind of. Some days I wish she'd stop fighting me on every single decision and just do what I say.

I encourage her independence. I anticipate and accept the hurdles that arise during these tumultuous teenage years. Hiccups.

But Spectacles, I'm scared.

I wish this was just a teenager overreacting. Yet, I suspect something terrible has happened. This might upset some of you, but you know me. If you want to make it sparkle, you gotta start with a clean surface.

The police suspect abduction.

Chloe's window was open, her bedding thrown askew on the floor. Her phone was still on the charger. You know she'd never go anywhere voluntarily without her phone.

Jackson, JJ, and I searched the whole house. And she was just . . . gone. How? Why? Who would do this? If you have any ideas, share them in the comments.

Too much? I scrunch my face in consideration before deleting the last sentence. People will comment without me telling them, especially after the press conference this morning. Repeating it here could come off as superficial.

I'm sorry. I'm a mess, and somehow, the blog makes me feel like I can keep going. I can do this. For Chloe. Because of you.

And the revenue your clicks will bring.

I ask you: what would you do if your child disappeared? We think we know what we'd do, but in reality, there's no way you could ever anticipate the impact of losing a child.

Scratch that.

Discovering your child has been taken.

Better.

I keep scrolling through her pictures, ones I've shared with all of you over the years.

The cursor blinks at me, waiting for my command, but there's a gaping hole where my inspiration should be.

Emilina ran off to the search party ten minutes ago. What did they find?

I dial Jackson's number, but it goes straight to voicemail. That ash-hole.

"Jackson, turn on your phone!" I scream into the recording, pausing after each word so he can fully comprehend how dumb he is. I try once more for good measure and leave the same message but with a forking thrown in.

Downy eyes me cautiously from the door. I can see the gears turning in his head, wrestling with the pros and cons of inserting himself into a conversation before finally deciding.

"I know this isn't easy, Mrs. Scarborough. Situations such as this can bring out the worst in us, regardless of our intentions. Stress and fear is an awful combination. I have a bit of a temper myself. Even spanked my oldest once."

"Why?" I ask, closing my laptop and sitting up straighter.

"This was years ago, mind you. My boy's finishing up his last year at Ithaca, and he'd be mad as hell I'm telling you this story. Anyway, Connie, my wife, was at work. I had the day off. Put the *Wizard of Oz* VHS in so I could run to the bathroom." He blushes at this, deepening the red I didn't think could get any redder. His modesty is endearing. Like Patton Oswalt tweeting. "Well. Lennie was only four at the time and had the attention span to prove it. Little did I know, he'd become quite adept at turning locks."

"No," I say, with what I hope is the appropriate amount of shared surprise.

"Yes. When I came back, he was gone. Front door wide open."

"That must have been terrifying."

"It was. I'm standing there on my porch in my undershirt and ratty shorts, shouting his name at the top of my lungs. Neighbors must've thought I was a lunatic. A million worst-case scenarios ran through my head before I caught his mop of hair bouncing by a row of bushes halfway down the block."

"Oh, my goodness. Where was he going?"

Downy chuckles. "He said he was following the yellow brick road. He had his favorite stuffed dog and had put his red sneakers on all by himself. He wanted to find Glinda and the Wizard. It was November. Some of the neighbors had scarecrow decorations in their yards."

I laugh. The sound shaky and full of nerves. It feels good to let it out, though. "Kids, huh? They put us through our paces."

He comes closer, leaning against the archway separating the rooms. "That they do, Mrs. Scarborough. Nothing scarier than being responsible for a child's well-being. And I'm sorry one of yours has gone missing. I understand that fear—and the beast that lives right below it."

Officer Downy's wrinkles carve his face, telling their own stories of joy and despair. How he can deal with the stressors of being a parent and an officer of the law is beyond my comprehension. It's admirable, really. Not many people are built for that kind of wear and tear.

"I would never hurt my children, Officer Downy."

I believe this fiercely, and yet the truth is never black and white. Hurt comes in many different forms.

He rubs a dry hand along his brow, leaving little white specks of dried skin on the front of his uniform.

My insides feel like they've been caught inside a Vitamix. I clutch at my throat and curl forward. "Is she in the woods?" I ask. "Did they find her?"

Downy doesn't look up, purposely avoiding my gaze. He removes his hat and scratches absently, and I have to fight the urge to get a broom and sweep the floor around him.

"We'll know soon," he says.

I nod, and when nothing more comes, I tuck my head to my chest and stay that way until we hear the pounding of footsteps.

The search parties have returned.

Officer Welsh pushes her way to the front of the pack. JJ and Jackson are close behind. I almost don't recognize them. Pallid and worse than distraught. Demolished.

No. No, no, no.

I run to them, throw my arms around Jackson's neck and press my body into his, wishing he'd reciprocate.

Maybe if I wish hard enough, none of this will have happened. Things will go back to the way they used to be. Other people get their wishes, why can't we?

But he doesn't hold me, doesn't even try.

Jackson stays wired in my embrace. Taut and alert, like my touch is sending electric currents into his muscles. JJ drops to the couch and smothers his face into his hands. Everyone else crowds into the kitchen, the dining room, the alcove closest to the staircase.

Filling the empty spaces. All these people and not one of them is right. I just want my Chloe.

"Jackson." I stick two fingers under his chin trying to make his eyes meet mine, but they're glued to a spot on the wall over my shoulder. I feel my patience cracking. "Look at me. What happened out there?"

A choked whimper comes from JJ, and I can't bear to hear it again. The sound of a baby lamb discovering he has been sent to the slaughter. Bleating and broken.

I shake Jackson, dig my nails into his arms until blood mushrooms.

Good. I hope it hurts. "Jackson!" I hiss. "Tell me. Please. Did you find her?"

He finally sees me. I search his drawn face for a trace of hope, but I only find resentment.

"You did this," Jackson sneers. He lurches out of my embrace and bumps into me as he passes to the living room. He pats JJ on the back. Rounds the coffee table and plummets to the floor. One second he's upright, the next he is cross-legged in a sad pile.

What the fork. "Jackson."

"Jennifer." The address comes from the back door.

I spin to Emilina as a siren blares in the distance. My stomach drops ten feet. Tears blur my vision. Collages dance together on the walls and crumble beneath the slideshow in my mind. I hear her first cry, dimming the lights in the delivery room to take her first picture. Her little toes, dry but perfect.

It's like someone is fast-forwarding my life. The red and white lights of an ambulance flash in time with the milestones. The first bite of real food: homemade sweet potatoes. She was covered in sweet orange goo. Flash. Her first steps, leaning on the refrigerator for support. Flash. Baking sugar cookies. The counter covered in flour and dough bits while she ate fistfuls of frosting. Flash. Her first tooth falling out. We named her tooth fairy Sparkle Glittery and slid chocolate coins under her pillow. Flash.

Dances and laughs. Flash. Hugs and cuddles. Flash. Piggyback rides. Flash. Photo shoots, costumes, auditions, and skits. Flash. Flash. Flash.

I exhale a massive sob. "Oh, no, my Chloe, my Chloe. No, no. No." The last one lingers in the air.

I don't know who catches me. The carpet doesn't break my descent. Through the floor, I go. Down the rabbit hole. And in that free fall, darkness descends. I see Abby's face stitched onto every horrible creature that flies out at me. Snowmen made of dirt. Owls flitting out of knotholes where blood trickles from the bark.

This is what you wanted, they say. Mocking and judgmental. *This is what you wanted all along.*

How does it feel to finally go viral?

I scream. "No! No, this isn't what I wanted! No!"

The tunnel extends. Someone pushes me. My teeth knock together. Hard. The metallic taste of blood fills my mouth. Hairy knuckled and calloused hands. They're too rough for her, I want to yell. Or did I actually speak? Too rough. Be gentle.

She's delicate.

"She's coming to," I hear near the end of the tunnel. The high-pitched ringing in my ears recedes. "Jen? Jen, are you with me?"

Emilina.

"Yes," I answer. I think.

"Are you with me?" she repeats, and her hands grab my shoulders.

"Yes."

"Good." Emilina's mouth is set and her eyes are watery. I haven't seen her so shaken since that night at the water tower.

"Why?"

"Come with me," she says.

She takes me by the wrist and leads me out the door while Abby pirouettes between the spaces of the living room, golden tutu sparkling, feet never touching the ground.

EMILINA

I lead Jen toward the tree house. There's no obvious trail, but she doesn't trip over the rocky landscape. There's no hesitation at all in her movements. She dips under low-hanging branches and dodges bristly pricker bushes with ease. Maybe the shock's increasing her ambivalence to the scratches on her hands. Or maybe this isn't her first time walking this expanse.

"You come out here a lot?" I ask.

"Not during the winter," she says. Monotonous. Vacant.

"What about Chloe? You said she likes being outside. Exploring and whatnot."

Jen ponders in silence for a moment then shakes her head. "I don't think so. Abby's outdoorsy in that she likes finding butterflies or pretty flowers; occasionally she'll help pick the herbs, but she doesn't exactly like to get her hands dirty, if you know what I mean."

"Kids have a way of getting into all sorts of things when we're not looking."

She scoffs, automatically on the defensive. "And you're supposed to be an expert on children, Emilina? Do you even have kids?"

"I remember what it was like at her age," I say.

"Give me a break. Abby doesn't *get into things*. Abby doesn't have many chances to be on her own. We've been incredibly busy this year. Between her lessons and the blog, she doesn't get a lot of downtime. And when she does, she prefers activities that are intellectually stimulating, like puzzles or chess."

I haven't heard her use Abby's real name before. "She sounds like a great kid."

Jen's mouth folds up. "The best."

"Has she ever mentioned a tree house?"

"No, I don't think so."

"What about JJ?"

"What about JJ?" she asks defensively.

"He got home late last night, correct? You told Downy and Welsh you had no idea he'd gone out."

She stops. "JJ and Ryan are practically inseparable. They like baseball and girls and horror movies, and they're certainly not hanging out in the woods."

"Are you sure? He's what, fifteen? From what my colleagues have told me, these woods are a popular spot for parties." I kick at a rusty can to my right.

Jen plants her feet and grabs her necklace, running the charms along the chain. "I don't like what you're insinuating, Emilina. My son doesn't drink. He doesn't party. He doesn't know about the tree house."

Color rushes up her neck, and the charms move faster as her agitation grows. She's shutting down, and when people shut down, they clam up. I need her to keep talking.

"Okay," I say. "I believe you. Let's keep moving."

I high knee it over a narrow fallen tree, and Jen follows. "Fine," she says. "But if you question my son's integrity again, I'm reporting you for harassment."

Her comment sneaks under my skin, but I swallow down my sarcasm and switch directions. "Have you noticed any unfamiliar cars on the street recently? People you don't recognize?"

"No."

"What about at photo shoots?" I ask. "A number of those are done on location, correct? Various parks, trails, entertainment venues. Have you gotten the sense recently that you were being followed? Anyone paying more attention to Abby than normal?"

"No, nothing like that."

Too short. Too quick. "Is it possible she had a boyfriend?"

"Jesus, she's thirteen, Emilina."

"You had your first crush in third grade."

"There's a big difference between an innocent crush and having a boyfriend. Abby's too young to date, and if she were interested in someone—which she's not but I feel like you need to hear me say it—*if* she were, then she would tell me. What are you implying?"

I shift my weight from one foot to the other. "Jen, I found some things in her room that are concerning. If you're holding back, you need to tell me."

"What things?"

I have a feeling she doesn't know about the journal. I debate telling her but decide to hold onto the detail a little while longer. "A photograph."

"What kind of photograph? I'm afraid you'll have to be more specific," Jen says with that same unreadable expression.

"A Polaroid of Abby."

Jen hugs her arms to her chest. "I take Polaroids all the time."

"Why?"

She counts off on her fingers. "To test lighting, outfit composition, angles. We've also been using them to stage flashback collections. The nineties are making a resurgence and throwbacks like Polaroids are incredibly popular right now. Chloe did a whole series of OOTDs last month, kind of like a day-in-the-life series. She's really got a good eye for it too. We considered making it a blog staple, but we decided to wait a bit longer to see if the trend sticks. I'm sure whatever you found is nothing."

The dark background. The way she covered her face. The out-of-focus body shape. That is not a picture of a girl trying on outfits for an Insta post.

"But you're positive? No boyfriend or girlfriend or anything like that?"

Her eyes close, chin upturned slightly. Sunlight trickles through the low-hanging branches and spiders across her face. "I don't know. If you asked me yesterday, I would've said no way in hell. Actually, heck." She titters. "But today . . . I feel like I opened a door to an alternate universe. Lying to Jackson and me? Sneaking around on her own socials? That's not my girl. That's not the Abby I know."

"People are rarely who we think they are."

She glowers at me. "I'm a good mother, Emilina."

I didn't say you weren't, I think. But she's not talking to me anymore. She's trying to convince herself.

"I'm a good mother. I am. I have done everything for my kids. Given everything I could to make their lives great. My body, my time, my—" She stops abruptly and turns away, ending in a whisper. "I've done the best I could for them. How could someone do this to me?" she squeaks.

There it is. The martyring, self-indulgent pity sinks its teeth and spreads like venom. "To *you?*" Years of suppressed anger rises in my chest. "Oh, poor you. Ever since we were kids, you blamed everybody else for your problems. Me, Carol—"

Mary and Nicole.

I snip their names on the tip of my tongue, but understanding spreads across Jen's face.

"How we react to shitty people matters just as much as the shitty things people do to hurt us, but you haven't seemed to have figured that out yet. You see that grove up ahead?" I ask, pointing to where an edge of yellow tape is barely visible. "Your daughter is lying over there. Left dead in an old tree house while you were plotting how best to exploit her in the next online campaign. What about her, Jen? What the fuck about her?"

Her slack-mouthed expression reminds me of a fish. Bobbing hopelessly from the line as the hook digs deeper into its gut.

Then she lunges at me.

It isn't the first time Jen's attacked me. That night at the water tower she came after me too. Chased me through the field in the dark. Burrs stuck to the cuffs of my socks. Sticks clawed at my arms and legs like they were alive. *Stay with us*, I heard them whisper as I ran. *Stay with us, Emme. Be here forever like her.* I knew if I stopped, they would pounce. The rough limbs would tangle around my ankles, between my legs, pinning my arms to my sides. Covering my mouth, eyes, nose until I couldn't breathe. Couldn't see.

Jennifer Scarborough has the same unpredictability as Jen Groff does in my memories.

I, however, have changed. I'm not the scared girl I used to be. I've had years of experience and training for this type of situation. I don't flinch or falter. Twisting her extended arm, I hike it higher up her back until she falls to her knees. Grunting in frustration and pain, she roars as I push her face into the thick layer of decaying leaves.

"Get off me!" she shrieks.

"Think about what you're doing, Jennifer. Think about what *we're* doing out here. Abby wouldn't want this."

Jen stops struggling. I release her arm, and she curls into a ball at my feet. Big, heaving sobs rack her body.

"Get up," I say, when I can't take it anymore. Her cries taper off as I clap mud off my jeans. "I need you to hear me because I won't say this twice. If you're hiding something, we will find it. We're going to comb through your records. Your social media. Your finances. Every shred of evidence we collect today."

She finds her feet, a baby deer learning to walk. "Am I supposed to be scared by that? Thanks for setting me straight, Emilina, but I don't buy the big bad detective act for one second. Walking around like you're high and mighty. Better than me. Once upon a time, we were cut from the same cloth, and that's the difference between us. I know exactly how I got here. You're the one incapable of telling the truth. I am a good mother. Just look at the blog. I have nothing to hide."

"You have plenty to hide."

"I could've killed you, you know." She grits her teeth against the dirt in her mouth as she speaks. Black mud and rotten foliage cling to her hair in clumps. The child of Swamp Thing and the Creature from the Black Lagoon. It's frightening.

"I know," I say. "But you didn't. Whatever the reason, you chose to let me go—and now it's my responsibility to make sure the person who took your daughter's life is caught and punished."

She studies me, trembling and uncertain. "Not a trick?" she asks. "She's really dead?"

"I'm sorry," I say, and mean it.

Her chin quivers. "I can't. I can't do this." She retreats toward the house, swaying a bit until she finds her balance, wiping muck from her limbs and picking at the wet shirt clinging to her torso as she goes.

I call Downy as soon as she's out of sight. "Mrs. Scarborough is heading your way. Keep someone on her at all times."

"Heard. I'll handle it."

"Thanks, Brian." I'll feel better with someone watching her.

I rub the dirt off my hands and arrive at the clearing where the ME is bent over the body. Jocelyn Abreu has been the Albany County Medical Examiner since her transfer from Atlanta after Hurricane Katrina. Horrible circumstances brought her here, but we're lucky to have her. The last coroner stored autopsy supplies in a mini fridge next to his lunch.

Joss is short with hazel-gray eyes and sharp features. She styles her straight black hair in a no-nonsense ponytail and her eyebrows are impeccably arched. She's also the only person I've ever met who mixes cereal with orange juice. I guess when you spend your days in the morgue, strange habits can be forgiven.

We've worked our share of unfortunate cases together, consoled too many families torn apart by grief. I can tell by the way she cradles the gold cross on her necklace, a Mother's Day gift—*Hector's a sweet boy*, she always says of her six-year-old son, *A sweet, sweet boy*—that she doesn't like what she sees. Leaning over the stretcher, I take in the shape of the body. Small. Too small for this place.

Jocelyn pinches the sheet between the tips of her fingers, peeling it away for closer examination and scratching her observations down on a clipboard.

I look from the body to the tree house and shudder. Tree houses aren't meant to hold the bodies of dead children. I join her at the foot of the stretcher.

Jocelyn glances up but quickly returns to her notes. "Emilina. Wish I could say I was glad to see you."

"Feeling's mutual. What do you have for me, Joss?" I ask.

"I thought we might be looking at an overdose given the location, but I'm sorry. Homicide, for sure."

"Any chance they don't know yet?" By *they*, I mean Albany's Homicide division. As disgusted as I am by the discovery, a murder ruling means her case is no longer in my jurisdiction—which makes someone else responsible for bringing the assailant to justice.

And in this case, that someone would be Devon Blaisdell, a husky man with crooked teeth and a chip on his shoulder, especially when it comes to CFSU trampling on his territory. He's been on the force longer than any of the other detectives, and his disdain for teamwork is well-known among our colleagues. Dealing with Devon is like shoveling snow during a blizzard.

"Sorry," Joss says. "They've been notified. Should be here soon. I saw the press out front, though, so I told the bus to come through the park. Buy you a little more time before they're hounding you for a statement."

"Any idea how long she's been out here?"

"Hard to say definitively. Body's cold but not stiff, so fairly certain rigor's passed. The skin is starting to blister. Moderate bloating and enzyme leakage—see there, around her nose and mouth?"

I nod at the pink foam crusted around both. "What about these marks around her neck?" I ask, turning my gaze toward the tree line. "Ligature marks? Or a knife?"

Joss scrunches her nose. "I'd say those are more likely from a small animal. Significant presence of blowflies, as well. She's probably been dead somewhere between three and seven days."

My head whips around. "That doesn't fit with my timeline," I say, gears turning. "My girl's only been missing since this morning. Could the temperature have sped up decomp?"

"Some, but not this much. I can't speak to your case, Emilina, but this body has been dead for longer than twenty-four hours."

The hair on the back of my neck rises. "Cause of death?"

"I'm not certain, but most likely blunt force trauma to the cranium. See this area here?" I have to look away as she turns the head. I cover my mouth and nose as she motions to a section of concaved skull covered by a mass of brown hair matted slick and black. A sliver of pink sweatshirt peeks out from the top of the sheet. "It appears to have been crushed. With what, I couldn't venture a guess at this point. I'll know more when I get her on the table. I will say I doubt this is where it happened, though. Too clean."

Blunt force trauma to the skull would leave a lot more blood than the splatters I found leading to the property line. And from what I can see of the tree house, the amount of blood there doesn't match with what you'd expect of such an injury. Head wounds are notoriously messy.

"You're thinking she was moved?"

"Almost certainly."

"Could it have been an accident? A fall?"

I picture Abby tumbling out of her bedroom window and landing hard on the muddy ground. But that wouldn't explain the discrepancies on the

Scarborough property. Or how she ended up a quarter mile away in the tree house. Or the timeline. If she's been dead for almost a week, why did they only report her missing today?

Jocelyn offers a noncommittal shake of her head. "I can't be sure. It's possible, but—"

"But not likely," I finish.

"Even if she did somehow trip inside the tree house, there's nothing she could've hit that would've done this level of damage without making a huge mess."

"Agreed," I say, motors whirring. "Listen, I know it's kind of poor form, but do you mind if I take a few pictures of the crime scene?" I motion toward the gurney. "And her?"

Jocelyn props the clipboard against her hip. "This isn't exactly a CFSU matter anymore, Emilina."

"Come on, Joss. Whatever happened to team effort?"

She holds me with a steady gaze before relinquishing a stiff nod. "Go ahead—but not a word to Blaisdell. Last thing I need is his stank breath breathing down my neck."

"My lips are sealed," I say, sliding to the camera app. I snap a shot of the ladder. The tree house. A second of the tree house from a slightly different angle. The stacks of logs. The trampled area around the bushes. When I'm satisfied I've got enough to reconstruct later, I tell Joss I'm ready for the body.

Jocelyn carefully folds the sheet down to reveal the girl's bloated face, the light pink fabric around her collarbone stained red. I angle my phone and take a quick succession of photos. I take a step closer, studying the body, the wound, her face. And pause.

Oh, no.

I rotate my head to the side, comparing the decomposing features to the very much alive girl in the photo Jen provided.

"Shit." Every muscle in my stomach revolts. I gag hard and run to the edge of the clearing, unable to hold back the vomit.

The smell of rubber and nature is overpowering, but it's nothing compared to the stench of the body. It clings to my skin, my hair, inside my nose. I can't escape it. I gulp for breaths, openmouthed to lessen the stench, but the retching begins again.

This isn't the first dead body I've seen. The horror doesn't wear off. I don't care what anyone says; it's not something you get used to. But as crass as it sounds, it's not the sight of a brutally murdered girl that upheaves my breakfast.

"Take it off," I say, walking back toward the body on shaky legs.

"What's wrong?" She's confused. So am I.

"The sheet. Pull it down."

"Why?"

"Just take it off," I snap.

Just as I understand the significance of her cross, Joss knows I'm alarmed when I forgo niceties and bark out orders. "Okay," she says, hesitant but complying.

Jocelyn stuffs the clipboard under her arm and begins peeling the sheet back when a baritone voice rumbles through the forest nearby. *Crap,* I think, as Devon Blaisdell stumbles into the clearing. He'll be pissed to see me, but if I'm right, it won't matter.

"What in the holy fuck is going on here?" he blurts.

I ignore him, looking intently at the body in front of me. "Son of a bitch."

"Did I miss something?" Jocelyn whispers and fusses over the stretcher. That's another thing I like about her: Joss hates making mistakes almost as much as I do.

"No," I say, letting out a rush of air in hopes of steadying the ground. I pop a breath mint into my mouth and roll it around my tongue. "I did."

Blaisdell waves at the EMTs. "Body haulers, let's go." They've been waiting for Joss to finish but hop to at his crass command. I half expect to see smoke billowing from his ears and nostrils. "Did I stutter, ladies? Anyone want to tell me what the fuck is going on?"

"Oh, hey, Devon. Didn't hear you," I say, not looking up from the girl on the stretcher.

"You're on my crime scene, Stone."

I take another picture.

"What the hell, Stone?"

"You're not getting rid of me that easily, Blaisdell." I nod to Jocelyn.

She covers the body and addresses the EMTs lingering behind us. "She's ready, y'all." They position themselves at opposite ends of the stretcher, lift in tandem, and exit through the trees in the direction of Western Park.

"Why's that?" Blaisdell asks, widening his stance. I read once that it's instinct for men to take up more space. Spreading their legs on trains, public transit, movie seats, airplanes—it's all a way of asserting their masculinity in an act of domination. Devon Blaisdell's performance thus far has been a prime example of that.

Instead of minimizing, I stand taller. The ticking crescendos in my head. The countdown has been working toward zero this whole time.

"Because," I say, watching the stretcher depart, the white sheet floating through the shadows. "That's not Chloe Cates."

Abby's Journal

If I had to say when all of this started, I'd have to say my birthday.

For the 2 weeks leading up to it, Mom was on a rampage. She studied Pinterest boards and style websites trying to decide which theme would be best for the celebration. This year matters more, she said. Thirteen is THE year. It has to be perfect.

I wanted Harry Potter. *I love HP. I haven't finished the books yet, but I binged the movies last weekend with JJ.*

Which character's your favorite, Abby? *See? I AM practicing for interviews, MOM.*

My favorite. Hm. Not Ron. He whines too much. Harry's the obvious choice. His family sucks, he lives under the stairs, and Daniel Radcliffe is pretty cute in a nerdy kind of way. I love Hermione. She's super smart and witty without being annoying. I love the leviosa *scene and her dress at the ball.*

So, just her spells, Abby?

Well, I'm so glad you asked.

I guess the real reason is her courage. She's not afraid to be herself. She doesn't change who she is because other people tell her she's too smart or not magic enough. She proves them all wrong.

I created a vision board because I thought Mom would like that better. I found pictures of other HP parties. They had personalized wands or glitter bath bombs for party favors. Lightning bolts and candles on the tables. Hogwarts houses. Butterbeer in copper mugs. But:

"HaRrY pOtTeR iS sO oUtDaTeD, aBbY. No one's gonna stop scrolling for a Potter Party. Besides, J. K. Rowling is too controversial right now, we can't risk being associated with that train wreck. I've got a better idea. What if we did Existential Mermaid?"

What does that even mean? Mermaid party? What am I, 4? Her pictures were freaking crazy. Sparkly seashell bikini tops and Lycra fins. Mermaid hair. Reiki crystals. Essential oils. A girl doing yoga??? Starfish decor. Waterfalls. Three-tiered pearl cake with a fork as the centerpiece. Rainbows. Rainbows? She'd already ordered seashells. Like, thanks for letting me know.

Wtfffff.

So Birthday Week comes and we're posting every day. Decor and favor ideas. Ten tips on successful "age-appropriate" party games. The big debate: cake vs. cupcake. Ten perfect gifts for your beautiful mermaid. Barf emoji. She says the numbers are CC Spectacular (ha, right), but I don't believe her. We only did 2 paid partner photos—a vegan frosting that tasted like pennies and a birthday cake–flavored lip gloss—and both only got a couple hundred measly likes.

I made a wish the night before the big day like I used to when I was 5 and thought stars actually had magical powers. For my 13th birthday, I just want to be Abby.

Mom woke up extra early to prep and decorate. Dad asked if I wanted to have a lunch date since JJ had practice. Lunch was fine. Dad's . . . well, Dad. Makes a lot of stupid jokes and talks about how cute I was when I was a baby.

Mom called while we were on our way home. FREAKING out of course b/c the streamers she ordered came in cobalt not coral and everything was RUINED!!!

Like who tf cares, it's a streamer. Basically colored toilet paper taped to the ceiling. I don't even care.

I had Dad drop me off at the park b/c I didn't feel like spending my birthday waiting in line at the party store. You could be dying and they'd still make you take a number.

I like the park, tho and I wanted to be by myself before I had to put Chloe on. There's a rose garden and small pond with koi fish with this arched stone bridge. I always feel so grown up when I'm on it, like that is where adults go to have important talks.

Maybe that's why I did it.

Did what, Abby?

I DMed *him* and asked to meet up.

OK, he said. WHEN. WHERE.

Where?!?!?! ahhhhhhh!! I told him now, the bridge, and I waited. And waited. And waited.

Journal, he never showed. I sent him a million msgs like I was thirsty af and didn't care—and rly, I didn't. I just wanted him to answer me. Didn't read my DMs.

Boys are trash.

I texted Dad to pick me up but he was still waiting at the party store, shocker, so I cut through the woods. Nbd. I saw a cardinal and wondered why some birds fly south for the winter and some don't. How do they find food? How do they stay warm? It's not like they can eat old french fries. Can they? I read that McDonald's food never molds, it's like radioactive or something, so maybe they could live off that. Sounds like the start of a graphic novel, tbh.

When I was almost home, I also saw this tree house. It looked pretty old. I remember Hallie Forest used to beg her parents for a tree house when we were kids. They didn't have the right kind of tree or something in their backyard, so they built her a huge playhouse instead. It had two floors and working electricity. Made a great clubhouse for a little while. There's even a CC Spectacular video somewhere of us playing with chalk paint a random third-party company sent us to promote. Mom prbly deleted it, but I remember her filming. Hallie's rainbow wasn't in the right order and she asked her to redo it. ROYGBIV.

I wanted to check it out but there was no way to get up to it. I've been thinking about going back. Seeing if anyone's been using it or if I could make it a place I go that no one else knows.

Anyways.

Back to birthday drama.

I get home. JJ was stringing a row of seahorse lightbulbs from a Command hook and cursing. I waved and ran upstairs to change. I decided on this mint skater dress with a scoop back. I really *didn't want to walk around in the sequined bra Mom picked for me. Hermione would cry if she had to wear that.*

*I went downstairs. Cardi B streaming through Alexa b/c Mom's so cool *eye roll**

Mom was taking a mirror selfie and didn't see me right away. Dad and JJ screamed HAPPY BIRTHDAY!!!

And there's merch everywhere. Balloons and a hot pink banner and confetti and a giant cake—not pearled and bedazzled like in her picture but shaped like a mermaid tail and covered in edible glitter. And everything says the same thing.

HAPPY BIRTHDAY CHLOE

In big cursive writing. There are CHLOE candies, CHLOE plates, CHLOE photo props with the hashtag #HBDChlo.

I'm standing there just like . . . wtf. WHY.

Mom wore this . . . IDK how to describe it . . . hula skirt? It was made of these puffy flower buds and straw and a crown made of real seashells. She kept making a big deal about it. "These are REAL! There's one for you, too, and those shells are REAL."

OoOoOoOoO like I've never seen a clamshell before.

That's nice, Mom, but is it just us? I asked.

Mom smiled at me from behind her phone, filming everything. She handed the phone to Dad and wrapped her arms around me. "Chlo. Come on. Of course it's not just us. I have a surprise."

Really? I said, getting hype. I can be gullible. One time JJ told me that chocolate milk comes from brown cows. I believed him for a year, pointing out the chocolate milk cows every time we passed a farm.

"Thirteen is such a special age, and we decided we had to go above and beyond to celebrate the beautiful woman you're becoming—the spectacular *woman, I should say.*" *She laughed, the fake one that sounds like glass breaking, and waggled at the camera.*

Oh, I'm such a fun mom.

So . . . what's the surprise? I asked.

She took my hands and gave Dad the signal. Two little flicks of her thumb mean BURST. Dad switched hands and held the circle down, hundreds of photos saving to the reel for her to pick through later.

"You've worked so hard, and we wanted you to have the chance to unwind and enjoy turning thirteen. So we, Chloe, are going to spend the evening at the spa at Crossgates. Aaaaaaaand I invited all your girls!" *She hung on the word like a soccer announcer. GIIIRLLLLLLLS.*

OMG seriously? You're not kidding. You're serious? OMG! *I screeched and cheered and looked around like they were gonna pop out from behind the couch or something.*

She took the phone from Dad and ended the recording and everything just . . . fell. FLOPPED. No more smile, no overly excited announcer voice. Just her, pressing play to review the vid. "This is good, Chlo, but can we go again? I want to get a shot of you coming down the stairs, and why aren't you wearing the bikini? Go up and change. Laurel's Boutique paid good money for us to tag them in that for their upcoming spring break sale. And this time can you try not to shriek so loud? It's cutting into the mic too much. Not cute."

What? *I asked. I didn't get the joke. This was my birthday party, my THIR-TEENTH BIRTHDAY that she'd just said was SO SPECIAL, and she wanted me to fix all these things to reshoot my entrance . . . b/c of a sponsor.*

Because I was too happy.

"Just once more, I promise, it's almost perfect." She pushed hair off her shoulder and fixed her stupid shell crown. I wanted to throw it at her. "Just go get changed quick."

No. NO.

"Chloe, stop being difficult."

I'm Abby, *I said.* Remember? A-B-B-Y ABBY. *I clapped at her. She flipped.*

Dad tried to smooth things over. I don't think he knew she was setting the whole thing up to shoot for the blog. They don't seem to talk. Like, ever. How can you marry someone and not talk to them? If I ever get married, my husband will know the boring stuff AND my secrets.

When I told her I didn't want to do blog stuff on my birthday, she just laughed. "We have an ObLiGaTiOn to our sponsors. Our followers have eXpEcTaTiOnS. We can't disappoint them."

If there was ever a sound bite that described Mom, that's it. All about the followers. Never about me.

It wasn't "once more" either. I put the stupid, scratchy sequin bikini on and did my entrance seven MORE TIMES. S-E-V-E-N. So she could get the right amount of excitement and plenty of shots for the Laurel's Boutique #ad and a believable cut away to "add the girls later."

Elle Woods would never.

She wouldn't let me have my cake until I plugged the bakery that made it (4 times) and then we had to do her specialty drinks (5 times and 3 different scripts with plenty of affiliated links). Link in bio for the recipe, Spectacles! Don't forget to hit like and subscribe.

We didn't even go to the spa. She wrote about how the manager didn't allow cameras inside for "privacy reasons" and uploaded pictures from their website, tagging them and RAVING about the seaweed facials and hot stone massages.

In reality, JJ and I ate cake alone on the couch watching Harry Potter *until he went to Ryan's and I gave up and went to bed. It wasn't even good cake. Fondant is stupid. It tastes like wax.*

I hate this. Some days I hate her.

JENNIFER

Staring at the living room walls, I realize I must've been sleep deprived when I chose such an awful color. Buttercream yellow. I thought it was supposed to be relaxing. I remember thinking that while I flipped through samples. Cheerful without being obtrusive. The perfect neutral. Yet, here we are, and the longer I look at them, the more aggravated I get that I have to sit in a room that is simultaneously too bright and strangely dark. Like a sick ward, where they use happy colors to try and distract you from the fact that you're dying.

But how could anyone forget that they've been given a death sentence?

"You're certain?" I ask.

Crust, I need a shower. I'm covered in mud and god knows what else. I'm tired. I'm hungry, and my emotional capacity is at zero. Five minutes ago, my daughter was dead. The last thing I need is mind games—or the woman currently scrutinizing me who seems determined to play them.

Emilina sits on the edge of the couch, stiff and uncomfortable. "We'll have to wait for official confirmation from the ME," she says, "but I'm sure. It's not her."

A knot in my chest loosens. "But . . . JJ saw her. Jackson saw her. You told us she was dead, Detective Stone. And now you're telling us that the girl in the tree house *isn't* Abby? I mean, what are we supposed to do with that? How can we give credence to anything you have to say? Maybe that is Abby and you're wrong now. Like you said, we can't be sure until the tests come back."

"I didn't see her," Jackson says. Pale and fidgety, he pulls at invisible threads on his jeans.

"I'm sorry, what?" I glare at him but he ducks his head into his hands, rubbing his face. "You said you saw her."

"I didn't."

"He didn't go up the ladder." JJ's words are shortened punches. He won't look at me.

I can't believe I hit him. "You saw her, JJ," I say softly.

"I saw a body," he responds. "Her hair. Her clothes. Her face was . . . it was too . . ."

Not Abby.

"Jesus," Jackson mutters.

JJ turns to Emilina. "If it's not . . . if she's not . . . who is it?"

Emilina sighs. "We believe it's another child reported missing about a week ago."

"The cheerleader?" JJ asks, mouth dropping wide. "Missy?"

"JJ," I say with an edge of warning.

"Yes," Emilina says reluctantly, looking from him to me. "Missy Crawford. Did you know her, JJ?"

JJ's eyes flick to me.

"No," I say, filling in the gaps. "I don't think so. She went to a different school. I mean, their paths might've crossed at one tournament or another, that's definitely possible. Between baseball and football, six degrees of separation. We talked about that when we saw the news talking about her disappearance, sort of like a warning to the kids, you know? Hit a little too close to home." Or so I thought. "JJ's participated in so many competitions and round-robins, but pretty much every district in our division attends those invitationals."

Missy Crawford. Her face flashes in my mind.

"JJ?" Emilina asks, like I hadn't just answered her question. "You looked like you were going to say something."

He kicks at the carpet with the toe of his shoe and runs a hand through his hair. "No," he says. "I didn't know her. Just from the news, is all. Everyone at school was talking about her."

"What were they saying?"

"Just a bunch of rumors. That she was doing it for attention or she ran off with her boyfriend. I don't know. Ryan was saying we had to watch out for Pennywise crawling around the sewers. He's dumb, though, so," he trails off.

JJ sounds like a kid again, the same morbid curiosity he demonstrates when he's writing about alien invasions and creature features. I probably shouldn't let him watch scary movies for a while.

Emilina smiles. "I don't think a killer clown is responsible. Monsters are a little trickier to pin down in real life because they look just like everyone else."

She stares directly at me.

JJ shakes his head and flops back on the couch. "Fucking weird."

"Language, JJ," I say.

He shoots daggers at me before diving into his phone.

"So, Abby—she is still alive?" Jackson stammers. He could use ten in a tanning booth. A healthy dose of UV and maybe a Prozac. I've never seen him like this.

"We obviously can't say for sure yet. What I do know is she's not in that tree house."

Jackson flubbers, a shiver that starts with his bottom lip and rocks through his body. "I can't. I can't—"

Losing it.

"Detective Stone," I interject, "what I'm hearing is that there's a *murderer* on the loose who's already killed one girl and might have taken Abby and you've got yourself parked in my living room. Wasting time. Why aren't you out there looking for him? What if he hurts my daughter?"

"First, it would be premature at this point to assume the homicide is connected to your daughter's case."

Premature, sure, but I can tell from her reserved demeanor that she's at least considering it. We all are.

"Is there a second?"

"Until I say otherwise, we continue to investigate every legitimate lead that comes in about your daughter."

"Have you gotten anything from the tip lines?" Jackson asks.

"Nothing useful, but I assure you, my team is adept at sorting through the weeds. If there's a credible development, I'll be the first to know. And, actually, I was hoping you could help me with something." She pinches a floppy white square between her fingers. "Have you seen this picture before?"

The Polaroid.

She tips it to JJ first. He glances up from his phone, squints, then shakes his head. "No, I don't know what that is."

Jackson next, mouth chiseled in a firm line of concentration. "No," he says. His knee twitches, and he revolves in his seat to look out the window.

Me last.

"Do you know who could've taken this?" Emilina asks. "Or who the other person with her might be?"

"Are you sure that's a person?" I stare down at the image. The butterfly necklace. Her pink cami. "Looks like . . . a thumb over the lens or even damaged film. Could be a number of things, really."

"It's dark, I'll give you that, but the colors seem too consistent. Why don't you take another look?" She pushes the Polaroid closer like that will magically draw an answer.

"I'm not convinced that blur is anything," I say, "but I do know when it was taken. The night of our last mall appearance. A few weeks ago at Crossgates."

"This could've been taken at the show?" she asks, scribbling in her notebook.

I shake my head. "I don't think so. Crossgates has windowed ceilings and is very bright. We staged in the atrium right outside the Apple store. It was *supposed* to be at that new bowling place, you know, with all the vintage arcade games and neon pins? But there was an electrical issue and that was apparently the best they could do on short notice."

"I see, and who was your point person?"

"The event director, Harold Forest. He's a neighbor. Lives in the next development over, actually. We've worked with him a number of times."

"Okay, I'll need his contact information."

"I can do that," I say, scratching a flake of dried mud off my wrist before flicking through my contacts to Harold's name. I pass the phone to Emilina and watch her assess the screen. I suppress the urge to rip it out of her grasp. She seems like the kind of person who would ask to see a picture and then proceed to scroll through every other photo in the gallery. Not that I have anything to hide, but people are inherently nosy.

She copies down his information and hands it back without further exploration. "How many people attended this event?" she asks.

"Over a hundred, it was swamped. We only had thirty spots for the VIP meet-and-greet session afterwards, though."

Scribble, scribble. Emilina's hand zips across the page. "I know we touched on this briefly, Mrs. Scarborough, but did anyone seem out of place? Someone who didn't fit in with the crowd?"

"I don't think so, but my attention was on Chloe. It was an excellent turnout."

JJ snorts. "Yeah, just peep the videos on the blog." I'm not prepared for the rancor in his response. *Blog.* Like it's vermin.

"I've got Luke, the detective you met earlier?" She pauses briefly for us to acknowledge we know who she's referring to. "He's got a team going through the online stuff already. But it's possible you noticed something that didn't show up in the footage. You'd be surprised at how equipped our memories are for this. Someone who stood out or just didn't feel quite right. Mr. Scarborough?"

"Hm?" He startles to focus. "Oh. No. I was backstage. I didn't see anything." Jackson practically bounces in his seat, how fast his feet tremor. It's also the fourth time I've noticed him checking his wrist for a watch that isn't there. "I mean, that was a *day*. I was just glad to get the hell out of there."

"Jackson." Honestly, the stupidity in this man sometimes is enough to blow my mind.

"What? It's not like she's not going to find out about it on her own," he says.

"Find out what?" Emilina asks.

"About the incident," he says.

"I'm sorry, I missed a step. What incident?"

I could throttle Jackson.

"What incident?" Emilina repeats, a hint of exasperation coloring her tone.

I close my eyes and count to ten. This is a forking nightmare.

"Abby got her . . . you know. Her time of the month," JJ says. He scrunches up his nose and shoulders.

Emilina offers that soft smile again, making friends with my son. Trying to get him on her side. Conniving troll. "Ah. I see." Then to me, "That's not exactly what I'd call an incident."

"It was her first time," I exhale. Weariness settles into my bones. I'm ready for bed. It seems like light-years since I opened that Bow-tastic! box. Another inch of anxiety tightens my throat. Abby missed breakfast and lunch. She won't be here for dinner.

"Oh," Emilina says, grasping the implication.

I was Abby's age when I got mine for the first time. And, while I'm sure she doesn't want to admit it, *I* was the one who taught Emilina about feminine products. She thought you had to have sex to use tampons. Almost fell out of her chair when I reached for the box because *virgins were supposed to use pads.*

Abby, at least, has me to teach her the ropes.

"She wore this sky-blue jumpsuit with iron-on patches," I explain. Adorable, but another thing we argued over that day. Abby thinks rompers are adult onesies.

I don't want to wear this, Mom.

I close my eyes to shut out her voice. "She was in the middle of a skit and someone threw a teddy bear on stage. She bent down to pick it up, and I saw the stain. So did the audience."

"Oh," Emilina cringes, the pen resting on her lap as full awareness dawns in the stretch of her eyelids.

"They were already livestreaming; there was nothing we could do about that." I frown in disgust and wrap my arms around myself. "The hashtags . . . well, let's just say they were less than flattering. #ChlosFlow and #ChloesPeriodParty and #PlugItUpCC."

"People can be assholes," Emilina says, offering an apology to JJ for her adult language. Completely unwarranted. I see the admiration in his eyes and want to punch her square in the jaw. "How did Abby take it?" she asks.

I massage my temple, fighting away the images of the crowd. Their laughter. Echoes of my own mortifying youth scurry forward.

Hey, Henny Jenny . . .

"Not well," I say. "She didn't know why they were making fun of her at first, but when she realized . . . she ran off the stage crying."

"And then you made her finish the show," Jackson says, nursing the bitterness in his response. We won't find a way to bridge that gap any time soon. "Just a pat on the back and a *get back out there, Chlo, we're all counting on you.*"

Emilina frowns. Wrinkles form around her mouth. She should really use a moisturizer. "Without changing?" she asks.

Hey, Henny Jenny . . .

"Nope," JJ says, an enthusiastic agreement with Jackson. "She wrapped my hoodie around Ab's waist and sent her back out there. Because being dragged once is never enough for my mom."

Crust. "There wasn't time!" I exclaim. "We only had one more segment left to get through. Her outfit was provided by one of our sponsors. They didn't send a second look, what was I supposed to do? Cancel the show and refund the tickets?" Like we could afford that. "The damage was already done. It would've been worse if we'd skulked off like she had something to be ashamed of."

"I see."

You're a horrible human being, her tone implies. The nerve of this woman, criticizing me in my own home. Just when I think I've come to terms with her reappearance in my life, here she comes with another ash-hole comment.

Before I can give her a larger piece of my overloaded mind, Jackson chimes in. "Tell her what you did when you got home."

Shut up. Shut. Up. Shut up. "Why is any of this relevant? The show's old news. How is this helping us find Abby?"

Jackson persists, turning his attention to Emilina. "She uploaded the audience footage on her blog. Made a whole thread about Chloe becoming a woman and how it was such a special time for a mother and daughter to bond."

Emilina's mouth twists. "And how did Abby feel about you contributing to her very personal experience being dissected online?"

"She was *pissed*," JJ says. I've heard him swear before but not so blatantly. I want to reprimand him for the language—and Emilina, that cow, for setting a bad example in front of my son—but how can I? I lost his sister and slapped him all in the same day. I'm not exactly in a position to enforce parental guidelines.

"Did she talk to you about it, JJ?" Emilina asks, scratching down more notes that probably say something along the lines of JEN'S A TERRIBLE MOTHER, SHE'S GUILTY NO MATTER WHAT.

"Yeah, she did," JJ replies. "I'm pretty much the only person she can talk to lately."

Fork.

He puts his phone away and scooches forward on the couch, elbows on his knees. In his practice jersey, he looks like he's on the dugout bench. "She was totally embarrassed," he says. "I was glad she wasn't in school that night. I know that's a bad thing to say, but I read the comments, and they were sick. Peopled gifed her reactions. Made memes. I told her to lay low on her socials until it blew over. She said she'd never forgive Mom. Cried for like an hour in the bathroom and then ran out the back."

"Ran out the back?"

Fork.

JJ nods. "Yeah, she took off into the woods. I saw her from my window. I thought about stopping her, but I figured it was probably better to let her go."

"JJ, stop," I say, on the brink of losing my temper. "Abby did no such thing."

Emilina gives me an abject look of disapproval. "When I asked you earlier if Abby's run away before—you didn't think this was relevant?"

I focus on Emilina, the slightly crooked tilt of her nose. I wonder if I did that to her in the woods that night.

"She didn't run away, Detective Stone. She went for a walk; we knew exactly where she was."

"How long was she gone?" Emilina asks.

"Barely thirty minutes," I say.

"A couple of hours." JJ seems determined to counteract everything I say. "I went to get a snack around midnight, and she was at the kitchen table. I tried talking to her, but she blew me off and went upstairs."

"He's making it sound much worse than it was. Abby needed some time to cool off. So did I. Later, I showed her what I was writing, and we talked about how important it was to discuss these things in a healthy, open way. She understood why I made her continue the show and gave me the okay to post." I clap my hands together so I don't scratch at the muck on my arms anymore. "She was *fine* with it. Abby is very mature for her age. She knows she can come to me with anything. I will always put her needs first. Always."

"That is such a bullshit," JJ says.

I glare at him as he flops backward into the cushions. "Young man, you're on thin ice."

"Whatever, you're the one lying to the cop like Abby didn't run away. She said you're ruining her life and she'd never forgive you."

"Stop!" I shriek. "Abby wasn't upset. She didn't run away."

"She was and she did." JJ yanks his phone back out and taps the Instagram icon. He clicks on the name he's looking for, scrolls through the gallery, and shoves the picture in my face. "See for yourself."

It's Abby with a mouse-ear filter. Teardrop stickers pour from her eyes, but she's got the weepy, swollen cheeks of someone who's been crying in real life. A pout on her pout.

"Mom's the worst. #MOMSTER," I read the caption out loud. "Momster." I scroll through some of the other pictures and push the phone away.

JJ shows the picture to Emilina.

"Seems like maybe the situation wasn't resolved," Emilina says, but she sounds more empathetic. This paltry show of kindness, however, is worse somehow.

"Excuse me, detective, but this is a family matter, and what goes on in my family is none of your business. I admit, I made a mistake with how I handled the mall show. It's not the first time and it won't be the last. That's what parenting is. I don't need to explain myself to you, because last time I checked, your job isn't to judge how I decide to parent my children. Your job is to bring Abby home, and I don't see how you could possibly be doing that by sitting around my living room, fixated on something that *doesn't matter*. Go find my daughter. Get out of my house."

Emilina stands but doesn't leave.

I blink and see myself grabbing two handfuls of Emilina's dark hair and slamming our foreheads together until her skull cracks. Her wail of surprise and the thunk of pain as skin separates from bone. It would hurt me, too, but the payoff would be worth it. The satisfaction of watching her bleed.

Instead of addressing me, she turns to JJ, somber and attentive. "If you think of anything else that could help, you can reach me at that number." She puts a business card in his hand. He reads the information and nods.

"He's told you everything, but thank you for being so thorough," I say. "I'll show you out."

"Where are you going?" JJ asks, and my heart aches. He used to cling to my leg if I had to leave the house. Nothing eased his fears. Bribes of candy. New toys. A special trip to McDonald's. Nothing. He'd wait at the window, nose pressed against the glass until his legs got tired. Then he'd slump to the floor and blubber until I returned.

This pang of desperation is directed at Emilina, though. Not me.

She snaps her notebook shut, slips the Polaroid into her jacket pocket, and checks her phone. "I have to run some evidence down to the station. Visit a few more people. I'll be back in a couple hours."

"Who are you visiting?" I ask.

"I'll start with Harold Forest."

"Sounds like a waste of time to me," I say.

"We'll see." She crosses the foyer, and it's everything in my power not to yank her to the ground by her horrible excuse of a messy bun. I skirt around her and open the door, grasping the knob until the urge passes.

Emilina hangs back. "You need to stop lying to me, Jen."

"I'm afraid I don't care much for your tone, Emme. How many times do I have to say this? I've been nothing but honest—"

"Was it you?" she interrupts, her hazel eyes dull in the afternoon light.

"What do you mean?"

"Did you call the press?"

Yes. "No," I stress.

Face full of distrust, Emilina lifts her elbow and holds up a notebook.

Okay? Am I supposed to be afraid? "What's that?" I ask when she doesn't offer further explanation.

"Abby's journal."

"Abby doesn't have a journal," I say, crossing my arms. But I immediately second-guess that statement. I've learned a lot about my daughter today.

JJ steps between us, dark hair sweeping across his brow. Handsome, but he needs a haircut before the next game. He sneers at me as if he can hear my thoughts and can't believe I'd suggest something so trivial at a time like this.

"Yes, she does," he says. "I gave it to her. You're welcome."

Before I can respond, JJ runs upstairs, slamming his door behind him.

"Jesus, JJ." Can't anyone in this family listen?

"A journal?" Jackson asks, joining our discussion. He stands a few feet away from me with his arms dangling at his sides. "Like a diary?"

"Your kids are keeping secrets from you," Emilina murmurs, the condescension returning to its rightful place. "There's a reason."

"Yeah, because they're *kids*," I say. I cast an exasperated eye at JJ's room before focusing on the red notebook. "You can't take that."

"Yes, actually I can," she says.

"I don't give you permission." I grab for it, but she shoves it farther under her arm.

"Mrs. Scarborough, it's imperative we explore every possible angle of Abby's disappearance. This journal could give us the insight we're lacking."

"What does it say?" Jackson asks. "Have you read it?"

"We'll know soon enough," she says, peering over her shoulder at the lingering reporters.

"Fine." I release the door, my skin itching under the camera orbs aimed at our interaction. "Fine. You win."

"This isn't a game, Jennifer. There's no winners or losers. No consolation prize. I either find Abby," she says with a pause, "or I don't."

"Start by getting her name right," I say. "It's Chloe."

She scoffs and pulls keys from her pocket. "You know, most families tell me that not knowing what happened to their loved ones is worse than death. They don't get answers. They don't get closure. They just get this . . . purgatory. Stuck between the likelihood of death and the hope that no news means a miracle could happen. I've been doing this a long time. I've never seen a miracle."

I gawk at her, desperately trying to eliminate her words scuttling around my head. *I've never seen a miracle. I've never seen a miracle. I've never seen—* "Get out of my house. Get out." I swing the door wide, put a firm hand on her back, and push her forward into the ravenous onlookers. Once she's across the threshold, I clasp my throat, the initials of my babies clenched tight in my fist. "You're our only hope, Detective Stone! Her life is in your hands! Find my baby!" I shout as reporters snap picture after picture. I make sure not to strain my face—don't need any second chins on display—but really give into the sorrow. "Find my Chloe! Bring her home!"

Emilina doesn't turn around. I don't need her to acknowledge me, though. She heard me, and she knows better than most how this will play out on TV.

Because she's wrong about our situation. This is a game. And I'm playing to win—not just for Abby, but for the rest of our lives.

Abby's Journal

I just got a DM from *him.*

  He apologized and said he felt SO bad about standing me up on my birthday. He was nervous about getting caught b/c his mom and dad were home and I guess they're super strict. I wonder if I'll meet his parents. Would they like me? Most parents like me.

  He asked me to give him another chance and said he'll make it up to me.

  I said NOPE. Thank U, NEXT.

  JK I said how? He really seemed sorry and I'm not a total bitch. I totally get having parents who are always sticking their nose in your business.

  He said he got me something for my birthday but didn't know if I'd accept his apology so he left the present at the park. I can take it or leave it.

  A present?!??!

  AHHH.

Oh. Cool. Thanks, I said. Like it's whatever. But I was FREAKING. OUT.

So . . . *drum roll* I snuck out after Mom and Dad went to sleep. I've been doing it for years and they haven't figured it out yet—our little secret—but I've never gone to the park alone at night.

I cut through the woods past the tree house. I wanted to see if anyone was out there. I mean, those trees didn't cut themselves down, right? It has to belong to someone. TBH I was a little worried the light on my phone would blow my cover, but Mom wasn't following me, and the tree house was empty. Didn't look like anyone's been there either.

It was so quiet other than my boots crunching. It was low key scary but also awesome.

When I was just about at the park, I msged him and he said the box was on the bridge.

Part of me thought it had to be a joke or something b/c why would he hide a present on the bridge, ya know? It's not like we met IRL where he feels like he needs to be nice to me. But I found it on the corner right where he said it would be.

A little blue card on the top said 4 U. I looked around hoping maybe he'd be waiting for me, but I was alone.

So I opened it. A butterfly necklace. I don't think they're real diamonds or anything and the chain's a little short but I don't care.

It's perfect.

I'll never take it off.

EMILINA

The Forest residence is a typical McMansion at the end of a winding cul-de-sac. I take in the wide yards and expensive toys: luxury vehicles, RVs, playground equipment, and four-wheelers. One house has an Olympic-sized swimming pool. I clock half a dozen people weeding flower beds or raking debris. A group of polished women in matching workout gear jogs by with friendly, yet curious waves as I round the sidewalk to the front door.

Their eyes pick me apart, and I can almost hear the conversations they'll have once I'm out of range, debating my identity and presence. I offer a stiff smile and tuck the flyaways behind my ear. I've had plenty of practice to hide my insecurities, but this much wealth still makes me uncomfortable.

The doorbell is attached to one of those ring security cameras. We have one, too, although it wasn't the fear of stolen packages that prompted our upgrade. Drew installed it after a particularly brutal case left me with a series of threatening letters and a dead bird on our stoop.

People are unpredictable, he said. *Doesn't hurt to put up an extra barrier when your job is to break down other people's walls.*

The certainty that I'm being watched by several sets of eyes makes my skin prickle. I doubt much happens on this street that the neighbors don't know about.

Unfortunately, according to Cap's latest update, the same can't be said of the Scarboroughs' neighborhood. Despite the onlookers and active Nextdoor community presence, the initial canvass has been a moot operation. They've talked to more than half the houses on the street, and so far, no one saw or heard anything during the time Abby was alleged to have gone missing.

Footsteps approach, and the door opens to reveal a man with slick black hair and the easy gait of a golfer, a weekend Clark Kent. He's average height and weight, but he wears a T-shirt and sweater beneath his North Face jacket, which gives him a bulkier appearance. I never understood how people could put on so many warm layers at once. I'd sweat through like a pig if I added a sweater to my ensemble.

The man twitches a smile, trying to make sense of the stranger standing on his porch. "Hello, can I help you?" he asks.

I present my badge. "Harold Forest?"

His expression becomes grave. "That's me. What's going on? Has something happened to Vikki?"

His wife. Victoria Forest is a high-level executive at Google and splits her time between New York and Nashville while she gets their new division up and running. Luke ran a quick background check on the family for me while I was shaking off the worst of my nerves. Being around Jen is mentally and physically draining.

"I'm sure your wife is fine, Mr. Forest. I'm Detective Emilina Stone, CFSU, and I was hoping I could ask you a few questions. Is it all right if I come in?"

He steps back with a mixture of relief and concern. "Of course, of course. Please."

I follow him down a spacious hallway into a well-lit living room. Tasteful family portraits dot the walls. Two built-ins framing an enormous stone fireplace are decorated with various abstract sculptures and vases.

We sit in oversized leather chairs that probably cost more than my entire year's salary, and Harold offers me something to drink. I decline and take out my notepad while he pours himself a lowball of good whiskey from an impressive bar display.

"Mr. Forest," I begin, "I'm not sure if you're aware of the situation, but I'm investigating the disappearance of Chloe Cates."

His mouth drops. "The Scarborough girl? Oh, geez, no, I had no idea. That's horrible."

"We're exploring several leads, but I'm in a bit of time crunch, so I'm gathering as much information about Chloe as possible."

"Of course, anything I can do to be of help."

I flick through my notes. "I spoke with Mr. and Mrs. Scarborough, and they said that you were the organizer for their most recent mall show?"

"Yes, I was in charge of the venue, which basically entails obtaining permits, scheduling security, setup, and breakdown."

"Just you?"

"I've got a team under me. Varies from show to show based on the anticipated size and particular demands of the performer, but for Chloe's I had seven—no, eight—of my guys, not including mall security and the vendors."

"Anyone new on the crew?" I ask.

He shakes his head and sips from the crystal glass. "No. I've been lucky. Turnover can be high in the industry, but we've had the same group going on three years this summer. We've done hundreds of events together. Never had a problem."

"Could you give me their names?"

He does. I record them with my notes and send them to Luke to cross-reference with the followers lists.

"Can you tell me about the show?" I ask.

"As much as I can. I was behind the scenes, coordinating with the tech department and DJ. But I caught bits and pieces. Lots of glitter. Some dancing. T-shirt cannon. I think her brother joined her on stage at one point. Mostly, it was Chloe doing her, whatever you call it, spectacular shtick."

I detect more than a little resentment in his tone. "Was there anyone in the audience that stuck out to you? Doing so many of these events, you probably get a feel for the type of guest you'd expect to attend?"

"That's true, I do, but I'm sorry, detective, I don't think there was anything out of the ordinary. Our mall security had to separate a couple of rowdy groups before they pushed onto the stage, but there were no other concerns noted in the post-show documents. Everything was in order. Besides the . . . you know." I nod, leaving the taboo topic of menstruation for another day. "Our lawyers discussed the possibility that the Scarboroughs would sue but ultimately agreed we were clear of any legal wrongdoing. We couldn't have anticipated *that* would happen, nor the scope and spread of the video."

And a nonexistent legal dispute doesn't narrow down my suspect list. Time to switch gears.

"Mr. Forest, Jennifer mentioned that your daughter and Abby used to be close. Do you know if she's heard from her at all?"

"I doubt she has. It's no secret that we don't associate with that family outside of professional obligations anymore, but we can ask her." He clutches his glass and pads down a different hall. "Willa? Can you come here for a second, please?"

He returns but doesn't sit, pacing slowly in front of the fireplace.

"Have you known the Scarboroughs long?" I ask.

"Too long. Almost ten years," he says.

His disdain for them piques my interest. Clearly, there's more to this story than Jen let on. "Did something happen to cause a rift?"

Elbow on the mantel, he takes a bigger sip of whiskey, smacking his lips. "We moved here from Boston when Willa was in preschool. My wife often travels for work and my biggest events are on weekends, so we decided that being closer to my parents would be the best situation for us. We're headed to Tennessee this summer. Vikki's blazing trails, and I've got a position lined up with the largest event planning firm in the South. Figured it would be easier for Willa to transition to a new high school than it would be to rip her out of her last year at the middle school. I'm rambling, I'm sorry."

"No, please, continue."

"The Scarboroughs were one of the first families we met. Jennifer showed up on the doorstep with Abby in tow one day. Had this giant gift basket full of gourmet condiments. Truffle hot sauce and fermented honey aiolis, what have you. Trying too hard maybe, but they were friendly enough, and Willa got along with Abby just fine."

"Until they didn't?"

"What're you guys talking about?"

I turn to the source of the voice. Willa Forest's long black hair frames her heart-shaped face. With her light blue eyes narrowed in my direction, she crosses her arms over a cozy white sweater and sits on the leather couch opposite the chairs.

"Willa, this is Detective Stone. She's looking for Abby Scarborough."

"I know," she says, not without attitude. "I saw the press conference. It's been all over my feed. Everybody's talking about it. Chloe Cates missing. It's crazy, but honestly, I'm not surprised."

"Why do you say that?" I ask.

She rolls her eyes. "Abby was always super dramatic. Like, we would be playing, and she'd trip and fall down and pretend to be really hurt. One time, she showed up crying and told me her cat got out. We spent two hours making flyers and searching for Sir Meows A Lot until her dad asked us what we were doing. Turns out, she didn't even have a cat."

"I see," I say.

"She just loves attention. I mean, look at Chloe Cates's Insta. I don't follow her anymore, but that girl loves drama."

"So, you've spoken with her recently?"

Willa clucks her tongue. "I didn't say that. We haven't talked in like a million years. But I don't need to talk to her to know this is all probably one big skit." Her fingers bite into air quotes around the word and she shifts in her seat. "Every time we hung out, we pretended we were on some dumb reality show. *ANTM* or *Teen Mom* or whatever."

"Willa Mae," Harold says, regarding her with an unreadable expression, a father-daughter communication. I used to have the same dynamic with my father. The blip of nostalgia is sharp.

"I'm fine."

Harold frowns at me. "I apologize. Willa and Abigail used to be very close. It's still a sensitive subject."

"Dad," she drawls, adding emphasis on the final *d. Dad-duh.*

I turn to Willa. "Do you mind if I ask what happened?"

"Nothing," she says. "Literally, we were like besties one day, and the next she wouldn't even talk to me."

Sounds familiar. "She never said why?"

Shrug. "Nope."

"Did you have an argument?"

"No."

A lie? "She ghosted you for no reason?"

Willa makes a noise of frustration and shakes her head. "She didn't ghost me, oh my god. She just couldn't hang out with me anymore because her mom said I was—"

She cuts herself off, eyes darting to Harold.

"Go on," he says, after a moment. "You can tell her."

Willa chews the inside of her cheek and focuses on the ceiling. "Fine. Her mom basically called me the f word."

"F word?"

Her chin trembles, but her voice is steady. "Fat."

"Mrs. Scarborough said you were fat?"

Willa flips her hair and stuffs her hands under her legs. "We were hanging out in the Confessional, messing around with her camera and props. Mrs. S came down and tried to get me to pose differently. She said the way I was sitting made me look like a turkey." Her pitch wavers as her emotions grow. "So I moved or whatever, but then she was fixing my hair and pulling my shirt away from my stomach. Abby told her to leave me alone, but it was like she didn't even hear her. Zoned in. Finally, she, took me aside and said that I had a pretty face but might want to leave the on-camera stuff to Abby. That with my quote-unquote weight issue, I might be better off holding the microphone."

My anger kicks up a notch. "That's terrible."

"Yeah, well," she says, shrugging her shoulders. "That's Mrs. S. Then Abby flipped out, started screaming and, like, throwing stuff. I'd seen her get mad before, but she was out of control, and after what Mrs. S said, I did not want to be in the middle of that."

"Did she fight with her mother often?" I ask.

"I guess. They butted heads a lot, but then she'd rave about some event they went to or some show they booked, and Abby'd be hype again. Crazy dysfunctional. I ran home crying. We never spoke again. That was the last time we ever hung out."

"Did Mrs. Scarborough ever reach out to you about what happened?"

Willa shakes her head. "Nope."

"I could've murdered that woman myself." Harold Forest holds up his hands and sits down. "Poor choice of words, I apologize. But Jen had no right to speak to Willa that way."

"Can I go now?" Willa stands, wiping her palms on her leggings. "Not trying to be rude, but I need to get my stuff before Ashley gets here."

"One quick question." I scan my notes, the underlined word that stuck out to me. "You said you and Abby hung out in the Confessional. What did you mean by that?" I picture the boxy curtained bench in a church, whispering to a priest through an ornate grate.

"The Chloe Confessional. You know, from the blog?" I give a beats-me gesture and she continues. "It's like this room in the basement where Abby gets interviewed one-on-one like a Kardashian by Mrs. S. The reality show version of therapy or something. Anyway, technically, we weren't supposed to play in the Confessional, but we snuck down when her mom was busy." She shrugs. "Tons of ridiculous costumes and backdrops. It was fun. Like our own fort. You know, before Mrs. S took over."

The gears in my head lurch forward. I can't shake the feeling that I've missed something. And while it seems like it should be obvious, the missing piece might not be as clean a fit as I want it to be.

"Willa, why don't you run upstairs and get your things? I'll keep an ear out for Ashley." Harold Forest smiles warmly at her, but it seems forced.

"Okay . . ." she drawls, arching her eyebrows. "I'll be right back, I guess." Tugging at the sleeve of her sweater, she bounces off with a timid wave.

Harold Forest waits a beat, then ambles to the hallway, checking that she's out of sight.

"Forgive me," he says, lowering his voice as he sinks into the chair. "But for Willa's well-being, I didn't want to talk about this in front of her. Vikki and I are in agreement. That woman should be ashamed of herself. It's utterly despicable what she's capable of."

Heat chases up my chest. "Can you be more specific, Mr. Forest?"

He sighs, a weary, pained sound. "We knew something was wrong. Not right away, I'm afraid, but we weren't blind to the changes. Willa stopped eating breakfast." Here, he chokes up. "She'd lie to us about lunches and skip dinner altogether. She'd come home from school and go straight to the treadmill. She lost eleven pounds in three weeks. She had big bags under her eyes. She was always tired, but she kept telling us that we were worrying too much. That she felt fine. Better than ever. It wasn't until . . ." He finishes off the whiskey with a polite gulp. "We'd gone out to dinner to celebrate Vikki's promotion. Four courses at our favorite Italian place downtown. Later that night, my wife walked in on Willa in the bathroom. She was bent over the toilet with her fingers down her throat."

Jesus.

I try to make sense of the beautiful girl I met deliberately vomiting the contents of her stomach. Because Jennifer insinuated that she was fat.

Harold selects a coaster from a stack and places his glass on the coffee table. "I never thought my child would develop an eating disorder, let alone when she was eleven years old. We got her help and continue to participate in therapy, but we are acutely aware that there may be triggering situations and try to provide her with as much support as we can."

I'm familiar with the statistics. A disturbing number of tweens are developing eating disorders compared to even a decade ago. It's estimated that forty percent of nine-year-olds have already dieted for reasons outside of a medical recommendation. Why? Peer pressure. Photoshop. Social media. My phone buzzes in my pocket. Caller ID reads SOUTH. "I'm sorry, I need to take this." I pluck a card from my pocket and pass it to Harold. "If you think of anything else."

"Of course."

"Thank you both for your time. I'll be in touch," I say and head for the front door.

A gust of cool breeze hits me as I hit *Accept* and duck into the car. "Stone."

"Emilina, hi, it's Rosie Thompson from South."

I riffle through my mental catalogue to put a face to the name. Despite our shared titles, South and Central don't pair up often. Each district runs with its own resources and staffing coordinators, so outside of the occasional professional development training, we don't have reason to.

An angular face shaped by blunt bangs and a cluster of freckles above her top lip. Rosie hasn't been with CFSU for long, but she's hungry. If I had time for new friends, I think we'd actually get along well.

"Rosie, hi, thanks for reaching out; it's been a hell of a busy morning."

"Fucking bet. Luke said you wanted to talk about the Crawford girl's case."

"Yes," I say, switching to hands-free and rounding the cul-de-sac. "You've heard?"

"Fucking tragedy. That boulder from Homicide stopped by to copy my files. Think the family just went in to get a positive ID on the body. She was found near your missing girl's house, is that right?"

I ease around a group of kids on bikes and turn back on the main road. "Yeah. So, I'm hoping I could pick your brain about how you approached Missy Crawford's case."

"Fire away," she says.

"What was your impression of her disappearance? Did the story ring true to you?"

"Yeah, I mean, it was all pretty straightforward. Found no hard evidence of drugs or foul play. Her parents were concerned, but her friends didn't seem too surprised. Said she'd been more preoccupied lately."

"Did you happen to check CCTV footage from the night she went missing? I know it's a long shot, but maybe a traffic camera in the area picked her up?"

Rosie huffs into the receiver. "Come on, Em, you know we don't have the resources to pull that shit. The parents had no fucking clue where she was going. No one watched her leave. No witnesses came forward to say they'd seen her. South wasn't about to approve a digital comb-through without a solid lead."

"Right."

"Kid was under enormous pressure, from what I understand. An over-achiever. To be honest, I thought I was dealing with a runaway situation. She'd taken off once before. No-showed for a final exam and crawled home a day later saying she needed a break, according to her mother. Over twenty thousand missing persons reported last year in New York. Nineteen thousand of those cases were runaways, but only three thousand of those are still open and unresolved. Odds were in my favor that she'd get tired of running and go home. Do I wish I'd pushed harder now that she's turned up dead? Fuck yes, but I did not think she was abducted."

A *ding* interrupts her next statement. Text coming through. The dash display shows a number I don't recognize. I dismiss the notification, but a second text follows. I thumb the home screen on my phone, and the first line of the message stops me cold.

Detective, it's JJ. I have a . . .

Shit.

I signal and screech to a stop while Rosie asks repeatedly if I'm okay.

"Sorry, I'm good. Listen, I have to get going, but thank you again for the chat."

"Sure, girl. We're in this together. Let me know if you need anything else. I'm off in ten, but you've got my cell, yeah?"

"Yeah," I say, but I've already checked out of the conversation.

I speed-read the text, then have to go back and read it again. I must've misunderstood.

No, I read it right.

JJ Scarborough wants to confess.

JACKSON

With the detective gone, I breathe in the reality of our current situation, which is . . . shitty. Very, very shitty. Less than an hour ago, we emerged from the woods in an eerie parade of mourning. The search party. *Party.* Odd name for such a gruesome task. The others were informed in whispers, as if saying it quieter would make it any less true.

It's her.

Only it wasn't.

I lied when I said I don't believe in divorce. I tell myself I'm against it. Constantly. It's become a mantra I repeat every night before I fall asleep—so that I *can* fall asleep. *I took a vow. Divorce is wrong. I took a vow. Divorce is wrong.*

I don't pray. Haven't been to church since I made my Confirmation in eleventh grade. I wore my best blue and white plaid button-down from American Eagle with khakis and brown shoes. Gelled my hair and made sure my nails were clean. As if I could get into God's graces by fooling the priest with my wholesome exterior.

My grandmother was my sponsor. I took the name Michael while she placed a hand on my shoulder at the altar.

"Michael," the priest said. I don't remember his name. We called him Father Bald. Father Bald made the sign of the cross on my forehead. "Patron saint of the sick. Of soldiers, doctors, police, and grocers."

"Grocers?"

"Everyone needs a saint, Jackson," he said. "Grocers are responsible for our health and nourishment, providing us the food and water with which we survive until Christ is reborn."

I wanted to say they spent most of the time talking to other cashiers, but he was on a roll. I nodded along, eager to return to the pew until the ceremony ended so I could go home to my PlayStation.

"Michael is a fine name. A noble name. The Archangel Michael escorts the faithful to their heavenly judgment when the hour of their death is upon them. But he's also a leader, controlling the army of God against Satan's forces. A true symbol of goodness in the battle against evil. Tell me, Jackson, will you be this leader? Do you plan to embody the same principles as your Catholic namesake?"

"Uh, yes." What else was I supposed to say? No, I don't want to fight the Devil? No, I don't believe in this stuff? Do you know how many versions of the Bible there are? Father Bald, no, I will not fight in God's army because that doesn't exist. There's no golden chariot waiting in the sky to rain down vengeance and justice.

"The word of the Lord."

"Amen," I said.

For all the good that word has done for me.

I thought when Jen and I got married, it would be forever—for better or worse, sickness and health, the whole gamut. My parents divorced when I was eleven. Watching them berate and degrade each other, I swore that when and if I found my proverbial soulmate, I'd marry once and make sure I did it right.

Things, shockingly, aren't quite that simple as an adult. Personalities grow. Needs shift.

The blog was supposed to be an anchor for Jen. An outlet to give her purpose and motivation when she felt like shit and wanted to spend her days lounging in bed with the shades drawn.

I didn't realize that supporting my wife's innocent venture would tear my family apart.

I didn't realize I would stand idly by as my daughter lost her independence one decision at a time. The birthday party was a wake-up call. That should've been a day devoted to Abby, but Jen had to take things too far. As usual. She has no self-regulation.

But in the week following the birthday disaster, I thought we'd actually arrived at a compromise. A light at the end of the proverbial tunnel. Jen agreed Abby could enroll at the high school for her freshman year if Abby agreed to continue the blog—if she could really commit to pushing "CC and Me" to the next level.

Maybe deep down I knew Jen would never let her enroll. CC Spectacular is more than her career. It's her life. In its prime, the blog brought in thousands of dollars through endorsements and advertisements. It also shielded Jen from having to take the next step. Gave her an excuse to *stay*.

Now, she's stuck. We all are. But unlike me, Jen would be perfectly content to live in this Insta-bubble. She wants Abby to find an agent, segue into film.

Be a star.

"Chloe's got what it takes," Jen told me. She'd just booked the mall show with Harold Forest. Hard to think of him as a neighbor, let alone a friend, when our interactions haven't been friendly since Jen went too far with Willa.

"A lot of people have what it takes. Weren't you just telling me we're losing engagement?"

Her eyes glimmered, with red carpets or dollar signs, probably both. "True, our numbers haven't been as promising lately, but something like this will boost us over the top. I've got a good feeling about this, Jackson.

Chloe has the It Factor. We'll never forgive ourselves if we let her squander away her talents in a classroom."

"What if a classroom is what she wants?"

"She's thirteen, Jackson. And as much as she may want to believe she's grown, she has no idea what she wants or what's good for her. We're the adults here. Us. Start acting like it."

We try not to fight in front of JJ and Abby, another one of my sticking points. Kids shouldn't hear their parents arguing. We both say things we don't mean in the heat of the moment, but it's the things we do mean that hurt the most. Anger brings out the worst of our truths.

Sometimes, lies are better.

If you ask her when she's off camera, she'll tell you we've had some zingers. Who doesn't? Every married couple argues.

Ask Jennifer Cates, Super Mom and Wife Extraordinaire, however, and she'll tell you we don't have any major problems. A few spats over silly stuff like leaving the toilet seat up or the correct way to load the dishwasher. She uses lots of buzzwords. Transparency. Honesty. Communication. Mutual respect. How our love flourishes, and *yours can, too*—as long as you subscribe to her blog for candid relationship advice.

If the birthday party was a wake-up call, the mall show was an air raid siren for the shitstorm to come.

That night, Jen was at the desk in our bedroom. The laptop screen reflected in the lenses of her glasses as she typed merrily along. I read the words over her shoulder, a habit I know she finds annoying but continue to do anyway.

Don't get me wrong: I wish Chloe didn't have to go through this ordeal on stage, but what woman doesn't have an embarrassing story about her first time? Period mishaps are a given. A rite of passage. Who am I to take that from her? She'll laugh at it the way we all do, looking back on the absurdity of our insecurities. I can't think of anything that defines a woman more. And that's what Chloe is now. A woman. She's in the club.

And really, isn't it time we stopped being so secretive about our periods? We all get them. Why is there such stigma around them anyway? We whisper the word tampon *like we're summoning demons with blood sacrifices. I mean, look at the audience! How many young girls and women in the crowd laughed at Chloe just to mask their own fear of the very same thing happening to them? I'm not mad, I'm disappointed. I'm angry that we've gotten to this point where women tear one another down instead of building one another up. Our bodies are beautiful. Menstruation is natural—something we have no control over.*

When I got mine . . .

Two zoomed-in photographs divided her words. The first showed Abby, the horrified look on her face when she saw the blood. The fear of not knowing what was happening or what she should do. I didn't know Jen had taken that picture.

The second showed the audience. A collection of laughing faces and wide-mouthed *oh*s of surprise. Phones held in the air capturing the embarrassment.

"You've got to be kidding me," I said.

"Spare me the lecture, Jackson. I've had more than enough attitude for one day." The keys clacked away, as oblivious to my concerns as Jen was pretending to be.

"We can't do this anymore."

Clack, clack, clack. "*We can't do this anymore, Jen*," she mocked. "Do you ever stop?"

"Do you? Come on. You know you can't post that."

"Why?" The clacking increased, a fury of words plopping on the screen.

"*Why?* You're a piece of work, you know that?"

Jen finished her sentence, saved her draft, slammed the chair into the desk, and finally faced me. "How many times are we going to have this discussion, Jackson? Huh? You really want to do this? My readers expect honesty. Raw, unfiltered life—a glimpse into motherhood without the glowing Facebook-worthy moments. Stretch marks and tantrums. It would be a glaring mistake to ignore what happened today."

Always her first defense. "That won't cut it this time. We're well past tantrums and playgroups. What you're doing is harmful, Jen. It's not right."

Jen blew past me and grabbed her phone off the charger. Her next move was to show me how much money we have in our bank account. The deposits from my paycheck versus the deposits from "CC and Me."

Because in Jen's mind, when personal gratification fails, she can rationalize her behavior with finances. This is about the money. A pissing competition for who contributes most to our family. Whoever has the biggest number next to the dollar sign deserves to have more weight in the decision-making process.

Jen cares about material things. There's nothing inherently wrong with that. She didn't have little comforts growing up. A paycheck-to-paycheck situation like most of the families in the area. But where's the line between justification and excuses? There isn't one person in this world who doesn't have a story. Am I supposed to dismiss what she's doing to our family because twenty years ago she was bullied for wearing clothes from Walmart?

She tapped her foot waiting for the page to load. Our checking account. Too predictable. "Here. If you're so comfortable up there on your high horse, your majesty, why don't you tell me which one of us is keeping the Scarborough household afloat?"

"Get that out of my face," I said, slapping her phone to the bed. "That's not your money. It's ours. You use us to create your content. We deserve that paycheck just as much as you do. Abby most of all."

"And she'll get her share when she turns eighteen."

"If you don't spend it all first."

"Bills, Jackson. Someone has to pay them. It's not like I'm blowing our savings on St. Barts and a BMW. Your salary doesn't get us this house. Our cars. JJ's football and baseball equipment."

"We could downsize," I said. Seemed like a practical solution. If we can't survive within our means, we have to decrease our expenses. Our house is in a prime location. It would sell easily in this market. But I know it's not a realistic solution to Jen. The word "downsize" equates to poor in her book. Some ingrained fear she has about losing her things.

I might as well have told her we could light ourselves on fire.

"We will do no such thing. I can't believe you'd even suggest it," she said, pushing her knuckles into my chest.

"So, you're willing to sacrifice your daughter for a bigger house? A nicer car? Tell me, Jen, how much is our children's health and happiness worth to you?"

"What about *my* needs?" she shouted. "What am I supposed to do without this? It's all I have. The only thing that's mine. Something to *be* other than a mother. Killing the blog would kill me."

"It's killing us."

I've been thinking about divorcing her ever since. As soon as the words left my mouth.

Is divorce a sin? I don't think so, but I'm not about to google the answer. Knowing Jen, she probably tracks my browser history. I imagine her outrage. Tossed between sports updates and porn sites is a stack of IPs on the morality of leaving your spouse.

The thoughts creep in randomly. I'll be drafting a proposal or sending an email and the glint of my wedding band will stop me midtask.

I take it off at work. The imprint around my finger fades after an hour or two but doesn't disappear completely.

Today, it's the only thing on my mind besides Abby.

What would my morning be like if I woke up as a single dad? I'd make the kids breakfast, wave when they got on the bus, and head to work. JJ would go to practice. Abby would too. She'd play basketball or volleyball—maybe both. She'd laugh off any recognition from "CC and Me" and find a group of friends who loved her for who she is. She'd go on dates and have her heart broken, but she'd learn from every experience.

I didn't think things would escalate. Abby's gone. A different girl is dead.

Dead.

The detective is right. Missy Crawford's hair is a little darker than Abby's, but the resemblance between them is striking. An intelligent investigator wouldn't chalk that up to coincidence.

I'm crying. Leaking is more accurate. Water pours from my eyes in rivers. What's the point in trying to stem the flow? I deserve to drown in salt water.

What kind of father can't protect his child?

The same father who encouraged his daughter to play along with a blog to avoid an altercation with his wife.

Wife. Another one of those words whose meaning has completely changed in the last twenty-four hours.

Jen looks at me from across the room, the first time we've been alone since this morning. The chasm that separates us cracks and stretches.

"So here we are," she says, the antithesis to the hysterical woman who threw herself on the ground moments ago in a show of despair for the cameras. This woman is composed, shrewd. There's sadness in her expression, but it's muted. After all these years she still doesn't know that I can read her like one of her posts.

I open my mouth and close it again. I'm not ready to ask the real questions yet. "How much of Abby's disappearance have you recorded?" I ask instead.

That digs at her. I can see the resentment perched in the creases of her brow. She studies me for a second before turning to the stairs. "I'm too tired for this," she says. "I'm going to take a shower."

"Why didn't you tell that detective about Abby running off after the mall?"

"She knows now, doesn't she? Don't worry about it, Jackson."

"I will worry about it, Jennifer. That was a stupid thing to do. They'll think we're lying."

She plods up the stairs.

"What aren't you telling me?"

Her response is sealed in the firm slam of the bathroom door. I could go after her, try to apologize or demand the truth, but I don't. I'm tired of bending.

And I can't stay here anymore. My legs bop, arms twitch, unable to contain the building energy. With a final glance out the window, I walk upstairs and tap lightly on JJ's door.

"What?" he asks.

I see him propped on his bed with his back against the wall. He continues to scroll through his phone without looking up. Seems to be the only activity anyone does in this house.

"She hasn't posted anything," he says, adjusting the pillow. "Abby, I mean. There's nothing on her accounts."

Because she doesn't have her phone. "Good thought to check, though," I say.

"I was sure it was her in that tree house. You don't think it's weird? That it was Missy up there?"

I shrug, out of responses. "I don't know."

"I didn't realize how much she looked like Abby. And the outfit she was wearing. It was Abby's pink outfit."

The thin line of pink fabric flashes through my mind. "A lot of people probably have that set—or a similar one."

"Uh huh." The phone drops in his lap. "I guess. I don't know. This is all so messed up. What do we do now?"

More answers I'm supposed to have. "You should eat something."

"I'm not hungry."

"Abby wouldn't want you to go on a hunger strike because you're worried," I say. If she were here, she'd probably give him a swift kick to the shins and a noogie for the trouble. *JJ, you weirdo, go get a Pop-Tart.*

"It doesn't seem right," he mumbles.

"I get it."

"Where's Mom?"

"Shower."

He nods and returns to scrolling. "I can't believe she hit me."

"Yeah. Yeah, I know. Me too." Yesterday, such an event would've been headline news in our house. With Abby gone, however, Jen's slap has been benched for the immediate future.

"She's crazy," he says, still staring at his phone.

"She's stressed."

"She grounded me for a week when I popped Lawrence Parsons after he hit me with that curve ball on purpose. But she gets to hit me and walk around like nothing happened? There's just no consequences for her because she's *stressed*?" Venom drips from his words. "We're stressed and we're not hitting anyone."

A canyon of silence sits between us as he taps through his feeds.

"How about I run out and pick up a pizza?" I say, at a loss. "Hunger makes it worse. Pepperoni and mushroom?"

"Abby would love that." Head low. Shoulders slumped.

"They'll find her, Jay. Any minute now she could come home."

"Or she won't. She could be dead like Missy."

"Stop; you can't talk like that. We have to stay positive."

"Okay, I'm *positive* she could be dead." He punches his pillow. Once. Again. Then he chucks it at his headboard and buries his head in his hands.

My stomach hardens. "You can't blame yourself. This isn't your fault."

"You keep saying that, but it's bullshit."

"I know it's hard, but try to relax. I'll call in a pizza and be back in twenty."

"I'm going to head next door for a bit to chill with Ry. Find something on Netflix."

"I don't know, Jay. Don't you want to be home in case they find her?"

Huff. "I'll come back for dinner. Just text me when you get back."

"All right." I ruffle his hair like I used to when he was a toddler. He hated haircuts. Screamed any time I came near him with the razor. Jen had to restrain him while I trimmed away the unruly mess. Working carefully through his bucks and shoves, and that "wet noodle" move all kids seem to master. By the end of every epic grooming battle, we were covered in acres of sheared droppings, itchy and damp from tears and drool.

I'm glad he grew out of that fear, but I'd gladly take one of those brawls over today's series of events.

JJ asks me to close the door on my way out. He doesn't want to see Jen, and I understand why. I don't know how they're going to work through what she did. It'll be easier if I divorce her.

There it is again.

I hear water running in the master bath. There was a time in our marriage when I would've gotten in with her. Pushing her against the wall, kissing her neck, working my lips down her body while she clawed through my hair.

The sadness I get from these memories is enough to push me in the opposite direction. We're not those people anymore. Maybe we never were.

I turn to the stairs and head for the kitchen. The forensics team has set up small tents around the area of the fence at the bottom of the yard. Floodlights block most of the view, but I see shadows of the people collecting samples.

I have to get out of here. Grabbing the keys from the hook, I scratch a quick note on a pink Post-it and leave it on the corner of the counter.

Going for pizza. JJ's at Ryan's. Be back soon.

Good. Keep going.

I take the side door into the garage and bump into Officer Welsh. "Jesus," I say, startled. "Sorry. I didn't realize you were still here."

She bites her thumbnail and quickly wipes her hand on the side of her pants. "Ah, sorry. I used to be a smoker but can't exactly do that with a baby at home, you know? Replacing one bad habit with another. Anyway, yeah, Detective Stone asked me to hang around in case a ransom demand is made in the next few hours. She wants someone ready to intercept, which would normally be one of the guys from digital forensics, but they've got their hands full right now."

"Oh. Right. Good."

"Going somewhere?" she asks.

"Um, pizza." I feel my face flush at the word. I wonder if she thinks I'm a terrible father. Going out for food when my daughter's missing.

"Phone on you?" she asks.

"Of course."

"Keep the volume on max."

I click the slim button and show her the blackened sound bars. "Done."

"See you soon, Mr. Scarborough," she says but she locks on my face like she's not ready to dismiss me just yet.

"Something else on your mind, Officer Welsh?"

She brings her fingers to her mouth, then jerks them away when she realizes what she's doing. "I know this isn't exactly my place," Welsh begins, pulling out her phone. "But I'm a new mother myself. I can't imagine how this feels for you."

"Thank you," I say.

"I'm also a subscriber. I've followed 'CC and Me' since a month before my little girl was born."

"Well, we appreciate your support. Abby will be happy to hear."

"However." Welsh holds up a hand like I've missed her point. "After the press conference, we really don't need to give the public any more reason to get involved. It gets messy. People can get hurt. You might want to encourage Mrs. Cates—Scarborough—not to post any more details about the investigation without discussing it with Detective Stone first."

I feel like I was clubbed upside the head. "I'm sorry?"

Welsh rotates the phone to me. The most recent "CC and Me" article loads. There's a picture of our house surrounded by reporters and police. Beneath that is an announcement of sorts. Jennifer Cates, concerned mother of Chloe Cates, listing the specifics around her disappearance and asking for the public's help in finding Chloe.

A picture of the woods.

And of Missy Crawford. Her face runs parallel to Abby's latest headshot with the caption: *Missy v Chloe. Possible serial abductor/MURDERER on the LOOSE??*

My fists clench. "When did this go up?"

"About ten minutes ago," she says. She looks guilty. Like she did something wrong by ratting on my wife. "There was other stuff before this but mostly what Stone covered in her statement." A pause. "We haven't even received confirmation that it is Missy Crawford yet. They have to ID the body. If they see this before Homicide is able to notify them . . ."

Guess that all-important shower played second fiddle to the likes.

"We don't want to start a panic," Welsh says, and sticks the phone in her pocket. "A girl is dead. Her family deserves privacy. And respect."

"I'll talk to her."

She nods, clearly relieved the talk is over and I didn't attack her for being the one to tell me. What good does it do to shoot the messenger? Welsh isn't the one using her daughter's disappearance as a money-grab.

I hop in the car and smack the garage door opener. Bruce Springsteen floods the speakers and drowns out my thoughts. For one incredible second, our family is happy, Abby is safe, and I'm lost in the melody, dreaming of running and highways and far-off destinations.

Fucking Bruce.

The cluster of reporters surrounds me as soon as I reach the bottom of the driveway. Puppet hands producing microphones and recorders. Pouncing, hoping I'll roll down the window for an impromptu chat.

Any comment on the girl in the tree house . . .

Have any demands . . .

Mr. Cates, was your daughter depressed or . . .

Do you think Chloe's dead . . .

I'd kill for an ounce of anonymity.

I check the clock on the dash, grimace against the weight of passing time, and pray I'm not too late.

JENNIFER

I post the article and put my phone on the vanity. The notifications begin immediately.

Yes.

I rotate the showerhead, waiting for the water to get hot. I avoid my reflection in the mirror, opting to reroll the washcloths in the linen basket. Next, I straighten the decorative vase of fake orchids, aligning it with the soap dispenser and hand lotion.

Missy Crawford turned up dead.

Abby's still missing.

I shouldn't care about the numbers.

But.

Clicks. Likes. Shares. People all over the country are searching for Chloe and tagging our accounts. Sorting through "clues" and posting videos as they try to figure out who the kidnapper is. Chrissy Teigen even retweeted a TMZ article. *Worst nightmare*, she said.

A-list engagement.

Is it possible to be addicted to social media? There are studies about the effects on toddlers, but what about competent adults? Hearing the notifications *ding! ding!* verifies that people care about what I have to say—that what I'm doing matters.

And that feels good. There's no other way to describe it.

As I step into the shower, my thoughts drift to starting a podcast. Those are so forking popular right now. Current events, pop culture, fairy tales, and scary stories. A podcast for every occasion. Cold cases are gold. I could do a whole true crime series. "CC and Me: The Abduction." I'd hire the best writers to draft the scripts. Interview the detectives and officers. Maybe even the Crawfords. The kids could reenact the scenes.

The kids.

And just like that, I'm out of the clouds and wrestling with my guilty conscience. Seems like no matter how busy I am, there's always enough time in my schedule for a heaping mound of guilt. More reliable than Jackson, that's for darn sure.

He's going to be upset about the post.

I'm just not sure I have the emotional capacity to care about hurting his feelings this time. He's not the kind of person who forgets or forgives. He holds grudges worse than an ex-girlfriend in a choreographed rom-com. It used to bother me. How he'd do something wrong then convince me I was making the whole thing up.

Gaslighting is his specialty, and he's had years of practice to perfect his technique.

On the blog, I've built Jackson up as the All-American Dad. It was a conscious choice, and he more than fit the part, but I wonder if I could've done better.

The affair should've been my out.

This was before we had kids, but I'd be lying if I said I haven't suspected another indiscretion a time or three over the last decade. A whiff of perfume here, a questionable stain there. How many late-night meetings do marketing teams have?

I could've walked away after the first time, when we were young and hadn't made promises to each other.

Now, though?

Jackson majored in Education, but with how serious he made it sound, you would've thought he was campaigning for president. He spent hours in the library working on lesson plans and rubrics. Putting learning centers together and stuffing binders—so many binders. I barely saw him. That was fine. I was busy with my own course load. I majored in Communications, which required me to attend school-wide sporting events, academic bowls, theater performances, literary conventions, basically anything that drew a crowd. I'd hand out fliers, promote on AIM and the school website. I was by no means a clinger.

We were independent, but we were good when we were together. He had a contagious energy. Charismatic and charming. And he was painfully handsome, with his broad shoulders and Tom Hardy swagger.

As things got serious between us, though, he became secretive. Deleting his texts. Locking his computer. The school required him to do it, he explained, unprompted. Student confidentiality during his practicum assignments, but really, he didn't want me snooping.

Luckily, I'm an expert at hacking passwords. Most of us are creatures of habit. We rely on the same basic information. Something easy to remember, because who has time to get locked out of accounts or wait for reset instructions?

Jackson was predictable. A combination of his first car and birthday.

I was in.

Yes, I know going through your partner's accounts is faux pas, a sign of distrust, but in my defense, I didn't trust Jackson. He was clearly hiding something, and I needed to know what it was.

I checked his email first. One by one, clicking the subjects and scanning the contents for whatever he didn't want me to see, then right-clicking them back to Unread to cover my tracks.

There were two from a woman, confirming their plans and professing her desire to pop his collar in a very colorful way. To be fair, Jackson always looked good with a popped collar, but as his girlfriend, I was the only one allowed to make that claim.

Those emails were scandalous, but not nearly as offensive as the texts I read on his phone later that night, turning my back to him under the blanket so the light wouldn't wake him up.

Her name was Ophelia, at least that's what he called her, and I'm sure you can imagine what their correspondence was like. The NSFW photos were the cherry on the perverted sundae. They were careful, no faces or identifying marks, but I knew Jackson's body intimately, and there was no denying it was him.

Ophelia.

I confronted him the next morning; there was no way I could sit on that kind of knowledge without it eating a hole in my brain. I was proud of myself for making it that long, fighting my initial instinct to burn his clothes and kick him out of my apartment naked in the middle of the night.

He cried because that's what Jackson does, part of his emotional sabotage routine. He cried and swore he loved only me. Begged me to forgive him. Promised he'd never do it again.

I replay that moment a lot. I think that's the exact point where the trajectory of my life branched off in a different direction. Who knows what I could've been if I hadn't said *yes*. If instead of *I forgive you* I said, *go fork yourself.*

I don't know why I married him.

And in a strange twist of irony, he's never forgiven me for going through his stuff. That act of dishonesty leaks into our arguments to this day. He tests me. Leaves his phone open on the counter, memorizes its exact angle, and if it's a centimeter off, he unleashes his fury, days of sullen, single-word responses and avoidance. Isolation and manipulation.

It's easy to explain his absence from the blog, at least, and I have plenty of material saved for just such occasions. I'll focus on some other area of my life that doesn't involve him or his impact on the kids. No one asks. That should tell him everything he needs to know about how important he is in this family.

God, I sound bitter.

I couldn't *not* write about Abby and Missy Crawford. Jackson will hold it against me—for days, years, the rest of our lives. Add it to the list, I want to tell him. He keeps score, but it's not like the points really matter when I control the million-dollar ticket.

The Ophelia pictures give me all the leverage I need.

My head's pounding, and my shoulder aches from the torque of Emilina's tackle. That haughty witch. The forking audacity.

I let the water run down my body and scrub the frustration out of my hair.

Does our water come from the blue tower?

The dense heat suddenly constricts my throat. I lean on the glass trying to steady myself against the dizzying tide.

The water tower.

My hand slips, and I almost tumble to the floor. Why is it so hot? My arm shoots out and fumbles with the wet nozzle.

You're trapped, my mind whispers conspiratorially.

"No," I gasp.

You're going to boil in here.

"No." I pull the handle, but the door won't open. The steam plops around me like wet snow.

Someone's locked the door.

"Please."

Like throwing a top on a hot tub.

"Stop."

They'll find your body covered in blisters.

"Help," I whisper, but my words sound distant, distorted and hollow.

She got what she deserved, they'll say.

I fall forward, pushing my weight into the fogged-up glass door. It swings open with a vengeance. Steam filters out in waves and I'm free.

Snatching a towel from the rack, legs rubbery and weak, I collapse to the floor.

Maybe I do deserve to burn.

My own voice, shocking in its clarity.

I deserve this.

After all, I am a murderer.

EMILINA

Looking at Western Park now, you'd never guess the decomposing body of a young girl was found just a few hours ago. The first tulip bulbs of the year are sprouting. The landscaping is crisp and clean with only a remnant of slush melting in the center of the greenery. Beyond that, it's quiet. Not even the traffic noise seems to break through. Between the darkening sky and the chill in the air, the place is nearly deserted. I dip my chin into my coat and trudge toward the koi pond.

My mind is racing. Abby to Missy to Nicole and around and around we go. Before CFSU, I never realized just how easy it is for young girls to disappear. Whether by choice or by force, there seems to be an infinite amount of cracks waiting to swallow them whole.

It's depressing when you think about it, really. The heartbreak and the unanswered questions. Rosie's stats were accurate, but saying *only* three thousand cases are open like it's a good thing is a problem in and of itself.

That's thousands of children across the state who might never be accounted for, and we're lauding that as a success.

I have a confession to make, but I can't do it with my mom and dad around. It's about Abby. Can you meet me at the park?

JJ has frequently been described as a nice kid. A good brother.

But I know better than most that appearances can be deceiving.

JJ stands with his back to me on the cobblestone bridge. I approach slowly, trying to assess his mood. Agitated? Distressed? Confrontational? I need to be prepared for anything.

Hands stuffed into his pockets, he bounces from foot to foot. I round the pond, and when he sees me, he straightens, taking a few hurried steps toward me before doubting himself.

"Hi, JJ," I say, prodding his expression for signs of guilt. He doesn't drop his gaze from mine, but his eyes are slightly puffy and skittish. They're rounder than Jen's and heavier lashed, but also flat, like a boy in a Norman Rockwell painting.

"Hey." He stares down at the koi pond. They bob along the surface, orange blobs with gaping mouths.

"Come here a lot?" I ask, breaking the ice.

"Not really."

"Like the fish?"

"They're all right."

"You know, my dad hated fishing," I say. "But he did bring us to the aquarium once, and there was this huge pool filled with koi. They had these long whiskers and beady little eyes—and they were always clumped together, fighting for the pellets the volunteers gave out. They bit my brother's fingers. He said it didn't hurt, but I didn't believe him. I thought they were tiny vampires."

JJ nods. "I can see that. You're not supposed to feed these guys, but everybody does. Sometimes they bring entire loaves of bread and just toss in chunk after chunk. But then the fish don't know how to find their own food, and they die, and the park crew has to bring in a whole new batch."

"I didn't realize it was so bad for them."

"They can't learn how to survive when they've been spoon-fed garbage their whole lives."

I study his face, the twist of his mouth, the serious scrunch in his forehead. "It takes perseverance to adapt," I say.

"Does it?" he asks.

"You know, JJ, I have to tell you that since you're a minor, I really shouldn't be talking to you without a parent present. Does anyone know you're here?"

"No. I told my dad I was going to Ryan's." He paces the length of the bridge away from me and sits on a bench stationed along the path.

In the summer, the park hosts a remote-controlled sailboat competition that launches from this spot. Retirees and sailing enthusiasts line up on the bank and race their model yachts around the pond. It's almost as much a spectacle as CC Spectacular, but without the pomp and circumstance.

I take a seat beside him and realize his shoulders are shaking. He hunches over, rubs his face as if he's tired, then rises to his feet.

"JJ, why did you send me that message?"

"I don't know."

"Confessions are serious. I'm not a lawyer, so whatever you tell me, I have a duty to report it and take appropriate action."

"I know, it's not, but—shit, I don't know what I'm doing." He sits back down.

"This is really something we should be doing at the station with your parents. Why don't you come with me, and we can call them when we get there?"

"No," he says emphatically. "I'm not doing this with them. I can't. Please, just hear me out and then afterwards if you need to arrest me or whatever, I won't put up a fight," he shrugs.

I angle myself on the bench. "Why would I arrest you?"

He drops his head into his hands. A noise of frustration escapes his throat and he rubs furiously at his glistening eyes. "This is my fault."

A twinge in my chest. "What is?"

"Okay, last week was really bad," he says. "Like, the worst it's ever been. Mom and Dad barely said a word to each other. And Abby . . . she wasn't in a good place."

"How so?"

"She was acting super weird. Basically ignored me, and when she wasn't ignoring me, she just stayed in her room. She stopped coming down for dinner. And my mom, I mean, you see how she is with this blog. I don't think they took a single picture, which is even weirder for them. They were arguing before I left for school and still going at it when I got home."

"About what?"

"No idea. I kept asking what was going on, but they just kept insisting they were fine. We're fine. Everything's fine. I couldn't take it anymore. It was like being in a volcano about to erupt. I started sneaking out to spend the night at Ryan's."

"So that's why you weren't home last night?"

He nods. "Barely feels like a home."

It's disconcerting when you lose that sense of safety. Home is supposed to be the place that keeps the danger away, a barrier between you and the rest of the world. How do you find peace when everything that's supposed to protect you feels wrong?

"Knowing how to take care of yourself is important. Sometimes your parents aren't going to be able to fix the problem—sometimes they are the problem—and recognizing you needed space is not the issue. I know it can feel bad to lie to your parents, but sneaking out to sleep at your friend's? That's pretty harmless."

He slams his hand into the wood, not quite a punch, but enough to redden his skin. The bench creaks in response. "It wasn't harmless. Are you hearing me? I wasn't there. I could've stopped this, but I wasn't there for her."

JJ collapses into tears.

I give him a minute to work it out before continuing. Truth be told, I need a minute myself. Either JJ is giving an Oscar-worthy performance, or his despair is genuine, and my ill-fated gut says he's telling the truth.

"Look, even if you had been home, there's no guarantee it would've made a difference," I say. "We don't know what happened, and we won't know for sure until we find Abby."

He wipes his nose with the sleeve of his sweatshirt. "You can't promise you'll find her. Look what happened to Missy."

The bloated corpse flashes in my thoughts. "Someone murdered Missy," I say.

"Yeah." He nods to himself like he's made a decision. "I need to show you something."

JJ reaches into his pocket, starts to pull something out, and pauses.

The hair on the back of my neck prickles, every muscle on alert. "What are you doing?"

"I don't want to go to jail," he says.

"I understand that," I say. "I can help. Talk to me." My hand floats to my hip, the acrid sting of nervous sweat clinging to my clothes. "Take your hands out of your pocket, please. Slowly."

Fear spreads across his face. "Oh, shit, no, I'm not—" Reluctantly, he takes them out and places the item in his lap.

I study it. I was expecting a weapon, but this feels more loaded.

A smart phone.

The screen is smashed to smithereens but otherwise in good shape.

My brain scrambles to catch up. "What is this?" I ask.

"I found it a few days ago."

"Where?"

"In the basement. I had a project due for Bio and I needed a trifold board. Mom's got shelves stuffed with props and crafting materials, so I went to see if she had anything I could use, and I found this crammed between two totes."

"May I?" He nods, and I take the phone. Trying to power it up proves futile, but Luke might be able to work his magic. "Whose is it?"

"I don't know, I don't recognize it. But Abby's been spending a lot of time in the basement."

"You think this could be Abby's?"

He shrugs.

"We took Abby's phone from her room, though. Your mom's made it clear that she wouldn't go anywhere without it. Did you buy this for her?"

"No way," he scoffs. "I'll get a job this summer after the season ends, but I don't have that kind of money."

"Could she have purchased it herself?" This isn't a pay-as-you-go. A newer model iPhone, judging by the size of the shattered screen. Not cheap. How would she be able to afford this on her own? And how would she be able to utilize it without a data plan? There are prepaid options, but again, how would she get the money and opportunity to do that herself?

"I don't think so."

"A sponsor?" I ask. "Does she have a partnership with a phone provider?"

"No."

"Have you ever seen Abby with this phone?"

JJ's patience boils over. "I don't know. I don't know, okay? I don't have all the fucking answers. I found it and thought it could be important. I should've told you earlier, but I was afraid they'd freak out. They were already pissed at me about the socials and the journal."

Lie.

I believe that he found it, but I'm struggling to buy his explanation for why he kept this from me for as long as he did. I'm not getting the whole story.

As if the timing could be worse, my own phone vibrates. I fumble with it and read the screen. Wonderful. "Detective Stone."

"You still got your thumb up your ass in the burbs?"

Blaisdell. A man of words. "I'm in the middle of something, Devon, what can I do for you?"

He chews into my ear. "Your DL called. You're sitting in on my interview, and I need to know when you plan on gracing me with your presence."

"What interview?"

"With the vic's parents," he says. "Media's making a connection between my dead girl and your missing girl and he wants to button up the loose ends before we've got a riot on our hands. I'll send you the address. Meet me there in thirty."

The line disconnects. JJ gapes at me.

"I have to go," I say.

"Is it Abby?" he asks.

"No," I say, tapping a new message thread. I send Luke a heads up that I'm dropping off another present. "But I do have to go. Listen, JJ. You did the right thing coming to me."

"Sure." He tugs up his hood as the wind whistles off the water. "So, what do I do now?"

I stand and adjust my jacket. "Your parents think you're at Ryan's?"

"Dad does."

"Go there and sit tight. I've got to take care of something, and hopefully I'll have some answers soon."

"Okay," he says, staring at the pond. The fish wriggle and writhe below the surface. "I, um, I love my sister, Detective Stone. I don't want to think about bad things happening to her."

The cracked phone burns a hole in my pocket. "I know."

After delivering the phone to Luke for processing, I park in front of the Crawford residence. No sign of Blaisdell's car. I message to let him know I'm here and scan the neighborhood.

The Crawfords' development is similar to the Scarboroughs'. Great park, a community garden, a hedge maze you couldn't pay me to walk through—I've read *The Shining*, I'm not dumb—and plenty of wilderness, as it's situated on the cusp of the Albany Nature Preserve.

Late for his own interview, Blaisdell texts to say he's running behind. Super.

It irritates him to have to share information.

Homicide isn't particularly common in Albany. We average about twelve annually, most of which are attributed to gun violence. Last year, Blaisdell caught a rough assignment. A confidential informant flipped on a known prostitute and drug ring that set up shop in a fleabag motel downtown. Paul Montgomery, the boss of said operation, had his own whisper network and discovered the betrayal before SWAT had a chance to make a move. Montgomery was apprehended, but not before he put a bullet in the informant's head and strangled the prostitute unlucky enough to be in his company.

Blaisdell's scheduled to testify in that trial, and I know he's got a mountain of prep to do. Criminal trials aren't nearly as common as television would have you believe. Most cases are settled out of court, and detectives are called for only a handful of trials over the course of their tenure. Blaisdell's good on scene. But put him on a witness stand? He's a hot mess.

With a full caseload and an imminent trial, I can't count on him for a secondhand debriefing of this interview, and if Cap's assessment of the media coverage is right (no thanks to Jen's blog, which, he informed me, was another subversion of my command), we need to address the rumors of a potential serial killer together.

I check my messages while I wait. Voicemail from Luke shortly after I left the station, saying he might have something from the social media dump and to call him when I can.

My thumb hovers over the number, but I decide to wait until after I talk to the Crawfords. If there is a link between the two girls, I want to know about it now before I start trying to connect the dots.

Audio messages from Drew. He sounds excited. Wants to know if I'll still be home for dinner. He hopes my day is going well.

No, babe, my day is definitely *not* going well.

I reply, IDK, I'll try, and drop the phone to my lap.

My hand gravitates to my stomach, some subconscious maternal gesture that feels strange and terrifying. I'm just shy of eight weeks pregnant, if my calendar is correct. I found out three days ago, but the reality hasn't sunk in yet.

Drew, on the other hand, is thrilled. He's talked about having kids since our second date, a shitty horror movie in a crowded theater. He's freakishly good at pointing out plot inconsistencies but not great at being quiet during the show. In the middle of the goriest scene, bodies strapped to tables and limbs being sawed off, Drew smiled. "His right arm was cut off, but his left arm's in the bandage. I can't wait to start a family. Two kids, maybe three. Big yard and a dog. Cats are dumb, though. Are you a cat person?"

I'm not now and never will be a cat person.

Neither is Drew, thank god. He's an excellent counterpart to my often-times stoic demeanor. Calm yet emotive. Sensitive but not to a fault. He's not afraid to call me on my bullshit or force me to take some me time when I get too much in my head.

It's not him I worry about. It's me.

What if I don't have the mothering gene? What if I'm already hardwired to fail? I picture the hospital, going through the labor, the hee-hee-who breathing method and the final pushes, the baby finally coming, and . . . nothing. I feel nothing. There's no bond, no rush of love. I look helplessly up at Drew with tears in my eyes, hand him the baby, and walk out of the room without another word.

I know that I'm my own person. I make my own decisions, and I won't let my life be dictated by the fact that my mother walked out on us.

But there's knowing, and then there's *knowing*, and the fears return relentlessly.

What if, for all the intentions I have to be a good mother, nature pilots me in another direction? A carbon copy of her departure.

Isn't that the saying? Every girl turns into her mother?

I have a stable career, a stable husband, a stable house—but am I ready to make it a stable *home*? Will I have to give up my career? This job is taxing, as unyielding as my doubt. Some days I leave without a shred of energy left to give to Drew. What happens to the equation if we throw a child into the mix? Whatever sense of balance we have, the equilibrium of happiness, I don't know if it can withstand all those winds.

More so if I'm programmed to leave.

A notification appears on my screen, interrupting my kaleidoscope of insecurities. Jennifer's blog post is going viral. Wonderful. The clickbait title. The pictures of Missy and Abby. Christ. This place will be crawling with reporters soon.

I pick up the journal and skim the first page to get a feel for what Abby wrote about. *When* she wrote. There could be answers in here too.

Blaisdell pulls up behind me a minute later. He offers an abrupt honk. I see his crooked shit-eating grin in the rearview, more yellow than white.

He slams the door and circles to meet me. His shoes squeak on the pavement, and he must've bathed in a vat of Axe. I have to take slow, shallow breaths or I won't make it through this interview in one piece.

"Detective Stone," he says gruffly. "Don't fuck this up. You're here because your DL called in a favor, but this is my case."

"Detective Blaisdell," I say, repeating his tone. "If you block me from finding my girl, I'll shove my foot so far up your ass, you'll puke blood for a week."

"Is that a promise?"

Foul.

We walk to the house, strides synched for the time being.

"Let me do the talking," I say.

"No fucking way," he says with a cough.

So much for teamwork. "She'll respond better to me," I say.

"This is my case."

"This is *our* case until I find Abby Scarborough."

"Thought her name was Chloe."

The screen door lurches open as we climb the stairs. Madeline Crawford is in her early to midthirties. Average height, dark hair, on the verge of being too skinny. Her eyes are as red as a Romero zombie. The last person a grieving mother is going to be candid with is Devon Blaisdell.

He clasps his hands in front of him like he's saying a prayer. "Hello, Mrs. Crawford," he says. "I'm Detective Devon Blaisdell, and this is Detective Emilina Stone."

"Hello."

"Terribly sorry for your loss, Mrs. Crawford," I say.

"Thank you," she says, expression unchanging.

"Can we come in?" Blaisdell asks. He pushes his shoulder into mine, nudging me an inch to the right.

"This way," Mrs. Crawford replies absently. We could've told her we were the Ghostbusters and her response would've been the same. She holds the door open with one arm pressed into the mesh screen and gestures us inside.

The house smells like lemons. An oriental runner with swirls of maroon, black, and ivory lies on the restored cherrywood floor. An antique telephone bench with a faded plush seat cushion is stationed at the base of an ornate banister.

A full-length mirror hangs above the bench. Like I'm crossing over into another dimension, I watch my reflection step onto the carpet. Madeline Crawford guides us into a modest living room and robotically sits on a stiff gray couch.

The walls are painted navy a shade too dark for the space. I suspect there's asbestos—all the old houses in this area have it—and the blue probably hides decades of lead paint. A built-in with hundreds of books lines the wall in an attempt to bring character.

You won't find charm like this in contemporary houses, but I'm grateful Drew didn't want a fixer-upper.

Mrs. Crawford doesn't look like she'll be worrying about lead levels anytime soon. She picks at a piece of her cuticle. A dot of blood spurts onto her skin. She wipes it with her opposite wrist and moves on to the next nail.

"Will your husband be joining us, Mrs. Crawford?" I ask.

"Madeline," she sniffs. "Everyone calls me Maddy."

"Maddy, then," I say, keeping a tempered tone.

"No. He's . . . he identified the body."

Blaisdell takes the seat beside her and offers a tissue. It's crinkled and there's not a box in sight. I hope it's not used.

Madeline dabs the corners of her eyes. "I couldn't bring myself to go with him. He's picking up his mother from Saratoga. She can't drive and she'll want to be here while we . . . make arrangements."

She focuses on the mantel above the stove at a framed photograph of Missy. Lasers have been replaced by charcoal-colored bubbles since my school days, but the signatures of a class package remain the same.

"I made her wear that shirt," Madeline points.

"It's lovely," I say. Royal blue, scoop neck, long sleeves. A nice complement to the flecks of green in her hazel eyes and the chocolate brown of her hair.

So much like Abby Scarborough's.

"She hated it. Said I wanted her to look like Violet Beauregarde." She cries again, perhaps weighted down by the understanding that fights with her daughter about clothes, about anything, are over. There won't be a day when she wakes up to a slammed door, a teenage attitude, or an exuberant shriek of celebration.

"I understand how difficult this is," Blaisdell soothes, "but I need to ask you some questions."

Sniff. Fresh tears slide to her lips. "Okay."

He scratches his neck with a meaty finger. "Have you ever been to Western Park?"

My thoughts float to JJ on the bench. The phone. Another piece that doesn't fit.

Madeline sighs and blinks to focus. "Yes. Of course. We've lived here our whole lives."

"Does the location have any significance to you?"

"I don't understand the question," she says.

"Would there be any reason . . ." He trails, shakes off his idea, and begins again. "Is it possible that Missy was left in the tree house because it's important to you or your husband?"

Is he expecting her to pontificate about motive? Come on, Blaisdell, this isn't *Criminal Minds*. This woman is hardly qualified to psychoanalyze her daughter's killer.

Madeline chews her cracked bottom lip. "We've only been a handful of times. Tulip Fest. Homecoming pictures. A show at the community stage once. I didn't know about that tree house until this morning, detective."

And now she'll never forget it.

Before Blaisdell allows this to go sideways, I take the wheel. "Would you mind just giving us a run-through? Your account of the day Missy disappeared again?"

A pregnant pause swells. "Sure." Madeline Crawford rolls the tissue into a ball and squeezes it as she speaks. "It started off like any other day. I woke her up for her music lesson. She's played the clarinet since fourth grade and takes it very seriously. She was going to be first chair this year." She sobs into her fist.

"Take your time."

Once she's able to collect herself, she continues. "Missy's lesson lasted for an hour. We stopped at Bowled for a couple of salads. I remember laughing because she stood on the chair to take a picture of our food." Madeline's chin quivers. "Uh, we ate there then headed to dance. She'd signed up for an extra class to keep her skills sharp until cheer practices start up again. They used to use the girls for baseball, but Brienna Tarpington got hit by a foul ball last year and her parents made it into a whole thing. The school decided they could only cheer at football games."

"Did you stay to watch the class?" I ask.

"No. I ran to the bank then stopped at the co-op for a few things. Just around the corner. When she was done, I picked her up and we went home. I got started on the laundry and she went up to shower before her study group."

The study group that didn't exist.

"How did her mood seem?" Blaisdell asks.

"Fine. Normal. Happy. I asked her if she wanted a ride, but she said it was close and didn't mind walking. I'd met Carolina's parents a number of times, so I didn't think anything of it. The kids were always getting together for some project or tutoring session, always alternating whose houses they went to and dividing up the work." She curls her fist to her lips and shakes her head. "I should've asked more questions. I should've realized she wasn't telling me the truth."

"You can't blame yourself, Mrs. Crawford," I say.

"Wouldn't you?" she asks.

Blaisdell clears his throat and silences me with an imperceptible nod. "When did you realize something was wrong?"

"She wasn't answering my calls or texts. That's one of our rules. I don't mind if she socializes while she studies, but she has to be available if we need to get ahold of her. Missy took her curfew very seriously. When half an hour passed and she still wasn't answering, I got worried. It's not like her to lose track of time. I had, you know, I just had a bad feeling."

I jot some key words down on my notepad. As much as apps have become second nature, I still prefer pen and paper for these situations. Puts people's minds at ease.

"Is that when you called the police?"

She shakes her head and squeezes the tissues a little faster. "No, we called Carolina's parents first, Albert and Jude. Wonderful people. Jude was confused. She said she didn't know about any project and put Carolina on speaker. She said, um . . ." She wipes her nose and takes a few deep breaths to steady herself. "She said there was no study session. That she hadn't seen Missy after school for weeks. I said that's absurd, she's been going to your house almost every day, maybe you're mistaken. And Carolina, bless her heart, she told me *I* was the one who was mistaken. She said Missy had been more distant; that's the word she used. Not weird, but distant. Busy. They assumed she had a boyfriend, which is just not true, detectives. Missy would've told me if there was a boy."

I have to wonder.

"Is that when you reported her missing?"

"Yes. They took our statement and told us to hang tight. That she'd probably turn up on her own. Kids will be kids, they said. She probably needed to blow off some steam. But I knew that was malarkey. Missy didn't have steam to blow off. She's a perfectly adjusted girl who loves her life." Her face droops. "Loved. Loved her life."

"Mrs. Crawford—"

She stops me with a stern hand. "My husband and I drove around the neighborhood for half an hour after the police left, asking neighbors if they'd seen or heard anything, but," she shrugs. "I, god help me, I was hoping we'd find her, like she'd broken her ankle or had a concussion or something. Do you know what it's like to *hope* that your daughter has had an accident? That something awful has happened to her, but it's a fixable awful? Just so you can have an explanation that makes sense? So your child comes home?"

Madeline's voice pinches toward the end, and the emotional buildup releases. She buries her face into her hands and wails.

Blaisdell shifts uncomfortably and gives me a sidelong look.

"Mrs. Crawford," I start, "I know this is a difficult discussion, but is it possible that Missy was seeing someone and she chose not to tell you? Or hadn't gotten the chance to tell you yet?"

Madeline vehemently shakes her head again, shreds the tissue into mushy ribbons, and rolls them together in her palms. "Absolutely not. Missy is a good kid. We're good people. Our friends are good people. We go to church every Sunday. No one we know could be capable of this. Everybody loves her."

I recall my conversation with Rosie. "Did Missy have a history of running away? Skipping school or not coming home when she was supposed to?"

She furrows at me. "My daughter is dead, detective." She pauses, her eyes skittering around the room. "She didn't run away. Somebody murdered my baby."

I allow Mrs. Crawford her tears.

When the worst of it is out of her system, Blaisdell asks, "What about someone she had a problem with? Someone who might've had a grudge?"

Blaisdell belongs in a knockoff mob show. Derivative *Sopranos*. Low budget. Bad accents.

Madeline Crawford seems equally unimpressed. "Like I said, Detective Blaisdell. Everybody loved Missy. She's student council president. Co-captain of the cheer squad. Volunteers for park cleanups. She . . . she *was* nice to everyone."

Emphasis on *was*. Tasting the new tense.

While I don't say it—since I have more tact than Blaisdell—I'm skeptical of this claim. My job warrants the doubt. Everyone wants to believe the best about their children, but middle school is tough for many kids. I've seen how jealousy can get the best of even the nicest girls. How they fight for their place on the social ladder—or become targeted because of it.

"Would it be possible for us to take a look in Missy's room?" I ask.

"Why?"

Blaisdell scowls. His nostrils flare. He looks like a bull about to storm the gates, clearly agitated with her reticence. "We might see something you don't."

Madeline moves farther from him. "Are you suggesting I don't know my own daughter, Detective Blaisdell?"

"Not at all. I was—"

"Because there was *nothing* we didn't share. Missy and I had a wonderful relationship. She trusted me with her secrets."

"I understand that, but—"

He's digging his hole deeper and doesn't know how to stop. "What he meant to say," I interrupt, "was that *we* need to get to know Missy better. See the world through her eyes. And the best way to do that is see where she spent her time. I remember how important having my own space was at that age."

Madeline stands, wipes tears from her eyes, but doesn't answer right away. "Okay," she says after a moment. "Come with me."

Blaisdell glowers but follows us up the stairs. We pass a wall with to-do lists, school announcements, and permission slips. A calendar without a blank space to be found. Practices, appointments, tutoring sessions, concerts, private lessons.

As if hearing my thoughts, Madeline says, "We color-coded to keep track of our engagements and synched our phone calendars." She plants a hand on the page and reluctantly moves on.

We stop in front of a door plastered with black and white shots of Paris. Eiffel Tower. Arc de Triomphe. Bastille. Louvre.

Her hand finds the knob but doesn't turn. She presses her forehead against the wood and breathes deeply. "I haven't touched anything," Madeline sobs. "It might be messy."

"That's okay," I assure her. Apologizing for a mess is a normal she can hold on to. Madeline pushes the door open and steps aside to let Blaisdell and me enter.

As opposed to the days of beaded curtains and boy band posters, Missy's room is a beautiful combination of chaos and simplicity. Her bed is made, beautifully creased corners and elegant lines. Pillows arranged by size and a lap desk perch at the headboard. A shaded lamp with a crystal base shaped into three balls.

It smells like almonds and expensive perfume. Definitely not going to find a bottle of Heavenly in here.

In lieu of a desk, there's a rolling laptop table stationed beside a beige chaise longue on a faux fur carpet. Chic and feminine yet functional. Above a distressed-style dresser and mini fridge, which Blaisdell determines to be full of bottled water and bagged apple slices, are four separate collections of collages.

Her core group of friends appears to consist of four other girls. They show up in some combination in basically every photo. Halloween costumes and spirit weeks. Cheerleading competitions and yellow choir robes. Beaches, restaurants, mall.

Mall.

Here I pause. I recognize Crossgates from the layout of shops and familiar blue tiles of the floor. They haven't changed since I was their age. The girls stand in front of Forever 21, a double-level excuse to spend five dollars on a skirt with TACO TUESDAYS stitched onto the pockets.

Forever 21, I remember from the few miserable times I've had to get my phone fixed, is right across from the Apple store.

The five of them pose with their arms around one another, giant bows in their ponytails. Their T-shirts are a gradient of colors ranging from neon pink to pastel peach. They each have a letter ironed to the front, spelling out one name.

C-H-L-O-E.

"Was Missy a fan of Chloe Cates?"

Blaisdell stops picking through the nightstand drawer and clomps to my side.

"CC Spectacular? Oh, yes," Madeline says, her voice lightening for the first time in our conversation. "She loved 'CC and Me.' I kept waiting for the phase to end, but," she holds out her hands in a what-are-you-going-to-do gesture. "There's a lot worse on the Internet these days. Some of these girls dress and act like they're grown. Chloe's page was more wholesome. I didn't mind her subscribing. Jennifer Cates seems to have similar values, and the family skits are pretty adorable."

"They're something, all right," Blaisdell scoffs, moving to the next collection of pictures. His scrunched forehead and squinted eyes make him look like a gopher trying to decipher a cryptic language. Under other circumstances it would be comical.

Madeline chokes on a sob and sits on the edge of Missy's bed. "I didn't love the idea of Missy having a phone, but with her late practices and tournaments, it made life easier. Plus, everybody her age has one. I didn't want her to feel alienated because I was too strict. I'm not unreasonable."

I sense this was an argument they had before and nod in agreement.

"I limited her screen time and reviewed her privacy settings. I monitored her feed so she didn't post anything too controversial or *revealing*." She draws out the last word, implying all the things no mother wants for her child.

I think of Abby and the phone JJ gave to me. "Have they been able to locate Missy's phone?" I ask.

"No," Blaisdell says. "Wasn't on her person or in the tree house. Trying to coordinate with the phone company for tower triangulation, but we're SOL if it's turned off or dead."

Madeline weeps.

I point to the mall photograph. "When was this taken?"

She examines the photo, her thumb caressing Missy's cheek. "That's from September. It was the CC Spectacu-palooza."

"What a mouthful," Blaisdell says.

"How would you describe that event?" I ask, flipping to a fresh page in my notepad.

"Shitshow," she says, and utters a laugh. She claps a hand over her mouth, as if showing any sign of happiness in this place is forbidden. I think it'll be a long time before she allows herself to feel anything but sadness.

"Meaning?" Blaisdell rolls his hand for her to continue.

"Detective Blaisdell, when was the last time you took a bunch of hyped-up thirteen-year-old girls to a concert?" she asks.

I suppress a smile.

"Never, but my sister loved *NSYNC back in the day, so I get the whole boy band craze. Kind of."

Madeline focuses on me. "It was insanity, and that's saying something because I've chaperoned four different cheer championships. Stiflingly hot. Hundreds of shrieking girls being crammed into the event areas. Music so loud my ears rang for days after. JJ Cates was there, too, and oh, they *adore* him. JJ 4 EVER and I LOVE JJ and JJ MARRY ME on glittery poster boards."

"How did Chloe take that?"

"She seemed to enjoy it. They did some prank skit and did a brief Q&A with the audience. Missy had a little crush on him, so it was cute to see her with hearts in her eyes. CC and JJ. As far as sibling relationships go, theirs seems good."

I love my sister.

Luke's message just became more pressing. "Was there a meet and greet afterwards?" I ask.

"Not for that show, but there was for the most recent one, and very well attended."

"You were there?"

Madeline looks at me like I've got three heads. "We were in the front row. I surprised Missy with VIP meet and greet passes. A reward for making honor roll third quarter."

Two missing girls. One dead. Both uniquely bonded by the imaginary creation that is Chloe Cates. Not a coincidence. Blaisdell realizes this as well. His ornery quips have taken a back burner to the details of the mall appearance. For once, we might be in agreement. We're chasing the same perpetrator.

"How would you compare the atmosphere of the last show to the previous one?" I ask.

She drops the photo on the bed next to her and sighs. "Fine? Mediocre? Strained, perhaps. Ugh, it was terrible, what she went through."

Blaisdell arches an eyebrow at me inquisitively.

"She got her period," I say.

From the stretch of his countenance, it's clear the idea is out of his comfort zone.

"I felt so bad for her," Madeline says. "All those people laughing, and to have it be live? I can't imagine."

"Did she seem distressed?"

"Wouldn't you be?" Madeline says matter-of-factly. "She actually finished the last skit, but that girl was mortified. I thought for sure they'd cancel the VIP, but they went through with it, and she seemed like her regular, sparkly self."

"What about the parents? Jackson and Jennifer, what were your impressions of them?"

"They seem like nice people," she says, leaving me to interpret what *nice* means. "Jackson Cates is great with the crowd, dancing and singing and just really friendly—incredibly popular with the late teens and young moms. Old moms, too, with those dimples and biceps, but not my cup of tea. To each their own. Jennifer doesn't seem to mind. She has an infinite supply of energy. And she loves Chloe."

As long as there's a camera on them.

"One last question, Maddy," I say, taking a final look at the collages. "Was there anything about the meet and greet that stood out to you?"

She almost dismisses the idea but stops herself. "There may be something," she offers, and tells us the story of the autograph.

Abby's Journal

*Whyyyy does she insist on booking these things? You don't see JoJo Siwa or Baby Ariel running around malls. But I don't have an agent. And I need an agent. And I just want to tell her, like, we've been doing this for **years.** Don't you think if the golden ticket was coming, we would've gotten it by now?*

When I was 6 I booked my first commercial for an orange juice company. National. Mom was hype. She spent 200 bucks at the salon getting her hair done to just sit in the waiting room and watch. I had pigtails. I sat at an old picnic table and drank careful sips from a glass as big as my head, licking my lips and exclaiming, "Oranges never tasted so fresh!" By the time it wrapped, I had about 3 gallons of that gross stuff swimming in my stomach and splinters from the stupid table. The director told her I was a natural but didn't call us for the next one.

After my bday, she told me that if I keep doing these Chloe Cates skits, I can start real school in September.

Which OMG huge deal, right? Except I don't believe her. She lies all the time to get me to do what she wants. Part of me REALLY hopes she's telling the truth this time. But I know her.

Sigh. Maybe I could go to school with *him.* Walk down the hall holding hands or hang out at each other's lockers. JJ says he doesn't go to his locker and I need to stop watching teen dramas.

OK OK. No more mystery. Real talk. *His* name is Chris. He's from Lower Madison and I think I'm in love.

He's HOT. Think Tom Holland and Ansel Elgort had a baby. Boy Next Door but dreamier. Brown eyes. Brown hair. Freckles. I love freckles. Tall, too. Mom's always saying it's better to date tall guys b/c short guys ruin pictures.

He loves:

1. *Science*
2. *Video games*
3. *Grilled cheese sandwiches*
4. *Cats (eh)*

He hates:

1. *Pickles (me too!)*
2. *Chores*
3. *Fallout (which . . . is a game, I guess? IDK, I'll have to google it)*
4. *Taylor Swift (Don't worry. I told him: Tay is *QUEEN*)*

He's also so sweet. I mean the messages, the butterfly necklace. V Adorbs. He told me about how his dad wants him to play football, but he doesn't want to. He wants to do this engineering club. Building robots. They go to national competitions.

He totally gets it.

He gets me.

I can't wait to see what he's like in person.

EMILINA

I think about that night at the water tower as I sit unmoving in the driver's seat, my brain running on overdrive.

I reread the first entry in Abby Scarborough's journal. Different subjects, different slang, but this could've been my own writing. I didn't dare write about what happened, of course, but in hindsight it probably would've helped me work through my issues.

There's nothing more deadly than a swallowed secret. You gobble it up, force it down, and pretend it's gone. You do everything in your power to convince yourself it isn't there.

But unlike the ones you bury, swallowed secrets are a constant battle. You can't just forget about them, cover them in dirt and walk away. I used to tell my father I had a moon in my throat when it got to be too much. I imagined a tiny yellow crescent growing inside me, stuck behind my epiglottis, pulsing through its revolutions until I eventually threw it up.

Our secret was that crescent moon, and I've put up a good fight until now.

We were thirteen when Jen killed someone.

Mary and Nicole were the proverbial Cool Girls, both revered and despised. For the most part, they left me alone. I was on the fringes of popularity, not defined by one social clique, which worked in my favor. Plus, I think Mary had a crush on Patrick and thought I'd talk her up to my brother if she was nice to me.

Jen didn't have a brother to impress and therefore had no immunity against the bullying.

The porno mag incident was bad. Should've been enough to keep her away from them for life, but it only seemed to make her want to hang out with them more. She craved approval. Acceptance.

That hasn't changed. If anything, I'd say it's gotten worse.

When we were thirteen, Mary and Nicole convinced Jen that one of the most popular guys in the school wanted to take her to the winter dance. Dances were a big deal. Everybody went, no exceptions. If you didn't spend months choosing your dress and planning who was going to be in your limo, you were doing it wrong.

And there they were, standing on her porch like the creepy sisters in *The Shining*, telling Jen that Adam Carrington—*the* Adam Carrington—was interested in her.

"You are *so* lucky," Mary said.

"All the girls are *so* jealous," Nicole added. "Adam is so hot."

"A heartthrob," Mary agreed.

"He's okay," Jen shrugged.

Her attempt at playing it cool fell flat. Adam had the whole Dawson Leery thing going on and she knew it. Jen was always crushing on someone, but no one more than Adam. Her notebooks were full of MASH games and unrequited confessions of love. Jen and Adam. Adam and Jen. J+A 4E.

Adam Carrington asking her on a date was a dream come true. I could see the stars in her eyes. How badly she wanted to believe them.

"He's waiting around the corner," Nicole said, barely suppressing her grin. "Didn't want your mom to catch you making out or whatever."

Jen blushed furiously. Beet red. "We're not gonna make out."

I tried to warn her. "They're messing with you," I said. "Don't go."

But Jen wouldn't listen. "Why would they lie? I'm just gonna talk to him."

"Yeah," Mary said. "No biggie. Aren't you happy for Jenny?"

I was stuck. I didn't know how to make her see what they were doing without her taking it the wrong way. I'd either come off as jealous or insulting. Pointing out the logic would only make it worse.

"Jen, come on. Stop and think about it for a sec," was all I managed.

"She's buggin', Jenny. Let's bounce before he gets bored." Nicole skipped off the stairs, and Mary followed. Crossed arms and hips jutted, tennis shoes bopping on the pavement, they waited.

"Jen," I said, hoping she'd hear the reason in my voice.

"Shut up, it's fine," she said and hopped after them.

I was going to stay on the porch, but the potential for catastrophe unglued my feet. I trailed at a distance. Watching. They followed her down the street, whispering and snickering behind her back and smiling like hyenas when she turned.

The pit in my stomach grew, iron butterflies scraping my insides.

She rounded the corner and no one was there. Obviously. I knew they were full of shit. What I couldn't figure out was how Jen let herself be fooled. Why she'd choose to believe them instead of following her gut. Until that moment, I didn't realize how dangerous desire could be.

Jen's eyes searched the houses, the porches, the street, still not understanding. She turned, confusion twitching her nose. "Did he leave?" she asked.

Nicole laughed and elbowed Mary. Her backpack lay unzipped at her feet, and in each hand, they held an egg.

Mary scrunched up her face in bewildered amusement. "Who?"

"A-Adam," Jen stammered.

"Wow, Jenny. The corner? I knew you were sad, but I had no clue you were a whore too."

Nicole launched first. It hit Jen in the stomach with a dull thud.

There was a pause, a slo-mo realization spreading across the group. The words. The egg. There was no taking it back.

Then, all at once, time unstuck. They threw the eggs, one after another, screaming, *Hey, HENNY JENNY, how many did you lay today?*

Over and over. I can still hear the excitement in their voices, shrill and hungry.

The eggs exploded against her arms and legs. One cracked against the side of her head. Another smashed her nose, and blood ran loose with the yolks.

Jen didn't move. She let them hit her until they ran out of eggs.

I expected her to cry. I know I wanted to, and I wasn't the one being pelted.

But she didn't cry. Not a single tear. Instead, she laughed.

Maybe it was nerves. The body reacts in strange ways to stress and embarrassment.

Maybe she thought if she brushed it off as a joke, proved she was tough, they'd do the same.

Whatever the reason, she laughed, shoulders shaking uncontrollably, doubled over, strings of yolk dangling from her lips. Hair stringy and matted to her face. The image of her cackling, covered in yolk and blood, is seared into my mind.

"*Freak*," Mary spat, one eye squinting through the lens of a disposable camera that seemed to materialize out of nowhere. The shutter snapped. She clicked the reel and took five more shots. "Ugh, you're, like, so gross."

"Pathetic," Nicole said and swung the empty backpack over her shoulder. "You're totally done, whore. Everyone's gonna know you love the corner."

They waggled their fingers at me as they passed, mouthing, *See ya*, like what had happened was the most normal thing in the world.

I wanted to scream. Knock them down and make them apologize. But like with the rest of the incident, I just watched them leave.

How could they humiliate her and just walk off? How callous and mean did you have to be to not care about hurting someone so much? I was pissed at myself for letting it happen. But whatever anger I felt was no match for what Jen was feeling.

Unwrapping my sweatshirt from around my waist, I held it out to Jen. "Here. Take this."

Nothing. No movement or indication she even heard me. "Are you okay?"

"What do you mean?" she asked. Vacant. Dead-eyed. Still smiling.

"I'm so sorry," I said.

"Don't." Jen pushed past me, yolk spattering the sidewalk. One careful step at a time, she walked home, an exaggerated smile glued to her face the whole way.

She didn't talk to me for two weeks. A lifetime in girl years. I understood she was mad. I should've tried harder. I should've done something when I saw the eggs, but I froze. Afraid of social persecution—of becoming the next target.

Because as much as I prided myself on not being labeled as one thing, the truth was I wanted to fit in, too; and in middle school, it seemed like that was the only thing that mattered.

A week later, the pictures were developed.

They circulated through the school like wildfire. Guys clucked at her as she passed, grabbing their crotches and calling her vile names. The girls were no better. Her locker was vandalized. By lunch, it was inescapable. She faked a cough and stayed home for the rest of the week.

When Jen finally decided to forgive me, she was different. Reserved. Cautious. Cold.

We stopped memorizing the dance moves to "I Want You Back" because she wanted to read *Cosmo* and learn how to perfect the day-to-night smoky eye. She started stealing. Maybelline eye shadow compacts and bags of

Hot Fries. A pair of sunglasses. Earrings. Car air fresheners. Nail decals. It didn't matter what she took as long as she did it.

Now I recognize those outbursts for what they were: cries for help. A young woman trying to fight through the bullshit of adolescence without any support whatsoever. Her dad died of a heart attack when she was two. Her mother worked night shifts at a nursing home and slept when she wasn't on call. I don't think Carol had a clue what went on in Jen's world. The ridicule she faced.

I'm not excusing Jen's actions, don't get me wrong, but sometimes I wonder if things would have been different if she'd gotten help. If one person had stopped to ask her if she was okay.

I certainly didn't. Not in any way that mattered.

And someone died because of it.

Abby's Journal

Chris asked about my family. I lied and said my dad's a lawyer. IDK why I did that.

I also said that my mom stays at home and organizes a book club. IDK why I said that either.

I could've told him about JJ, but I said I was an only child. What if by some weird turn of fate they know each other IRL? JJ's always meeting people at tournaments and all-star camps and he's not as into social. Like he checks it, but he's not on top of his followers like I am. They could be friends and not be friends on IG.

I told Chris to call me, but he said he doesn't like to talk on the phone—which I get. I haven't called someone . . . ever. In the olden days people had to share phone lines—dial-up internet sounds like the literal WORST—and anyone could pick up and listen. I'd die if Mom listened to our calls.

I wonder what he sounds like, tho. I'll be memorizing lines or scrolling through Mom's photo logs and I'll just . . . blank. Is he more of a Noah Centineo or a Timothée Chalamet? What does he smell like?

I look forward to DMs from him more than Christmas morning.

It's nice having someone who only knows me as Abby. Chris. Abby. Chris and Abby. Chabby? It needs work.

We're gonna meet soon. It's going to happen. And I have the PERFECT spot picked out.

I stole my dad's ladder and snuck it out there the other night. He still doesn't know it's missing. I cleaned out all the leaves and brought a camping lantern and some sheets so it's v v cozy.

I'm stressed af he'll figure out I'm lying before I get the chance to tell him. He still doesn't know about CC and Me. I know I should just be straight with him. I'm not trying to hurt him. And I'm gonna tell him at some point.

I just don't know when.

EMILINA

I read the next few entries in Abby's journal, but it's difficult to concentrate now that I've opened the can of worms I've so desperately tried to ignore for the last twenty years. My eyes skim over the words while my mind drifts backward.

Despite her drastic attitude shift, I hung out with Jen most days after school. The bullying had dwindled by that point, attention veering to the next scandal of Stefanie Jolinsky taking birth control, and I expected a typical Thursday night of finishing our homework, reading through her new supply of magazines (stolen), and trying on different combinations of chokers and butterfly clips (also stolen).

The evening sky was a milky blend of oranges, pinks, and dusky blues. I let myself in. Ringing the bell would've woken up Carol before her shift, and I did not want to make that mistake again. I was still scared about adults being mad at me.

I kicked off my shoes and ran upstairs to her room. If I hadn't been in such a hurry, I would've noticed that there were more shoes by the door than normal, but as it was, I burst through the door and came face to face with Mary and Nicole.

What the fuck, I wanted to shout, indignation, shock, and disbelief exploding in my chest.

"Oh," Nicole said, already losing interest. "Hey, Emily."

"Emilina."

"Whatever," she shrugged, her pencil-thin eyebrows arched with attitude.

"You should totally let me crimp your hair, Jenny," Mary said.

"Yeah," Nicole agreed. "She's like a pro. It'll look *so* good on you."

"Okay," Jen said, beaming from her spot on the bed.

I already knew how that would play out, and I didn't like it. "Jen, I need your help in the kitchen."

She scrunched up her face and sucked her lips to the side. "I'm busy."

"Yeah, she's busy. Makeovers are serious, and this could take a while. Hey, how's Patrick?" Mary asked. The crimper—a fat square with wavy gold plates set to 415 degrees—clacked in her hand. She took a chunk of Jen's hair, pressed it between the plates, then jammed the crimper into the side of her neck.

Jen hissed and jerked forward.

Nicole and Mary laughed.

"Jen," I said, yanking her down the hallway by the arm. "What are they doing here?"

She rubbed the angry red spot on her neck. "I ran into them before eighth period. They asked if they could come over."

"You have History eighth."

"I skipped," she shrugged, wincing at the movement.

"Think, Jen. Why would they want to come over? They don't even like you."

"Shut up," she spat. "You're just jealous."

"Jen, come on. Why are they here?"

She looked at me like I had asked her why the sky was blue. "Uh, because I told them my mom has a shit ton of vodka and lets me drink whenever I want."

"Why would you say that? What were you thinking?"

"Something to do." She brushed past me, knocking my shoulder, and screwed her signature too-cool-for-school smile into place. "Go home, Emme."

I should've, but I didn't. I followed her down the hall. The only explanation I've been able to come up with is that I wanted to protect her. And even though every nerve in my body was screaming for me to leave, I had to account for my lack of courage with the Henny Jenny incident.

"Looks like you got a hickey," Nicole said when we returned. "You guys were totally making out."

"Oh my god." Mary's words slurred together, *ohmigod*. "You totally were."

"Psh, no we weren't," Jen said, but I knew she was rattled. Catholicism creates a special mixture of guilt and fear, especially in someone like Jen who was already ostracized. There was an accusatory tone floating through their statements. The I-know-your-dirty-secret-and-I'll-tell type tone. Snakebites spreading poison under Jen's skin.

Nicole sputtered and cocked her jaw out, signature teenage attitude. "Are you a *lesbian*, Jenny?"

Jen was reaching for the crimper when she paused. No more than a couple of seconds, but a vein of ice ran through me in that hiccup of time. I couldn't explain it in the moment, but I realize now that on some level, at least, she'd made up her mind to act.

"Hey, how 'bout I make us some drinks?" Jen suggested.

They exchanged a look and shrugged. "Whatever," Mary said.

Jen fixed me with an inscrutable glare. "Excellent," she said. "Be back in a jiff."

Mary snorted. "Who says jiff?"

I watched Jen trot down the stairs, a spring in her step, and a few minutes later she returned with three solo cups of cherry-red liquid.

"What's in it?" Nicole asked, swirling the concoction around.

"A Dirty Shirley," she said. "You've had them before, right?" She handed the last cup to Mary and turned her chin up at me. "Sorry, Emme. None for you."

Mary took several gulps and wiped her mouth.

Nicole sniffed her cup and sipped. For all her talk, I'm pretty sure that was her first experience with alcohol. She didn't think Jen would follow through on her promises, but now that she had, Nicole had to maintain appearances. "This is okay," she said. "I prefer rum."

"I think we've got that too," Jen said, hitching her thumb toward the door.

"I'm good," Nicole declined with a frown and wave of her hand. I saw Jen hide the ghost of a smile as she passed around an assortment of trashy magazines.

Leaning against the dresser, I flipped through the pages distractedly. Ads for drugstore cosmetics and cigarettes interspersed between celebrity gossip and movie news. Every so often, I'd sneak a glance at Jen, trying so hard to appear nonchalant in her chair while radiating nervous energy.

Jen held her magazine up, some blonde model with a low-cut orange bodycon dress against an orange backdrop, and made a noise of irritation. "Is your itsy too bitsy? What the hell does that even mean?"

"Vaginas are not one size fits all," Nicole tittered. "Figured you of all people would know that, Jenny."

Jen sipped from her cup.

I opened my mouth to say something but was quickly interrupted. Mary lurched forward onto the page she was reading. *Seven Tips on How To Keep Your Pelvic Floor Strong.* She groaned and clutched her stomach. She blew out air and moaned.

"What's wrong with you?" Nicole asked with more than a hint of annoyance.

Mary doubled over. She burped, apologized, and burped again.

"Ew," Nicole said, slapping her shoulder. "What is your problem?"

Mary clawed at her stomach, a pained, terrified expression spreading across her face as she burped again. Thick. Wet.

"I'm pretty sure that's the opposite of what you're supposed to do for a strong pelvic floor," Jen laughed.

"I think," Mary belched, "I think I need to go home." Another wet belch and an even wetter squelch, and the stench of rotten eggs filled the room.

"Ugh, oh my god, gross," Nicole shuddered as we covered our mouths and noses.

"Oh my god," Mary cried. "Ohmigod, ohmigod." She pressed a hand to her mouth and bolted. A minute later, the front door slammed.

"Mary's lame. Can't handle her liquor," Jen said, tipping a cheers in my direction.

I knew she was behind it. She was being too cool, too . . . calculated. She'd done something to the drinks.

Part of me understood why she did it; part of me might actually have been rooting her on. Vindication. Revenge.

If that had been the end of it.

But it wasn't. Her intent was palpable, thick and prickly. She wasn't trying to just teach them a lesson.

Jen had other plans.

"My mom's going to wake up soon," she said. "She's cool about me drinking, but she might want to talk to your mom."

"Um, why would she do that?"

"I don't know, to be responsible," she said, matching Nicole's attitude. "You haven't had that much, though, if you're scared your mom'll be pissed. It's not like she's going to smell your breath when you walk in, right? I'm sure you'll be totally fine."

Nicole stared into her cup.

"Unless you want to go to the field?"

"We've got homework," I said. The rebuttal was spontaneous, my gut instinct working in overdrive, sensing Jen had something else planned.

"I did mine, Emme," she clipped. "You should go home. The two of us are just gonna chill for a bit. Right, Nicole?"

Nicole tucked her chestnut hair behind her ear. It was fluffy from the round brush she most likely used to blow-dry it and immediately fell back into place. She took another sip and shrugged. "Sure, whatever. Nothing better to do."

That might've been the last decision she ever made.

Abby's Journal

Today was the worst day of my life.

This is just . . . so messed up on SO many different levels. Like, I knew my family was nuts, but this blows everything else out of the crazy waters.

It's 1 A.M. I'm writing this on my bed with my back in the corner and all my pillows in front of me like a mini fort. I locked my door. I NEVER lock my door. We're all about open doors in this family, my mom says. We talk to one another.

Well, somebody isn't taking their own advice.

I don't want to talk to any of them. I'd run away if I could. But I have no one. As long as Mom's in charge, I'll never have anyone. She doesn't want me to have anyone.

I guess I should start at the beginning.

Today was the big mall show. I could do these things in my sleep, but she was making a huge freaking deal out of it. She was all, we need you to be on, Chloe. You have to take this seriously, Chloe. This is our moment, Chloe.

Our moment. Sure. 🙂

3 things happened today that changed my life forever.

1. *I got my period. Ugh.*
2. *My mother proved that she's a sneaky liar.*
3. *Ugh, I can't even. How do I even write this?*

We got to Crossgates and my stomach was killing me. I had a headache all morning. I wanted a pretzel. A big freaking pretzel from Auntie Anne's. With chocolate sauce to dip it in. I threw on JJ's hoodie and snuck to the shop. I ordered the pretzel, broke off the tiny leg—the best part, don't @ me—and dunked it in the warm chocolate.

Sugary deliciousness.

And then Mom the Bitch found me.

I was trying to hide, but she legit misses nothing. I'm convinced she has robot eyes on the back of her head. She snatched my pretzel and threw it right in the garbage. What are you thinking? Chloe Cates does NOT eat this trash.

News flash. We're the same person, but go off.

I walked away, her whisper-screaming about ReSpOnSiBiLiTy and bRaNd and how I was trying to ruin HER life. I blocked it out and ran behind this like temporary wall thing they installed so I had a place to change or whatever.

Should've just kept JJ's sweatshirt on but NoOoOoOo. I *had* to wear the outfit the preteen boutique on steroids sent. Rainbow sequins and patches with neon colors. Chloe Cates has to be dripping on stage.

I stayed there until Dad knocked to wire me up. Mr. Forest stopped by as he was finishing to get him to sign some papers and I peeked out at the crowd. Packed. Sold out. Which, on the one hand feels good. I want them to like me. The Chloe me. IDK, it's complicated, I can't explain it.

TLDR I was trying to hype myself up. Mom was running through her speech doing her best Meryl impression. Which is cringeworthy and she should forever stop.

Dad told me to hang in there. *He had a* feeling everything was going to be all right.

Of course he did. He's a liar too.

Then the show.

Flashing lights. Everybody cheering CC! CC! CC! Cue music.

I cartwheeled out and tried this new intro dance I worked on all week. A quick combo of a few TikTok dances I put together myself. They went nuts. Super into it. I honestly thought that I might see it dueted that night.

It's impossible not to feel good in those moments. I didn't even care that my stomach was revolting. Sparkles and jokes and skits, I was all in.

And then.

Then I noticed they were interrupting my lines. Laughing. Pointing. I tried not to because rly people do strange things sometimes, but I looked down.

When I saw the blood . . . I know this is going to sound stupid, but I flashed to what went down at the Ariana Grande concert in London. I thought I'd been shot and everyone was just staring at me.

And just like that, I knew. That's what the audience would *do as long as they could film it. Like, do I even really matter to them? They love the jokes and the dances and the sparkly, happy girl on the stage, but would any of them reach out to help me?*

Obv not, as my period is one of the top trending tweets rn. It's like they want me to be bigger just to see how great it is when I break.

EMILINA

I turn to the next page in Abby's journal and prop my head in my hand, the echoes of the past weighing me down, dragging me back to that night.

The night Jen became a murderer.

Jen shot a glance at her mother's bedroom door as we tiptoed past to the liquor cabinet. She danced her fingers along the bottle tops before grabbing the vodka.

Liquor in hand, we headed to the field.

My recollection has probably skewed with time, but I don't remember passing a single person. No cars or dog walkers. It's strange how isolated this moment feels. The three of us alone, side by side, huffing as we crested the steep hill and arrived at the field.

The first official snow of the year hadn't hit yet, but already the ground was frozen and unforgiving. Our footsteps crunched on the grass as we headed through the meadow toward the woods. I shivered in the open air, feeling exposed. We weren't supposed to be there.

"Drink?" Jen asked, offering the bottle to Nicole.

"No," she replied, her voice barely above a whisper. She looked around as if we were about to get caught.

We fell into a single-file line as we approached the path, the ground softening the closer we got to the trees. Mud splattered the backs of our jeans, and we hitched up our legs to save the hems from being dragged. Nothing was worse than wet cuffs.

The past overlaps with the present, and I see the tree house ahead of us, the creaky structure brooding over our clearing with the stump seats. Logically, I know it wasn't there that night with Nicole, but flipping to the next page of Abby's journal, my mind combines the two locations into one gruesome slideshow.

The woods.

The chill.

The dead girl.

Cold wind kicked up leaves, swirling them around in the darkness. Nicole plopped onto the stump and curled her elbows around her knees for warmth. Jen stood in front of her and gulped from the bottle. The liquid glugged with each swallow and splashed out when she was done.

I realize now that she must've been sneaking liquor from her mother regularly, to be able to drink that heavily without crashing; but that night, I thought she was possessed.

Nicole cocked her head to the side and pinched her face into a condescending scowl. "Wow, chug much?"

Jen laughed, the titter of a witch in moonlight. "Nicky, do you remember the first time you brought me out here?"

"Don't call me Nicky, bitch. That's rude. We're not that tight."

"You're right. You're right. Yes." Jen bowed, lifting imaginary skirts, and cleared her throat. "Your *majesty*, do you remember the first time you brought me here?" Cackle. Swig.

"My god, you're so weird."

"But do you remember?"

"Can't say that I do," Nicole exhaled, feigning boredom.

A blustery gust raised the hairs on my arms, but that wasn't the only reason I shivered.

Jen gawked at her. "The dirty magazine? The one you blamed on me?"

"Doesn't ring a bell," Nicole said with a smirk. "You would look at porn, though. Everybody knows it's the only way lesbians get off." She knew she was pressing Jen's buttons, but she didn't care.

She couldn't see Jen's spine unfurling, another inch for every jab and jeer.

"I just wanted to be friends," Jen said. The raw honesty in her voice scared me. Naked and unwavering. It was the kind of admission you save for your closest friends, your lover, your diary. It didn't belong in the thickening woods with the rotting leaves. "We're not going to be friends, are we?"

Not a question.

"Ha," Nicole snorted. "Me? Friends with Henny Jenny? *No* way, loser."

"You asked her to hang out," I said. "Why are you here then?"

Scoff. "'Cuz I was bored." She flipped hair from her shoulder. "Mary's got, like, a stomach thing. Probably caught some of your grody germs, Henny Jenny. And I wasn't ready to go home yet."

"Eye drops, actually," Jen said.

"I'm sorry? Did you say eye drops?"

"Why don't you like me?" Jen asked, flat but laser focused.

"God, you're pathetic," Nicole groaned.

"I'm not," she said.

"You are. I can't believe you'd even think I'd consider being your friend. Poor and dirty and so freaking weird. Always hanging around us like a puppy—"

"I don't—"

"—drooling over boys who will never notice you, never like you, never want you. Adam Carrington would rather get a handy with sandpaper than be seen with Henny Jenny. He wouldn't go near you with a ten-foot pole. No one would. You're the laughingstock of the whole school."

Nicole's bullet had clearly hit its target. Jen sucked in a tight breath and her chin quivered.

"Aw, poor baby," Nicole laughed. "Are you going to cry now?"

Nicole's voice floats forward as I read another random entry, Abby venting about how unfair her mother is. How *off* her behavior can be sometimes. Then I'm diving headfirst into the memory.

Jen sniffled and went blank. "Want some?" she asked Nicole, shoving the bottleneck into her face.

Nicole lurched backward and swatted Jen's hand away. "I said no. *Thanks.*" She rocked on the stump and sighed. "This is so lame."

Jen frowned at me, a curve of mock indignation. "She said no."

"I heard." My pulse escalated to a fever pitch.

Turning to Nicole. "You said no." Shrug. Chuckle. "No." Fake disbelief. Swig.

"Ohmigod, what is your—"

Crack.

What haunts me in the wee hours of morning, when the room is a bluish-black and cool air seeps from the vents, is not the secret. It's the gargling. I hear it now, alone in my car with this red notebook open to another girl's troubles. The thoughts of Abby Scarborough, daughter of a murderer, spilling over the edges.

Like the gargling.

Crack.

A second hit. Harder. A third, harder still.

Nicole, her head shattering on one side, choking on her own blood.

"Unggg," she grunted. The whites of her eyes fluttered in and out of focus.

"I'm sorry, I can't understand you when you're mumbling." Jen cupped a hand to her ear, the bottle slick with vodka and Nicole's blood.

"Ung nnnn unggggg." She clawed at the ground, but I don't think she knew what her arms were doing by then. Blood pooled around her in an inky black arc.

"Oh. Yeah, right. Duh. You're sorry for making up that nickname. Cool, yeah," Jen said, like they were having a normal conversation. "No doubt. Apology accepted."

I hadn't moved since the first three blows. Jen brought the bottle down again. And again. The dull *thud, thwump* was enough to break me from my frozen stance.

I didn't try to stop her. I didn't help Nicole.

I sprinted aimlessly into the trees. Away from the path leading to safety and deeper into the cacophony of the forest. I heard Jen behind me, years away from CC Spectacular and the suburban life, a bull charging a matador.

I ran without direction, completely on survival autopilot, but I couldn't escape the monster.

"Emme!" Jen shouted, chasing.

Farther from the path, the environment around me transformed. The faces, the same ones that have stayed with me all these years, I saw them earlier in the woods. Tree beasts opening their mouths to devour me whole.

Abby's words jump off the page, and bile rises in my throat.

There's something wrong with my mom.

Abby's Journal

Let me tell you. Getting my period for the first time in front of everyone? Not fun.

What makes it worse is that I couldn't just stop. She wouldn't let me leave. She forced me to go back onstage and act like nothing happened. Professionals don't quit. Wrap that hoodie around your waist and get out there. You can change before the meet and greet. It's a period for cripes sake, you're not having a baby.

There's something wrong with my mom.

I mean !!!! Who does that?!

So I'm literally bleeding everywhere, completely mortified, and still have to do the freaking MNG. Cool cool cool.

Once I realized what was happening, I knew I wasn't dying, but I still had questions, ya know? I needed my mom. I needed her to just understand that for one day, Abby needed to come first.

I guess that was too much to ask. I should've known better.

I ran to the BR and coming out of the stall was this girl who literally could've been my twin. She was washing her hands and staring at me in the mirror. I've seen the doppelgangers Reddit. Everybody has a twin that's not related to them. Someone you share the same face with.

I found mine.

Chloe! *She was super nervous.* OMG I'm Missy. I'm your biggest fan. I've been to all your shows, and you're just so amazing. Can we take a pic?

I'm like, yeah, sure. Other Me.

We took the pic. So weird. Like the ultimate faceswap.

Everybody says we look alike, *she said.*

I know, right? We really do, I said with my Chloe smile, but I felt like a giant puppet doll. Well, nice to meet you, DOPPELGANGER, but I gotta put a glitter shake on that.

She was in the MNG line 2 minutes later anyway with a woman who looked nothing like my mom. I guess doppelgangers don't necessarily have to have matching parents. One of my mom is more than enough, tbh.

I'm crying. The stupid ink's smudging. I bet that's why people started doing this online. But I have to get this out. I don't know what else to do. I thought the day couldn't get any worse.

I was so wrong.

EMILINA

I don't know how Jen caught up to me that night. The weight of her body straddling my stomach, her fists pounding my cheeks, I screamed until she crushed my top lip into my teeth. My ears rang louder than cymbals.

She's going to kill me too, I thought. I said goodbye to my dad, to Patrick. I told them I loved them and hoped they'd find out the truth someday. I thought I was dead.

Shaking and crying, I waited for the bottle to crash into my skull. Would it hurt? Would she have to hit me a bunch of times like Nicole? Would I know I was dying?

Seconds felt like hours, but the blow didn't come.

Jen laid on top of me and sighed. She pressed her mouth to my ear and whispered. "I need your help."

Goose bumps raised on goose bumps as I processed what she said. "What?"

She propped herself to a standing position and brushed debris from her clothes. "I told you to go home. You didn't want to listen. So, the way I see it, you have two choices. You can help me with the body."

"Or?" I grimaced, forcing myself up and inspecting the blood on my hand.

"You don't need me to tell you the other option, Emilina."

She was right. I didn't want to die, so I chose to help her dispose of Nicole's body.

"What do you say, Emme?"

"Okay, okay." I had to say it twice before it would sink all the way in. A moral stain that has kept me in check for the past twenty years. Where others have taken bribes, called in favors, pushed relatives for departmental recommendations, I've stayed the course. My soul's already damaged goods. I can't afford to make any more mistakes.

Missy's dead, my subconscious whispers. *You're responsible. That's a pretty big mistake.*

A stomach cramp steals my breath. I'm on the cusp of vomiting, the car suddenly too hot, the smell of clean linen from the air freshener too crisp. I thumb the window button and hang my head on the cool metal. How can I ever be a mother when I did such a terrible thing?

I'll do whatever it takes to make up for this, I promised, winded and terrified, dragging the body to the base of the water tower. *Just let me survive this night.*

Jen held her arms. I held her ankles. We didn't speak until we dropped her at the ladder. "There," she said. "We're going to put her in the tank."

"No way."

"We have to."

"Somebody will find her," I said.

"Not until she decomposes," Jen said. "Water erases, like, all the residual evidence. Besides, they only do inspections on this place every six months."

I don't know how she found that information, but her eyes showed no glimmer of lying. I tried to appeal to her rational side, assuming she had one and was willing to listen to it. "She's heavy."

"So?"

"So how are we going to get her up there?" I tried to estimate how tall the water tower was, but the more I tried to count the rungs of the ladder, the longer it extended to the sky. Hundreds of feet. Thousands. We struggled hauling the body when two of us were carrying her. How would we manage one handed, on a ladder, with gravity working against us?

I lift my head off the car door with a concerted effort. I close my eyes, count to ten, and slowly the spinning subsides.

The next entry in Abby's journal is markedly different. The slant in her letters is dangerously close to falling over completely. The loopy bee swirls are jagged and sharp, like she had to get her thoughts on paper before they exploded inside her brain.

How are we going to get her up there?

"She's not that big. There's a rope at the top. To the left of the hatch."

"How do you *know?*"

"I put it there," Jen said.

"You're kidding."

I waited for a joke that never came.

"One of us has to climb up and throw the rope over the railing," she said.

"And the other?" I asked, desperately wishing I was stuck in a bad dream.

"Will tie it around Nicole's waist and make sure it doesn't get caught on anything on the way up. Come on, Emme, try and keep up."

"I can't do this. We can go to the police. Tell them it was an accident."

"No." Jen grabbed my cheeks and forced me to lock eyes with her. "We can't. They won't believe us. We'll both go to jail. Kiss our futures goodbye. No prom, no college, no marriage—nothing. I won't spend the rest of my life in jail, Emilina. Not for this bitch."

"This isn't right."

"Right has nothing to do with it. None of this was right. Or fair. She would've ended up here one way or another." Jen didn't give me time to respond. She mounted the bottom rung. "I'm stronger. I'll pull from the top. All you have to do is bring up the caboose."

She scaled the ladder to the platform and threw down the length of black rope. It curled like a snake next to Nicole's body. Her eyes were half shut, glazed. Lifeless.

Clipped to the end of the rope was a harness. I felt a flutter of recognition. Before his heart attack, Jen's dad had worked for a utility company. Carol had stuffed his old safety gear—scuffed helmets and thick rubber gloves and a harness he used when he was out on the poles, among other things—into a box, storing it in the garage because she didn't want to see it but couldn't bear to sell it.

The realization hit me like a battering ram, how much thought she'd put into this. She wasn't acting in the heat of the moment; she hadn't made a mistake.

Jen had purposely taken her father's gear and left it at the water tower.

"Move your ass," Jen hissed from the top.

Numb hands aren't great for fastening straps to dead bodies. I struggled getting the harness over her shoulders and around her torso, struggled more securing it in a way that wouldn't send her tumbling down on my head. When I was sixty percent sure the buckles wouldn't unsnap, I signaled to Jen.

She braced her feet against the raised edge of the platform, wound the rope around her arm a few times, and tugged backward. She was wearing his gloves to protect her hands, too big but she'd thought to bring them.

Nicole flip-flopped, jerking awkwardly in the air. I held on to the ladder with my right hand and gave Jen as much leverage as I could. Slowly, I found my rhythm, and Nicole's body steadied. I put the brunt of the weight on my free shoulder.

Cheerleaders, I told myself. *We're practicing a new routine.*

Death smells terrible. It's clean on TV. The victims look peaceful and dignified. Nicole was none of those things. Her bowels had released—an interesting fact my biology teacher left out of the anatomy unit—and the mess leaked through the thin denim of her jeans. It seeped through my shirt, clogged up my breathing. Piss and shit and the sickly-sweet smell of her skin.

I went to a luau-themed party my freshman year of college. The frat went all out. Grass skirts and pineapples and a whole pig, roasting lazily on a spit that I could've sworn was Nicole's hip on my shoulder. I managed to vomit in the row of bushes to my right, and I never went to another luau.

"Hold up," I moaned, fighting the dizziness. I turned my head away, desperate for fresh air that didn't smell like Nicole. Forcing myself not to spew cafeteria lunch all over my shoes, I adjusted my grip and slipped. A tight scream escaped my lips, the jolt of panic sizzling as I slammed myself into the ladder. I caught her body around the thighs and hoisted her back up while Jen mumbled obscenities from her stoop.

My muscles burned, but I powered through. Onward and upward, as they say, until Nicole's shoulders cleared the platform. Her head banged hard on the metal base as Jen pulled her from my grasp. Jen's shirt was drenched with sweat, and the makeup she had applied another lifetime ago was smeared and smudged, but I've never seen her look so alive. So utterly present. Like she understood the universe and her place in the world.

I saw *that* Jen in the woods today. She hadn't disappeared with the destruction of her childhood nemesis. She'd merely been hibernating.

Together, we undid the harness and heaved her into the tank. Our eyes had long adjusted to the darkness, but Jen moved with familiarity that only comes with experience. Practice. How many times had she been up on that ledge before she pressed Nicole's palms together above her head in a morbid swan dive?

Or a futile prayer.

Her sides scraped against the metal of the tower, sending a shower of powder-blue flakes through the grated walkway.

Nicole's body splashed into the water with a hollow clunk. I didn't see her face as she descended. It was too dark, the drop too fast. But when I replay this moment, I see her lips part, a tear slides down her silvery cheek. Her dead eyes beg for help, locking on me as she plummets to her grave.

We were just kids, but look what we had done.

When we skulked down the ladder and hopped to solid ground, I was shaking. Jen was not. Calm and collected, she said, "Promise me, Emilina."

"What?"

"Promise me. Promise. You can't tell a soul."

"Okay." I just wanted to leave. I would've agreed to anything at that point to be as far away from Jennifer as I could get.

"No. Promise me. Say the words. You can't tell anyone, or I'll come after you next."

The commitment in her eyes. The gargle from Nicole's mouth. That was my reality, and I knew she was telling the truth. "I promise."

"Good. Now I need you to do something else."

"No. I'm done."

"This is important. You can't go home looking like that without an explanation."

I looked down at my soiled shirt, reeking of defecation. Nicole's blood sticking to my skin with Velcro strength. It was dark. The streetlights would be on when we got to the bottom of the hill. My dad would be in the beginning stages of worry. He might've even called Jen's house.

We're going to get caught, I thought.

"No, we're not—not if you do what I tell you to."

I didn't realize I had spoken the words aloud. "What's the plan?"

"You need to tell your dad I beat you up," Jen said.

"What?"

"We had a fight. I kicked your ass. Shoved you into a pile of dog shit."

"Jen, you know my dad. He's super protective."

"I'm counting on it."

"No, Jen. He'll ask for your head on a platter. He'll call the *cops*."

"Good. That's what I want."

"Excuse me?"

"It's the only way any of this makes sense." She motioned to my disheveled appearance and put her hands on her hips. "You won't make a big deal about it. A silly girl fight is what everybody'll think. Clothes, a boy—I don't care what you use as the reason. As long as we have the same story, no one will expect us to be involved in Nicole's disappearance."

"What about Mary?"

Jen smiled. "Mary will want to cover her own ass. She was drinking, remember? More eye drops than alcohol, but still. She'll admit to being at my house, that I gave you an attitude. She *will* probably make a big deal about it, like we were sworn enemies or whatever, but I don't think it'll get to that point."

"This won't work."

"It will. Nicole's going to be reported missing tomorrow, Saturday at the latest. Unless we do something stupid, they won't find her for months." She tilted her head and examined the water tower. "If at all."

Wind slithered against my damp skin until my teeth chattered. I could smell myself, the horrible stench of death and sweat and fear, and I wanted to run. Rewind to the moment I decided to follow them to the field and go home instead. Throw myself into bed and wake up to it all being a terrible nightmare.

"One more thing," she said.

"What's that?" I whispered.

"We can't be friends anymore."

I sputtered a laugh, saw the set of her jaw and realized she wasn't kidding. "You think I'd be friends with you after what you did?"

"What *we* did, Emme, and don't you ever forget it. I'll tell everyone you did it if you chicken out and change your mind."

"You can't do that."

"From this moment on, we're done. We'll never speak of this night again. We'll never *speak* again. Before long, it'll be like it never happened." Jen put her hands on her hips and surveyed our surroundings.

What else could I do but agree?

The beauty of hindsight is how often we imagine things would be different if we made the other choice. Took the road less traveled, as the saying goes. Everyone misinterprets that poem. That by taking the less-traveled path, you're opting for adventure, braving the unknown.

But that's what everyone gets wrong.

The paths are the same. It's the person who changes. We don't know that one choice over another brings us to where we are—or that reversing time and walking the other would have the opposite effect.

Perspective is what matters, the detail that gives hindsight its shimmery appeal.

Drenched in a cold sweat, I continue reading Abby's private thoughts, hoping this will lead me to the truth.

Abby's Journal

So when I got home, I locked myself in here and DMed Chris.

I need to talk to you, *I sent.* It's important.

I was not expecting him to answer. I've asked him a thousand times and he's never said yes before, so why would he start now?

CHRIS: *What's up*

ME: *CALL ME*

CHRIS: *OK*

OK?! I'm literally traumatized by how excited I was.

I was finally going to hear his voice. This boy who likes robots and gave me a butterfly necklace and understands who I am when I'm not Chloe.

Tay could write a song about it.

Somebody just knocked on my door. Nope. Prbly just JJ coming in from wherever but I don't want to see anyone.

My hands are shaking.

I'm about to break into Dad's stash and steal his bottle of SoCo. I've never *actually* drunk it but it smells like candy and I'm tempted.

Mom would kill me if Chloe Cates showed up to Bow-nanza photos drunk. Not a very good role model.

After what she did, tho, she's in no position to tell me no.

EMILINA

Nothing about this investigation has been straightforward—Abby's journal included.

Lying about socials to her parents is one thing, but a boy she met online?

If this really is a boy. Insta is breeding grounds for predators. I've seen too many catfishing scenarios, girls who are trying to escape bad home situations or their own ennui, but their Insta-Knight in Shining Armor turns out to be Larry Gilbert, thirty-seven-year-old sex offender.

I set the notebook down and dial Luke's extension. Luke's been a tech liaison on the team for the last four years. He spends almost as much time researching new hacking methods as he does lifting weights, and he'll talk your ear off about both, but he's a straight shooter and genuinely good at his job.

"Della Villa," he answers on the fourth ring. I hear the bustle of the station and the soft click of a keyboard.

"Luke, it's Emilina, I got your message."

"Oh, Stone, perfect timing. Cap's sending you the info in the next couple minutes."

"Info on what?" I ask. "Did you get something off the phone?"

"So, no, I'm still working on that, I just found a charger that fit. But I'm about done with the run-through of the family's social. Right off the bat, Abby's phone—the one we took from her bedroom—is clean. Like, factory reset clean. No pictures, no messages. No apps. I was expecting more from a teenager."

So was I. Could be she did have a second phone, after all. "This girl's monitored closely by her mother. Maybe she just deletes everything when she's done."

"That could be. According to the data, it was last reset about a month ago. Internet browser was wiped more recently, within the last few days, but I pulled the cached files, and there was nothing unusual there. Entertainment news sites, some clothing stores, Wikipedia."

"What else?" I ask.

"The blog's also clean; some overzealous fan emails, but nothing that raised a flag, you know? Same with the CC Spectacular Insta. The only messages I found were between the mother and MLM sponsors and some midlevel influencers she was trying to team up with. I dumped the deleted files, too, and found more of the same."

"You were able to access her deleted Instagram messages?" I ask.

Luke chuckles. "Everything's forever on the Internet, Stone. Clearing your caches doesn't do shit to protect against someone with my particular set of skills."

"Duly noted, Mr. Neeson."

He pauses to talk to someone in the background. "Sorry about that. Wild day here."

You don't know the half of it. "What about Abby's personal account?"

"Right, so, nothing suspicious on 'CC and Me' but Abby Scarborough's finsta is a whole 'nother story."

"Yeah, I don't know what that means, Luke."

"Finsta is a fake Insta. It's where you'd post something that doesn't fit with an account that you might want to keep more curated. Your Insta will have a polished aesthetic, all filters and color schemes or a theme, whereas your finsta will have . . . basically anything you wouldn't share with a mass following. Finstas are typically used for close friends, so where Chloe Cates has thousands of followers, Abby Scarborough's finsta only has a dozen."

"You can't just upload all of your pictures to a single profile?"

I hear the shrug in his voice. "You could, but an influencer who relies on a perfect image for income wouldn't be caught dead breaking from metrics."

Interesting choice of words. "All right, so this finsta. What'd you find?" I ask.

He clears his throat. "Messages from a boy who calls himself Fortnite-Chris. They go back a few months. Mostly innocent stuff. Griping about parents and schoolwork. But the last few got pretty heavy."

"How so?"

"They were talking about meeting, and from the gist of the messages, I'd say they did more than entertain the idea. I'd even venture a guess that they did meet in person, and it didn't go the way they planned. The communication stopped abruptly after."

Fuck. "Do you have any indication of whether or not FortniteChris really is who he says he is?" And not a forty-year-old man subsisting on cat food in a dank cellar.

More clicking. "Yeah, I checked out his stuff. A lot of these predatory accounts will have markers, as you're probably aware. Approachable pictures. Fun stuff that draws kids in, usually stolen from other accounts to make themselves look legit. For someone like me who knows how to access the embedded information, it's relatively easy to spot, but these guys aren't stupid. They'll try to cover their tracks. One thing I look for is how long the accounts have been active, right? An account created yesterday and has twenty pictures uploaded within an hour of one another is a huge red flag. FortniteChris, however, has had an account for three years. He posts pictures of his family and himself frequently, not generic stuff you can google for stock shots."

A string of tension releases. "Any chance of finding out his real name and location?"

"Way ahead of you, Stone. Cap talked with the DL at South and agreed to share information since we've still got a missing girl on our hands. He gave me the go-ahead to work my magic, so I was able to trace the IP to an address in Lower Madison. Got a hit. Registered to a Terrence and Amy Mitchell."

"What are the odds that out of everyone she could possibly meet on a secret Instagram account, a boy from Lower Madison was able to connect with Abby? Was her location turned on?"

"No, she had that disabled, but it could be as simple as clicking on a hashtag."

I thumb the corner of the journal like a flip book, concentrating on the *zwip, zwip, zwip* as I work through my thoughts. Minutes ticking by, making the most of daylight is pivotal. We're in crunch time now. Abby's words are important, but I need to see this guy for myself.

My phone buzzes. I check the screen and quickly scan Cap's text.

"Okay, 424 Hemmingford. The Mitchells, you said?"

"Yes, ma'am." Luke clacks the keys. "You want me to get dispatch to send a car to meet you?"

"No, but make sure Devon Blaisdell over in Homicide South knows I'm pursuing a possible lead. He was going to meet Joss to see about the autopsy."

"Will do."

I toss the notebook into the passenger seat. "Hey, can you do me another favor?"

"Shoot."

The real reason I called. "Radio Welsh. Have her bring in the Scarboroughs. Tell them we have some questions about Abby that need answering;

I really don't care how she swings it as long as they're at the station by the time I finish here."

"Okay, yeah, I'll do that now."

"Thanks, Luke." I end the call and enter the address into my map app.

As I drive past the uniform houses with their cute planters and budding spring decor, it's impossible to clear my mind. Nicole's gargle. Abby's disappearance. Missy Crawford's murder.

My pregnancy. Everything rushes together into a ball of anxiety. Do I really want to bring a child into a world full of dangers? Where we can do our best to teach our kids how to be good people but can in no way control the will or effort of others? Or guarantee that they'll take our advice in the first place.

I'm almost relieved when Siri announces I've arrived at my destination.

Lower Madison is the college part of town with an eclectic mix of residential and commercial property. This neighborhood was built in the '40s when one blueprint was used for an entire block. I park across from a gray two-story with a small but puritanically maintained front yard. A wind chime twinkles from the porch beside an American flag and a rustic wood etching that reads, THE MITCHELLS.

I ring the doorbell and step back. Two cars in the driveway. Light on in one of the rooms behind the gauzy curtains. After a beat, I hear footsteps approaching, and a short woman with a pineapple bun and the bowlegs of a practiced runner opens the door.

"Hi, can I help you?" she asks, eyeing me warily. Her blush sweater offsets a spray tan, and she tugs on a Pandora charm bracelet.

I show her my badge and watch the crease in her forehead deepen. "I'm Detective Emilina Stone. Are you Amy Mitchell?"

"Yes, I am. What's going on?"

"I was hoping to ask you a few questions about an investigation I'm currently working. Can I come in?"

She opens the door, scratching absently at her collarbone. "Please. Can I get you a bottle of water? Or I might have some iced tea."

"Water'd be great," I say, as she ushers me into the dining room. I take a seat at the far end of an expensive-looking banquet style table and study the pictures hanging above a vintage bar cart. Most include a teenage boy playing various sports; football seems to be the focus, though, as I count eleven shots of him in uniform, ball tucked under his arm or midtackle.

Amy Mitchell returns from the kitchen, harried and serious. "Is your son home?"

She hands me a bottle of water and rounds the table. "Yes, Chris is upstairs, probably on the PlayStation. He'd play that thing until his fingers fell off if we let him. Terry, my husband, says he can have two hours after practice as long as his stats keep improving on the field. I think his time'd be better spent outside, but kids don't really do that anymore. Go outside."

"Mrs. Mitchell," I say, "I hate to cut right to the chase, but I'm investigating the disappearance of a young girl from Upper Madison. Chloe Cates?"

Her eyes widen. "Oh my god, I knew you looked familiar. I saw you on the news earlier. That poor girl."

I feel my face flush. "Yes, well, I'm here because I have reason to believe your son may have recently been in contact with Chloe. I was hoping I could speak with him for a few minutes."

"Wait, you think my son had something to do with this?"

"I'd just like to talk to him."

"Christopher's a good boy."

"I'm sure he is, Mrs. Mitchell, but he and Chloe seemed to have gotten quite close over the last few months, and she may have confided in him. Sometimes kids share things with their friends that they might not want their parents to know."

Her eyes flicker to the pictures, trying to decide whether she wants to go along with this or see me to the door. Finally, she seems to make up her mind. She crosses her arms over her chest, slides her tongue over her teeth, and shouts, "Chris, come down here, please!"

"What?" His voice echoes through the house.

With an exasperated huff, Amy gets to her feet and stomps to the stairs. "Chris, get down here immediately or I'm cutting the Wi-Fi."

"Fine!" he shouts. Pounding feet above me. I follow his steps until I see him emerge on the staircase. We lock eyes, and his body goes tense. "Who's that?"

"Just come down here," she says. "We need to talk."

Dark haired and lanky, Chris passes his mother and makes it across the room in three loping strides. "Hey," he says.

"Chris, this is," she bites her lip and looks at me expectantly.

"Detective Stone. You can call me Emilina."

"Okay. Hi."

"How old are you, Christopher?" I ask.

Amy speaks for him. "He's fourteen. He'll be fifteen in a few months, though. Tall for his age. Got the height from my husband, but at least he got my skin."

"Mom, god, stop," he says.

I give a polite smile. "Christopher, this won't take long. I just need to ask you a few questions."

Amy reclaims her seat at the table and motions for her son to sit too.

He dumps himself into a chair and twitches nervously. "Okay . . . I dunno how I can help."

"I'm trying to locate a missing girl." I take out my phone and present him with a picture of Chloe.

"Who's that?"

"The girl from the news," Amy says. "Chloe Cates."

He shrugs. "Never heard of her, sorry. Is that it?"

Lie, and not a good one. His response is too vacant, his disinterest forced. I heard his sharp intake of breath when he saw her face. "Are you sure?" I flip to a picture of Abby I saved from her Instagram account next. "From what I understand, you and Abby spoke frequently."

His expression goes slack.

"Abby? Who's Abby?" Amy glares at him. "Have you been messing around with a girl from school?"

Chris cringes. "No."

Amy sighs. "How many times have we gone over this? Christopher, you know if you've been messing around with some girl during the season, your father's going to have a heart attack."

"I'm not messing around with anyone, Mom."

"Then who's Abby? And what does she have to do with Chloe Cates?"

"Abby's just a girl," he says. "She doesn't go to our school. I met her on Insta. We were just talking."

"An *online* girl?" Amy says.

"So, you are FortniteChris?" I ask, attempting to steer the conversation away from the argument they'll inevitably have after I leave.

"Yeah, that's me."

"And you've been talking to Abby via Instagram for months?"

"Chris?" Amy says the name with disdain, like I just served her roadkill on a silver platter. "What's she talking about, Christopher?"

His arms stretch across the table like limp noodles. He taps anxiously before drawing back into himself. "Nothing, it's not a big deal. Can I go now?"

"Not quite. Chris, Abby's missing."

Horror. Complete shock washes over him. He jolts in his seat and looks from me to his mother. "Missing? What does that even mean, like she was kidnapped?"

I put my phone away. "We think she may have been abducted. No one's seen or heard from her since last night, and we found some alarming evidence when we searched the home. I have to ask: where were you last night, Chris?"

"Home," he says without hesitation.

"The whole night?"

"Christopher had practice. An hour at the batting cages then an hour of field work and scrimmaging. They came back here for pizza after. All of them. Thirteen boys. Didn't clear out until almost one." Amy rips her phone out of her pocket. I hear the clicks as she taps out a message. "I'm texting my husband; he should be here for this."

"Do you have to?" Chris asks.

"She's asking for your alibi, Christopher, this is serious."

He gulps. A master criminal might be able to feign his terror, but Chris doesn't strike me as a particularly good actor. Plus, having your baseball team over for dinner is a pretty solid alibi.

If it's true.

"We will have to check with your teammates to verify that information. If you could give me a list of names that would be extremely helpful."

Amy dashes to the kitchen and returns with a printout of the roster. "The coach's number is listed on the bottom too."

"Thank you," I say, folding the paper. "Christopher, when was the last time you spoke to Abby?" I ask.

"I . . . dunno," he says, pulling out his phone. He taps and scrolls, shakes his head at the screen. "Like three weeks ago. Not since that night we hung out."

My ears prick. "So you did actually meet Abby?"

"Jesus, Chris," Amy says. "You *met* someone from the Internet? Are you out of your mind? What were you thinking?"

"Nothing, Mom, it's really not a big deal. Abby's not some rando girl from the Internet. She's just Abby. Kids do it all the time."

"No, they most certainly do not. Wait until your father hears about this."

"Come on, Mom—"

"Christopher, can you tell me about the last time you saw Abby?" I ask, speaking over them.

"He had nothing to do with that girl going missing," Amy reiterates. "He lied to us, yes, but he'd never do something so reckless."

Chris nods in agreement. "I really had, like, no idea that anything was going on."

"I'd just like to hear about the last time you saw her. Did something happen?" I ask.

"I guess, I dunno," he says. "There's not much to tell. We only hung out the one time. She'd been asking to chill for a while. I kept putting her off because I wasn't into her like that, but she was, like, really upset; and I wasn't supposed to do it, but I dunno, I said yes. I met her in the park and we hung out for a bit, and then my dad texted asking where I was, and I bounced." His eyes dart from me to the table and back again.

"I cannot believe you went behind our backs," Amy starts.

"I'm sorry." He scratches a freckle on his forearm, avoiding her gaze.

"What do you mean, you weren't supposed to?" I ask.

"What?" Christopher tries to act oblivious, eyebrows scrunched in confusion, but the table shakes from his jittering leg.

"You said you *weren't supposed to* meet Abby. I'm just wondering why you'd say that."

"Uh . . ." The table shakes faster. "Because of my mom and dad?" He rounds it into a question and searches my face for approval.

"But they didn't know about her."

His face reddens. "I, uh."

"You blew Abby off once before when you were supposed to meet, is that correct? On her birthday?"

He rocks a bit. "Yeah."

"But you went to the park and left her a present. A necklace?"

Amy sighs. "You gave this girl jewelry? How could you keep this from us? Do you have any idea—"

"No, I, it wasn't like that," he says. "She's cool. I was just trying to make her feel better."

"Christopher Thomas Mitchell, don't you dare lie to me. Right now, you'll be lucky if you get that phone back before you graduate from college, and I have half a mind to throw that game system in the garbage. I have to find out my son has a secret girlfriend who may have been kidnapped all in the same day."

"I don't have a girlfriend, Mom!" he whines.

"You gave her a necklace, but you didn't actually like her?" I ask. "You were using her?"

"No," he insists.

"So, explain to me how that works. Why give her the necklace? Why would you risk getting in trouble to meet someone you don't like?"

Chris runs both hands through his hair. "This is fucked up."

"Watch your mouth," Amy warns.

"Sorry, mom, but . . ." He flips his phone, wipes the screen, and stares at the ceiling. "This is not how this was supposed to go down. I'm, shit . . . she's really missing?"

I nod. "Chris, right now, you're not in trouble." Yet. Maybe he understands this, too, because he scoffs and crinkles his face. "But I need you to be honest with me. You seem like a nice kid. I don't think you meant to hurt her, but there are a lot of things that don't make sense here. I can't divulge details of an ongoing investigation, but I have to tell you, with the evidence we found and your relationship coming to light, you'd probably be the number one suspect if something has happened to her. We have her phone." Maybe both of them. "Tech's going through your messages as we speak. If they find something even remotely suspicious . . ."

"Do we need a lawyer?" Amy asks.

"I can't advise you either way on that decision, that is your right; but if your son is hiding something, we will find out."

"Christopher, if you know where Abby, Chloe—whoever—is, you need to tell this detective." Amy looks worried but alert. She links hands with her son and squeezes. "You didn't take that girl. He didn't take that girl," she says, raising her eyes to mine. "Check the house. She's not here."

He's sweating now. He withdraws from her grasp and puts both hands on his bouncing knees, leaning back against the chair. "I didn't do anything to her. Abby's . . . I dunno, okay? It just kind of happened."

"What happened?" I ask.

"This is so messed up," he mutters. "I just wanted the PS5."

I pause, his words filling me with dread. "I'm having trouble understanding you, Chris. What does a PS5 have to do with Abby's disappearance?"

His chest rises and falls faster. "She paid me to do it," he says.

I lean closer, attempting to piece together what he's saying. "Paid you to do what? Who is she? Do you mean Abby?"

Chris shakes his head. "No," he says. "Not Abby."

Abby's Journal

Good Girl Abby would never agree to meet a boy from IG in person. At night. In the middle of the woods.

Chris wasn't supposed to be like everyone else, though. He was supposed to be different. So when he said we could meet up instead of talking on the phone, I didn't bail. Mostly b/c I was pissed. I needed to talk to someone real and I didn't care if it was dangerous.

We met on the bridge at the park and ugh, swoon. I couldn't even look at him without giggling. He was literally the cutest boy I've seen IRL. Big Cameron Boyce smile. Dimples for days.

He said I was beautiful.

And I'm crying again, ugh.

OK. Trying to keep it together. I can do this.

I told him about the tree house. Suggested we go there. He wanted to hang out on the swings, but I was like

1. *There's too many people.*
2. *I have this rly cool setup where we can just chill and watch a movie.*

What I really meant was

1. *I don't want my Robot Eye Mother seeing us.*
2. *I don't want anyone recognizing Chloe Cates and blowing my cover.*

I could tell he didn't want to right away. He was going off about not liking the woods or how dangerous they were or something, and I'm like riiiight. Do you not want to hang out with me? He said we *were* hanging out but since it meant so much to me, then fine. Tree house it is.

It felt like I'd won a fight I didn't know we were having, but I was getting cold and just wanted to get away from the night runners and midnight dog walkers and weirdos.

We cut through behind the playground. I should've realized he was distracted, looking over his shoulder. Maybe I did and I chose to ignore it, IDK. I was distracted too. I thought he might hold my hand. I've never been alone with a boy before. Let alone kissed one. I thought I might have my first real kiss.

I couldn't stop smiling and wow, that makes me feel so stupid.

He didn't hold my hand. I brushed against him a few times but he stuffed his hands in his pockets and I gave up. We got to the tree house and he just stared at the ladder. I got this rly weird vibe from him and I got scared he was gonna leave, so I ran up the ladder before he could duck out.

If I had that charm Hermoine uses to be in two places at once, I'd rewind to that moment and GTFO.

He came up the ladder and sat next to me. He smelled like pizza and his leg was warm. I loaded Netflix on my tablet and he picked Umbrella Academy, *and for like 20 minutes, we just watched this superhero show. No talking or anything. Is this a date? I kept wondering. Is this what a date feels like? This jumbled question of does he like me or am I seeing something that's not there?*

He didn't move away from me, but he kept checking his phone. I could see it lighting up even though he told me he wasn't on it. I knew he was lying. Now I know why.

When the episode ended, he sat up and turned to me.

"All right," he said. "Abby, you're pretty cool."

Thanks, I said. You're cool, too.

"We should chill again sometime. I mean it," he said.

Yeah, that'd be ok with me.

Then he leaned in.

I can't. The butterflies in my stomach. I closed my eyes. This is it, this is it, this is it, my mind screamed. Like it was happening. Chris was gonna kiss me.

I held my breath. His lips brushed against mine. And then a flash went off.

My eyes were closed, so I thought I was losing it at first b/c why would there be a flash? Why would he be taking a picture while we kissed?

But when I opened my eyes, it wasn't Chris I saw.

It was a figure on the ladder. They moved so fast I wasn't sure I actually saw it at first but then I heard the clank of feet on the metal.

I screamed and fell back, throwing the freaking sheets over my head like a kid hiding from a monster under the bed.

"What are you doing?" Chris was staring at me like I was crazy.

I was like, tell me you saw that.

"What?"

Omgomgomg, there's someone watching us.

He stuck his head out. Shrugged. "There's no one out there."

I'm like I know what I saw.

He looked down again. I saw his phone light up but couldn't read who the text was from. "Ok," he said. "Stay here. I'll go check it out."

Um, NOPE. I tried to get him to stay but he kept shaking me off. He stopped on the ladder and stared at me with his big brown eyes and all the freaking butterflies went off and UGH.

"Don't worry, all right? I got you, just wait here."

That was it.

Alexa, play "drivers license" on repeat

I thought he was trying to impress me. My own personal superhero. Turns out I've just gotten so good at pretending I even fooled myself.

5 minutes. 10.

I tried texting him. Left on read. I called, went to voicemail. I was nervous. I couldn't wait out there all night. What if Chris got hurt trying to protect me from some psycho in the woods? I gave it another 2 minutes then got my shit and decided to go after him.

I was almost to the swings when I heard them.

Chris, holding his hand out with his back to me.

And my dad. With the camera. Giving money to Chris.

I didn't understand what the hell I was seeing.

My first thought was oh shit.

My second thought was nononononono.

Then it was a bunch of questions. Why is he here? What's with the money? Why did he take a picture? How did he know where I was? How does he know Chris?

Dad? I asked.

Chris jumped like he'd seen a ghost. Not my dad, tho. He didn't look surprised. He looked sad.

"Abby. Shit."

What's going on? I asked. My legs felt like spaghetti noodles and my skin was on fire. Chris? What is this? Why is my dad giving you cash?

"Sorry, Abby," Chris said, shoving the bills in his pockets. "I was gonna tell you, but I dunno. Sorry."

Sorry for what? Why are you sorry, Chris?

He wouldn't look at me.

Dad, what is going on? I asked. He wasn't talking either. I wanted to cry, but I tried to hold it in.

"I'm sorry we did this," he said. "You weren't supposed to find out tonight. We were going to tell you later. Together."

Did what? Tell me what?

"Yeah, I'm out," Chris said. "I don't want to be in the middle of this. Abby." *He shrugged and I swear I wanted to punch him right in the face.*

Chris? Chris!

He ran off. I started to run after him, imagining screaming at the top of my lungs in his stupid, beautiful face. No shame. I was gonna make him explain wtf he was talking about. But my dad grabbed me. I tried to push him off but he just squeezed harder. The camera fell.

"Stop, Abby. Stop. You can't—just listen!" *I finally stopped fighting. We were out of breath. It was dark but I could see he was crying. He grabbed the camera and made like he was gonna throw it but stopped at the last second.* "It was your mother's idea. Son of a bitch. Let me explain. She found your Instagram, Abby."

Shiiiiiiiiiit. How? I asked. I thought I was so careful but I should've known. Right away I was like wtf JJ. I didn't think he'd be that dirty and rat me out again.

"I know this is tough to hear, but I won't lie to you, Abby-girl. Not anymore. Mom installed an app on your and JJ's phones that let her track what you guys were doing. She found your account. She went through your messages and then made a separate account to reach out to Chris."

OMG.

"She told him who you were and asked for his help."

Why would she do that? I asked.

"Why does your mother do any of the things she does? She wanted to find a way to make you love CC and Me again."

I looked at the camera. He was carrying it in his arm like a baby.

What did she ask Chris to do?

"To keep talking to you. To—to act like he liked you. He screenshotted your conversations and sent them to her. I didn't know about this right away, Abby-girl, you have to believe me."

I broke down. The private things I shared. The lies. My mom. All of it.

I don't have to believe anything that you say EVER. How could she do that? I sobbed. And sobbed. And ugly cried. Kim Kardashian's got nothing on me. How could he do that to me? I asked. Why did he say yes?

He stared at his feet for a rly long time. "She paid him. A hundred bucks up front. And then tonight, he told her he was going to meet you. She said she'd double the amount if he kissed you at the park."

Gross.

He took the camera in his hands like a football. I couldn't stop looking at it.

So if Mom made the deal with him, then why are you here, Dad? Why'd you take a picture of us?

He sighed big. "You weren't supposed to see me. I've never used this stupid thing before." More curses before he met my eyes again. "Mom wanted a picture for the blog. Chris said he could take it and send it to her, but she said it had to be a Polaroid b/c she's got a vintage aesthetic picked out for some post she's writing that's supposed to be a huge success, I don't know. You know how she gets. She told me I had to come out here to make sure nothing got out of hand between you guys. That it was my responsibility as your dad."

Gross. Gross. Gross.

"And since I was going to be keeping an eye on things anyway she said it'd be no big deal for me to get one quick shot. You were supposed to be on the swings, but then you went in the woods and I had to follow. Did not expect you to be in a goddamn tree house, Abs. I was so focused on getting up the ladder without you hearing. I thought I pressed the button to override the flash but you saw how well that worked out. Christ, I'm the shittiest dad on the planet, aren't I? You probably hate me."

I just stood there. Everything hurt. Nothing made sense. Still doesn't. I don't know which is worse. Them lying or Chris agreeing to it. I can't trust anyone.

Why didn't you tell her no? I asked. You didn't have to listen to her.

"I wanted to, Abby-girl, I really did. But I can't say no to your mom." He got this scared look on his face, like pasty and washed out. Slenderman white. "Look, I don't have a good reason, ok? If I didn't do it, she would've done it herself, and I knew that would've been much worse. I couldn't talk her out of it, and I couldn't persuade her to change her mind. I thought this option was the lesser of two evils."

He pulled the picture out of his coat pocket and held it out for me. It's blurry. You can't see Chris at all. And I just thought, All of this, and she won't even have something she'll be able to use.

What's she going to do next?

I cried. He tried to put an arm around me and I jerked away. He made this noise like I hurt HIS feelings and he punched the swing set. Any other time I would've been worried, but I couldn't care less. I hope it hurts.

I'm hurt. I'm being raised by a crazy person. Held hostage in my own home. Forced to play a stupid part so Mom can feel important.

JACKSON

I take the left turn too sharply and the pizza slides in the seat. I slam the top of the box to keep it from tipping, but it'll be a greasy mess regardless. There should be a pizza seatbelt. A detachable carrier that hooks into the center console to—

A horn blasts. A bespectacled woman in a Subaru glares at me. Normally I'd give her a friendly wave of apology, but I hate Subarus. I jerk back into my lane and flip her off for good measure.

No friend-making on the road for me today.

I weave through the heart of downtown traffic and let my mind pick apart the last few months of my life.

The night Jen told me about Chris, I'd come home to a family I didn't recognize. Jen was chipper, attempting to bake a sourdough loaf while she hummed old-school Britney Spears. Abby, meanwhile, was upstairs belting out love ballads with her door closed. I rarely heard her sing anymore and hearing her harmonize the chorus to Usher and Alicia Keys's "My Boo" was like walking into the middle of a *Black Mirror* episode.

"Um. Darling Wife. What's wrong with Abs?" I asked her.

Instead of answering, Jen smeared flour down my nose and forehead with childlike glee. Her eyes glistened. She opened the camera on her phone and pressed herself into me. "You look good." She nuzzled close to my chest and held her arm out, above her head and angled slightly. "Tilt your chin down, Jackson. A little more. Perfect."

She snapped and swiped through the gallery. "Great. Let's do one more reel. My hair's a little flat." She dipped her finger into the flour and spread a dab on her cheek before touching up mine. "And maybe try to smile. We're experimenting in the kitchen. I'm your wife not your prison guard." She switched sides and recreated our angles. A husband prop.

I pushed away. I don't know why her cheery disposition set me off, but it did. I was at the end of my rope. I just wanted an answer. I didn't want to go through a dog and pony show to get it.

"Don't ignore me," I said.

"How am I ignoring you? We're taking a picture together."

"Okay, but why does Abby sound so . . ."

"So what?" she asked, grabbing a dish towel. "Happy? Enamored? Merry?"

"Yes." I said. "I mean, it's nice, I'm happy to hear her in a good mood for a change, but I wasn't expecting it."

She let her eyes rove over my face before leaning in conspiratorially. "Did you know Abby has another Instagram?"

"What?" She nodded, brows arched in our shared parental gossip. "No. We weren't going to let her have her own, were we? Didn't you delete it?" I deflated a bit. "Have you talked to her about it?"

And if you did, I thought, *why the hell is she serenading up there?*

Jen returned to kneading the misshapen dough ball. "*I haven't.*"

I didn't like the inflection. "So who has?"

Knead. Slap. Knead. Slap. "Chris."

"Who's Chris?"

I'll admit, I was a tad jealous. I pictured a man who slicked his hair with oil and took gym selfies with hashtags like #getswol and #legday. A man Jen had apparently entrusted to have important conversations with my daughter while I was at work trying to offset our spending deficits.

That pissed me off. I gripped the side of the counter. "You're seeing someone?"

"What?" Slap. The ball stuck to the counter. She wiped her hands on her apron then turned to the sink. "No. God, Jackson, is that what you think of me?"

Her denial fell flat. "Cut the bullshit, all right? I'm not playing this game. Who's Chris? Where'd you meet him?"

She dried off and tapped on her phone, the way she did when she wasn't interested in what I was saying. Do you know how hard it is to talk to someone who'd rather scroll through notifications? When we first met, she wouldn't even bring her phone on dates. She had a small hot pink camera she carried on a cord on her wrist, but she only used it for special occasions. Birthdays or parties or anniversary dinners.

Sometimes I miss those days.

"You know, I'm sick of this. I'm trying to have a serious conversation with you and I might as well be talking to a cardboard cutout. Head down, texting like I'm not standing right in front of you. Is what he has to say really that important? Or can *Chris* wait until we're done? Wouldn't want to impose."

"Oh, would you stop," she said, thrusting the phone in my face. "*This* is Chris."

A lump of concern swelled in my throat and dropped three levels. It was a boy, no older than JJ. Dark hair, dark eyes, doing what Jen called an

"Insta-pose." Not looking directly at the camera. That hazy lost look. A surprised-on-purpose candid.

"You can't be serious."

Jen laughed. "Jesus, Jackson. I'm not sleeping with him." Barely above a whisper. "Of course you'd jump to that conclusion."

"What's that supposed to mean?"

Her patented, "don't-be-dumb" smirk was the only response.

There was some inner debate about putting up a fight, but ultimately, I thought it better not to. With Jen, I have to choose my battles carefully. "Who is he then?" I asked.

"Chris is Abby's first boyfriend."

"What?" I asked. "How? When did she meet him?"

"Recently. They've been chatting," Jen insisted. "It's cute, actually. And this will be good for her. She needs to vent to someone."

Vent. "And you're really okay with this?"

Jen hemmed and hawed and rolled her eyes, as if she were also admitting this to herself. "Okay. So. Technically. The situation's a little more complicated."

There it is. "How much more?"

"A bit. Let me start from the beginning." She glanced toward the doorway before continuing. "A few weeks ago, I found out that Abby was talking to this kid on Instagram. Innocent, but they seemed to be getting along well. I could tell Abby was starting to trust him, but I was afraid of where that might lead—she's not exactly forthcoming with me at the moment, as you know—so I took control of the situation."

"What did you do?" I asked.

She sighed. "Everything's fine."

"What does *fine* mean, Jen? That's not an answer."

Upstairs, Abby tapered off a high note and rolled into the next song.

"We have an arrangement, Chris and I," Jen said. "I reached out to him, introduced myself as her mother, said I wanted to talk to him about his discussions with my daughter, and, you know."

"No, I don't know."

Plucking at her nails, her whole body jittered nervously. "It's nothing. I just offered him a deal of sorts. I didn't want him to disappear when she clearly was bonding with him. Could you imagine having her heart broken on top of all the other attitude she's got going on? No. We'd all go crazy. So, I took care of it. Abby gets a companion, the opportunity to really enjoy her first crush, and Chris gets a little monetary incentive to go along with it. Venmo is incredibly convenient, and considering what I've paid for editing programs, this is a steal. Win-win, really, when you think about it."

"And what do you get, Jen?" I asked.

She shrugged. "I get to enjoy my daughter's happiness."

"That's it?"

"And," she stretched the word. "Chris agreed to be featured as a love interest on the blog as long as we didn't use his name. Not a problem, a code name will be fun. I'm thinking something with a throwback vibe when I get this series of posts with their DMs edited. Dylan, maybe. Or Chad. Everybody loves a good Chad. I don't know, I haven't made up my mind yet, but I'm putting the pitch together. I've got a feeling this will be huge."

"Oh, for fuck's sake, Jen."

"What?"

The idea of tricking Abby tore at my gut, but it's not like I had a leg to stand on. I failed her when she was four and Jen implanted the idea of the blog in her head.

And mine.

I've learned from JJ. The mistakes I made, the loneliness I felt. I can help other mothers, Jackson. To feel less alone. To let them know the sleepless nights and diaper blowouts don't last forever. And we can make it a family thing. Chloe will be front and center, but there's a place for JJ. He'll be included, too, but girls are more marketable for something like this. It's perfect timing.

The dashboard clock reminds me that our timing is anything but perfect. I've failed her.

Jen took my bargaining chips years ago when she found those photos on my phone. That ship sailed, as they say, but I thought I was still on course. Turns out that I've just been navigating away from rocks and into icebergs.

The light turns red, and I ease to a stop. Out the window, I watch the evening bustle of the city. Couples strolling to their reservations at one of the four fusion places on this strip. The tail end of a pickup game at the community rec center, players filing out with jerseys slung over their shoulders.

So normal. Oblivious to my daughter's disappearance.

I could still turn around.

No.

Maybe.

I tap along to the music on the steering wheel. I'm not actually considering this. I'm going home. I have to.

I check the clock again. This damn light is so long.

My phone buzzes in the cup holder and my heart stops. I flip it over, chest constricting with anticipation.

TODAY ONLY. SAVE FIFTEEN PERCENT ON YOUR FAVORITE HOME ESSENTIALS WHEN YOU USE TARGET CIRCLE.

"Fucking Target," I exhale.

Discount notifications galore, but no updates on Abby since I left over an hour ago. An hour? Shit, how did that happen?

Turn around.

I can't.

Who's going to believe it took me over an hour to get pizza?

"Fuck." I roar, my voice reverberating. "Fuck, fuck, fuck." The release is welcome.

Finally, the light changes, and I turn left onto Western. The road stretches in the headlights before me as storefronts give way to housing developments, cheekily dubbed by allusions to Robin Hood. Sherwood Forest Ave. Marian Drive. Nottingham Terrace.

Must be nice to be a masked vigilante. Nobody but the villain questions whether or not Robin Hood is committing a crime, because in legends, the good guy can do something bad and not only get away with it, but be praised for the transgression.

I doubt anyone's going to want to give me a medal after today.

I'm filled with a sense of impending doom. The inescapable confrontation that's waiting for me.

What am I going to say to Jennifer? We have to talk about this before it's too late, but where do we even start? How do two people have an honest conversation when the road to truth is paved with lies?

As I slap the turn signal, the rearview lights up with flashing red and blues. A siren whoops. I stare into the mirror, palms slick on the wheel, unable to comprehend the police cruiser behind me. Did they see me? What do they know?

I'm done.

Throwing on the hazards, I pull over and squint into the side mirror. A silhouette emerges, nothing but a bulky shadow in the light, and slowly walks toward me.

"*Shit*," I groan, rolling down the window.

"Mr. Scarborough?"

The familiar voice breaks me out of my thoughts. "Officer Welsh?" My hand slips into the handle, but she stops me before I open the door.

"Please, stay in your vehicle, Mr. Scarborough." Cold. Distant.

I release my grip and give her a quizzical look. "What's the problem?" I glance at the speedometer. "I'm sorry if I was going too fast. I'm just—time got away from me and I really need to get home."

She bends to better see my face. "It's not that. Detective Stone asked me to find you." Her gaze flickers to the pizza box. "You've been gone for quite a while."

"Yeah, I—sorry. I needed to catch my breath. Rough couple of hours, you know?" I offer my best humble smile, somewhere between a smirk and a frown, and furrow my brow. "Is something wrong? Did you find her?"

"There have been some developments," she says cautiously. "We need to ask you some questions."

Developments? Questions. The band in my chest tightens. "Like what, what does that mean?"

"Mr. Scarborough, it would be easier if you could come down to the station. We don't want to do this here." She tilts her head toward the curb where I notice a few residents from Loxley Lane have gathered, drawn by the police presence.

Rubberneckers. I'm sure this will make excellent fodder on their HOA discussion board.

"All right," I agree. "I'll just swing by the house. Drop off the pizza and pick up Jen and JJ. We'll meet you in half an hour?"

"Actually, no need to go home. You can follow me to the station from here."

"Why?" I ask.

Welsh stands. "Save you the trouble. Your wife's already there."

JENNIFER

Something's happening.

Downy consumes the doorway with his evasive responses and one-word answers. *Yes. Certain developments. No. We'll discuss this at the station.*

"I don't understand. Am I under arrest?" I ask.

"No."

But his eyebrows scurry together into a solid caterpillar of everything he's not saying. Not under arrest. *Not yet.*

"Please, be honest with me. Is it bad news?" I ask, cupping my hands together. "Have they found her?"

"Detective Stone will answer your questions when we get to the station."

"What's really going on, Officer Downy?"

"Best we get moving," he says.

I run a hand through my tangled hair and feel my face flush in shame as I recall the moment I stepped out of the shower. The wave of shame. Until that point, my tears were controllable. A release from the overwhelming discoveries today has brought to light.

Those tears, though. They burned. I've never cried like that before and I'm paying for it. Not even James Charles could fix my face right now.

"All right," I say. "Sure. Anything we can do to find Chloe, right?" Suddenly, I can't keep my thoughts straight. "Um . . . right, let me just grab my purse. Have you seen my phone? Jackson should've been home by now. I should call him. Do you need JJ to come with us? He's at his friend's house across the street."

"Probably good he stays there," Downy says. "For now. Send him a message on our way out."

Well, that sounds loaded.

"Right." I bustle to the kitchen and root around stacks of bills and advertisements for my phone. I find it charging next to the Bow-tastic! box and have to fight the déjà vu rising in my gut. Focus. Okay. I bring up JJ's text thread and let him know what's going on.

Downy grabs the communicator on his shoulder. "87, be advised," he says, pressing his mouth close to the receiver. "10-5 Detective Stone, en route to station. No sign of Mr. Scarborough."

"He went to pick up pizza on Western," I say, but the response sounds like an excuse. Like I'm covering for him.

"Welsh is going to run a patrol over that way. I'm sure she'll pick him up." He sets his jaw, an unreadable expression crossing his face. "We should get going."

Scooping up my purse in a haze, I mumble acquiescence. Downy walks beside me to the car.

The cameras start immediately. I hope my expression reads confident yet concerned, but with the bombardment of flashes, I'm not sure I give more than a grimace. I imagine the stories they'll concoct. Headlines turning against us. MURDER MOM. CC AND MAYHEM.

People love to watch the mighty fall.

I would know.

What they haven't seemed to have figured out is I won't let myself fall. I will not lose control again. This *will* turn around. No more bottom-tier influencer luncheons where the swag bag is nothing but a Ziploc full of samples. No more we-can't-afford-its. We will go global. International ad campaigns. Interviews on every afternoon talk show. A tasteful indie film that solidifies Chloe's place in the celeb-sphere.

We can control this narrative. We can come out on top.

As long as I remember who I am and how I got here.

Downy opens the rear door of the police cruiser and steps aside.

I hesitate. Going in for questioning is one thing. Being escorted out of my home and shoved into the back of a cop car is another matter. "Is this necessary?"

"Hey, I'm not cuffing you."

"Cuffing me?" I say taken aback.

He opens the door wider.

We could've driven in together, a show of unity, if Jackson hadn't decided to go for a culinary joyride.

I take one last look around the neighborhood. Beyond the news vans and cameras, behind the flickering curtains and neighbors' curious stares, not much seems different. Snow melts. Daffodils add bright pops of yellow to the dreary landscape.

All of this, and none of this, the same as it was yesterday.

I duck my head into the cruiser and brace for what's to come.

Abby's Journal

APRIL FOOLS!

Story of my life, amirite? The joke. Is always. On me. Like remember that time Mom decided to ruin my life? Trick question! That's every day.

I told her I hated her when I finally came home from the tree house. I said it once and I couldn't stop saying it. I hate YOU. I HATE you. I HATE YOU.

Didn't make me feel any better tho. I'm still miserable. JJ's been at the Fletchers. And at practice. Basically anywhere but here. I don't think he knows exactly what happened but he knows something's going on and he wants no part of it.

Yesterday I was going to go to the park for a run but I can't even look at the bridge anymore. I took the butterfly necklace off and was def gonna throw it in the trash but I couldn't. It hurt too much, so I just put it in the bin in my closet so I wouldn't have to look at it anymore.

Mom's giving me the cold shoulder. Punishing me for not doing CC Spectacular. She's running out of emergency material. Stressed af but I don't care. Not my problem. I don't think I've ever gone this long without doing a skit. It feels weird. But good. Good I guess. It's strange. OK. IDK, it's whatever. I won't do it and she can't make me.

Mom and Dad are fighting. Pretty sure he's sleeping in the living room. I hear him creeping downstairs. I guess I don't blame him. I don't want to see her and he's supposed to sleep in the same room. Nope.

Wait, I think he's coming back upstairs. I hear someone.

OK. Wow. Um, so, Dad wrote me a note and put it under my door. He used to do that when I was a kid and sad I didn't get invited to any real slumber parties.

I don't know what it means. I tore it up and flushed it down the toilet.

It said: I think I have an idea.

EMILINA

Trips down Memory Lane aren't really my forte. I like my past in the rearview, a distant dot in the background. That night in the woods made me the person I am today—whoever that person is. Good or bad. Probably somewhere in between. I've taken children from abusive situations and placed them with loving families, ones who provide meals and hugs and tender words. I've reunited missing children with worried parents, abandoned children with guardians, and once, I negotiated the release of a hostage when a troubled girl's strung out boyfriend used her as collateral in a bank robbery gone wrong.

But I did nothing to stop Nicole from being murdered.

I also helped hide her body.

Jen was right in her assumption that my dad would hit the wall when he saw me. Hell, Patrick almost drove over there himself, he was so livid. I was disgusting. Bruised. Shaken. I cleaned up as best I could with handfuls of wet leaves on the ground, but the point was to look like I got jumped, so I didn't try too hard.

He called the cops. He wouldn't take no for an answer, but at least he let me shower first. I couldn't let them find a dead girl's blood on me. I burrowed my soiled clothes deep into the trash on the way out. He brought me to the station where a kind officer took pictures of my injuries and made me write a formal statement.

Jen and her mother showed up an hour later.

With all her planning, I don't think she quite understood that nobody was required to do things her way. In her mind, she thought she'd be verbally reprimanded. A proverbial slap on the wrist.

I wasn't supposed to press charges.

But I wanted her to think I would, at least for a little while. I was angry. Scared. I knew I wouldn't really go through with it. But she deserved to sweat for what she'd done to Nicole, and in turn, what she forced me to do.

That was the first time I lied about what happened that night. I did it again when Nicole was reported missing, and Mary told them she'd been with us the night before.

They interviewed everyone. As Jen's former BFF and one of the last people to see Nicole alive, that included me. I stuck to my story, but it took a toll on me. I couldn't eat. Couldn't concentrate. And when I managed to sleep, I had horrible nightmares. Every siren in the distance was coming for me. Every knock on the door was the police. We wouldn't get away with it. I was going to jail.

We didn't speak after the interviews. Attention eventually died down, her disappearance explained away as a warning not to do drugs or get involved with a bad crowd or whatever convenient excuse parents needed to convince their kids to follow the rules.

But Jen followed me in the halls, wanting me to know that she knew, and she was watching.

They never found the body.

To this day, Nicole is still listed on the Missing Persons website. Her mother calls the station on the anniversary of her disappearance every year. To keep her hope alive. To remind them that she's never been found.

That's a pain for which I can't atone.

I've thought about going out there a million times, calling in an anonymous tip to put her to rest, but something always stops me.

No, not something. Selfish fear. I can't tell anyone about what Jen did to Nicole without implicating myself. Statute of limitations doesn't apply to murder. Or accessory to murder, for that matter. I'd be arrested. I would lose everything—my career, Drew, everything.

Twenty years since that night, and for all the good I've put back out into the world, I can't escape my mistake. The *thunk* of the bottle. The stink of the gore.

Twenty years later, another girl is dead and one more is missing.

She will die if I don't get this right, I'm sure of it.

I stride down the corridor and open the door to the digital command center. Luke mans the desk, fretting over lights and switches and adjusting monitors until he's satisfied with their positions.

"Hey, Luke, how's it going?" I ask, handing him a cup of coffee.

"Still working on that phone," he says. "But almost set in here. I want to have everything ready to go if this turns into a formal interrogation. Think that's where this is headed?"

"I don't know."

He sips from the disposable cup and grimaces. "I cancelled my date for this. Third time this month. I doubt she'll hang around much longer, but honestly I'd rather be here. She has this weird obsession with couponing, and I'm just not in that kind of place yet, so—"

"Luke, catch me up on that later, all right?"

He gives a mock salute. "Will do."

Central District is old and compact compared to the spacious metallic and chrome of South, but I've managed to wrangle two interview rooms for the Scarboroughs. Side by side, identical in every way save for the person who fills them.

On the left is Jennifer, of many names and temperaments. As she waits, she sits calmly at the table, occasionally crossing her arms and shaking her head, as if she can't believe where she is.

On the right is Jackson Scarborough, all-around average husband in spite of his gold star profile. Generally inoffensive in his interactions and vanilla on paper. No priors. No documented history of violence.

Jackson hasn't stopped moving. He picks his teeth in the mirror. He tries sitting, but that lasts mere seconds before he's up and circling the table. Currently, he paces the compact room. One wall, pivot. Corner, pivot. Corner, pivot. Back to Go and around the Monopoly board again. Then in reverse.

The door screeches behind me and Cap enters in a flourish. He takes in the various digital setups we've got going to record these interviews, nods to Luke, and joins me at the window.

Cap is tall and lean with high cheekbones. The team jokes that he's Idris Elba's American cousin. Tonight, however, his usual pristine appearance is marred by dark circles and day-old stubble. His shirt is wrinkled at the elbows and waist and an extra button is undone at the collar.

He flips through the red notebook now, a befuddled whoosh of air releasing as he finishes the last paragraph. "Who's up first?" he asks.

"Haven't decided yet," I say, checking the acoustic bar and microphone settings.

"Bullshit, Stone, I know you've got a batting order."

I laugh. "Honestly Cap, this is like a two-headed coin. She's cool as a fucking cucumber, and he's got more ants in his pants than a picnic in July."

"Sounds like you've got some fumigating to do."

"Sick burn," Luke adds.

I tilt my head at the banter. "I'll do my best."

He passes me the journal. "Forensics get back to you?"

"Waiting on labs, but I called Devon."

"Homicide Devon?"

"The one and only. Jocelyn left a message with her prelim results on the body. Blunt force trauma, COD. Something round and flat for the weapon but she didn't have specifics yet. They were also able to pull three sets of fingerprints from the scene. One's a partial on the ladder. The second was on the tree house door but might be too degraded for accuracy. The third, however, was clean, she said. On the floorboard beneath the victim's head. She's got them processing with a latent print expert and I'll get that update by Monday, Tuesday, at the latest."

"Not bad for Homicide, but that doesn't do much for us now."

I chew on the next observation. "I invited him to sit in on this. Devon. He's on his way. Wants to ask them some questions about Missy Crawford. I know we wanted to be able to placate the public outcry, but they have to be connected, Cap. Luke's working on the second phone we got from JJ Scarborough."

"Spidey magic. Actually, Spiderman doesn't do tech, so I guess it's Ironman magic?"

"Luke," Cap says.

"Right." He turns back to the board and adjusts another dial. Behind him, Jennifer checks her watch and examines her nails, while Jackson continues his expedition around the room.

"Where are we with the former friend and Internet boyfriend?"

Despite the sleepless nights that come with this job, Cap remains level-headed. Rarely is he satisfied with a gimme clue, encouraging our team to go the extra mile. To identify, support, and confirm our suspicions before we make a move; because when you're dealing with the strain of missing persons, the margin for error is incredibly slim.

"I've got a couple of officers checking alibis for the Forests and the Mitchells. There's a lot of animosity brewing amongst these families, and we can't deny the common denominator between everyone is Chloe Cates."

He thumbs his chin and examines the Scarboroughs, eyes flicking from one to the other. "I see your point."

"Look at these." I unlock my phone and flip through the pictures I took at the crime scene. Connecting the dots. "We thought it was Abigail Scarborough in that tree house—similar build, hair color, even the clothes match the description we were given. Too similar for this to be unrelated."

Cap grimaces. "Fuck, put that away."

"Sorry."

"Where are you going with this, Stone?"

"Joss said it's possible that the body was out there for a week, but that makes even less sense to me. Where's the blood? That scene is not consistent with the COD."

"You found traces of blood in the yard, correct?"

"And the strands of hair, yes."

"Are you suggesting it might be Missy's and not Abigail Scarborough's?"

"I think it's possible. Lab's running DNA, but it's too big to dismiss as coincidental. Do we have enough for a search warrant?" I ask.

"Homicide can handle a search warrant if they deem there's adequate reason to investigate the Scarboroughs."

"But they don't have the same incentive to move. We need as much information as we can get if we want to find Abigail Scarborough alive."

He sighs. "It's late, but I'll make a few calls, pull some strings."

"Try Judge Alameda," Luke suggests. "He spends most of his weekends streaming *Downton Abbey* and researching a historical fiction book he wants to write. Had me look at his router a while back because his Wi-Fi is straight shit."

"I'll see what I can do," Cap says. "Might be enough to get the ball rolling on our end. You really think one of them killed Missy Crawford?"

Promise me, Emme.

"I don't know. I can accept that maybe they neglected to tell us about Missy at the meet and greet because they were distressed about Abby's disappearance; but something's not right. Between the DNA and finger-prints and their shaky stories, I think we'll have enough to send them to the DA on a silver platter."

"Let's not jump the gun," he says. "That's a hell of a lot of variables. I've seen cases with more evidence dismissed for less." He grazes a palm against his five-on-the-verge-of-eight o'clock shadow. "But, I agree. Clock's ticking. You better get started."

I pat Luke's shoulder. "Text me when Blaisdell gets here and be ready to go."

"I was born ready, Stone," he says, reclining in his swivel chair. I'm amazed it can hold his weight. He's built like an oak tree.

"Right, well," I say, giving my reflection a once-over before my gaze focuses on the person behind it. "Here we go."

If push comes to shove, my history with Jennifer will come out. It'll have to. This time, though, I'm ready for it. I might not be prepared for the fallout, but I'll worry about that after we find Abby.

I stick the notebook under my arm, shake out my nerves, and open door number one.

JACKSON

They make these rooms uncomfortable on purpose. The hard-backed chairs and bad lighting. The goddamn mirror, I'm like a zoo animal. Worthy of being observed from the outside, but not given the courtesy of explanation.

Pacing helps.

No, it doesn't.

What's going on? What's taking so long? Why am I here? That's what they want me to think. They want me to confess. Break down and admit to the crime.

I won't. I repeat it with each step. I won't confess. I won't confess. I will not tell a lie.

I'm on the nineteenth lap when I hear a click and the door opens.

"Mr. Scarborough," she says. "Sorry to keep you waiting."

"Detective Stone. Do you have any idea what's going on? I'd appreciate an update. Why am I here? Have you found her? Is she all right?"

"We're following up on a new lead, Mr. Scarborough. For now, why don't we take a seat and discuss the matter."

"Am I under arrest?" I blurt.

She looks at me quizzically. "No. We're just having a chat." She sits and motions to the chair across from her. "If you'd be more comfortable with a lawyer present, you're perfectly within your rights to do so. Up to you."

"No, I don't need a lawyer."

"Okay, well, if you change your mind."

"Got it."

"Won't you join me?"

"I'm good, thanks." That's when it all starts going downhill. Next, she'll ask me if I'm thirsty so she can take my DNA off a cup.

"Suit yourself." She shrugs and tosses a file onto the table. She wants me to ask what it is. Why else would she put it there?

When I don't say anything, she places the red notebook with the file. My traitorous feet move forward like a moth to a flame. "Is that Abby's?"

I'm screwed. Breaking my own rules in under five minutes.

"This," Stone says, caressing the cover, "made for some interesting reading."

"I didn't know she had one." I pull the chair out and sit. Strike two.

"To be fair, I didn't tell my dad I had a diary either. The whole point is to keep it a secret. Abby wrote a lot, actually. Lots of behind-the-scenes insight about the blog and your wife. JJ—she loves him, you know. What a great brother."

"He is. We're very lucky."

"Lucky," she clucks her teeth. "Is that how you'd describe your family? Lucky?"

"Luckier than some. We've been fortunate in many ways."

She retreats a bit, presses her back to the chair. It squeaks, a nails-on-chalkboard shriek that grates my teeth. "Tell me about yourself, Mr. Scarborough. Can I call you Jackson?"

"Sure."

"Jackson, then. Let's start there. You were born in Syracuse?"

"Yes. I lived there until I graduated from high school."

She smiles. "Go Orange, right? Love that mascot."

I nod slowly, not really in the mood to bond over Otto and college football.

"How did you meet Jennifer?"

This is an easy question, one that every couple in the history of monogamy is asked at some point or another. "We met in college. I was playing ultimate Frisbee with my friends on the quad when I saw her coming from the Communications center. A stunner. The most beautiful girl I'd ever seen." An embellishment, but it always gets me some brownie points. Usually. Emilina remains stoic. "I smiled and waved and completely missed my buddy's throw. Hit me right here," I tap the side of my head, "and I fell flat on my face. Not my smoothest move, right?" I chuckle. She doesn't reciprocate. "But I knew when she smiled back that she was the one I'd spend the rest of my life with."

"Aw. Cute," she says, but her tone is flat.

"Yes. A shame we're not meeting under better circumstances. I'm afraid we're not our best selves today," I reply.

"Understandable." She crosses her arms over her chest. The buttons of her shirt pucker slightly, and I make sure not to get caught noticing it a second time.

"Yes."

"So," she says, switching from scrutinizing detective to engaging interviewer. "Jackson Scarborough. Married to the most beautiful woman he's ever seen. Two kids—*beautiful* kids, I might add—living in suburbia in this modern-day happily ever after."

I offer a placating gesture and drop my hands to my lap.

Stone's eyes float across my face, slightly narrowed and searching. "What do you do for work, Jackson?"

"Uh, marketing. I'm an Associate Director at Ignita. Corporate accounts, but I handle most of the foreign markets, so you probably wouldn't be familiar with the companies."

Her eyebrows raise. "Wow, impressive."

"It has its moments."

"Did you go to school for marketing?"

"No," I say, clearing my throat. "Education."

"A teacher. Noble profession. I could never do it. Too much work and not nearly enough pay. Do you know the average teacher puts over two thousand dollars of her own money back into the classroom every year? They pay for their own materials and don't even get a tax break. Crazy."

"Yeah, that is crazy." Parrot.

"Sounds like you made the right choice getting out when you did. What changed your mind?"

Careful. "Mostly what you said. I realized I'd be paying student loans until I died."

"Of course." She taps the notebook and stares at me. "Are you happy, Jackson?"

"Sorry?"

She glances up, an infinite gesture of inclusion. "In life. Would you say you're a happy person?"

"Normally, yes."

"But not today."

"No, today my daughter was kidnapped and you're more interested in talking about my college years."

"You know what, you're right. Let's talk about the present instead. Tell me about the weeks leading up to Abby's disappearance. What were they like?"

"Stressful," I say before I can censor the response. It's hot in here. My shirt sticks to my neck and under my arms.

"That doesn't sound particularly happy. What made them stressful?"

"I'm sure you know, otherwise I wouldn't be here."

"Humor me," she says. I don't like how relaxed she sounds.

My eyes fall to the journal. What could be in there? What did you write, Abby?

"Ah, you know. Normal stuff. We spread ourselves pretty thin. My schedule's busy this time of year, all those first quarter lags ramping up for the bread-and-butter accounts. JJ's starting varsity this year, which we're very proud of, but that means we're shuttling him to extra practices and pitching clinics. Jen had Abby signed up for these promo test shots with new sponsors."

"You're referring to Bow-tastic!?"

"Yeah, that was the biggest, but there were a few others in the works."

"How did Abby feel about the deal?"

Why does she want to hurt me? "I'd say she had a mixed reaction to it. She's been down lately."

"Down." Stone gives a questioning frown.

"That's what I said."

"Elaborate. Please." She takes out a notepad and writes. The pen scratching against the paper is like wasp wings in my ear.

"Well, after the mall show, which again, I'm sure you've seen by now, Abby made it clear to Jen that she needed a break."

"A break from your wife?"

"The blog, but I guess they go hand in hand."

"*Jackson.*" Emphasis on my name, like we're a couple of buddies arguing over baseball stats. "Let me get this straight. Abby told Jen she didn't want to be on the blog anymore."

"No, she just asked for some breathing room. Wanted some time to figure things out for herself."

"But your wife continued to post about her."

"I don't know. That's Jen's thing. You'll have to ask her."

Stone takes some papers out of the folder. "I mean, where's the line? Babies don't have input over whether or not their lives are posted on social media. I can't remember the last time I scrolled through my time line and my friends weren't sharing milestones. Birthday parties, Christmases, Disney. That's the way things are today, right? If it's not posted, did it even happen?"

"I guess so. I'm not online much."

"I laughed at that TBT video Jen shared of Abby—excuse me, *Chloe*—a few weeks back. She had to have been two or three. Painting her face with peanut butter and running naked through the house. Do you remember that?"

I nod, the room blurring under my tears.

Stone pushes the papers across the table. "But Abby's not a baby anymore. She's old enough to understand the potential ramifications of having her entire life published on the site. To care about what other people think of her. She's certainly old enough to be keeping you afloat financially."

I stare at the information, blinking away the glaze. "You checked our bank statements?"

"Jennifer granted permission to the officers who arrived after the initial 911 call. Standard procedure in suspected kidnappings. We monitor the accounts for suspicious activities. Wireless transfers or ransom demands."

"I see."

"I'm no expert, but that red number there," she says, tapping the negative balance, "might explain some of the stress. It also might explain why Abby's requests to be removed from the blog fell on deaf ears."

Stone splays more bills across the table. I scan the numbers, first with disbelief, then with despair. The details pour out like soured honey. We've missed bonuses for months. *Months.* And Jen didn't say a word. The money we paid Chris. The specialized decorations for the new shoots. She bought personalized goddamn Chloe candies for Abby's birthday, but we can't afford a bag of groceries.

"You know, Jen offered a reward for Abby's return when she hijacked the press conference. Doesn't seem to me like you have much to leverage, though."

Two months behind on the mortgage and car. *Four* credit cards maxed and two more within a hundred dollars of their limits. Even if Bow-tastic! had paid a hefty advance, there's no way it would've covered half of our debt ratio.

"You seem surprised by this," Stone says, jotting more notes on her little pad.

"Jen's in charge of the bills," I say, skimming another page.

"Someone should tell her that."

I shove the papers away. "Money problems don't make us guilty."

"Guilty of what, exactly, Mr. Scarborough?"

"Of whatever it is you're trying to get us to confess to in this clown show. You should be out there searching for Abby. Going door to door. Have you even considered the registered sex offenders in our area? I checked that website myself this morning, and it's staggering how many live within a mile of our home. If she gets hurt, it'll be on your hands." I struggle to keep my composure. I feel the barriers cracking at the seams.

"We don't know who took your daughter—or why, for that matter. Let's look at what we do know, shall we?" Stone shuffles the bank statements and bills into a single pile, a neat stack of betrayal. Next to that, she places the Polaroid she showed us earlier and the journal, opened to Abby's familiar loopy handwriting.

"You said you'd never seen this picture before." She picks up the Polaroid and holds it in front of my face. Abby with her messy hair and the blurred form of a boy in the corner. My stomach lurches.

"I'll ask you again, Jackson. Have you ever seen this picture before?"

"No."

"And you don't know who took it?"

"No."

"Had you ever seen the tree house before today?"

"No." I sound like a broken record.

"Have you ever been inside the tree house before today?"

"How could I have been inside it if I've never seen it before?"

"Good point." She puts the picture down and turns the journal to face her, running a finger down the paragraphs. Looking for something. "Does the name Chris Mitchell mean anything to you?"

The lurching is replaced by a succession of explosions. I could tell the truth, but if I slip—admit something that Abby didn't write down—I could be screwing myself. "Can't say that it does."

Stone actually laughs. "I don't give advice very often, Jackson, but I'd recommend you avoid gambling. Your poker face can use some serious attention."

"I don't know what you're talking about."

"Okay. For argument's sake, we'll use hypotheticals. Hypothetically speaking, what if I told you that Abby wrote all about her online relationship with a boy named FortniteChris." Air quotes. "And then, again, hypothetically speaking, she thought she was going to meet said online boyfriend after a particularly brutal lesson in puberty."

"*Does* it say that?" I ask.

"It's an exceptionally awful moment."

"Uh huh." I wish she'd take the photo off the table. I can still hear Abby crying.

"I can't imagine what it'd be like to find out my mother had paid a boy to like me and my father condoned it."

Why?

I can't. "Please, stop." I push back from the table, the chair screeching with rusty protest.

"Here's what I really want to know, though." I start pacing again, but I see Stone point to one of Abby's entries and glare at me. "Hypothetically speaking," she says, "what would the father's 'idea' have been?"

I stop. "The idea?"

"You slipped her a note. 'I think I have an idea.' Right here, and she mentions it again—about a week later—when she describes how volatile things had been in your house."

This isn't good.

"Well, I can't speak for this hypothetical father, but if that were me, I'd say it sounds like he was trying to make things right," I say.

"Maybe he was," she nods sympathetically. "Or maybe he was trying to save his own ass."

Coward. She's calling me a coward. "Am I being charged with something?"

Detective Stone leans back in her chair and removes a container from her pocket, her eyes never leaving my face. She pops a mint into her mouth. "No."

Good. "I'd like to leave now."

"You're free to go any time, Mr. Scarborough, but as a courtesy I'll tell you it doesn't look good if you do."

"I don't care how it looks, and I don't need your advice."

Stone picks up the notebook and clears her throat. "'I have to make a choice.' One of the last things she wrote. What did she mean, Jackson? What was your brilliant idea?"

My hand lingers on the knob. I finally look at the mirror and don't recognize the slovenly apparition staring back at me. Mustard-hued and weak. I choose to focus on my shoes instead, but even they seem to mock me.

"Could I have a cup of coffee?" I ask.

"Sure." Gathering up all the items save for the picture, she pauses at the door. "I'll be right back."

The door clicks shut behind her.

I'm a liar, and I'm alone, neither of which is worse than what I've done.

JENNIFER

Fourteen clicks.

Right back where I started.

Only this time, I'm counting minutes, not likes.

According to my watch, it's been fourteen minutes since Downy stuck me in this bunker, and each one that passes adds a new layer of emotion.

I started at calm. I tried to maintain that Jennifer Cates persona I've nurtured the last decade. Wholesome, vibrant, and eternally optimistic. Can't be the mother of CC Spectacular if you're a miserable bitch all the time.

Yet, here we are, and I am one miserable bitch, indeed.

Making me wait is part of her game. She has all the time in the world, apparently. She's not worried about finding Abby.

Finally, she arrives. No golden chariots or adoring fans, but you wouldn't know that looking at her smug upturned nose.

"Detective Stone," I say. "Good of you to come."

"Sorry to keep you waiting. I've had quite the interesting afternoon which was punctuated by a riveting discussion with your husband."

"Jackson's here?"

"He is."

"Does that mean you've found Abby?"

She tucks a loose hair behind her ear and shakes her head. The messy excuse for a bun flops around. She needs a dozen bobby pins and a decent styling gel.

"I have to tell you," she says. "He's giving us an awful lot to think about."

She's lying. "Jackson's not much of a talker, and when he does decide to chime in, it's usually with some ridiculous story he saw on Yahoo. He loves the advice columns."

"Geez, Jen, tell me how you really feel."

"Have you found Abby?" I ask.

"We're working a solid lead. While we wait, though, I'd like to ask you a few questions."

I run my tongue along the ridges of my teeth, reading between the lines of what she's actually saying. "Is this an interrogation?"

"Would you like to call your attorney?"

"I told you. I have nothing to hide. Ask your questions."

"Okay." Emilina sits at the table and waits for me to join her. Always vying for control. "Let's start with what Abby wrote in her journal."

I tsk and tilt my head to the side. "How invasive of you to read my daughter's private thoughts without our permission."

"Invasive," she says, opening the notebook. "This coming from the woman who tricked her own daughter into falling in love with a boy who was using her for a gaming system. Now, where have I heard that story before?"

She's got nerve to bring up our past, even in a vague reference like that. What I did to Abby is nothing like Henny Jenny. I wasn't trying to be cruel.

"I'll take full responsibility for that," I say. "Paying Christopher was a shortsighted intention on my part, but my heart was in the right place.

I was trying to protect Abby. I didn't want to leave anything to chance. You never forget your first love." I've never forgotten mine. "I just didn't want her to get hurt. I know how painful it can be when feelings are unreciprocated."

Or exploited for the entire school to mock.

"But she did get hurt. She found out about your arrangement, and how do you think she felt when she realized what you'd done?"

"A lot better than she would've felt if Chris had dropped her without explanation."

"You didn't give her the chance to get that far," Emilina says, and I clench my hands together to keep from reaching across the table and slapping her. "What kind of mother hijacks an innocent dialogue and pays a boy to pretend to like her daughter?"

I can't believe I didn't anticipate a journal.

"I did it for her own good," I say. "That's the last I'll say on the matter."

"I'm being raised by a *crazy* person." She reads from the notebook in punctuated bits of emphasis. "Held *hostage* in my own home. *Forced* to play a part online so my *mom* can feel *important*. What part of that is for her own good, Jennifer?"

"You're not a mother. You wouldn't understand."

Her nostrils flare and her fingers flutter on the table. I've hit a nerve. "Okay," she says. "So, if your goal was to protect Abby from getting her heart broken, then why did you enlist your husband to break her heart on camera."

Come on, Abby. *Every* detail?

"It was supposed to be her first kiss, but Jackson messed that up too. I told him he needed to push the flash override, but he apparently didn't listen. Typical husband, you know? In one ear and out the other."

"You're putting this on Jackson?" she asks, ignoring my attempt at small talk.

"I already said I had an error in judgment. It was a terrible idea."

"I agree with that assessment. While we're on this subject," Emilina flaps, "still want to stick with your original story about not being to the tree house before?"

"I said I'd never gone up there. I never said I hadn't seen it."

"Pretty sure I remember our conversation accurately, Jennifer."

"Was that before or after you threw me to the ground?"

Emilina purses her lips so tightly they almost disappear. I'm not an idiot. Someone is watching on the other side of that mirror. Probably her boss. Every word I say in here counts. And when it comes to boosting likes in my favor, I'm the best.

"For the record, you're stating that you knew about the tree house, but you've never been inside. Is that correct, Mrs. Scarborough?"

Touchy. "We're not on the record, Emilina. This is a friendly chat."

"Did you know about the tree house, Jennifer?" she says pointedly.

"Yes," I say innocently. "I knew there was a tree house. I found out about it when Jackson followed Chris Mitchell and Abby into the woods."

"I see." She pauses, eyes downturned at the journal. "Why have Jackson take the Polaroid?"

Sigh. "For an upcoming series I was planning to run on the blog. Cell phone pictures are fine, but they don't have the flair that we need to make this segment work. Chloe Cates has shared every aspect of her life with our subscribers. I doubt you know much about what it takes to make it in this field, but it's a constant battle. New talent. Fresh faces. People love babies. Babies are cute and new moms have a lot of time to browse when they're nursing a baby at three A.M. Parents of teenagers, though? You have to be authentic and original to keep your status, and Abby's burgeoning love life was the perfect hook. Everybody loves new love."

"Especially when it's paid for," she says.

This forking journal. "Look, Abby and I have our moments, but I love my daughter. She means everything to me. That diary doesn't give an accurate depiction of our lives. It's the emotional ramblings of a teenager with rushing hormones and mood swings."

"Are you saying we can't believe what she wrote?"

"I'm saying you'd be hard pressed to find a diary that wasn't dripping in dramatics. Kids exaggerate to feel better. Get their frustrations sorted out." I regard her with my friendliest we're-a-team smile. "You remember. Being obsessed with someone only to have that person betray you. And what'd we do in response? Curse them out in our diaries and cross out their pictures in the yearbook."

That was a little too close to the truth for my liking, but I'm breaking through her leathery exterior, at least. God, she needs a moisturizer. Emilina's eyes flick to the mirror and back to me, muddled with anger. I stare right back.

You wanted to play this game.

She clears her throat "That's not the same thing."

"Isn't it, though? Abby loves the blog. She loves taking pictures, especially with the Polaroid; I told you that. She has a real knack for lighting, but she likes being in front of the camera just as much as she likes to be behind it. She wants me to post about her. Does she get frustrated with me? Sure. But at the end of the day, she loves what we do."

I sense Emilina's doubt. It pours out of her skin like dew. Sweaty dew. She could use a shower, the slick sheen coats her skin, but pointing that out won't make her doubt me any less. She opens a folder and sorts through a stack of papers. When she finds what she's looking for, she holds it up. A picture. "Do you recognize her?"

"Missy Crawford," I say, voice full of sorrow. "So awful."

"That's right." Emilina assesses the picture then drags her eyes back to me. "She looks a little like Abby, don't you think?"

I crinkle my nose. "I don't see the resemblance."

"Really?" She offers an exaggerated expression of disbelief. "I don't know. Maybe take another look. I can pull up your post, if that would help. The side-by-side comparison was a nice touch."

Bitch. "That won't be necessary. I'm familiar with the content. I stand behind everything I post."

Emilina lets half a smirk curl before hiding it with a serious frown. "Did you know she was a huge CC Spectacular fan?"

"I did not." I sweep loose strands of hair off my brow and shoulders. My skin feels clammy and dry at the same time. "She was a beautiful girl. Such a senseless tragedy. How dreadful for her family."

"They're devastated."

"You've spoken with them?"

"Oh, yes." She slides the picture to me as her phone buzzes. "Ah, excuse me a second. Stone," she says pushing the phone to her ear and stepping out of the room.

Pain needles through my right eye, threatening a migraine. On the other side of the windowless door, I imagine Emilina rattling off about any number of things. Her impressions, her concerns, the evidence. Could there be evidence? What could she have? And am I entirely certain Jackson won't talk?

No.

The clarity resounds in my chest like a bass drum. Jackson is unpredictable. He could go either way. He could tell the truth. He could lie. Given the circumstances, I'd say it's increasingly likely that he's going to choose whichever option best serves himself—wife and kids be damned.

The groundwork for my next go with Emilina is taking shape. I close my eyes and picture myself speaking the sentence. I've been crying on demand since I was thirteen, a surprisingly useful skill. If I offer it up as a confession, she'll be forced to take it seriously. She won't have a choice. Personal grievances aren't admissible in a court of law.

And we both have a reason not to air our dirty laundry.

Okay, I can do this.

When the door opens, however, Emilina isn't alone.

Can't anything be easy?

"Mrs. Scarborough," she says, indicating the man on her right. "This is Detective Devon Blaisdell. He's investigating the murder of Missy Crawford and asked to join us today. Is that okay?"

No. "Of course."

She retrieves her spot beside the portly man. The way his eyes slide over my body makes me recoil. His presence is bad. But the other person she dragged with her into this shithole is worse.

"And you can have a seat next to your wife," Emilina says, addressing the sloppy toad at her heel.

Jackson radiates nervous energy. He doesn't meet my gaze, intently focused on burning a hole into the floor. "Jen," he murmurs.

I push my chair an inch to the left and cross my arms. "Jackson."

"Well, isn't this a cup of sparkling sunshine, Spectacles," Emilina says, and this time, her smile stretches to the corners of her eyes.

I should've killed her when I had the chance.

Abby's Journal

Chris keeps DMimg me. I read them but don't answer. I don't know what to say. Thanks for making a fool out of me? Hope the PS5 was worth it?

Obv I still care about him, but it's not the same. I can't stop thinking about how he just left me that night. Would he have stayed if he knew I was Chloe?

UGH I HATE that the idea even crossed my mind, but it did and it matters. Would she have been enough? Would he have taken the $ if it meant he got to hang out with her instead of boring Abby?

And as if that's not enough, something seriously weird is going on. Mom says she has a surprise for me. IDK but with her, surprises are never a good thing. Esp lately when every convo we have is an excuse to fight.

I didn't bother asking Dad if he knows what it is. He never knows anything, and even if he does, he just lies to me.

No more talk of the plan. I think he's given up. Prbly for the best.

EMILINA

This is the truth behind the carefully crafted masterpiece they present to the world.

We're just shy of twelve hours since I got the call from Cap. The Scarboroughs, no longer the shiny plastic model of domestic bliss, sit before me, perplexed and angry. I imagine this is what it must be like when two starving wolves finally decide to eat each other. Survival of the fittest: marriage edition.

"Mr. and Mrs. Scarborough, let's cut to the chase, shall we?" Blaisdell says. He has his own files. He puts a blown-up print of the body next to Missy's smiling school portrait. The juxtaposition is jarring.

Jackson is visibly uncomfortable, like he swallowed a live tequila worm.

Jen studies the pictures with objective interest. "This is absolutely horrific, Detective Blaisdell. Emilina informed me she was a fan. Please, send her family our deepest condolences."

"How kind of you," he pauses. "Cause of death was determined to be blunt force trauma. See that caved spot in her skull, there?" he says, pointing to the mass of bloodied hair. "Kind of hard to see with the bloating and all those bits stuck in."

"Yes," Jen says and smooths the front of her shirt.

"Now," Blaisdell continues, "head wounds are notoriously bloody. You ever hit your head on anything, Mr. Scarborough?"

Jackson jolts. "Me? No."

"Nasty stuff." Blaisdell confides. Just two guys shooting the shit at a bar. "You know, twenty percent of the blood pumpin' from your heart goes to your brain. Even a small scalp laceration will gush because of all the arteries. Like Carrie at the prom."

Jackson shudders.

I scribble a random line in my notepad. This makes him more nervous; his legs jitter as he follows my hand with his eyes.

Blaisdell and I exchange a furtive look of understanding and he continues. "For an injury like this one," he taps the photo again, emphasizing the gore, "we'd expect to see a lot more blood in the tree house. Which is why I'm havin' trouble with this scene." He takes out a second photo, an interior shot of the tree house I haven't seen until this moment. The flash illuminates the plank walls and floor. Other than a few smudges and some coagulation, there's no blood. "You can see for yourself. That floor's basically clean enough to eat off, if you could stomach it."

"I wouldn't go that far," Jen says, craning her neck away from the table. She peers into the mirror and wipes under her eyes.

"Here's my question," Blaisdell directs at Jackson. "Why isn't there more blood?"

Jackson shoots past pale to gray.

"Could it have washed away?" Jen suggests. "I mean, we don't know how long she was out there."

Blaisdell shakes his head. "We know she was out there for about a week, actually. And to answer your question, no. It's not possible that liters of blood just *washed away*. The tree house is old, but it was dry. Even if there had been exposure, forensics would've found traces on the ground, on the ladder, through the floorboards. Degraded, but it would've been there. There's nothing. Almost as if she was killed somewhere else and her body was moved after."

Jackson rests his chin in his cupped hands. Blaisdell's line of questioning is affecting him.

"Are you okay, Mr. Scarborough?"

"What? Oh, um, good, I'm good."

"Did either of you know Missy Crawford?" he asks.

"No." This from Jennifer, taking the lead. This was her method when they questioned her about Nicole's disappearance too. She was forthright and humble and expressed concern about Nicole's well-being.

We had our differences, but we weren't enemies. I hope Nicky's okay.

Blaisdell flips another picture over. The shot that was hanging in Missy's room. Five happy girls in their matching C-H-L-O-E T-shirts.

"Madeline Crawford, the girl's mother, said her daughter loved CC Spectacular. Read your blog and followed her social media. Attended several 'CC and Me' live events."

Jen shrugs. "I apologize, Detective Blaisdell, but you can't really expect me to remember her after all this time."

"I can't?"

"That was weeks ago. We had a sold-out show and have done several virtual events since then. She could've been any face in the crowd."

A third photo joins the bunch, one I haven't seen before. The two girls together, Chloe and Missy, shoulders pressed against each other, the camera flash reflected in the mirror behind them. Missy is preening, the freckles on her cheeks pop through the blush. Abby's smile is more modest, but they look companionable. Friendly.

I'm Missy. Your biggest fan.

The words flash in my mind, and I recall reading about this moment in the journal. For how hard Jen tried to convince me there's no merit to her words, everything Abby's written so far has panned out.

Blaisdell watches Jen and Jackson's responses. "We pulled this from Missy Crawford's Instagram account. The date matches your mall show."

Jackson doesn't make a sound.

Staring at the picture, Jen finally blinks before regaining her composure. "That was probably taken at the meet and greet. Which again, we have so many followers and do so many of these events . . ." She trails off. "If she says we met, then yes, we may have met her, but I have no recollection of that. Tons of fans want selfies with Chloe. As I'm sure you can imagine, that was a stressful day for all of us. Everything after that is a blur."

My phone vibrates. I glance down at the screen to see a message from Luke.

Need to talk asap

Blaisdell lines up the photos like he's preparing for a carnival game. Choose the right one and win the prize.

"Blaisdell, a word?" I say.

"Can it wait?" he asks.

"It'll just take a minute."

He mutters under his breath but moves to stand.

"Excuse us," I say, tucking the file under my arm.

Jen and Jackson unceremoniously watch us go.

I don't wait for Blaisdell to close the door.

"The precinct better be on fucking fire, Stone," he grumbles at my heel. "What kind of janky operation is Central running?"

"Luke wouldn't have messaged if it wasn't important."

"Who the hell is Luke?"

"Digital Forensics specialist."

He's not in the command room, so I hustle down the hall toward the tech sec—a unit off the secondary wing that's become the unofficial Geek Squad headquarters.

I find him hunched over his desk, squinting back and forth from a computer to a tablet. The glamorous life of a computer investigator. Luke's going to need glasses soon. He shifts in his seat, and I notice the smartphone connected to a data retriever.

"Luke," I call.

He snaps to attention. "Hey, sorry to interrupt your mojo flow, but this couldn't wait."

"What's up?" I ask.

"Okay, so first: the guys you had running follow-up checked in, but Cap intercepted the messages to me. Harold Forest's alibi checked out. We've got ticket receipts from the theater and the Stew's manager sent over timestamped security footage from that night. I also did some digging on social and found four tweets from his daughter between the hours of midnight and two A.M. One of which is a selfie from her room." He tabulates and Willa Forest's face pops up on the laptop, an angular view of her room visible in the background.

"He's angry, but he didn't strike me as the violent type," I say.

"On top of that, Forest and two of his neighbors voluntarily granted access to their home security records. None of them showed street activity from the night Chloe Cates went missing."

"Doesn't seem like he'd have time to plot and execute an abduction."

"I still want to run through traffic cams in the area, but I'm waiting on approval. For what it's worth, all things considered, I'd say that's a safe assumption."

"Any word on the Mitchells?"

Luke closes out of Willa's feed and reloads another page. "They're still working through the roster, but the coach vouched for the pizza party."

Blaisdell huffs. "This is why you cut my questioning? I'm trying to find a murderer, not gossip about sleepover attendance."

"That's only half the reason," Luke says, hitching a thumb at the screen. "I broke the phone," he says.

Blaisdell frowns in confusion. "What phone?"

"It was already broken," I say.

"No, that's not, I mean I got in. I bypassed the pin code. Obtaining the user information sucked since the screen was a bucket of glass shards, but I was able to access the settings and pull the registration number. Not my best work, but I figured going for speed was better than achieving total operational control. I'm sorting through the data modules now. Whatever was backed up, we'll know in a matter of minutes."

I pore over the tablet and watch the synch stats. "Great job, Luke. Photos? Emails?"

"Texts too. Probably her deleted folder, as well, as long as my caffeine fix doesn't expire."

"I want to know who she was talking to before she went missing."

"Should be doable, as long as she wasn't some criminal mastermind with a penchant for firewalls."

"What phone?" Blaisdell repeats.

"Abigail Scarborough's brother came to me earlier with a phone he found in their basement," I say. "I think she was using it to talk to her boyfriend, but I couldn't get it to turn on in its condition."

Luke whistles. "Actually, about that, Em. The phone's not registered to Abigail Scarborough. Or Chloe Cates. Or any of the other Cateses for that matter."

I cock my head to the side. "Then who is it registered to?"

He nods to Blaisdell. "Missy Crawford."

Abby's Journal

I only have a minute. OMG I can't believe this is happening. I just. I'm shaking. I have to—I don't know what to do.

I'm scared. So scared.

This can't be real.

EMILINA

Blaisdell's presence seems to swell. The red of his scalp is visible through the short cut of his hair. "The victim's phone was not recovered with the body. Our tech guys tried to get a GPS track on it but no dice. The last location ping was three minutes away from her home, and subsequent search of the area turned up nothing."

I feel my insides freeze.

"Makes sense if it's been dead this whole time," Luke says. "And the Find My app was disabled."

"You said the son just gave you the phone?" Blaisdell asks.

"Yes." I reconstruct the rest of my conversation with JJ. "He said he didn't want to give it to me when his parents were around, but he thought it could be important."

"That doesn't sound suspicious at all," Blaisdell says sarcastically.

"Why would Missy Crawford's phone be in the Scarboroughs' basement?" Luke asks.

Blaisdell shuffles toward the desk and examines the data retriever. "Exactly what I'm wondering. Okay, I need you to stop whatever digital extraction you're doing and bag that up. Anything you've already done, get it documented and copied to my DL. I cannot deal with another bullshit case toss because you were technically altering evidence."

"I didn't know this was your victim's phone," Luke says and rushes to locate a Faraday bag, one of the only ways to block signals and protect cellular evidence from being deleted once it's in police possession.

"Stone, let's get this photographed." He slips a latex glove on with gritted teeth. "I swear to fuck, Emilina, a goddamn cell phone. Better knock on every piece of rotting wood in here that he didn't destroy DNA or prints mauling this playing Tetris with his hacker code, or it's your ass on the line."

I swallow my pride and start photographing the phone. "Blaisdell, I had no idea. JJ gave me no indication this could belong to Missy Crawford."

Or I chose not to see it if he did.

"Here." Luke returns with the bag as we take the last shot.

"Get this to forensics like yesterday," Blaisdell says.

"Sure thing."

"Luke, can you update Cap and see if this'll speed up the warrant?"

"On it." He dodges around us with the agility of a speed skater.

Blaisdell steps away to make a brief phone call to Homicide South. I stare blankly at the computer screen while my thoughts percolate.

JJ was anxious. I thought he wasn't telling me the whole truth, holding something back, but I assumed he didn't want to get in trouble. Or get Abby in trouble.

How did he wind up with the phone of a murdered girl?

"All right," Blaisdell says, disconnecting his call, "I'm not fucking around when we go back in there."

"I wouldn't expect you to," I say. "Again, Devon, I'm sorry. If I had known the phone could have any connection to the murder investigation, I would've turned it over immediately."

"Yeah, well, too late for that. We have to make sure everything else is done by the book."

Sure. Shit. The pressure to confess my prior relationship with Jen mounts, and I almost blurt out the truth of our past to him right then. The more complicated this gets, the worse it is that I haven't disclosed this information.

"Let's see what they have to offer," I say, as we round the corner and push into the room. Jen and Jackson are where we left them, although their postures scream of conflict. Angled away from each other, arms stiff against their bodies.

Jennifer perks up as we enter, her interest stretching like an accordion. "Did something happen? Is it Abby? Any news?"

Blaisdell sits like a stone. "Have you had a chance to look at these photos?" The blow-up of the body is now facedown. Blaisdell turns it over and slides it to the table's edge.

Jen fumbles. "We did, but like I said, and I'm deeply sorry to admit this, I don't remember meeting Missy Crawford. She's one of a million girls Chloe has touched in her journey."

"Mr. Scarborough, do you agree with your wife's statement?"

Jackson's response is automatic. "Yes." He sounds hollow, though.

"So, it is your position that neither of you recalls meeting Missy Craw-ford," Blaisdell states.

Jen nods once. "Yes." Her gaze lands on me. "Detective Stone, I thought this was an informal chat, and it's becoming decidedly hostile in here."

"Hostile?" Blaisdell muses. He gathers the pictures into a pile like he's packing up. "Wouldn't want that. Okay, well there's just one more thing I need to ask then."

"Of course," she says.

"How did you come to be in possession of her cell phone?"

Jackson's mouth drops.

Jen strings her words slowly. "I don't . . . have her cell phone, Detective Blaisdell."

I swipe to the first picture in the reel and lay it on the table.

Jen leans forward, curiosity replaced by dawning revulsion. Her face slackens. The mask she's worn since this morning slips, and I'm able to see the truth underneath.

Jennifer is terrified.

"I've never seen that phone," she mutters.

Lie.

Stirred from his stern avoidance, Jackson's eyes float to the picture of the phone and narrow. "What is that?"

"Missy Crawford's phone."

"She was found near our property," Jen says. "Maybe the killer tossed it into the brush, or she dropped it beforehand. We don't own the woods."

"True," I say, locking the screen. "But this was recovered from your home."

"Oh my god," Jackson moans.

"Jackson," Jen says. Her attitude is more on par with a boxing coach ignoring the swollen eyes and three-inch gash on the cheekbone of her prized fighter. Ice it up and get back out there, sport.

"I can't do this anymore."

"Jackson." This time I hear a twinge of panic in her response. Her face softens. The Jennifer Cates mask has returned, however briefly. "You're having a panic attack, sweetie." She rubs his back and looks to Blaisdell. "He's having a panic attack. He'll be fine. Breathe in, Jack—"

"Don't fucking touch me," Jackson says, pitching her arm aside.

They're unraveling.

Jackson is a bundle of exposed nerves on the brink of imploding, much like how I imagine I was the night I had to give a statement about Nicole's disappearance.

Jen, however, hasn't changed. She portrays the same detached demeanor she embodied at thirteen. She holds her breath. Eyes upturned and mouth set in a deep frown, she fiddles with her wedding ring, twisting it in half circles until it slides away. I have a strong feeling this will be the last day she wears that band.

Once it's off, she exhales. "I want to confess."

What.

Blaisdell grunts. "Mrs. Scarborough, I think I should advise you that you have the right to remain silent."

"Consider me advised," Jen says.

"Wait, wait, wait. She can't confess," Jackson says, kicking to his feet.

"Mr. Scarborough, I suggest you take a seat while we get this sorted out."

He sputters. "No—no, I want to confess first."

"Oh, that is just perfect," Jen laughs drily. "Typical spineless antics."

The whole room seems to be tipped on its side and void of oxygen.

The nausea hits me square in the throat, a full-on crescent. "Excuse me," I mutter to Blaisdell. The door hasn't even clicked before I retch into the wastebasket of the adjoining room.

Cap rushes in behind me as I wipe my mouth on a rough brown paper towel. It smells like a hamster cage, wet and musky, and almost sends my stomach into revolt for the second time.

"Hell, Stone, you okay?" he asks.

"Good," I say. Better now that I'm not in there.

"Take a minute. Get your bearings. Luke's on standby in the control room. Downy and Welsh are going to give them a proper Mirandizing, but both are refusing lawyers. Good news for us."

"Wonderful," I say.

"We'll separate them. I want you with the husband. That woman's angling for you something hard."

"Yeah."

Cap frowns, deep lines of disapproval. "You should've told me you know her."

He's right. Skirting protocol isn't like me. We're supposed to work together, especially when there's a homicide to consider in the interim.

"Knew," I say, spitting into the trash. "We knew each other."

He sighs. "Yeah. Well. I don't want her statement thrown out because you guys have history."

"Heard." The dizziness recedes.

"How much history are we talking? Between us."

A life's worth. "We were best friends for a while growing up. Haven't spoken in twenty years."

He grunts. "Boy troubles?"

Murder troubles. "Something like that," I say.

"All right. From this point on, you don't speak to her alone."

"Abby's out there somewhere, Cap. I'm the only one who's going to be able to get the truth out of Jennifer Scarborough."

"I wouldn't get cocky, Stone."

I know. "Sorry. I'm just really scared for this girl."

He nods. "Blaisdell will take her statement. You take the husband. Let's see what shakes out."

Two confessions.

Both of them will lie. That's a given. I wonder if there's been a single moment of truth in this entire day with the Scarboroughs and their made-up world.

The question, then, isn't which one will lie. The question is which one will do it better.

JENNIFER

A light in the corner of the ceiling switches from red to green. For a lot of people, this is the moment they freeze. It takes skill to keep your wits about you when you *know* you aren't the only one listening. I've seen the most confident public speakers paralyzed by crippling stage fright when they realize the cameras are rolling. No concern for me. I have more experience in front of a camera than everybody else in this building.

Knowing how to lie when you're accused of murder is an added bonus. Technically, I wasn't accused of murder since Nicole's body has never been recovered, but I have a unique frame of reference.

"As a formality, I have to inform you that this is being recorded and anything you say here could be used against you in a court of law," Blaisdell recites, sorting through his papers.

"I understand," I say, and we proceed with the rest of the formalities. Name, date, time, attendees, and the subject of our meeting.

"Can you tell me, in your own words, Mrs. Scarborough, about your relationship with Missy Crawford?"

"Define relationship."

"Look, you were the one who wanted to confess. I've got zero bullshit tolerance left, so what's it going to be?"

I wait a beat, weighing what I want to say next. On the other side of the table, Emilina has been replaced by Officer Brian Downy, who scowls at me unabashedly. You'd think I confessed to being a cannibal and would prefer to eat his liver with some fava beans and a nice Chianti.

"We knew Missy Crawford," I say slowly.

In the movies, I'd be shrouded in mystery and speak with the ease of a seasoned criminal. Effortless and smooth as butter. My makeup would be flawless, a bright red lip and four coats of mascara on my lash extensions. A close-up of my mouth would reveal the slightest hint of seduction in my half smile as I spun my tale. Cut to the next scene and the camera would follow my hip-swaying saunter to a chauffeured car, black and sleek, windows subtly tinted, awaiting my grand exit in a cloud of smoke.

My reality couldn't be further from that chic Hollywood daydream. My hair's flat and frizzy, my skin's blotchy, and I'm too tired to muster a handshake, let alone a voluptuous victory walk. I haven't felt this drained since JJ was a baby.

"Start at the beginning," Blaisdell says.

Which beginning would that be? I want to ask him. When I murdered Nicole twenty years ago? When Emilina had me arrested? When I caught Jackson cheating on me? I wish he'd be more specific.

I sip from the water bottle Downy begrudgingly shoved at me before retreating to whatever hole from which the others are observing. He'd rather see me die of dehydration.

" 'CC and Me' has been a family venture since Abby was a toddler," I say. "It started as a hobby, a way for me to keep my sanity with two kids and no friends. I was lonely. I felt very isolated from the rest of the world."

"Uh huh," Blaisdell says with a blank stare. Either he doesn't have children—which I'd put money on since I don't see a wedding ring and he's demonstrated as much compassion as a potato—or the damsel in distress tactic won't work on him.

I switch gears. "And then it wasn't just a hobby. It was like we blew up overnight. People responded to us. They engaged with our stories and wanted more from our family, and before I knew it, we were getting offers from some big-name companies wanting to partner for promotional campaigns. One post has the potential to bring in thousands of dollars in revenue."

"A lot of money," he says.

"It is, especially when we get competing offers from multiple outlets. You can make a genuine career out of being an influencer." At least I did until our engagement waned. And the stream of bot purges, crackdowns on sponcon, and algorithm changes. "'CC and Me' has been our primary source of income for five years."

"Big weight on your shoulders?"

More than you'll ever know. "I love what I do, but yes. Sometimes it's an enormous pressure."

"How does Jackson feel about it?"

Abbreviated chuckle. "He's fine as long as I don't nag him too much."

"Why would you nag him?"

Segue. "Jackson used to be a great husband. Attentive and loving. Sometimes he still can be. Traces of the man he used to be peek through, and it's almost like it was when we first started dating. He'll surprise me with flowers or leave little notes with poems around the house for me to find."

"And when he's not like that?"

"He's aloof. Careless. Honestly, it's like living with a third child. He piles dirty bowls at the table instead of loading them in the dishwasher. Leaves wet towels on the floor for me to pick up. Laundry magically folds itself, don't you know?"

"My wife has said as much."

So, he is married. The financial tactic is working much better. "Sounds like a smart woman."

"How does this connect to Missy Crawford?" Blaisdell asks. "How did her phone end up in your house?"

"I'm getting there," I say assuredly. "The blog is largely focused on my writing. My experience as a mother and how it relates to our audience. We call them our Spectacles."

"Spectacles."

"We thought Abby needed a stage name. Lots of celebrities do it. Gives them a little more protection from the public. We decided on Chloe Cates for a number of reasons, but CC Spectacular was a cute nickname that garnered glowing support and name recognition from our Spectacles."

"Doesn't it make you ashamed? Pimping your daughter out like that?" His thick eyebrows waggle with condemnation.

I'd love to take a razor to that eyebrow. Shave the whole thing off in one fell swoop.

"I'm not *pimping her out*, as you so crassly put it, Detective Blaisdell. I'm helping her meet her potential. That's what mothers do. It's no different than if she played a sport. I mean, would we even be here if we were talking about me pushing JJ to play in the majors? There's much more wiggle room when it comes to boys and athletics, but we can save that examination of gender and social constructs for another day." I gather my hair together and smooth it into a wave off my shoulder. "Abby's talents don't pertain to a playing field, but she has every bit as much potential as those high school superstars being recruited by the pros."

"Isn't that a lot of pressure to put on a thirteen-year-old?" Blaisdell asks.

"For a normal kid, maybe, but Abby's got the right disposition for this business. And it's not just her. As I said, I write. Abby performs. We're a team."

"What about Missy Crawford?" Blaisdell asks. He shuffles his materials into an organized pile. Eliminate chaos. Regain control.

I fight the urge to wipe everything off the table and let the emotion creep into my voice. "Abby's hit a bit of a rough patch lately. Sulking and withdrawn. And when it comes to the blog—ugh, it's like pulling teeth. We had a big fight after her last appearance. One of our worst."

"Which was?"

"The show at Crossgates Mall. It was a huge clustermuck, excuse my language." I keep my hands in my lap. Exaggerating in any way could ruin this, and the opposite—wrapping my arms around myself, hunching, fidgeting—is an implication of a guilty conscience. "She asked me not to post about her anymore. Not to tell stories about her, not to use her pictures or videos. She was one hundred percent done."

"But you knew better?"

"I'm her mother. I know when she's overreacting and when she's serious. Abby needed a day or two to cool her head and then she was back to her normal, spectacular self. Jackson, on the other hand, was insufferable."

"How so?" Blaisdell asks.

"He heard Abby and me arguing and basically attacked me."

"Physically?"

"Not then, but his temper is unpredictable. My mother calls him a loose cannon. He's never been aggressive toward me with the children present, but I wouldn't put it past him. He stormed in between us and said I was a terrible mother. Can you believe that? He wouldn't stop. The vitriol he spewed." I sniff and look up toward the ceiling. "He told me that he was going to take Abby and JJ somewhere I'd never be able to find them."

"Did you think he was serious?"

"God no," I say. "He makes threats like that all the time. He knows the kids are my world, and he just wanted to hurt me—to keep me on my toes. In reality, Jackson wouldn't know what to do without me. I told him as much, and he eventually conceded. If I had known what he was planning, what he was capable of . . ." A falsely nervous shake of my head.

"What's that exactly, Mrs. Scarborough?"

"Jennifer, please." I raise my hand to show I've removed the band. It's strange not wearing it. The ring's become an extension of my skin.

"Jennifer, I need you to be clear. What are you claiming that your husband did?" Blaisdell, somber yet considering, maintains steady eye contact. I wouldn't go so far as to call him open-minded, but he's amenable to my explanation, at least.

I suck in a breath and continue. "We love doing meet and greets—that includes Jackson. He schmoozes the crowd like a pro and enjoys every minute of it. Maybe a little too much, but we all have our faults. It's not like we could do away with the postshow events. They bring in a tidy profit, but more than that, we want our fans to feel connected to us. Those relationships are very important to the blog and to our family morale. Anyway, Missy Crawford was a VIP at our last event."

"You remember meeting her?"

"I do."

"So your previous statement was a lie?"

Such hostility in his voice. "No, it wasn't a lie. I didn't remember at first, but once you showed me the picture of her and Abby together, it all came back to me."

"Uh huh," he says. "What else came back to you?"

Blaisdell's sniffing around the bait. "Jackson saw her before I did. Pointed her out in the crowd. *Look at her*, he said. *She looks like Abby*. I didn't see her then because I got wrapped up with Harold Forest about our permits and capacity limits." Because that man also insists on making my life difficult every opportunity he gets. "When that was handled, I turned around to find Jackson talking to Missy and her mother."

"Madeline Crawford."

"Right. She seemed enchanted. Jackson can have that effect when he wants to. He knows how to turn on the charm. He's handsome and courteous and complimentary. I wasn't surprised. But Madeline Crawford wasn't the only smitten kitten. When her mother was distracted, I think she was getting her ticket scanned, Missy handed Jackson a sheet of paper."

"Do you know what was on the paper?"

Henny Jenny.

No. I rotate my watch and breathe through the memory. I will not be broken by the girl I was or the stress of this moment.

"Yes. I do the laundry, remember? He left it in his jeans pocket. It was her number and social media handles."

"Why would he take those things?"

This is it, Jackson. You did this to us, and I'm done swimming in your river of shit. "I didn't know at the time. But I should have guessed. I knew who he was when I married him."

Blaisdell sharpens. "And who was that?"

"You tell me. Ask him about Ophelia."

EMILINA

I'm just getting into my groove. Jackson's talking—slowly, but he's cooperating—and I think we've established a decent rapport. Positioning myself as a perceived ally, I prepare for my next round of questions, harder hitting than the last but not accusatory. It's a fine line, not a tango but an equation.

A recipe.

Drew makes these incredible soufflé pancakes. They're light and fluffy yet melt in your mouth. The trick, he says, is the flour. You need to have the right blend of cake flour and all purpose. I didn't know there was more than one type of flour before he explained the baking process. Once you have your blend, it has to be sifted, weighed—not scooped; measuring cups don't suffice—and incorporated in specific increments alternating wet to dry.

The batter is unforgiving. An eighth of an inch over and your pancakes are dense. Under, and they're runny and flat.

Balance is key, and like Drew's soufflé pancakes, it's my favorite part of interrogating.

As I tick off the boxes of my strategy, the door opens with a creaky groan. Blaisdell and Downy flank Jen, like a prom queen being led down the red carpet by her two dashing escorts.

What the hell is going on?

"Session is terminated at," I check the time and recite the details before ending the recording. I imagine Luke on the other side of the mirror doing the same. "Detective Blaisdell?" I ask.

"We've had a breakthrough," Blaisdell announces.

"Oh?" I say, hopefully disguising the irritation in my voice. How quick he is to forget that only minutes ago, he was ripping me a new one for messing up his case.

Officer Downy hustles to rearrange the chairs to accommodate the growing presence in this cramped and heated space. With a stiff look at the Scarboroughs, he makes his exit, leaving me to ponder what Blaisdell's endgame is.

Blaisdell throws me a wiseass smirk, like we're in on the joke together. "Mrs. Scarborough has just confessed that Missy Crawford was targeted by Mr. Scarborough. He obtained her information at a meet and greet and attempted to initiate a relationship with her online."

What is he doing?

"You told them I did what?" Jackson says, throwing daggers at his wife.

Jen doesn't return the animosity, choosing instead to look straight ahead like a doll, vacant and unbothered.

Jackson isn't deterred. "Jesus, why would you make something like that up? I'm your husband. I wouldn't hurt a child."

Jen tucks each arm neatly into a fold. "I'm tired of covering for you."

"How so?" I ask.

Jen flutters her lashes, a gesture I'm sure she means to be endearing but I find theatrical. "This isn't the first time Jackson's proclivities have gotten out of hand."

"Don't do this, Jennifer," he growls. "You can't trust a word that comes out of her mouth."

"Ask him about Ophelia," she says.

What little color remained drains from Jackson's cheeks. "No, no, no, don't do this. This is not the same thing, and you know it."

"Who's Ophelia?" I ask, pivoting to Jackson.

I'm not sure anyone is prepared for his response. I thought he was the lesser of two evils. The one who'd get her to break.

I should've been asking myself what kind of man would fall for someone like Jennifer.

Jen's confidence bubbles to the surface. "Better yet," she adds, "ask him about the *real* reason he didn't become a teacher."

"Not everyone is cut out for the classroom, and there's nothing nefarious or weak about accepting that I'd be best suited for an office job. Wasted a lot less money than you did on a bullshit degree you use as a photo prop."

This is going south quick. The heater clacks to life, and I pull at the collar of my shirt, fighting a sudden wave of dizziness. I thought morning sickness was only something I'd have to deal with in the morning. I close my eyes and rub the back of my neck until the spinning subsides. "Stop. No more games, Jennifer. If you have something to say, just say it."

"Fine." She ruffles her hair, and the scent of her shampoo wafts in my direction. Fake strawberries, fat bulbous nodules from chemical additives. I hold my breath and wait for the moment to pass while Jennifer finally speaks.

"Jackson has a taste for young girls," she says.

The reaction is instantaneous.

He stands so fast the chair flies out behind him. "Liar!" Jackson shouts. He slams the table, repeating the word over and over as he beats the surface. Blaisdell and I are ready to grab him should he make a move toward Jen. Instead of attacking, however, Jackson cries. Crumbles. Fists clenched and sobbing on the floor. The sight is rattling, a deconstructed human suit.

"That's a lie," he moans.

If she's shaken by his outburst, she hides it well. She folds her hands in her lap and looks only at him. "We were in college. In love. I could see our whole future in the making, and yet I couldn't shake this feeling. Like when he was with me, he was somewhere else. It was like he had this wall around him, a shell that grew harder the longer we were together. Impenetrable. He insisted that I was creating problems that weren't there. I actually started to feel crazy because I couldn't trust my judgment. So I went through his email. His phone. I saw *messages*." She emphasizes this word, *messages*, wobbling her head in nostalgic shock that we aren't privy to. The gesture is intimate, like she's forgotten everyone else is in the room, and I'm reminded of that moment just before she attacked Nicole in the woods. How she'd receded while still being wholly present.

She said no.

"It wasn't in my head. He was involved with someone else. A girl named Ophelia. There were dozens of inappropriate messages I can't bear to repeat. The things he said, the things he did with her? I was heartbroken."

Jackson's cries diminish. He props his elbows on his knees and cradles his head.

She remains fixed on him while Blaisdell and I hang on her story. I've been convinced that Jen was lying throughout the day, but this feels genuine, that same naked vulnerability I heard in her voice that night.

I just wanted to be friends.

"So, one Friday night he told me he was going to the library to work on lesson plans. The library? On a Friday night? Please. Jackson worked hard, but he partied just as much as the rest of us. Could've been president of his frat if he'd just stopped getting in his own way." She curls her lips inward and bites down. "Anyway. I followed him. It's embarrassing to admit. I should've broken it off, but I wasn't as independent as I am now. I thought I needed him in my life. Wanted him to love me."

"I did love you, Jennifer," he says. "Why are you doing this?"

Jen blinks away the tears glazing her eyes and turns her attention away from him, letting her gaze land on each of us as she continues. "He picked her up from this pizza place not too far off campus," she says. "There was a dead end close by. I parked up the street and crept up to his car. The windows were fogged, which is like the biggest cliché in the world, isn't it? Not too foggy, though," she says, staring at Jackson with what appears to be genuine hurt. "I could still see Jackson cozying up to her, bodies pressed together, hands tangled in her hair. I waited for him to realize what a mistake he was making cheating on me, but he never did." She sniffs. "When I couldn't take it anymore, I banged on the window."

"Jen, please," Jackson begs.

"She was so young. Here I was expecting to have it out with some unwitting college freshman who'd been seduced by his upperclassman status, but Ophelia? She had to have been a high schooler," Jen whispers. Her eyes glisten slightly. "He'd dropped the student teaching so suddenly, I thought maybe he'd failed his certification tests," she shrugs. "His mother would've withdrawn his stipend, and that would've been tragic. Learning how to survive on a minimum wage job." There's sarcasm, but it's masking the pain and anger. Her nostrils flare and her voice wavers. "When I saw him—when I saw *her*—I knew she was the real reason he quit."

Jackson's head bumps against the table as he stands, and I jump at the sound.

"There was never an Ophelia," he says. "She's making shit up to make me look bad. I cheated on Jen in college, yes, but with not one of my students."

She *is* diverting attention, but that doesn't account for his panic.

"Did you go to the police, Jen?" I ask. "Can anyone corroborate your account?"

"No, I never told anyone else. As far as I know, Jackson didn't see Ophelia again after that night. But I suspect there have been others."

If what she says is true, Jackson is a predator. Student teachers aren't vetted before they go into schools. With no safeguards in place to protect against student teachers, he would've had free rein to take advantage of a vulnerable situation.

"Mr. Scarborough?" Blaisdell asks, keeping his fists balled tight at his waist. If the cameras weren't rolling, I wouldn't have blinked if Devon had thrown him through the wall.

"I would never hurt her," he says.

"Is this true?" I ask him. "Did you have a relationship with one of your students?"

"It wasn't a relationship."

That's a yes. Explains my quandary about what type of man Jen attracts. How did Madeline Crawford describe him at the CC Spectacular shows? Dimples and biceps. Popular with the older teens.

"Did you have a relationship with Missy Crawford?"

"No."

"Did you try to initiate a relationship with her?" Blaisdell asks, jaw clenched.

"No, I wouldn't do that. Jesus, I'm not some dumb horny college kid. I'm a father. I love my kids."

"I saw the way Jackson looked at Missy at the meet and greet," Jen says. *"Oh, Jen, look at her.* The puppy-dog eyes. The brazen flirting—"

"I wasn't flirting."

"He was obsessed with her," she continues. "Scrolling through her old pictures at night when he thought I was asleep."

"I haven't logged on to my accounts in months, you can check!" Jackson exclaims.

"He thought I wouldn't notice when he started coming home later from work. He'd take JJ to practice and message Missy while he waited so he could delete them before he came home. But a wife knows when her husband doesn't want her anymore." She wipes tears with the back of her hand. "I know it looks like we're this happy couple on the blog, but Jackson has a horrible temper. You saw him a moment ago. Imagine the kind of rage he showed me when he realized what I knew. I was scared for my life." Jen shrinks in her seat.

"This is insane," Jackson says, utterly disbelieving. "I've never threatened you, I'm not violent. And I had no relationship with Missy Crawford."

It's too late though. The more he denies it, the guiltier he looks.

Jen directs the connections now. "He tried to manipulate that girl into doing unspeakable things, and when she wouldn't, when she rejected his advances, he got scared that she'd turn him in."

"There wasn't a reason to be scared because this relationship did not exist. I've been faithful. Unhappy, but fucking faithful. I didn't kill anyone! It's Jennifer, can't you see that?"

We can subpoena the college for his records. Find the host school and subpoena them for attendance rosters. Possibly interview the girl—*woman*, now—if she's traceable. See if the Ophelia allegations have merit. We'll dump his cell phone records, and if there is correspondence with Missy, we'll find it.

But even if what Jennifer says holds credence, we still need more. Because while Blaisdell is getting plenty of information to build his case, I'm no closer to finding Abby Scarborough than I was an hour ago.

"Tell us about the phone," Blaisdell says.

Jackson pounds the table. "I've never seen her phone."

Jen settles into a seat, adjusting the hem of her shirt, comfortable and unbothered. The hairs on my arms prickle despite the smothering heat. Is she as calm as she seems?

"Last week, I took the kids out for frozen yogurt," she says. "Jackson stayed behind to work, some big case he claimed, but he was really sneaking Missy into the basement. Hiding her like a toy. When she was all set up, he went on like it was a normal night. Can you imagine? I even brought him a to-go cup. I had no clue she was in our house—not then, anyway. But I couldn't stop thinking about the infidelity. It was eating at my sanity. It was one thing when we were in college, but we've been married for almost sixteen years. We have the kids to think about."

"This is bullshit," Jackson moans.

"He didn't come to bed that night. I just kept picturing him scrolling through her feed and remembering Ophelia, and I couldn't take it anymore. I confronted him. I heard him in the basement and started down the stairs, but Jackson stopped me halfway. I said I knew what he was doing, that it was wrong, and I was going to go to the police. He told me he'd kill me if I called the cops. He knew exactly how to do it so he wouldn't get caught."

"And you believed him?"

"Of course, Detective Blaisdell. Before this nightmare, Jackson and I used to listen to true crime podcasts every Saturday morning. And Ophelia could be just fine somewhere now, but I also can't prove that he didn't do something awful after I found them in that car. It's not like I kept tabs on her."

"Jesus, you can't be serious." Jackson drags his face down into despair. "What is wrong with you?"

Jen locks on Blaisdell, tears spilling down her cheeks. "I was so frightened of what he might do to me. Or to the kids. And now Abby is—"

Jackson lunges across the table.

I don't stop him. I could easily subdue him, but for a fraction of a second, I want Jackson to succeed. Want to watch as he wraps his hands around her throat and squeezes until her eyes bleed.

Christ, what am I doing?

I move to restrain him, but Blaisdell is surprisingly nimble. He finds his feet and pins Jackson against the wall. Downy bursts in for the assist.

Throughout the entire altercation, Jen doesn't flinch.

"I'm taking him out," Blaisdell says, pushing Jackson toward the door.

Jackson bucks against him, gasping and wild. Spit flies from his mouth as he roars at Jen. "You're fucking done, do you hear me? Done. I didn't touch Missy Crawford."

Jen stands, daring him to try again. "Then how do you explain the blood, Jackson?"

The commotion stops, the calm before the storm.

"What blood?" I ask.

JACKSON

Everyone's watching me now that Jen's convinced them I'm worse than a child murderer. I have to keep my shit together. I need them to believe me.

"The blood was everywhere," Jen begins.

Blaisdell's giant hands are clamped around my wrists. He urges me to the door, but I dig my heels into the linoleum. "Just hold on a second, hold on. I'm calm. I need to say my piece."

"This has already gone far enough," Stone says.

I glare at her. "Jennifer is lying. All of this is bullshit, and you're being played."

"How?"

Blaisdell nudges the back of my knee, but Stone holds a hand up. "It's all right, Devon, I think Jackson can control himself."

Reluctantly, he releases his death grip. "Try that again, and I'll throw you in holding. Understand?"

"You're not actually entertaining this, are you?" Jen asks. "He's a monster. He killed Missy Crawford and threatened to kill me too. He belongs in prison."

Detective Stone turns to her. "Whether you like it or not, we need to work through this now. Your daughter's still missing, and she's running out of time. So, Jackson," she says, rotating to me, "how are we being played?"

I home in on Jen, her expression both crestfallen and vindictive, and let the words spill out of me. "Jennifer's using bits of the truth to distort the facts and you're eating it up like fucking coyotes. I'm innocent. Jennifer killed Missy. She lured Missy to our home. She earned her trust. And then she killed her."

"Why?" Stone asks, equally perturbed and skeptical.

"May I?" I ask, motioning to the chair. Blaisdell grunts, and I assume my place at the table. "When Jen gets an idea, she runs with it. I stopped questioning her a long time ago; the arguments are just not worth the headache because I always lose. So, when she told me I needed to talk to Missy Crawford and her mother, I did."

"Oh, okay, Jackson, sure." Jen flounders. "A grown man can't make his own decisions? I forced you to talk to a nice woman and her beautiful young daughter? Can we end this charade now so you can find my daughter, Detective Stone?"

"That's what I'm trying to do," she says. Then to me, "You didn't find that request to be weird?"

"When it comes to 'CC and Me,' nothing surprises me. I mean, you know about the train wreck that was her thirteenth birthday and what happened with Chris and the Polaroid. That's the tip of the iceberg. We could all feel Abby pulling away from the blog, but Jen was determined to keep her going."

"How?"

"Jen saw this girl coming out of the bathroom with Abby and a lightbulb went off. Abby wanted friends. Real friends. She wanted to go to school.

Be an average kid. But she couldn't do that without Jen making a sacrifice she wasn't willing to make. Missy was the answer to that problem."

"Wanting to have friends is a problem?" Stone asks.

"It is when you're Jen."

Jen scowls. "That's really unfair, Jackson, especially coming from you."

I wonder how much longer she's going to play the victim card. Villainizing me to make herself look good. I used to respect her blunt honesty. When did that twist into blatant manipulation?

"Didn't you find it alarming that your wife was essentially trying to isolate your daughter?" Stone asks.

"Yes, I—"

"Are you flipping serious?" Jen interjects. "I wasn't isolating her. Abby is the most social, outgoing girl you'll ever meet."

"Calm down, Mrs. Scarborough, or we'll have to escort you out."

Jen whips to Blaisdell. "I'm calm. Why is it the woman who's always told to calm down? Why not put a leash on my husband who tried to assault me in front of everyone in this room?"

"Jennifer," Stone says, somewhere between an admonition and an appeal.

"I didn't know this situation would play out this way. If I had—"

Stone holds up her hands. "Let's slow down a bit."

Easy since she's not the one in the hot seat.

"You're wasting time," Jennifer says. "It's dark and the temperature's dropping. What about Abby?"

And all at once, my resolve dissipates. What am I doing? I didn't think this through.

"Jackson?" Stone asks.

Jennifer could turn over the pictures of me and Ophelia. If she actually has them. I've never called her bluff before; but then again, I've never had a reason to. Can they prove it's me in them? Probably. Who knows what Hercule Luke can decipher. What would that mean?

Prison.

For how long? Years. They don't make people serve life sentences anymore. Do they? I don't have a record. First-time offense. I'd have good character witnesses. Coworkers. My parents. My boss. They'd say I'm a decent guy. Friendly.

What would people say about Jen?

Laying my hands down, I move my gaze from Stone to Blaisdell, maintaining eye contact with what I hope is dignity. Almost forgotten what that feels like. "I want a deal."

"I'm sorry?"

"A deal. I'll tell you everything you want to know. Testify against my wife. But in exchange, I want immunity."

Jen extends her neck with exaggerated attitude, an irritated gesture I've seen many times in our marriage. I've always thought it made her look like an ostrich.

"You conniving prick," she says.

Stone shares a measured look with Blaisdell. "That's not how this works, Mr. Scarborough. Trust me when I say the DA doesn't blindly hand out free passes for undisclosed crimes."

"I don't want to go to jail," I say. I feel nothing but terror. I don't belong in jail. A month ago, my biggest concern was an Ignita deadline and JJ's cleats being a hundred dollars too expensive.

"No one does," Stone says. She takes an 8 x 10 photo of Abby out of her folder and flips it around so I can see it. I prefer this one to the Polaroid. Give me a match and I'll gladly burn that myself.

My Abby-girl. She beams at me from the confines of the photograph. I'd give anything to take it back.

Okay, Abby. Here we go.

"Jen loved Missy from the moment they met: the perfect fan. She knew everything about us. She had our skits memorized. She dressed and acted like Chloe Cates. But more importantly, Abby loved Missy. The girls really hit it off. I actually couldn't believe it at first: one, because Jen's plan was working and two, that Jen had relented and given Abby what she wanted in the first place. I should've known the other shoe would drop. Jen just can't help herself."

"Sounds like you're talking about yourself, Jackson," Jen says.

"What happened, Jackson?" Stone asks.

My heart hammers in my chest. "Missy was an untapped talent, my wife's words." I feel like I need to insert addendums into anything that might be taken the wrong way. "She was a natural. By the end of the first week, she and Abby were choreographing their own dance moves. Abby was like her old self, and Jen saw dollar signs. Missy was supposed to be the link that would solidify the future of 'CC and Me.'"

You'd think I'd be able to ignore that damn green light in the corner after years of being in front of the camera. But I want to crawl under the table and hide from its beam. In some ways it's worse than Jen's festering presence.

Stone shifts her weight forward. "She wanted Missy to join your blog?"

"Jen convinced her she'd be famous," I say. They'd start small, a few test shoots to feel out sponsors. There was going to be a whole comprehensive business plan in place for a new integrated venture: *CC and MiMi*. MiMi being Missy. Jen saw them as the next Charli and Dixie D'Amelio."

"I don't know who that is," Blaisdell says.

"Sisters," Stone explains. "Two of the most popular girls on TikTok. They have over a hundred million followers. Net worth at least eight million dollars even after the backlash about their questionable behavior. Now they're segueing that infamy into their own reality show."

"Wow." Blaisdell releases a whoosh of air. "That's a hell of a lot of ambition."

"Missy—she was just a kid, a starstruck kid, at that. Of course she said yes. Wouldn't you have done the same if someone handed you an opportunity like that at that age?"

Stone's eyes are slightly pink. Tired. But I don't underestimate the spark in them. "We spoke to Madeline Crawford. She didn't mention anything about this alleged opportunity. She didn't even seem to be aware of the fact that the girls were friends. Are you suggesting she withheld this information?"

"No, not at all," I say. This is going well. I think. They haven't put handcuffs on me, so that has to be a good sign. "Jen told Missy she had to keep their friendship a secret for a little while. She conveyed how serious it would be if Missy told someone about the launch beforehand. No more blog. No more swag bags. No million-dollar future. Nothing."

The cutthroat side of Jen hasn't suffered under the guise of Jennifer Cates. I think I see a hint of a smile before she covers her mouth and murders me with her glare.

"An ultimatum?"

"I guess," I say. "Not that she needed it. Missy had no problem lying to her parents, telling them she was at a study group. The impression I got was Missy led a very structured life." Much like Abby's. I don't say this, but the implication is understood. "She was coming to our home two or three nights a week to create new material with Abby. Everything was going according to her plan, and Jen wanted to keep it that way."

"Now I know where JJ gets his fantastic imagination," Jen mumbles.

"Mrs. Scarborough," Blaisdell clips.

"Level with me, Jackson," Stone says. "Missy's handed a golden ticket by one of her idols and you expect me to believe she didn't tell a single soul? Not her mom or her friends or even some random stan Twitter account? No one could agree to that, let alone a thirteen-year-old."

"What you have to understand, Detective Stone, is that these kids have grown up on reality TV and social media. The idea of saving the big reveal for the cameras, it's second nature to them. They'd rather wait to spill their dirt in a confessional as long as the clip goes viral. This was huge for her; she said so herself. If Missy was worried about anything, it was maintaining her other extracurriculars once they made their debut."

"If that's really all it was, why hide it? Madeline Crawford seems like a reasonable woman, and she spoke very highly about 'CC and Me.' Wouldn't she have been thrilled?"

My head feels like it's been weighted down by anvils.

"Maybe," I say. "But it wasn't a sure thing. Not everyone wants their kids to be Internet famous. Quantifiable proof of success goes a long way when you're trying to convince someone to do what you want them to do. Jen had a pragmatic solution for that, as well. They would loop Missy's parents in after we got a better idea of audience response. She wanted to test engagement metrics before they got everyone's hopes up and let the cat out of the bag."

The detective remains stoic but attentive, seemingly unsure about whether to believe me.

I run a hand through my hair. Greasy. Like my lies have turned to oil and are seeping out of my scalp. I thought confessing was supposed to make me feel better. I feel like a dumpster fire and Emilina Stone's holding a can of gasoline.

Blaisdell confers with Stone quietly. She jots something down and angles the pad at him. He replies with a grunt, thumbs his nose, and says, "Mr. Scarborough, I don't get it."

"What's not to get?"

"For starters, you've painted a lovely picture. Sunshine and friendship and sparkles—I'm gathering you guys like sparkles, but stop me if I'm getting ahead of myself—everything was copacetic in the world of CC Spectacular. So, how did we go from happily ever after to a bludgeoned thirteen-year-old girl shoved into a musty tree house?" One solid finger jabs at the crime scene photo of the body.

"I don't know," I say. "But I could never do that."

"So, Jen killed her?"

Do it, my mind urges, but the words stick in my throat.

"This is ridiculous." Jen asserts. "Jackson hurt that girl and he'll do everything he can to save himself. That's what he does. He's selfish and manipulative and—"

"I'm not a predator," I say. "You know that. I'm sorry I hurt you back then, but I guess I didn't realize how deeply it has affected you. That's on me. I failed you as a husband. But don't use my mistakes to justify your own."

She sputters. "Gaslighting, Jackson, really?" She frowns at Blaisdell. "Look, I don't want to sound callous. What happened to Missy Crawford is undeniably a tragedy, but my daughter is still missing. Giving him the stage for smoke and mirrors is insulting when Abby's life is on the line. Why doesn't anyone want to find Abby?"

Stone locks her strained eyes on me. "Jackson, if you suspected Jen killed Missy, why didn't you go to the police? Missy's been dead for almost a week. You could've come forward anytime, but you chose not to. Why?"

That's *the* question, isn't it? Why.

"Have you ever gotten caught up in something you thought you had complete control over only to discover you're totally free-falling? The answer so far above your head you can't see the surface? I didn't realize we were drowning. It wasn't supposed to be like this," I say. "I didn't think anyone would get hurt."

"Didn't you, though?" Stone says. Her face is pained, voice thick and on the brink of wavering. "On some level, whether you want to admit it or not, weren't you choosing to ignore the very real possibility that someone would get hurt as long as everything worked out for you?"

"My life is in shambles, and you guys thinks I'm guilty of murder. Thank god it worked out for me," I say sarcastically. "I didn't ask for any of this, detective. I was doing my best to salvage what was left of a rock slamming into a hard place."

Blaisdell scoots his chair an inch closer to me. "You want to talk about rocks and hard places?" he asks, dangling another crime scene photo in my face. Missy Crawford's bloated, lifeless form on a sterile stretcher burns into my brain. The bright red of her innards, wet and exposed, congealing at the forefront.

"I really don't."

"You killed Missy Crawford, didn't you, you sick son of a bitch? Wishful thinking sure as shit didn't crush her skull and put her in that tree house."

MANDY McHUGH

The magnitude of what I'm up against rams into me with hurricane force.

I wait for them to understand. They have to know that I didn't, couldn't, kill anyone. Let alone a child.

But there's no token of comprehension, and Jen doesn't say a word.

I'm not betting my freedom on Jen's stubborn streak. "I wasn't sure what Jen had done until you told us Abby wasn't in the tree house," I say. "I had doubts when I heard Missy was missing, sure, but we're talking about *murder*." I clear my throat to stem the tears burning my eyes. "I had to weigh the truth with the consequences."

"The truth." Stone crosses her arms. "Did you see your wife attack Missy Crawford?"

Don't panic.

"No."

This room reeks of sweat and mold. Or maybe it's me. This secret rotting inside me finally venting into the open.

"I think I need a minute to regroup," Stone says. Her coloring is off, but it's nothing compared to the yellow hulking beast of my reflection.

"I think we all do," Blaisdell gruffs. He motions in the air, and a few seconds later, Downy appears.

"Sit tight," Stone says, closing her folder. The detectives exit the room, and I count the minutes until my world ends.

EMILINA

Blaisdell stomps to the coffee pot, grabs a Styrofoam cup in his bear claw, and pours the burnt liquid in a wide splash. He doesn't offer me any, an omission of manners for which I am grateful. The stench of the grounds churns my stomach. I'd really like to refrain from throwing up again so soon.

"You're not seriously telling me you believe a word that comes out of his pedo mouth, Stone," he says.

Cap bustles in behind us and shuts the door. The harsh fluorescents bounce off the top of his head. "Popcorn confessions," he says. "Devon, the Crawford girl is your jurisdiction. What's your take on all this?"

Devon gulps and goes for a refill. "I'd book them both, if it was up to me. Take out the trash in one big haul." Glug. Wipe. Toss. He misses the can and leaves the used cup on the floor. "But that's above my pay grade, DL. Your detective isn't ready to clear out yet—"

"Not until we find Abigail Scarborough," I interrupt.

He gives an exasperated expression. "And your tech guy might've seriously fucked me with that data pull. Regardless, the phone was allegedly found in their basement."

"Allegedly?" I ask.

"You're taking the kid's word for it, Stone. Kids lie all the time, and he's got one hell of a reason to claim he just found it. Can't rule him out yet."

"He's a kid, Blaisdell, he didn't murder Missy Crawford." I say this with conviction, but I remember the fear that flooded my body in the park. How certain I was that JJ had a weapon.

"Well, let's ask my victim what she thinks, shall we? Oh, wait."

Anger laps my doubts. Even if Blaisdell has a point, he doesn't have to be such a smug prick about it. He has time to gather his concrete proof to find a murderer. Abigail doesn't.

Cap nudges me. "Where's your head?"

What am I thinking? That's a good freaking question, Cap, so glad you asked. Carefully, I work through my thoughts. Predator. Stage mom psychosis.

JJ?

"I'm not saying I believe either of them when it comes to Missy Crawford's murder. I'd just like to have one hand on the shovel before we go back in there and they feed us another pile of bullshit."

"So, let's look at it from both sides," Cap suggests. "Say it was the wife."

"If Jennifer Scarborough plotted this whole thing, we've been two steps behind since the 911 call."

Murky, day-old coffee dribbles out of the cup. The sight of it forms a stone in my gut. I pick up his cup and toss it in the garbage, giving Blaisdell a side eye.

He snorts and shuffles to the basket of snacks on top of the microwave, chooses a packet of chips, and crunches one slowly. "Either they did it together or they're covering for the son. Seems pretty cut-and-dried to me."

"Or one of them acted alone and the other is a pawn. Unless we find love notes, texts, or photographs—or Joss finds physical evidence on the body—this is all circumstantial. We need more facts. Where are we on the warrant, Cap?" I ask.

"Luke's tip was good. Judge Alameda came through. Should have it in hand within the hour. I touched base with your DL," he motions to Devon, "to coordinate execution, and officers from both stations are en route to the Scarborough house," Cap says.

Which is great for Devon but doesn't get me closer to Abigail Scarborough.

If she's still alive.

She is. I have to believe she is.

Blaisdell dusts crumbs from his shirt and removes the tiny pad from his pocket. He flips through the pages of surprisingly neat lettering and scans his notes. "Are we booking one of them now or not?"

I glare at him. "Do we have enough conclusive evidence for that, Blaisdell? You feel confident that a halfway decent lawyer won't get the charges dismissed before Monday if we guess wrong?"

His face burns. "No."

The furnace sputters and I crack the small window above the sink, relishing the cool air. The familiar sounds of the station filter in from the hall. Clanks and conversation. The occasional shout of a drunk demanding to be released from the tank. A typical Saturday evening in so many ways.

"They think they're smarter than you," Cap says. "Give them a dose of their own medicine."

"How?"

"Use the kid," he says.

"Abby?" I ask.

"JJ."

He must see the surprise on my face. His suggestion, while not against protocol, is out of character for his straitlaced demeanor. "Arrest JJ Scarborough?"

"We'll have to bring him in anyway. I don't know where I stand with him as a suspect yet, but frankly, what I think doesn't matter. If they think we're arresting him for murder, they might cave. Tell us where Abby is."

Cap's implication is clear. *Or where she's buried.*

Nobody needs to remind me of the stakes. "Risky. If one of them changes course and decides to lawyer up, it's Abby we're throwing into the flames."

Blaisdell checks his watch. "I'm okay with this."

"All right," I say, pausing at the door. "Let's go tell them their son is a murderer."

JENNIFER

"You're crazy," Jackson's mutters—to himself or to me, I don't know, nor do I care. "And they see that."

"Name calling won't change what you've done, Jackson," I bite back. "Try to accept the consequences. It'll be easier in the long run."

Downy stands between us, arms folded, caterpillar eyebrows united into one thick, serious line. Beckoned to babysitter duty, probably to make sure Jackson doesn't try to attack me again.

So formal. So serious. Certainly not sharing any heartwarming parental anecdotes now.

I roll my head, left, right, center. I knit my fingers together and count to twenty. This nightmare will all be over soon. It has to be. Nightmares don't survive the daylight.

"They can't make us wait in here forever," Jackson says. "I need to get out of this room."

I let my eyes travel his face, his body, not looking for anything in particular but curious nonetheless. His blue eyes are tired and drawn. His brown hair is unwashed but the same healthy brown that he gave to JJ and Abby. His slumped shoulders force a blip of a gut to cling to the slub knit of his shirt.

There's a haze to him, a filmy layer coating his once-shiny exterior.

This is the man I married. Always has been. This isn't a matter of being blinded by love, of lifting a veil and finally admitting to myself that he has faults and flaws.

It was a filter. I took the dull penny he was, set him to Mayfair, and convinced everyone he was gold.

I did that. Me. And I can tarnish him just as quickly.

The door swings open.

I can't conceal the fine lines or highlight the shadows away, but I smooth the unkempt hair around my chin and cross my ankles like royalty. Class can be bought, no matter what people tell you about mettle or substance, and I've spent too much of my life accounting for Henny Jenny.

Whatever Emilina throws at me, devastating or otherwise, I'm prepared. I have to be.

EMILINA

I open the random folder I grabbed from the desk in the break room. "We just had an interesting discussion with the Medical Examiner. Forensics was able to pull a set of prints from the crime scene. We collected both of your prints from the house earlier. Do you remember that?"

Silence.

"Abby's, too, of course, latent from her room. Elimination purposes."

"Okay?" Jen says.

"We also took JJ's." I let the information settle. Jen's breathing quickens. "And as a precaution, I asked them to run those prints against the ones at the tree house." I pretend to scan the paper. Calculated pauses are useful. There's something about the deliberate quiet that elicits fear. People feel compelled to fill the void.

Jen's eyes widen, just for a second, but I don't miss her reaction. "I'm surprised you were able to get results so quickly," she says. "Those tests are backed up for months, sometimes years."

Everybody's an expert. You watch one Netflix documentary and suddenly you're an unparalleled authority of the legal system.

"Under normal circumstances, in a bigger city, that can be accurate," I say. "But this is Albany. One missing girl turns up dead during the course of an investigation into another girl's disappearance—one with a large following, whose mother went on television and provoked a public outcry, I might add—and boom, priorities shift. Either of you want to take a guess as to who was the match?"

More silence.

"What if I told you that we could connect JJ to both Missy's phone and her body?"

I watch the thought-worm wriggle deeper as they consider what I've told them. Resisting the urge to lay on more details is tougher than I imagined. I've given them doubt; no need to push my luck, but is it enough? Will they fold?

"You can't," Jennifer says, leaning back in the chair.

"We can. JJ is the one who turned the phone over. He messaged me earlier and said he wanted to confess."

"Jesus," Jen doubles over, pinching her temples. "This isn't happening."

"He climbed up that ladder pretty fast, too, didn't he, Jackson?"

"That explains the print, then," Jen says, head snapping up. "Your incompetent officer allowed him to tamper with a crime scene."

"The print was taken from a place JJ would not have been able to access based on Welsh's description of the event," I say.

"Detective Stone, what are you accusing my son of?" Jackson says.

"We're bringing him in now," I say. "He hasn't been charged yet, but it's only a matter of time until the DA hears the news and pulls out all the stops."

Jennifer squints. "You're—you're arresting JJ?"

"We're sorry to have put you through this. I recommend you call your lawyer—he's going to need one—and you'll have a chance to speak with him once he's been processed."

"Processed?" she squeaks.

"You can't arrest JJ. He's not a killer," Jackson says. He scans the room. "You're wrong. He barely knew Missy."

"That's not for us to decide." Blaisdell stands and motions to the door. "I'm afraid we can't discuss this further with you at this time. If you'll come this way—"

It's Jennifer who speaks next. "The prints aren't JJ's."

Yes.

"And how do you know that?" I ask.

"Because I know whose they are."

I look from her to Jackson. "Whose?"

When she speaks, her voice is barely audible, a whisper of her normal disposition. "Abby."

Around me, the room sizzles.

"Jennifer, what are you doing?" Jackson asks.

My eyes rove over her face for any sign of deception. I see none. "You're lying," I finally say.

"I most definitely am not." She slumps in her chair. It's almost like her muscles are too weak to hold her upright anymore. "I didn't see it happen, but I know it was her."

"How." Not a question.

"I heard them fighting in the basement." Her hands shake. She presses them together between her knees. "Missy wanted to bring a friend from school to the Bow-tastic! shoot. I told her I'd think about it, and that didn't go over well."

"With Missy?" I ask.

"With Abby. She was really upset. It hurt her that Missy wanted to invite someone else. Honestly, she overreacted. Abby doesn't do well with the intricacies of interpersonal relationships."

"And whose fault is that?" Jackson sneers.

"You want to have a pissing contest over who's the best parent, Jackson? Because I guarantee you will lose every goddamn time."

This is going to keep happening: the two of them devolving into sniping matches. This is an endurance competition. A thousand tiny cuts instead of one ultimate blow.

"What was their argument like?" I ask.

Jennifer glares at Jackson but jerks her eyes to me. "They were screaming at each other. I can't remember exactly what was said, but it escalated. Missy said she was leaving—that she might not do the shoot."

My phone buzzes in my pocket. I glance at the screen and see a text from Cap: Teams on scene.

I flash the screen to Blaisdell and chew on Jen's words.

"So, the girls are arguing. Missy leaves. And somehow she ends up dead, but you had nothing to do with it?" Blaisdell asks.

"I tried to intervene before it got carried away, but I was just making it worse, so I went upstairs. To give them a chance to work through it on their own." Her voice grows thick with emotion. "I put my earbuds in, blasted my music, and ignored them." Jennifer sniffs and wipes her nose. "A little while later, I thought I heard this noise. A thud."

"You thought you heard a noise," Blaisdell says.

"Yes. But I couldn't be sure. I took the buds out, but I didn't hear anything else." She inhales deeply and continues. "I went to the top of the stairs and listened to make sure they were all right. Abby appeared. Scared the bejesus out of me. She was crying. Said Missy had left and didn't know if she was coming back. That she needed some privacy and would be up when she was ready. But in my heart, I think I knew something was off."

Jackson surges to life. "Taking advantage of your daughter because she's not here to defend herself. Really? You're caught, Jen. Stop the games."

"She did it," Jen insists. Calm. Woeful. Confident. "And you know she did."

"No, Jen. I *know* you're lying," Jackson says with the same conviction.

"You think this is easy for me? I wish it was Jackson who killed her, but it wasn't."

But is that the whole truth?

"If Abby bludgeoned Missy in the basement, that would've made a huge mess. You heard what Detective Blaisdell said about head wounds. How would she have gotten that by you?"

Jen rubs her face. "I don't know. There were some stains on the carpet in the Confessional. I saw them a few days later. She said she'd knocked over one of the paint cans and tried to clean it up herself. I was so preoccupied this week, I didn't consider that she would lie to me about something like that. I had the carpets steamed right before the Bow-tastic! shoot."

"We have a warrant to search your house," I say. "If there's blood, they'll find it."

"I'm sure they'll find it," she says.

I try to work through the kinks in her story. "I can't accept that Missy would fall off the map and you'd just forget about her."

"I didn't forget about her," Jen says, pointing inward. "I tried calling and texting. She stopped responding to me after her last message."

"Which was what?"

Jen's lip trembles. "Two words. I'm done."

"How could a dead girl text you?" Blaisdell asks.

"She couldn't," Jen says simply. "Abby must've kept her phone."

Jackson shakes his head in a daze.

"Did you see the body?" Blaisdell asks.

"No."

"So who put her in the tree house?"

"It had to be Abby," Jen says, and leans tiredly on the table. "I had no idea Missy was out there. This whole time, I thought Missy was angry. Avoiding me. I didn't think her disappearance had anything to do with Abby. I don't know how I didn't see what was really going on."

Blaisdell examines the photo of Abby. "This girl—she carried a dead body across a quarter mile of rough terrain, in the dark, and managed to hoist her up a ladder. By herself? Without anyone seeing or hearing a goddamn thing?"

"I have no other explanation. Unless Jackson helped her."

But I do. In my mind's eye, I see Jennifer at the top of the water tower, straining under the weight of another dead girl, and I know it's possible.

Blaisdell blusters. "Look, you spent half the time trying to convince us that your husband is a serial rapist and child killer, and two seconds later, you're insisting that, no, your daughter's the murderer. And you," he says, tilting a chin to Jackson, "want us to believe your wife is a fame-obsessed mastermind capable of murdering her way to the A-list. Doesn't work like that. We have the prints. We're bringing your son in. Unlike you people, DNA doesn't lie."

"Okay, no," Jackson says, starting to rise. Fear grips his muscles. "You can't. Just hold on." He turns to his wife. "Jen killed Missy in our basement. Fact. She moved the body hoping it'd be months or years until someone found it. Fact. And now she's blaming it on her own daughter. I can't believe I didn't see who you really were."

"I am her mother," she spits. "Nobody will ever love her like I do."

"I should've taken the kids as soon as you started seeing them as dollar signs. Likes and trending and *viral*. You are the virus, Jennifer. You infected our kids with this mentality that they're only worth the traffic they bring to your website. That who they are—who they want to be—doesn't matter, and now someone is dead because of it."

"I'm the only one who loves those kids," she says. "You're not doing her any favors by covering for her, Jackson. Abby needs real help, more than either of us can give her. She *butchered* that girl in our home and left us to bear the consequences."

"What do you mean left you?" I ask.

Jen drops her head. "Come on, Detective Stone. Does anyone in this room actually believe Abby was kidnapped? Because I don't. Not anymore. She has to be hiding. If I had to guess, Chris Mitchell must be helping her. He's the only person I can think of who she might go to for help. I doubt she's told him the truth, but if I know anything it's that Abby can be a very convincing actress. We wouldn't have made it this far if she wasn't."

Except Jen doesn't know that I've been to the Mitchells'. Abby isn't there.

"No," Jackson says. "The lies stop now. Detectives," he rotates back to us, "if you won't believe me, then you have to listen to her. Abby will tell you herself. She didn't murder Missy."

"Good idea, Jackson," Jen says. "How do you suggest we do that?"

The ringing in my ears kicks up a notch as everything screeches to a halt. "Mr. Scarborough?"

Jackson pushes the hair off his brow, exhaustion and something resembling resignation shadowing his face.

"You can ask her," he says quietly. "I know where she is."

JACKSON

Exhaustion pummels my body, but I can't quit. The damage Jen's done is irreparable.

Who am I kidding? The damage we've both done is irreparable.

"What do you mean you know where she is?" Jen asks. "What do you mean *you know where she is*?" She moves to grab me, knocking the chair in her pursuit, but Blaisdell pushes her off.

"Sit down, Mrs. Scarborough," he commands.

Her breath is ragged and when she speaks, her teeth are bared. She looks like a hyena. "You know where she is?" Jen asks. "The whole time?"

This is it.

"Abs hadn't come out of her room for more than a shower in days, shut down whenever Jen came within five feet of her. I was really worried. I kept asking her what was wrong, but I was totally at a loss. Finally, she broke down and said Jen had done something to Missy. Something bad."

"I didn't—"

"She was terrified of Jen. Of what she'd do if Abby didn't do the Bow-tastic! shoot. And, quite frankly, so was I. Last night, I saw Jen take a sleeping pill before she went up to bed, and it came to me. I opened the window to make it look like she'd snuck out. I didn't know where we were going until we were in the car, but I knew I had to get Abby out of there."

"You bastard," Jen says through streams of tears. She looks defeated. Broken. But even in her sorrow, I recognize her anger bubbling. She cracks her knuckles, rubbing her hands rhythmically up and down her legs.

I'm out of remorse.

"Jen hadn't been in the best mindset, as I'm sure you can imagine, and the melatonin hasn't been as effective lately, so I knew we had to act fast. I didn't want to risk her waking up."

"Where is Abby?" Stone asks.

I exhale a lifetime of guilt. "In the early days of our marriage, Jen and I used to drink. A lot. We'd buy a jug of wine on a Friday night, do a puzzle. And we'd talk. It didn't matter about what."

Blaisdell brandishes his impatience. His large foot bounces double-time on the linoleum. His stubble stands out like black stumps, remnants of a forest fire. I take in the coarse stubs and imagine the clearing at the top of the hill.

Stone tips her head, peering at Jen from the corner of her eye.

"Jen didn't talk about her childhood often, but when she was drunk, the stories would come pouring out of her. How hard it was that her mother was never around. How mean the girls in her neighborhood were. The constant thread was this place she hung out when Carol was working."

"You didn't," Jen says.

Stone pales. "Mr. Scarborough, are you talking about the field?"

"You know this place?" Detective Blaisdell asks.

She waves him off. "Jackson, is she in the woods?"

I shake my head.

Jen answers for me. "That land was turned into condos last year."

I pluck at a scratch on the table. "I made her promise to stay put. Gave her the flashlight and fleece blanket we keep in the emergency car kit. I tried to get to her earlier. When I went for pizza, but I couldn't. Too many reporters. Police cruisers everywhere. Too many people looking for Chloe. They were replaying the press conference on the TV at the pizza shop, and I just couldn't."

"Where?" Blaisdell says.

Abby. My Abby-girl. I stare at the woman who used to be my wife. Her eyes are beady and dark in the fluorescents and no matter how hard I try, I can't remember what I used to see in them. I look from Stone to Blaisdell, hoping they'll throw me a bone, but knowing I'm unworthy of forgiveness. "Behind the condos. There's an old blue water tower."

Stone jumps from her seat and raps on the mirror.

"Jackson, why would you bring her to the water tower?" Jen says, ashen and near hysterics. "She's in the water tower? You left Abby in the god-damn water tower?" She lunges for me again. This time, I feel the tips of her nails graze against my cheek. They don't draw blood, but the zing of the scrape pulses.

"Jesus Christ," Blaisdell says, pulling her back. It takes effort though.

Jen roars in frustration. "No, no, no. You have to get her out of there! You have to get her now! How could you bring her to that place, Jackson? What the hell were you thinking?"

"It was just a stopgap, a place to hide for a few hours. I was going to move her once I figured out how to do it without you knowing, but this was the best I could do on short notice. Then you insisted we call the police, and everything blew up faster than I expected."

The door swings open, revealing a small group of officers clad in black uniforms led by the Detective Lieutenant I was introduced to earlier.

"Where?" he asks.

"The water tower off South Lake Avenue." Stone throws a coat over her shoulders. "I'm coming with you."

"Me too." Jen starts.

"The hell you are," Stone says.

Welsh breaks off from the group and approaches Jen—who immediately begins to struggle.

"No!" she shrieks, throwing her body into Welsh and grabbing for me. She tears at my collar, scratches my neck, her face red and monstrous. Welsh manages to hook an arm behind her back, but Jen continues to wail. "Emilina, no! Wait! Get your fucking hands off me. Jackson, you son of a bitch. Let me go! I need to see her!"

While I'm not proud of it, her despair gives me the slightest satisfaction.

Downy's at my side next. "Let's go," he says, looping a hardened hand into my armpit.

I don't struggle. I let Downy lead me to the cell, Jen's cries echoing off the walls, and press my head against the metal as the gate clanks shut. The bars aren't as cold as I imagined.

EMILINA

The water tower.

Standing at its base, craning backward to see the small latch just beyond the ladder. Nicole's body isn't strung up on a rope this time, but shadows of that night flash with every blink.

It's not as tall as I remember it being, not up close. The powder blue has faded and cracked with age. Serpentine mazes of orange, brown, and black speckle the surface. Several NO TRESSPASSING and DANGER signs hang around the perimeter.

"Be careful." Cap hands me a flashlight.

I nod, unable to respond. I have to go up there.

Two decades of submerged nightmares are the only thing standing between me and Abigail Scarborough.

It's much easier to navigate without a body encumbering the process. Where once the ladder seemed to stretch infinitely, I'm surprised when I reach the top in a handful of breaths.

I swoop a leg over the barricade and test my weight on the catwalk. The metal groans in protest but holds. I grip the railing regardless, unable to shirk the image of Nicole dangling from its height. I peek over the edge, just once, and swear I see myself. Thirteen and covered in gore, shuddering beneath the cold night sky.

Time is fluid in this place. Warped and shimmering and thin.

The flashlight sputters, and I give it a stern smack until the beam steadies. "I will not fall," I whisper. "I will not fall. I will not fall."

Why not? I did.

I know her voice is in my imagination, but I jolt and spin, expecting Nicole's corpse to be at my heel. My breath expels in dry, fast hitches. Heart racing, I clutch the railing until the worst of the shock passes.

Okay. I can do this.

Noises from below sound distant and strange. Bendy. Like I've been transported to a parallel universe.

There's another sound near, though. Imperceptible for anyone on the ground where it's safe from the ghosts of murdered children.

A clunking from inside the tank.

One step. The catwalk screeches and I freeze, gulping down air in short bursts to hear better.

Two. Three. Fo—

There it is again. The scuttle of movement.

The door is barely five feet tall. I lay my hand against the surface. Freezing. Rusted studs dot the outside, feathering in dusty orange bullets. I press my ear against the icy steel and listen.

She's in there, the younger me whispers.

I step back an inch, noticing the amber ashes speckling the catwalk. Someone's opened this door, and recently. I grab the handle with both hands and yank.

The hinges creak and squeal but oblige.

Someone screams. A high-pitched, vulnerable wail that doesn't seem to stop.

Nicole, my mind whispers.

"It's not her," I respond. "You know it's not her." The dead can't scream.

Really? Come on down and join me. Find out for yourself.

I stare into the abyss with naked fear. Decades of fighting the horrors other people create, and now I've come full circle: this is where my demons lurk, where every bump of terror originates.

She's in there with Nicole. A dead-girl party. Bloated and rotting and pissed—and they know what you did.

Stop. I can't think about Nicole right now.

"Abigail Scarborough?" I say, shining the light toward the door.

The scream ends abruptly.

"Abby?"

At first, nothing, but faintly, from the impenetrable darkness, I hear a tiny voice. "Hello?"

"Abby?" I repeat, slipping my head and shoulders through the frame. It smells like (*death*) rust and wet iron. The absence of light inside the tank is disorienting. A sensory deprivation chamber. I move the flashlight in wide arcs and almost drop it when the figure illuminates.

Nicole.

No. Abby.

Alive.

The basin still holds a few inches of water. She props herself on the cold metal, barefoot and shaking. Her chattering teeth are masked by bluish lips and stringy hair zigzagging across her forehead. Old pipes run the length of the wall beside her. There's a ladder, but it's missing several rungs and impossible to see without the beam of the flashlight.

Shielding her eyes from the light, she raises a ghost-pale arm. The skin of her fingers is waxy and pruned. "Hello?" she cries.

My heart breaks, an actual snap in my chest. "Hold on, Abby, I'm coming." I push out of the tank and shout to the team. "She's here, I need a medic!"

I don't wait for them to respond. I don't let myself question the integrity of the forgotten ladder. I clench the flashlight between my teeth, find the rung with the heel of my boot, and plunge inside.

Come on in, the water's fine!

Nicole beckons me from the depths, her skeletal outline splashing in the darkness.

Concentrate, I tell myself, biting down hard on the flashlight. *One step at a time.*

The bars are slick but navigable. I reach the bottom, sweating in spite of the chill. Stagnant water ripples around my feet, and I feel something graze my ankle.

Marco!

No.

Polo!

How long can bones stay intact under water before they start degrading?

I spit the flashlight into my hand and swing it to the other side of the tank where Abby struggles to maintain her footing.

"Stay there," I say.

I don't know the symptoms of hypothermia, but I'm fairly confident that hours in a freezing vault without proper clothing or a source of heat would be a good way to get it.

"Please." Abby wraps her arms around herself and shakes harder. "H-help me. Cold. So c-cold."

"I'm coming," I say. "I'm coming."

"I d-dropped the f-flashlight looking for the l-ladder. I t-tried to c-catch it, but s-slipped. The blanket f-fell into the water. Please."

Marco!

I scale the side and extend to meet her. I feel her flesh, deathly cold but alive, but even then my mind refuses to cooperate.

She's alive.

She's dead.

Abby.

Nicole.

If Jackson's timeline is accurate, Abigail Scarborough has been trapped in this water tower for almost twenty-four hours with the bones of his wife's first victim.

"My name is Emilina," I say to the quivering child. I unzip my jacket and swaddle her inside, not feeling the cold air or the shiver of the past. "Everything's going to be all right. I've got you."

"Detective Stone?" A concerned voice floats down, a blue silhouette against a starry black sky.

"Here."

The floodlights come next, so stark and bright I'm blinded by their arrival. Abby inches closer. "You're a d-detective?" she asks.

I rub her arm and rest my chin on top of her head.

Her voice is a cold whisper in my ear. "I was s-so scared. I think there's s-something down here."

Nicole.

I search the murky water, my mind playing tricks with the floodlights on the surface. Every ripple is her. The tip of a femur, the jut of a tibia.

I hear footsteps on the ladder.

No one's being added to this watery grave. Not tonight. "You're not alone. We're going to get you to a hospital."

Her teeth clink.

"I know this has been terrible, but I need you to be prepared, okay?"

What am I doing? She's too fragile. I look at her shaking, so small yet so resilient. She's terrified, yes, but she survived.

It'll be worse for her if the press drags her through the mud. "We found Missy," I say before I change my mind.

"Missy? Oh, my god." Abby rocks. The zipper of my coat hits the tank with delicate *clink, clink, clinks.* "My m—mom. My mom. Killed her." She cries.

And there it is.

No more assumptions. Here is the truth. Here is absolution.

What absolution? a voice scratches from the depths of my conscience. *Are you really going to leave me down here, bitch?*

I stare at the water.

The tears that follow are frigid and raw. I let them soak the fabric of my thin shirt until I'm also racked with shivers. From the rectangle, I see Jennifer and me, lugging a broken body to the steely edge. I blink, and the mirage disappears, replaced by two responders sending down a rescue stretcher secured with canvas straps.

A scratchy blue blanket materializes around Abby's shoulders, and the extraction begins.

An EMT anchors at my side. I grab his elbow and point to the bottom of the tank. "Hey," I say, hoarse and thin. "I think there's something in the water."

Drew leaves the light above the sink on for me. He knows I don't like coming home to a dark house. I crave the reassurance on a night like this. I kick my shoes onto the welcome mat by the door. They're caked in dried mud, and dead leaves dust the floor like rusty confetti.

I leave a trail of damp clothes behind me. Socks, pants, shirt. Abandoning them sporadically as I slog up the stairs to the bathroom.

It's after midnight. I'll have paperwork, mountains of it, but all of it can wait.

I brush my teeth, conscious of the fact that I threw up multiple times throughout the day and didn't stop to do it earlier.

Better get used to it.

"Hey, Wonder Woman," Drew says as I shimmy under the covers. The sheets are cool, but he's as warm as buttered toast. My own personal space heater. I curl into his side and sigh as the stress dissipates from my muscles.

"Hey, yourself." I kiss the soft spot between his shoulder blades.

"Bad day?"

"The worst."

"Want to talk about it?"

"Not yet," I say. We fall into comfortable silence. I soak up his acceptance, but it doesn't stop my nerves from firing. I can't shake the events of the past couple hours. Phantoms, old and new.

Drew rolls to face me. Soft moonlight filters in through the shades. He's handsome and attentive, and it makes me want to cry. "Did you find her? Chloe Cates?"

How do I answer that?

"Yes," I settle on, "and no." I tell him everything I can, everything that's not decades-old, and the tension evaporates with every word.

"A second body?" he asks.

"Bones. They think they've been down there a long time. Joss is going to be busy this week."

"Jesus. And Chloe was in there with it." He shudders. "What a nightmare."

Not it. Nicole.

"She almost died in that tank, Drew. Because her mother was too crazy to let her have a normal life, and her father was too scared to leave."

"I can't imagine," he says.

"No blankets. No light. Twenty-four hours alone in the dark." With the remains of my past. "Not knowing what was going to happen to her."

"That's horrible."

"You know what's more horrible? Having a mother who tries to blame you for a murder she committed."

"That's an oddly specific example of horrible."

"Drew."

"Emilina."

"Doesn't it scare you?" I ask him, shrinking into myself to lay bare my other unspoken fear.

"Doesn't what scare me?"

"This. Us. Having a kid. The enormous, not even slightly improbable chance that we'll mess her up for good."

"Her?"

"Or him. You know what I mean. Don't you feel how irreversible this is? One mistake, one bad choice, and we're fishing our kid out of a water tank or dragging her out of a tree house."

He doesn't budge. "Is that really what you're scared of?"

"Yes," I grimace "and no."

Why is it that the most important things we want to say are always the trickiest to string together? Words slip out of reach and leave bread crumbs of what they should've been in their wake.

Try.

And for once, I don't jump out of bed or change the subject. Once you've battled your darkest secret, it's hard to find excuses to be afraid.

"I didn't have a mother, Drew. I have no clue what I'm doing, and I have no idea where to start. What if I'm not good at this? What if our child hates me? What if—" (*just say it*) "what if I'm not supposed to be a mom?"

What if I'm not *here* to be a mother?

I haven't been able to silence the fear that the bones will lead back to me. Guilt renewed.

Drew grips my shoulder, a warm mix of strong and gentle, and in his face, I find nothing but adoration. Certainty. "That is never going to happen," he says. "Our child is going to love you, and you are going to love him."

"Him, huh?"

"Our strapping young lad," he winks. "Or lass. Yes, we're going to make mistakes, a ton of them, but we're going to work through them together because that's what families do."

"Yours maybe."

"Yours too. Patrick and your dad may not have understood everything you experienced."

That's for sure.

"But they were a damn good support system. Do you know how proud they'd be of you right now? Em, you saved a girl's life tonight. How could you possibly doubt you'll be a good mother?"

That girl is traumatized because of me. "You have to say nice things about me because you're my husband."

"Shouldn't I say awful things about you because I'm your husband?" he asks with a playful nudge.

"Such a jerk," I say, but I'm laughing and crying and enjoying the unfamiliar tingling of his hand on my lower belly.

"I love you." He states it with the ease of someone spouting a universal fact. The sky is blue. There are twenty-six letters in the alphabet. *I love you.*

"I love you too." I lean in for a kiss and stop short of his lips.

"What? Do I have morning breath already?"

The gears inside my brain whir and wiggle.

Drew starts to pull away. "Okay, I was joking, but now I'm getting self-conscious."

"It's nothing." It's something. I can't put my finger on it, a detail just outside my reach. I kiss him and shuffle back to my side of the bed. "Nothing. Sorry. Turning it off for the night."

A ping of doubt surfaces. Abigail is only thirteen. A child.

And yet.

A young girl is still dead.

Two young girls, my mind hisses. *Can you live with that?*

As I close my eyes and wish for sleep that will not come, I know that I cannot.

ABIGAIL

She'll be here any minute.

I slide my arms into the sleeves of my sweatshirt so only the tips of my unpolished fingers peek out of the cuffs. I can't remember the last time I didn't have some uber-bright color perfectly manicured and gelled with a sparkle topcoat.

I could get used to this natural look.

I've been home for two weeks. Although I guess I can't really call it home anymore.

Dad's putting the house on the market. He has a realtor coming over to take pictures tomorrow, which means he's been busy shoving "knickknack bullshit" into boxes and stacking them in the garage.

Most of the knickknack bullshit belongs to Mom.

Wardrobe, picture frames, shoes. Not to mention every accessory from "CC and Me." I can't believe how many backdrops and sparkly tablecloths we have. And don't even get me started on the pallets. We could build a mini mansion, but who would want to live there? Splintered wood doesn't scream home sweet home.

I lift the corner of the blinds and stare out at the street. It's cloudy—and quiet, thank god. I'm sick of the news vans parked on our lawn. I can't even get the mail without someone taking my picture and asking stupid questions.

How did you survive? How does it feel to know your mother murdered your friend? Can you ever forgive her?

I'm just trying to get the mail, guys.

JJ's at Ryan's. What else is new? I see his lime-green scooter tucked between the porch rails in its normal spot. All this crazy stuff going on and he's still afraid to practice driving. Maybe Ryan will convince him. The brother JJ's never had. Pretty sure the Fletchers have adopted him at this point. He barely looks at me. Any time we're in the same room for more than a couple of minutes, he gets super awkward and makes up a reason to go somewhere else.

Dad says he's "processing." And I'm like, shouldn't I be the one "processing?" It's not like he was there that night or had to stay in that dumb tank with a heap of bones. I think he just doesn't know what to say to me. I hate that. We used to be able to talk about anything. Now it's like he's afraid he might catch whatever germs I got from Mom when she did those awful things.

Mom.

I flop back onto the couch and pull the drawstrings tighter around my face. A scrunchy cotton cocoon.

Dad says she'll try to fight the listing. I guess her lawyer sent something called an injunction, but *his* lawyer made it go away. Dad's lawyer is probably the skinniest man I've ever seen. He has knobby knuckles and wears suspenders because his pants are too loose around the waist. But he wants to help, so I guess that's okay.

Why would she want to keep this place anyway? That's just creepy. One of the papers called it the Murder House. So creative.

Whatever, we're leaving. I don't know where we'll end up. Some place far away from Upper Madison where people have never heard of CC Spectacular. Nebraska. Or one of the Dakotas. Nothing bad could possibly happen in a state like North Dakota, where there are more cows than people.

That's what we need. I'm "coping" according to my therapist. Dad's "struggling." JJ's being harassed at school. Shockingly, kids don't trust a murderer's son walking their halls. He still gets up and goes every morning, though, I know it sucks for him. Being the butt of the joke. Feeling like you're under a magnifying glass. Yeah, I get it.

Leaving could be, like, my chance to find out who I really am. To start making my own choices without Chloe Cates.

Isn't that what I've wanted?

The slam of a car door brings me back. Emilina—she says to call her by her first name—ducks into the back seat and pops up holding a folder. She tugs her jeans up, adjusts the front of her shirt, and squints at the house. I wonder what she's thinking about, so wrinkled and serious. The other detective, Blaisdell—Blaze-dell is how I think of him; he always smells like he just got done vaping and stopped at McDonald's for a Big Mac—he looks at me like I'm some porcelain doll about to break.

It drives me nuts.

Emilina though. When she looks at me, it's a little scary. Like if she stares hard enough, she'll be able to pick apart my brain and read my thoughts like fortune cookies.

"Abby-girl," Dad calls from the foyer. "You have a visitor."

Like it's some big surprise. She arranged this meeting.

"Hi, Abby," Emilina says. She has a nice smile, but it's a little too big. Too many teeth showing. Mom would've photoshopped some of them out. She turns to Dad and drops the smile. Not happy to see him then. They wanted to charge Dad with "obstruction." They settled for *filing a false report* since I was never *technically* missing when he knew where I was.

But he agreed to testify against Mom and they released him the next morning. I was in the hospital when all that happened, though. Emilina explained most of it when she came to check on me.

"Mind if we speak in private? A little girl talk?" She may be talking to Dad but she's doing that thing where she stares at my face. Forehead. Eyes. Nose. Chin. Up and down like an elevator. Doesn't she need to blink?

"Sure," he nods. "I'll be in the kitchen if you need me."

She joins me in the living room but doesn't sit. "Wow," she says, hands on her hips. "Strange without the pictures."

I scan the walls. Dozens of tiny holes mark the places where Mom pinned our lives for the world to see.

"Do you miss it?" Emilina asks.

"Honestly, I'd be happy to never see another camera ever again."

"I bet. How're you holding up?"

I don't trust that wounded puppy dog look she's giving me. "Fine. I'm not, like, permanently damaged, if that's what you're asking. At least that's what the shrink keeps saying. But the press has been bad. I'll be happy when all of this is over."

And I can get on with the rest of my life. I've read the headlines. I may not have a phone anymore—Dad says we'll talk about it after things calm down—but JJ leaves his laptop unlocked. Willa wouldn't talk about me, but she had plenty to say about my mom and her "psycho ideas." Chris did multiple interviews. His mom wore a cross necklace and hugged him while she cried and said what a *good boy* he is. He wished me well.

Vomit.

Less annoying than the nicknames, though. Have I literally just traded Chloe Cates to forever be The Girl in the Water Tank?

I freaking hope not.

"So," I say, playing with the plastic end of the drawstring, "do they know any more about . . . you know. The bones?"

"They're still trying to get a match, but they're close," she says flatly. "Any day now."

"Oh." I run my thumb along my lip. "Why did you want to see me today? I mean, other than the girl talk."

Emilina removes pages from the folder. "Look, I won't sugarcoat this. You've been through a lot, but you're stronger than most people give you credit for."

"Thanks, I think."

"I'm just wondering how you're feeling about the trial," she says.

"I haven't thought about it much," I say. "Trying not to think about the bad stuff. It's hard."

She nods. "I know it seems like some abstract concept, but it'll be here before you know it, and as someone who's had her fair share of court appointments, I know how nerve-racking it can be. Taking the stand is difficult."

"Yeah, it'll suck, but whatever, I'll be all right. I've got months to figure it out. My dad'll be there. And you. You've been super helpful."

"And your mom."

I pause, thinking about the last time I saw her. The bags under her eyes. The dry, red skin on her hands. She doesn't have any lotion or makeup. Didn't even look like my mother.

"Dad says I don't have to look at her, and she's not allowed to talk to me. Yeah, I'm scared, but I'm also like, I can do this. I'll be okay."

"You're a brave girl, Abby."

"Whatever. Thanks."

"Do you mind . . ." she trails off, chewing the inside of her lip before trying again. "Curiosity is getting the best of me here. Is it okay if I ask you a few questions?"

You're going to do it anyway; I don't know why you bothered asking for permission. "I guess."

"You said your mom killed Missy."

Is that a question?

"Because she did."

Yesterday, Mom entered her not guilty plea and begged the judge to set a reasonable bail. She needed to be home, she said. For her kids.

For her kids. Riiiight.

Hair from the fence and traces of blood and other stuff from the basement. They found the murder weapon: a vintage spotlight we used for formalwear shoots for an *old Hollywood vibe*. It was wiped clean with bleach, but Missy's blood had seeped into the cracks. I don't know everything, but I know that's bad.

They also have my testimony. I'm taking the stand against my mom.

The judge couldn't pound his gavel hard enough. Murdering a kid? No bail. Duh. She has to stay at Albany County Jail until the trial.

"You witnessed her attack Missy?" Emilina asks.

"No," I say, equally unblinking. "We were arguing, and Mom asked me to give her some time alone with Missy. She had that look, though, you know? Like the *mom* look. I think she knew we weren't going to work it out when we were both so pissed. Sorry. Mad. And she wanted to make Missy see things her way. My mom loved making people see things her way." That's an understatement. "So, I went to my room," I shrug. "Watched *The Deathly Hallows*. Maybe if I hadn't had my headphones on, I would've heard something. Could've stopped her."

I've told this story so many times, I could do it in my sleep. Usually, I'm met with poor-baby frowns, but Emilina, she's not pitying me.

"If you didn't actually see anything, how are you so sure it was your mother? Couldn't it have just as easily been your dad? Or JJ?"

Missy's voice blasts in my head. *You're so weird.*

"No," I say. "It was definitely my mom. She came upstairs maybe an hour later and told me that Missy had left and I wouldn't be hearing from her again. *Missy never existed*, she said. Like Willa. But why would she leave without saying anything to me? That's so rude. And Missy wasn't rude. I didn't get it. I was about to text her when I heard my mom moving stuff around in the cleaning cabinet. And I was like, why is she cleaning this late? Weird. So, while she was doing that, I snuck downstairs." I wipe real tears from my eyes.

"Mm," she says and tilts her head. "Why didn't you call the police?"

Sniff. Wipe. "I told you."

"Tell me again."

I sit up straighter and huff. "Do I have to? I don't want to sound like a baby, but going through this again is super painful. I'm having nightmares. I mean, this is a *lot*. I'm not even allowed to watch R movies."

"You'd be doing me a favor. I'd really appreciate it," she says softly.

I throw out a big sigh because this is the last thing I want to do. Whatever gets her out of here faster, I guess.

"Fine. I didn't call the police because I didn't even know what was happening. My shrink says I was in shock. That my brain literally killed a switch to protect me from the trauma. There was so much blood, Emilina. I can't even. I didn't know what my mom was going to do to me. I was so scared."

"I understand."

Do you, though? "Yeah. So." I shrug.

Emilina glances down at the folder.

"Is that all?" I ask after a minute of nothing but Dad thumping cabinets.

She turns the folder so I'm able to see an 8x10 photo of clothes separated by numbers. A shirt, pants, a bra. "We found blood on your clothes. Mixed in the washer with the other stuff. The blood matches Missy's."

"Okay?" I ask, dragging out the question.

"Not your mom's clothes, though. And from your description, she would've been covered."

I give a noncommittal shrug. "I don't know, maybe she got rid of hers?" What does she want me to say?

"How did blood wind up on your clothes?"

The door. The floor. Everywhere.

"I don't know," I say. "I hid when I heard her coming down the stairs, but she heard me make a noise and everything gets fuzzy after that. Maybe it got on me then? I don't know. It all happened so fast."

"Uh huh." She stuffs the picture back into the folder. "I just have one more question."

"Go 'head."

"Your mother accused you of murdering Missy."

That's definitely not a question.

She lifts an eyebrow expectantly. It could use a tweeze.

I scoff. "I'm thirteen."

"Age doesn't give you an exemption. You'd be surprised what people can do when they're pushed past their limits."

I smooth the hood off my face but won't look at her. I don't like how she's staring at me, all skeptical and judgy. Missy looked at me that way too.

"You were upstairs watching a movie when she murdered Missy," Emilina says. It feels like a trick.

"Yeah, I was. With my headphones on."

"Okay."

Mom always said she knew when I was lying. "It feels like you don't believe me."

No. Yes. Her expressions shift.

"Do you actually think I did it, Emilina?"

"Did you?" she asks.

Geez, way to put it all out there.

"Missy and I were best friends. I really miss her. For the first time ever, my life didn't seem so messed up."

"But your mom couldn't let you be happy, is that right?"

"Not if it meant the end of the blog."

"Mm."

Again, with that annoying sound. *Mm.* Like, what does that even mean?

"Mm," I repeat.

"What were you fighting about?" Emilina asks. "You and Missy."

Are we doing this? "I told Mom Bow-tastic! was a stupid idea. She shouldn't have agreed to do it in the first place. Missy couldn't follow the rules and we hadn't even started yet. Why did she want to invite someone else? Why wasn't she happy just hanging out with me? Why couldn't she just listen?"

"That's not really an answer."

I shrug. "I think it is."

Her lips pinch together like Mom's do when she's big mad.

I hear Dad in the other room. Wrapping dishes in newspapers. We've never gotten the paper delivered, and suddenly they're everywhere. Grandma Carol brought them over, Mom's face on the front page of every single one. And now Dad's using them to keep bowls from breaking when we move without her.

It'd be so easy to end this. Call him in and tell him I'm tired of talking. So tired. But Emilina's keeping something from me. I can't let her go until I know what it is.

I stand and stretch. "Mom loved making up problems for me to solve. Did you know that?"

"I did not."

I take two steps toward Emilina and lower my voice. The last thing I need is for Dad to come in right now. "We played the 'what-if' game a lot. What would you do in this situation? How would you respond to this question? Said it was good practice for interviews."

"I can see that."

"Right, yeah, so, if we're playing this game, I'd say something like, what if I told you Missy called me a jealous freak? That inviting her friend did not need to be a whole thing, but I was *making* it into a problem just to be dramatic. Me. Dramatic. Seriously?"

"I remember the first fight I had with my best friend," Emilina says. Her gaze wanders like she's reliving the good old days. "It was awful. We didn't speak for weeks."

"So you get it then. One second we were disagreeing, and the next, we were literally screaming at each other. I don't even know where it came from."

"Where what came from?" she asks.

The spotlight.

"The blowup. I'm usually so chill."

"But something about Missy asking to bring another friend into the mix set you off?"

I stare at the ground. Blood pools around my shoe and I blink it away. "She said she didn't want to do the blog if I was going to be *weird* about everything. That we straight up couldn't be friends if I was going to be such a loser."

"I'm sorry she said those things. How did you respond?" she asks. Like we're talking about jeggings.

All the blood. I clench my teeth together. "This is just pretend, Emilina. You have to say *what if* for the game to work. I'll show you: *What if* I said I was pissed? *What if* I said she was nothing without me? Nobody knew who Missy was. Nobody cared. She hadn't even made her first post and already she was acting like Mariah Carey."

How can Chloe Cates be so cool when you are such a freak?
Freak.

"I'm not a freak." I snatch the folder out of Emilina's hands and rip it in half, watching the pieces float to the floor.

"Abby," she says. Just once, but I feel the shift between us.

When I speak again, nostrils flaring from the adrenaline rush, I try to steady my voice, but I still can't look at her. "Don't do this. Please. You saved my life, Emilina."

Emilina frowns. She's prettier when she's sad. A moment passes and she says, "Your mother's going to be tried for second-degree murder, Abby. Do you understand what that means? She could spend the rest of her life in jail."

My thoughts are photographs. I think of four-year-old me in the gold tutu. Flashing lights. CC Spectacular. The tree house. I think of Chris. The blood. The weird goat-noise Missy made when the spotlight connected. Her hair snagging on the corner of the fence. Me in the dark. Shivering, alone.

"I'm okay with that," I whisper. Tears sting my eyes and I blink them away. "I had a lot of time to think while I almost died in that tower. I didn't ask for her to make me famous. I never had a choice about being online. She told me I was special, but all I've ever wanted was to be normal. She wouldn't let that happen. She wanted me to be more. All of this is her fault." I dab my eyes with my sweatshirt sleeve.

Emilina looks like she swallowed a bug. And you know what? That's exactly what the truth feels like. Gulping a big nasty fly you didn't realize was floating in your green smoothie.

Her disgust is gone just as quickly. Cold and critical. "I could bring you in."

I gasp, a little whistle of surprise. "Why would you do that?"

"You know what you did."

"We were just playing a game." I move to the window and open the blinds, casting black lines over our faces. Through the slit, my reflection stares back in the glass. I look so different without Chloe. Like Mom.

"This isn't a game, Abby. Missy is dead."

She wouldn't. Mom's already charged. She can't arrest me.

Can she?

"Good thing none of that was true, right? That'd be wild." I try to chuckle to show it was supposed to be funny, but it's too sharp. Raising my hood, I slide my hands into the oversized pocket. "Sometimes I think I'll never get warm again. Like a part of me is still in that tank with the bones."

A ghost walks up her spine. She shivers, studying my face a minute longer before turning away.

I win.

"I should really go help my dad," I say. "Lots to pack."

Emilina scoops up the torn pieces of the folder. "I was a lot like you when I was your age," she says. "Figuring out the world when you feel like you're backed into a corner is like running with blinders on. You're bound to make a mistake, and you won't even realize it until it's too late."

My lips stay glued.

She walks toward the foyer. "The thing about mistakes is you either learn from them or spend the rest of your life running from the consequences."

"Okay." My heart pounds a hundred miles an hour. Waiting. "Emilina?"

She spins, her face another mask, blank and unreadable. "Abigail."

My name. A dream come true. What I wanted to hear for so long. So why am I wishing she'd said Chloe?

I peek around the corner to make sure Dad isn't watching and move to her. "What are you going to do?"

She clutches the pieces to her chest. "The right thing," she says. Grasping the knob, she pulls the door open and pauses on the step. "I'll see you soon."

Then, she's gone.

I bolt to the window and watch until she reaches her car.

Go, I think at her. *Just. Go.*

As if she hears, Emilina's gaze lands on me. There's a look, a secret we share that stretches a minute too long. She waves once, a short goodbye flick, and the butterflies in my stomach go soaring.

ACKNOWLEDGMENTS

It's true what they say: the first draft is nothing like the final book. *Chloe Cates Is Missing* was a wild ride from conception to production, and I am grateful to have so many people in my corner who helped me discover this firsthand.

To my husband, Sean, thank you for keeping the kids busy with countless games of Go Fish and War, trips to the playground, and superhero gym classes so I could throw myself into revisions and edits. More than that, thank you for being my Huckleberry and always being the first to read my words.

Mackenzie and Jack, thank you for being so excited that I write "scary chapter books" and keeping me company while I write. This book wouldn't have been the same without Lego piles and Barbie games. Love you 3,000.

To my amazing agent, Anne Tibbets, I am forever grateful for your guidance and support. The journey was strange and winding, but I couldn't ask for a better person to help champion *Chloe Cates* into the world.

From beginning to end, it has been a privilege working with Luisa Smith and the team at Scarlet Suspense. Luisa, your keen editorial eye has been invaluable. Thank you for believing in *Chloe Cates* as much as I do.

Like many others, I've wanted to be an author since grade school, and I was lucky to have a father who encouraged me to read often. Dad, thank you for years of Barnes and Nobles gift certificates, for driving me to Walden's for my first *Goosebumps* books, and for giving me a paperback copy of *Misery* when I was ten.

Along those lines, to my little brothers, Mike and Trev, thanks for asking me to tell you bedtime stories and not being too traumatized when they were recaps of *Are You Afraid of the Dark?* episodes.

To my family and friends, thank you for your unwavering support and encouragement, especially during these uncertain times. Finishing a novel during the pandemic was nuts, and I couldn't have done it without your love.

I also had some excellent teachers who helped me realize my love for writing. Dan Hayes, thank you for emphasizing the basics despite my surly teenage attitude about spelling tests and grammar checks and inspiring me to explore my own writing. Ann Ryan and the entire Le Moyne College English department, you pushed me to be a better writer, taught me the importance of constructive criticism and the value in never being afraid to ask a question. And to the wonderful professors and peers of the College of Saint Rose English program, thanks for enduring my melodramatic short story drafts and limericks.

To Austra, Meg, Kaitlyn, Katelyn, Jenn, and Amy, thank you for reading random chapters and helping me laugh when I got too stressed. From Tik-Toks to memes to unflattering selfie mode candids, you guys are the best.

I'd be remiss if I didn't give a shoutout to the writing communities on Twitter. I had no clue when I joined that I'd find so many talented writers I'm lucky enough to call my friends.

Last but not least, thank you, thank you, thank you to the readers, bloggers, reviewers, librarians, and indie book shops that help spread the word about books like mine.